The Erra

Having lived and worked on three continents, Kate Innes has settled near Wenlock Edge in England, and it is this beautiful historic landscape that has inspired most of her writing.

Formerly a teacher and museum education officer, Kate now writes fiction and poetry amidst the benevolent chaos of husband, dogs and children.

www.kateinneswriter.com

info@kateinnespoetry.com

The Errant Hours

KATE INNES

Mindforest Press

Published by Mindforest Press www.kateinneswriter.com
Copyright © Kate Innes 2015

ISBN 978-0-9934837-0-7
A catalogue record for this book is available from the British
Library.

Set in Garamond
Cover design by MA Creative http://www.macreative.co.uk
Maps by James Wade http://jameswade.webs.com

Cover image: 'The Taymouth Hours – Woman Shooting'
British Library, Yates Thompson 13, f. 68v

For Sonja
and
Freya

The Hours

Matins	one or two hours before dawn
Prime (first hour)	daybreak
Tierce (third hour)	approximately 9:00 am
Sext (sixth hour)	approximately midday
Nones (ninth hour)	approximately 3:00 pm
Vespers	early evening, approximately 6:00 pm
Compline	darkness/sleep, approximately 9:00 pm

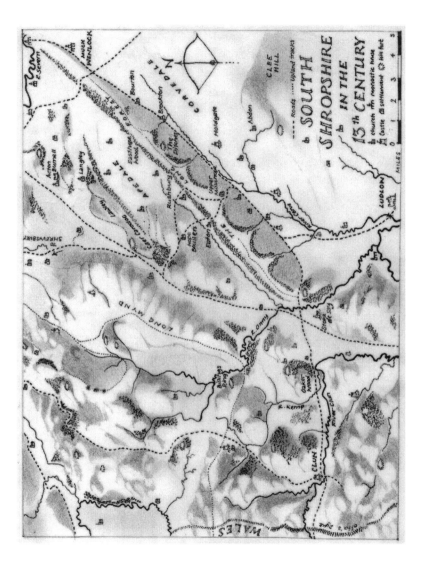

SOUTH SHROPSHIRE IN THE 13th CENTURY

Part One

Acton Burnel Manor
The 12th day of September, 1266

Vespers

There were no shouts from the yard, no sounds of hooves or carts. The silence was unnatural, like the pricking absence between lightning and thunder. Guiliane turned on her side and called again.

"Marjorie!"

The chambermaid was usually just outside the door, but Guiliane's cries brought no response. Her pains were close together now. If she went to look for someone, she would not reach the stairs before the next one made her writhe. Her soiled clothes were piled by the bed and the smell of them made the bile rise in her throat. She pushed herself towards the edge of the bed and vomited on the linen. The next pain followed. Guiliane closed her eyes and sobbed through it.

Her own breathing was so loud that it must have masked the sound of the door opening. When she pushed herself on to the pillow and looked up, Alianore was standing in the doorway, her hand still on the latch.

"Marjorie is ill. She cannot come."

"She is ill?" Guiliane remembered the maid at her side when she had run to the privy during prayers. Then she had fallen into bed, overwhelmed with tiredness, and after that, it was a blur of sickness and pain. She tried to raise herself on her elbows, but the effort made her stomach turn. She swallowed carefully. "Madam, I am ill also, and the baby is coming."

"I know. You have been sick since vespers yesterday." Alianore's voice was tinged with disgust. "We have been watching you while you slept, as Marjorie could not. Your pains began at prime."

"Since prime?" Guiliane pushed the hair out of her eyes. "What is the hour?"

"Almost vespers."

"I am thirsty. Bring me a cup, for God's love." Her mouth felt cracked; her tongue was a flyblown fleece. There was silence.

Alianore could not refuse her a drink, surely. She refused her friendship and even courtesy, but a cup she must see as her Christian duty. Nothing else would arouse her to help 'that French whore', as she called her. Even to her face.

"Please, Madam, for sweet Mary's sake."

"I have ordered the serving women to attend you, but they will not." Alianore's voice was flat and distant, her face hidden behind the door. "They fear God's judgment and have no wish to suffer the fever, like you and your servant. Only your little pet from the kitchen was willing to come. He does not understand that beauty does not bring God's mercy." There were two handclaps. "Edwin, bring a flagon of wine and water. Then come back with fresh linens and some oil."

When the next pains finished, Guiliane was shaking violently. A cup was held to her lips, but she spilled more than she drank. Seconds later she heaved over the side of the bed. The hands that held her were Alianore's hands. The coverlet and sheets were pulled from round her and replaced. Her face and neck were washed in cold water, and she was laid down on fresh linen in time for the next spasm.

In the absence of pain, Guiliane craved sleep, but she forced her eyes open. The lank form of Edwin, the scullion, was tucked in the corner by the fireplace. Alianore was standing next to the prie-dieu, looking through the window, her long fingers drumming on the shining wood. She must have felt Guiliane's gaze because her shoulders twitched and she turned round. The deep crease of disapproval between her pale eyebrows pointed down to her thin, pressed lips, and she quickly averted her eyes from the bed.

"I can do no more for you, Lady. The servants understand your fate and want no part of it. It has happened just as I told you it would." Her fingers were busy again, flicking imperfections from the stiff fabric of her skirt. "Bearing the baby of a Priest and not repenting of it has provoked God's righteous wrath against you. Perhaps in France the Priests can make their choice of women and then shrive themselves of their sin, but that is not the way here. We have given you the chance to repent, but you have only laughed at us and shown disrespect to our saint. This household is not a brothel. I must take Matilde away now. Pray to God that your folly has not condemned the innocent."

Alianore beckoned Edwin and he came forward slowly, trying not to look at her. The poor boy. She should not have protected him from that beating. Alianore would never forgive him.

"As the servants have all gone, Edwin will have to tend to you. I hope you realise that in this country it is improper for a boy even to set foot in this room. But I don't expect that will worry you." Alianore moved towards the door. "The village midwife is also heavy with child. I will send for her, but she may not come," she said with something like satisfaction.

"Wait," Guiliane gasped. "Alianore, I am sorry for what I have done to you."

"It is not what you have done to me, it is the contempt you have shown for God's law and for the Saint's book!"

Guiliane shut her eyes. Robert couldn't have known what his cousin's wife was like. He would never have sent her here to be humiliated like this. But then he always assumed the best of people.

"I am sorry. I do not know where it is. I was reading it and the next day it was gone."

Alianore's expression was outraged. Guiliane had to grip the edge of the sheet as the next pains came. When they subsided, Alianore was pointing at her.

"You see now, Edwin. It was for good reason that God cursed women with pain, as it humbles the vain and frivolous."

"Did you send to Robert? Will he come?" Guiliane panted.

"I sent a message to him at Kenilworth, yes, and at my own cost. But as you know he is in the service of Prince Edward and you are his mistress, bearing his bastard child. He cannot leave the Prince at the siege and run to his whore whenever she calls him. He should have explained that to you."

Guiliane shut her eyes. She could no longer look at the face of this woman who hated her. No matter how hard she had tried to make her laugh or smile, it had only made the hatred grow. But without Alianore, there was only death. She raised her palm like a beggar.

"Madam, please do not leave me alone. For the sake of my babe, stay with me."

"You are not alone, Mistress Guiliane. You wanted the company of men and boys, and now you have it. Pray for God to have mercy on you. Perhaps the midwife will come soon."

She left through the open door.

Compline

Ursula arrived at the manor, out of breath and in pain. It was an uphill walk from her cottage by the wood and the night was close. The chamber was at the top of a steep spiral stair. Edwin went ahead of her with the light. At the door, the stench of disease met her. Only one lamp was burning near the bed where Lady Guiliane lay under thick embroidered coverlets, her dark hair wet and matted. She looked older. Ursula had last seen her as a pretty carefree girl walking in the lane the week before. The bulge of her baby had been lying well, and there was colour in her cheeks. Now her skin was like milk after the cream has been skimmed. Ursula wondered how long she had been left alone, labouring and ill.

"Where are the serving girls and my lady's attendants?"

"Lady Alianore has taken her child to Langley. The chambermaid is ill with the fever and all the other serving women have gone." Edwin was edging towards the door. Normally such a boy would not be allowed in a lady's chamber. He looked terrified.

"The Priest?"

"We sent for him, but he has not come."

Ursula was not surprised. Father Bernard was well known for avoiding the sickbed. Even a summons from the manor couldn't always rouse him to his duty.

"Edwin, we need hot water and any clean cloths you can find. Go quickly." She turned her back on him. Lady Guiliane was shivering. She did not respond when Ursula took her hand.

"My lady, how long have you laboured? Is the baby still moving?"

The French girl did not reply or open her eyes, but lines of pain deepened across her forehead. Ursula smelt the sickening sweetness of her breath. She was too weak for birth pangs. They had not called her in time.

The problem was obvious when Ursula moved aside the heavy bedclothes and began her examination. She could feel two feet where the head should have been. The footling would die if she could not pull it out; the mother was half dead already. Usually the assembled birth attendants and servants would be offering their various advice, but today it seemed a blessing to be the only one at the bedside. She would not have stood up to their scrutiny. She could not hide her loss for long.

"These are all I could find, Goodwife." Edwin was at the door with an assorted pile of cloths and a bronze ewer.

"Pray God they're clean," muttered Ursula, taking them in her arms. "Get some wood and stoke the fire. We need to keep the room warm." Edwin turned and ran. More like a rabbit than a boy.

Ursula sat on a stool and, bending close to Lady Guiliane's ear, she began a gentle but insistent stream of Latin. The martyrdom of Saint Margaret, patron saint of childbirth, was read out from the family book whenever a baby was to be born in the manor. The phrases describing the Saint's triumph over the dragon were like a childhood song in Ursula's head.

"*Once the sign of the cross had been made, that fearful dragon split open in the middle and she came forth from its womb unharmed and without any pain.*" *

As she came to the end of her recitation, she began to wonder where the book of Saint Margaret was. Lady Alianore had great faith in it, especially in the power of the golden image of the saint on the last page. Surely she would have brought it to this young girl in childbed, despite her state of sin.

Ursula had a sudden longing to kiss the image of the saint herself, and to weep over it on her knees. She felt her own womb contract. Her labour the previous night had been short and violent. The baby had already died in her womb. She had known it the day before, when the movements stopped. Ursula had delivered the baby girl herself, washed and wrapped her in the cloths she had prepared and prayed for a miracle, laying her on the bed next to her sleeping son. But even Saint Margaret could not bring a baby back from the dead.

Ursula had covered her in a wool blanket and taken her to the end of the garden, near the cherry tree. Un-baptised and unnamed, her daughter would not be granted burial in holy ground. She had dug a hole and lined it with flowers from the wood. By the time Kit had woken, she was washing in the icy well water from the bucket, hiding her tears.

But she could not afford to give in to that sorrow now. Ursula took a deep breath and stroked Guiliane's cold hand.

A scraping sound at the door made her start.

"How does she fare?" Edwin entered and crouched by the fire, feeding it sticks, his silhouette absorbed in not looking at the bed.

"Very ill. Go quickly and get Father Bernard. I can baptise the baby if it lives but I cannot give the lady last rites."

"Yes, Goodwife." The sound of his footsteps rebounded on the stone stairs.

After making Lady Guiliane as comfortable as she could, Ursula began the slow, patient pulling, manipulating the baby's legs. They kicked against her, and she gave thanks that it still lived.

"Come forth."

Hair stood up on the back of Ursula's neck. It seemed as if the strange, foreign voice came from the Saint herself.

"My lady?" Ursula stopped pulling and looked at the French girl's face. The manipulation of the baby would be causing Guiliane great pain, but the voice had sounded strong. Her eyes were open, fixed on a point on the far wall where a crucifix hung.

"*Come forth. If you are male or female, living or dead, come forth for Christ summons you, in the name of the Father, and the Son, and the Holy Spirit, amen.*" *

Guiliane finished the prayer with a sob. Ursula recognised the words. It was the final invocation from the Passion of Saint Margaret. Lady Guiliane's eyes closed; her face knotted with pain.

Ursula was shaking, covered in sweat and her arms had lost all feeling when the baby finally began to come. The head emerged last, covered in a mat of dark hair. Ursula quickly tied the cord with a piece of linen and took the small iron knife from her belt. The blood from the cord was dusky red and the baby looked cold and listless. Ursula rubbed her quickly with the rough linen cloth, and she began to cough. She cleared the mouth, and the baby let out a wail like a newborn lamb. Ursula held her close, feeling the intake of breath, her breasts hot and full.

There was a warm jug of oil near the fire. Laying the baby on the cloth by the hearth, she rubbed her with the oil until she was a good colour, then carefully swaddled her in the few clean pieces of linen she could find. The baby was asleep, but her mouth sucked hopefully.

"Lady Guiliane, you have a baby girl. Lady!" Ursula squeezed her hand tightly and placed the baby next to her on the pillow.

The new mother's eyes opened, but did not seem to see.

"Give thanks to God, you are delivered of a baby girl. She is here beside you. Try to sit up a little."

Guiliane twisted her head with effort and looked at her baby, lifting one hand towards her.

"Illesa."

"My lady?"

"Illesa." She touched the baby's cheek with the back of her hand.

"Is that her name?"

Lady Guiliane looked suddenly frightened, and she gestured beside the bed.

"The Saint's book. It is lost." Her voice was just a rasping whisper.

Ursula looked all around the room. There was no sign of the book amongst the discarded bedclothes or near the prie-dieu, where it should have been placed. She got down on her knees and felt around under the bed. After several minutes of blind searching she felt something near the wall, trapped behind the bed curtain. She sat up with it and ran her fingers over the smooth parchment, tracing the stately procession of the words and the fine swirls around the pictures.

Ursula put it into Lady Guiliane's hands and she clasped it, her eyes open wide.

"*Illesa sine dolore*. I want to look upon her."

Ursula took the book and turned to the last page. The image of the saint was smudged from repeated kissing.

"*The Father is alpha and omega, the Son is life, the Holy Spirit is medicine. Amen,*" * Lady Guiliane murmured and put the image to her dry lips. She shut her eyes and let the book slide onto the coverlet.

"You take," she muttered, and did not speak again.

Ursula was desperate to get away, but Lady Guiliane could not be left to die alone, and the Priest still had not come. She recited the prayers for the dying and held the girl's hand until her breath stopped and her face slackened. The words of baptism and the marking of her forehead with oil did not wake the swaddled baby. Ursula covered her with one of the fine scarlet and gold blankets from the bedchamber and cradled her against her chest. She picked up the book with her free hand and went out into the dim light before dawn.

A cow was lowing, waiting to be milked; otherwise there was no sound or sign of anyone. Heavy dew dragged on her skirts as she came through the meadow. All was quiet in the cottage. Kit still slept under the green woolen blanket she had woven for him when he was born, five years before. Ursula put the baby down and touched Kit's halo of golden hair. He turned over, bringing the blanket across his crumpled face, but did not wake.

The baby girl was stirring; soon she would cry with hunger. Ursula picked her up, sat in the chair by the hearth embers and put her to the breast. By the time the babe was asleep and full, Ursula knew what she would do. This motherless girl would not be wanted. Lady Alianore had made her feelings about Guiliane's condition known to all. After the bodies had been buried, when Lady Alianore returned from Langley, Ursula would go to her and explain how Lady Guiliane had died with the words of the Passion on her lips giving birth to a girl who had lived only an hour.

Ursula carefully unwrapped the sleeping baby and set aside the finely woven cloth. She took the lid off her old linen chest, emptied it and put the book of Saint Margaret at the bottom. Over it she folded the old clothes and placed the baby carefully on top of them, cushioning her with the rough wool blankets. The baby did not stir. She would sleep a long time with all that milk inside her.

Outside she found the spade next to the woodpile and took it to the cherry tree. The pain she had felt in her breasts and belly was gone, and she dug quickly. When the loose soil was cleared away, she knelt down and scraped the dirt off with her hands. Her dead baby girl was still wrapped tightly in the blanket, unmarred by the day underground. Ursula touched the alabaster of her cheek.

Going to the well, she drew water and added crushed hyssop leaves from the garden. She set her baby's body on the ground, cleaned her carefully and wrapped her in the scarlet blanket. It would do. No one would be looking carefully. They were all too ill or too scared.

Ursula rose from her knees, picking up the bucket. She carefully emptied the hyssop water on the ground, reciting a prayer under her breath.

"Mama."

Kit was standing on the path, blanket in one hand, looking at her.

"You're awake, my love."

"What is it?" he asked, moving to touch the covered form lying on the ground near the well.

10

"Come and see, poppet. It is a baby, but she has died." Ursula uncovered her face for the last time and held Kit while he looked at her. His hair brushed Ursula's cheek and she smelt his sleepy breath.

"Where did she come from, Mama?"

"She is Lady Guiliane's baby, who was staying in the Manor. She died in the night. God rest her soul." Ursula watched his face carefully.

"Can I hold her?"

"No, Sweetheart, but kiss her and say a prayer. She will be buried by the church with her mother. I have washed her and made her ready."

Kit bent down and muttered *"Pater amen."* When he straightened, his face was perturbed. "But Mama, there is a baby inside. Its eyes are closed. Is it dead too?"

Ursula bent down and put her finger on his lips.

"No, Sweetheart, she is just sleeping."

"Who is she?"

"That is a surprise for Papa. She is your sister, but we must keep her a secret for today. If anyone comes to the house, you must tell them to go away because you are not well."

Kit frowned. His eyes were still crusted with sleep.

"She is my sister? Where did she come from?"

"From my tummy. Feel." Kit's hands pushed at the loose skin of her once taut belly. Finally he smiled and turned to run back inside. Ursula grabbed his hand.

"You can stay and look after her while I take the other baby to the Priest. But Kit, don't forget. She is a secret. Don't let anyone come in. Remember, it is a game so we can surprise Papa." Ursula squeezed his hand and smiled.

"Will Papa be back tomorrow?" he asked and pulled hard on her arm.

"Maybe. Now get your tunic on."

"Can I let out the chickens first?"

"Yes, and see if there are eggs." Ursula turned aside to hide the tears that began to swell in her eyes. Kit disappeared round the wall of the cottage, abandoning his blanket.

Ursula looked down at her own baby. The scarlet and gold cloth around her face gave her the colour of the living. Her features had the perfection of innocence. She did not deserve to be

11

excluded from the presence of God, and she would not be. Ursula covered the baby's face and stood up. She would walk to the church and deliver up this baby to be buried in holy ground. Her labour pains would begin at the church door, and the Priest would send her away without delay. And then she would come home to her new daughter; the sleeping, unharmed *Illesa*.

Chapter I
Friday the 12th day of July, AD 1284
The 11th year of the reign of King Edward I
Holdgate

It was midday, and those who had food were eating by their plough strips or at their hearths. Illesa pressed her hollow belly to ease the spasm and turned west. If God favoured her today, she would soon eat well, and until then she would not think of it. Her fingers found the end of her belt and rubbed the worn patch, but she had long outgrown her childish habit of chewing leather when she was hungry.

Along the narrow track, a fence of white, splintered stakes surrounded a plantation of elm saplings. There was a hint of smoke in the air and in the smoke was a whiff of meat. A high-pitched bark echoed from the hills on either side. She must be near.

Illesa slowed her pace. She could see no distance ahead, only the mottled sky above the steep banks of trees, hushed and still. The track turned left, opening onto more level ground where the new fencing stopped abruptly at a tall chestnut tree. Beyond it were thick, grey walls. The Forester's lodge and his gaol stood on weed-ridden ground. The stone was un-softened by weather and the narrow lancet windows were freshly cut. She went a little further. In the north wall was a thick timber door reinforced with iron.

The dog had stopped barking. It might be watching, waiting for her to go through the wattle gate. Illesa retreated a few steps into the shade of the chestnut. The smoke came from a low timber building across the cobbled yard. A stable door growled on its hinges, as if someone had just opened it, but there was no one in sight.

Her brother, or half-brother, was not likely to come into view of course. He hardly ever did, and now he had managed to get himself locked up when he was meant to be on his way home to her. He should have been back months before, in time for their mother's burial if not for her death.

Illesa shivered with sudden cold. Maybe he wasn't here at all. Maybe Kit was already dead, and they had fed his body to the dogs. She jerked her head to dislodge the horror and crossed herself. Kit would not die here. If necessary he would gnaw away at the stones with his teeth. Brother or half-brother, he was his father's son. That was certain. They were both as stubborn as mules.

A door banged and footsteps sounded on the cobbled yard. Illesa hurried to the gate. The man had his back to her and was heading for the kitchen.

"Sir!" Illesa called.

The man turned, stood still for a moment with his hand on his dagger hilt, and then strode towards her. His clothes were worn and stained and his beard untrimmed, sticking out from his chin like a goat. Not the Lord Forester, obviously. Probably the guard. On the belt around his waist hung a chain and two iron keys. He gestured her inside the gate, letting his eyes take in the length of her.

"Who are you?"

"The smith of Holdgate's daughter. I've come to speak to the Forester."

"About what?"

"It concerns my brother."

He shot a glance at the gaol door.

"Is your brother in the cells?"

Illesa nodded.

The guard snorted, then spat in the dust. A bruise on his cheek was just turning greenish-yellow.

"The arrow smith? You've come to see him? Guilty as sin. He's going to be here for a long, long time," he drawled, coming three steps closer. She could smell his breath. "So, what have you got for us then, sister?"

Illesa drew back. Her fingers went to the pouch, safe between her breasts.

"I have coin to pay. Where is the Lord Forester?"

"He is riding." His hand shot out and gripped her wrist. "I will look after the coin for you until the Forester returns, and I'll be sure to tell him who brought it."

Illesa twisted her arm, and he let her go suddenly, pushing her away from the open gate. She whirled round to face him, stumbling. He was watching her with his mouth open and legs apart. Enjoying himself. The next time he would not let her go. If she tried to run, he could come after her easily enough on a horse, if his goat legs weren't fast enough. She could only hope to find some people on the road.

Illesa crossed her arms over her chest.

"Let me see my brother," she demanded. But her voice was high and unsteady, and the guard only pouted mockingly. He could not stop fingering the heavy keys hanging from his belt.

"No one goes into the gaol unless they are going to stay there. And your brother is not coming out, unless he is on a bier." He made the sign of the cross over the imaginary corpse.

But he wasn't dead yet. Illesa shot a glance at the gaol. Perhaps Kit was near a window. He might hear her.

"Be merciful, for Christ's sake," she cried. "I am poor. I have no other coin, nor any more virtue once mine is spent."

The guard's smile showed red, swollen gums.

"You're wasting all your fancy words. The Lord Forester isn't here, like I said."

Behind her, dogs began barking in sharp, frantic yelps. Illesa held her hands out in supplication.

"Please, master, all my family are dead, except my brother. I have no one to help me. God will reward you if you have mercy on me." With each word she took a small step away from him, her feet hidden under the sway of her skirt.

The guard turned his head towards the yard and whistled. The dogs stopped barking. He took his fingers from his mouth and licked the specks of saliva from his lip.

A second man was approaching from the side of the stables.

"For sweet Saint Mary's sake," she pleaded.

"Look, Destrey," the guard called. "That bastard's sister has come to set him free. I can think of a way to pay him back for his blows. We'll put her in a cell next to his, so he can watch."

She took the warm leather pouch from between her breasts and held it on her hand, jingling it to make the coins ring. Two shillings was not going to be enough. Not for both of them.

"You can count the coin, master. There are thirty silver pennies, and I also have a jewel my mistress gave me," Illesa lied, glancing at him through lowered lids, while her fingers fumbled to untie the knotted wool. "Sardonyx, a powerful amulet."

The other man was coming up behind her. She turned so both of them could see what was in her hand. The new man was short and wiry, chewing on something in his swollen cheek.

"Let me show it to you," she said as the yarn came free. With her other hand, she gathered the fabric of her skirt to her ankle.

Illesa threw the coins in a wide arc at their faces and saw the bright silver fall into the weed and mud. Then she ran, clutching her skirt, through the gate and out onto the road. Behind her, the men were shouting.

"That's mine, I saw it first!"

"Where's the jewel?"

"Get her, you idiot!"

"I'm no fool. If I go after her, you will take all the coin!"

They were on their hands and knees. The dogs had started barking again. There would be a fight before the end.

It was a mile before she slowed to a walk. The road was still not busy, but she found a cooper and his gaunt wife, travelling to Wenlock with a donkey and a cart loaded with barrels, and they allowed her to walk beside them.

"What've you been running from? You are all of a sweat," the woman said, squinting at her.

"A vicious dog."

The cooper tutted.

"Did you throw stones at it? Most dogs will run if you just raise a hand to them."

"Yes, Master. I did."

There was a long silence.

"Shouldn't be out on your own, girl," the cooper's wife muttered out of the side of her mouth. "You'll deserve any trouble you get."

If the guard came after her, the wife would tell the cooper not to help her, and he would do what she said.

"I'm sure she is grateful to be safe now, wife."

"God be thanked," Illesa replied and fell a few paces behind.

They were silent until they reached the turning for the church, standing high on the hill at Holdgate. From there it was only a mile further home.

"God guard you," the cooper called, as his wife whacked the donkey's haunch to make it pull up the hill.

Of course she should thank God for guarding her. Saint Margaret had not forgotten to give thanks when God saved her from being raped by the Roman Governor. Saint Margaret had been imprisoned and tortured, but had not wept or despaired, even though she was just a girl. Saint Margaret had defeated the dragon of Satan through her faith alone.

Illesa pinched the soft skin at her wrist and twisted it between her nails. The pain would take away her fear and calm her. It was only the coin that was lost, after all. The coin that was going to pay off her debts and get her brother back. When she was home she would be able to quell the bile that rose in her throat.

God damn those thieves.

Once she reached the end of the miller's field, the cottage came into view with the forge beside it and the small plot around it, close by the wood. There was no smoke coming from her thatch and no smell of a seething pottage or valerian being simmered for a poultice. There were no hens in the yard, and the sheep in the pasture were not hers. Ursula was dead these past two months, and still it was not easy to return to the empty hearth and the silence. What she had was only what she could grow, debt being the most abundant crop of all.

She stopped at the water butt by the side of the croft and did what she had often been scolded for doing; drank like a dog and splashed the water on her face and down her hot neck. Her undergarments were still damp from her run. Illesa squeezed her plait out. Wiping her hands on the linen of her skirt, she took the key on its leather thong from around her neck and unlocked the door. There was a flurry of dust and air, but all else was still. She walked through the shafts of light coming from the facing window and unlatched the shutters.

The few things left were all in their places: the trestle and the small table, her father's chair, the old stools, iron tripod pot, bowls for pottage, distaff and spindle, empty of wool. The last piece of bacon, mostly rind, still hung over the hearth. It would be Sunday soon, when she would be allowed to eat it with leeks or onion. The hoe, axe and leather bucket stood by the back door.

Fear and running had quelled her hunger at least. Perhaps later she would find some acorns in the wood and make some flour with the remains of the beans. She felt breathless, and there was a deep shuddering in her chest. All was gone, except these few things. She must make sure the most precious thing had not somehow vanished while she was away.

Rushes caught at Illesa's feet as she went into the sleeping chamber and knelt in front of the wooden chest. She removed layers of clothes and cloth, knowing each one by the feel of its weave on her fingertips: Father's old tunic, Mother's best wimple, Kit's threadbare hose. She placed them carefully in a pile.

When the chest was empty, Illesa pressed the side of the thin elm base and felt it tip, releasing a waft of fragrant air. Mugwort and tansy. She lifted out the false bottom and reached inside. A strap with a pierced silver tab secured the whitened leather binding. The pin on the cover was also silver. It was only the size of her spread palm, but heavy, as if each word inside could be weighed in gold.

Illesa carried the book to the small table in the hall, but did not open the shutters above it. There was no knowing who would see her if they walked past. Unpinning the strap from the binding, she opened to the page where the saint's halo was brightest: the scene on the mountain, before the torture, before the death. A breath of air moved the fine parchment, raising hairs on Illesa's arms.

Whenever Illesa opened the book of the saint, the feeling was always the same. She became a hawk lifted high in the air, and with the hawk's eye she could see the sparrow in the hedge and the fearful beasts at the edge of the world in an instant, and all the detail of their beauty and horror.

But the last picture in the book disturbed Illesa. The image of the saint was smudged, and the features of her face were like a reflection seen in the water at the bottom of a well. Ursula said that many women had kissed the saint, smearing the paint in their devotion, for as she had come out of the dragon's belly unharmed, so Saint Margaret had the power to bring forth healthy infants and spare the lives of their mothers.

It was years later that Illesa realised the kisses must have been from the book's previous life, before it came into Ursula's hands. She never brought it to the childbed. Instead she recited the story by heart, fixing frightened women with her dark eyes whilst she did her best to birth their baby. Most survived, if they had called her in time.

Illesa placed her fingers on the book's margins and closed her eyes. She could see her mother before the illness in the same posture, her still face framed by a green wimple, strong thin body bent forward, lips forming the words, frowning as she read.

Illesa jerked her head up from the table. She must have slept. There were familiar sounds outside, coming from the direction of her crop. Rustling leaves, snapping stems. She sped out of the back door and ran past the empty hen house, down the path to the wattle-fenced plot. The damp soil was strewn with pods and printed by delicate hooves. Three does and their growing fawns, already sleek and muscular, were trotting away into the shadows of the coppice. This time they'd had the beans as well as the rest of the cabbages.

Everyone in the village would be smug. She'd heard their whispers. What did she expect, living alone near the wood? It was just stocking a larder for the deer and foxes. If she had any sense she would marry one of the cotters, live in the village and farm her strips with everyone else.

Illesa knelt down among the scattered leaves, her boots sinking into the soft ground. Only the onions in her garden were untouched. She dug them up through tears. They would be safer hanging inside. Cradling them in her skirt, she went through the gate, brushing her mother's herbs with the hem of her tunic. They were growing vigorously despite months of neglect. Illesa could not understand this unfair reversal. She had nurtured Ursula like a tender plant, kept her warm and nourished in a soft bed, steeped the comfrey and sage for stomach pain, rubbed her with oil. It did no good. Her mother had withered like the vine sent to Jonah by God.

The front door ground on the flagstone and Illesa stopped, frozen mid-step, listening. There were no voices inside. If it was someone demanding payment, they would have shouted for her, not crept in like a thief. So, whoever it was did not know she was there. She could still hide.

But, inside the cottage, the book of the saint was lying on the small table. She had not returned it to the chest. Illesa bit her lip and her mouth filled with the taste of blood. She bent down and let the onions fall into a pile on the soil. The back door was closed. She went to it, hearing nothing but the hammering inside her chest. Gripping the hilt of the knife at her waist, Illesa lifted the latch and threw open the door.

"Who's there?"

The person in the shadow cried out and stepped back.

"Oh, Illesa, you gave me a fright!" It was a woman's voice. "Don't do that, I thought you were the devil!" She came into the light of the open door. Agatha, the bailiff's daughter, was wearing another new surcoat of blue cloth with a matching veil. She pressed her hands on her pregnant belly and breathed out slowly.

"Good day, Madam." Illesa replaced the knife in its sheath before stepping into the room and curtsying. The shutters were still closed above the table where the book lay. Her only hope was to keep Agatha away from that corner.

"I knew you must be somewhere, but I didn't think you would spring out at me, ready to slit my throat," Agatha said, coming towards her. "By the saints, what's wrong? You are as white as a shroud." She lifted Illesa's chin slightly. "I didn't scare *you*, did I? I was only coming to see how you are."

"I'm unused to visitors, I'm afraid. It's kind of you to come," Illesa said, crossing to the other side of the room and pulling her father's chair from under the trestle table. "Sit down; you'll be tired after your walk from the keep."

It was Agatha's first pregnancy and she was making the most of it. Being widowed after only three months of marriage seemed to suit her. She had returned to her father's house with more land, new clothes and a status far above that to be found in the village. Agatha brushed something off the polished wood and lowered herself onto the chair. She looked at Illesa appraisingly.

"Goodness. You look dreadful. What has happened, Illesa? You look quite wild."

"I am well, I assure you."

"You look half starved," Agatha grunted. "Here, I've brought you a little something to celebrate the Feast of Saint Veronica." She took a small cloth-wrapped packet from the bag at her waist and put it on the table. Cheese. Illesa could smell the sweet cream.

"Ellen in the dairy is quite good, although her face is ugly enough to curdle milk." Agatha sat back, looking at Illesa's bent head. "You aren't going to cry are you? For heaven's sake, girl, what is the matter?"

The irony of the situation was too much. It was only because Illesa had been forced to give her livestock and most of her pans in lieu of rent that she was not making cheese herself.

"You are very generous. I feel ashamed that I have little to offer you," Illesa managed, keeping her eyes on the table.

"Just a cup of ale will do, really. It's such a hot day." Agatha paused. "You do have ale don't you?"

"No, I'm sorry, Madam."

Agatha sighed loudly.

"By Christ, this is absurd! You are being a silly fool living here on your own, starving like a madwoman. Everybody thinks so. Why suffer like this when its not even Lent?"

"But I am not suffering."

"Anyone would think you were doing penance for something," Agatha continued. "Except, what could that be when you've lived here so long and been as quiet as a mouse?" She tiptoed her fingers across the table. Illesa smiled warily.

"There now. That's a bit better. But don't get any plainer or none of the poor old cotters will marry you and you will have to stay here, all alone with your water and onions." Her look was mocking. "Now what's this I hear about you on the road on your own this morning? Where were you going, without permission or a chaperone?" Agatha cocked her head and smiled. "Don't look like that. You can't expect to go off by yourself and it not be noticed."

No, she couldn't. The whole of the village knew the fastest way to get in the bailiff's favour was to inform on someone else.

"Kit's been gaoled."

"Yes," Agatha stretched her back, and set her knees wider apart to give her belly room. "I know. It's such a shame."

Of course she knew, and she wasn't sorry either.

"How long have you known?"

"Oh, a few days." Agatha waved her hand in the air as if swatting a fly. "The messenger always comes to the keep first. I can't think why Kit would be so stupid as to poach a deer, and when he was so close to home as well." Her small mouth twisted in a parody of sadness. "I hope that isn't where you were going, Illesa?" She tapped her finger on the table. "It wasn't, was it?"

"They say the Forester will take a bribe. Kit would have been able to pay off our debts if he came back here. You know he is skilled, and a good ploughman."

"You took the two shillings to bribe the Forester? The money from selling the rest of your herd? You thought that would be enough?"

Illesa ran her fingernail along one of the cracks in the table.

"Yes."

"And what happened?"

She couldn't wait to hear the latest disaster. It was better than watching a mummer's play.

"The Forester wasn't there and his men threatened me."

Agatha got up surprisingly quickly, her face almost triumphant.

"They saw *you* coming! A young girl on her own." Her voice was full of scorn. "And took the coin, no doubt." Agatha did not wait for Illesa's nod. "Well, you really have been a fool this time. Now you have no way of paying off your debts except to give up your land."

The bailiff had been planning this for a long time. The more credit he offered to them through his charming daughter or by any other means, the more chance he had of acquiring their property in the end.

"You could get something for this table and maybe for the bed or this chair. But really, that is it." Agatha ran her hand over the chair back and looked around the room. "You will have to give this place up."

She began to cross the room, assessing the contents. Illesa couldn't stand it anymore. She ran to Agatha, blocking her view of the shadowed table, took her hands and let the tears run down her face.

"Ask your father to stand surety for Kit. He knows the Forester well. He will listen to him, and, by God, I swear we will pay off the debts we owe you."

Agatha pulled out of her grip.

"You know he won't do that. Father has not forgotten Kit's insults." She pushed Illesa sideways slightly and leant over. "Is that a book?" She gazed at the shining gold halo and put her finger tentatively on the edge of the page. "It's beautiful." Agatha sat down in front of it. "Open the shutter."

Illesa did, her stomach churning. The sunlight fell onto the open page where the young saint was watching the sheep on the mountainside. On the left, the prefect Olymbrius rode past. Mountain birds perched in trees coloured like rainbows. A raven regarded the scene, its beak open. She stood silent by the table watching Agatha leaf through the book. When she finally closed it, Illesa let out her breath.

"Is it the story of Saint Margaret or Saint Marina?" Agatha frowned up at Illesa.

"They are the same holy saint. Here it is written as Margaret."

"I have never seen a book so fine. It must be worth a fortune. Who did you steal it from?"

Illesa watched the motes of dust falling towards the book's bright silver clasp. If Agatha accused her, the bailiff would convene the manorial court.

"I didn't steal it. It was Ursula's. She was Saint Margaret's guardian."

Agatha's eyes narrowed.

"What on earth do you mean?"

"My mother kept the book so that Saint Margaret would help the women here to birth their babies. It is one of the Saint's promises that her blessing would rest wherever there was a book of her Passion."

"But where did she get it from?"

"I don't know. She would never say." The lie was easy. It had been true for so long.

"She must have stolen it." Agatha ran the tip of her finger along the strap to its bright silver point. "This should belong to a holy order or a wealthy family."

"No, Madam, I assure you, she was charged to keep it."

Agatha arched her back, blinking in the strong light coming through the barred window.

"And now you are doing the same? Is that why you are living here like a hermit?"

"She told me to keep it safe." And hidden. Certainly not to let this she-serpent and her avaricious father see it.

"I don't believe it." Agatha shook her head. "This must have been commissioned for many pounds, and you claim it was given to the wife of a smith? Don't treat me like an idiot, Illesa. Father will find out who you took it from."

"I swear I am speaking the truth. Look." Illesa opened the book and turned to the page at the very back. "Here is the promise, written from Saint Margaret's own words." She pushed the page towards Agatha. "The blessed Saint has given her help to many women in Holdgate since my mother came here. If the book had been stolen, she would not have done so."

Agatha pushed the book back to Illesa.

"You *are* full of surprises. I cannot read Latin, but it appears that you can." She got up awkwardly and folded her arms across her belly. "I need to talk to Father. You should have told him about it as soon as your mother died. It casts suspicion on you that you didn't. The sale of this book could have paid off your debts a hundred times."

"No, it must not be sold!" Illesa squeezed her hands together to stop herself reaching out to take it. "Saint Margaret will only help us if it is kept safe and hidden. If you tell your father, it will be taken away and we will lose her blessing." Illesa took a gulp of air and met Agatha's gaze. "She will protect you when your time comes."

Agatha looked down at the book and opened the cover. She traced the loops of tendrils and snakes that adorned the first initial *O* of *Omnipotens*.

"If your mother had it legitimately, surely the Priest or the Brothers would have known of it. I cannot imagine a smith's wife being chosen as a suitable guardian for such a holy book." She turned a few pages. "But, let us say, that it does give protection in childbirth. I have heard of the Passion of Saint Margaret being used in that way. If that is so, it should stay in Holdgate." She glanced around the almost empty room. "But not here, in this hovel."

Illesa swallowed the lump in her throat.

"I will give it to you, in lieu of the money, Madam. If I pray to the saint and read you the Passion, your baby will be healthy. That is her promise."

Agatha looked at Illesa, her pupils very small and piercing.

"You cannot bargain away your debt. You know that I could take you to the court on a charge of stealing this book. If you haven't paid back the money by harvest time, as we agreed, then your land will be forfeit." She caressed the silver pin between her thumb and forefinger. "I will take the book with me now and keep it hidden in my chamber so it is with me when my pains begin."

Illesa put her hand out as Agatha began to rise from the stool.

"I swear by the Saint herself, the book will protect you," she said quickly, "but leave it here with me so I may appeal to Saint Margaret for you. We must not lose her favour by doing things in a hurry."

"What do you mean?" Agatha had sat down again, but her plump fingers still rested on the leather binding.

"The book of her Passion represents the Saint herself. We cannot bundle her from one place to another without proper prayer and supplication, Madam. If we do, she may remove her protection." Illesa kept her eyes lowered. "She will only favour those who show her due reverence."

Agatha snorted dismissively, leant back and folded her hands in her lap.

"Very well. You may say the prayers required. But once that is done, it must be brought to the manor and into my keeping. Saint Margaret will be more honoured there."

"Yes, Madam."

"And if my baby is not safe, I will know that you have been lying, and you and your mother are guilty of stealing the book. You know what the law is about theft."

Illesa had seen men convicted and hanged, but never a woman. Guilty women were taken to the river and drowned.

Agatha got to her feet and moved towards the door.

"My time is near, Illesa. I want it within two days." She turned in the doorway. "No later or I will have the constable after you."

Illesa heard the toft gate slam. She went to the window. Agatha was struggling up the hill, past the coppice and the reeve's penned pigs. When she was the size of a spider Illesa could crush between two fingers, she returned to the book and sat down hard on the stool in front of it.

If Kit were here he would laugh at her now. He had always made light of her disasters. But he was never likely to be here again. They would hang him, if he lasted long enough to make it to court. His gaolers were determined to make him suffer as much as possible. Kit had that effect on people in authority.

She closed the book and carried it to the wooden chest, fitted the plank over the book and began replacing the pile of clothes and blankets that had seemed such a comfort before. Amongst them was her mother's fragrant packet of herbs and roots for making her simples and poultices. Even it could not mask the smell of Kit's sweat and the smoke of his forge that clung to his old jerkin. Holding it, she allowed herself to cry. He was not a careful man, but he would never have risked so much for the sake of his stomach. She would not believe it of him. He had been on his way to her; had nearly made it.

Illesa unrolled her mother's leather bundle without thinking, checking the contents as she had been taught. The strong herbs were all there. Henbane, black poppy, bryony root. To make the sleeping draught she would only need darnel, and she had seen that growing near the miller's land. Pound it in a mortar until it was a fine powder, her mother had said. She had used it only on the very distressed, girls who had lost their babes and needed the emptiness of sleep to calm their grief. But it would work on men, if she used enough.

She could not risk going back to the gaol in the same clothes. Illesa ran her fingers over the seams of Kit's jerkin while fear pricked the back of her hands. It was stained and patched in several places, but skillfully with Ursula's tiny stitches. All the clothes were too big. She would have to work quickly to make them ready. After that she could only rely on God's mercy.

Bending down into the chest, she took the book out again.

It could not be left behind.

Chapter II
The 13th day of July, 1284
Myllichope

From the fork of the widest branch of the oak, Illesa could see the gaol door and the back of the stables. On the west end of the stone lodge was a stairway leading to a windowed room. Two men, armed with crossbows and short swords, attended the Lord Forester. She recognised the short, lithe one, Destrey, from the day before. They all rode out mid-morning. While they were gone, the guard opened the gaol door, threw the contents of a slop bucket into the road ditch and pissed on the ground. There was a stable boy no older than ten and a woman's voice shouting in the courtyard.

Illesa had found her hiding place before dawn, skirting the compound at a safe distance until she found the pollard oak and scrambled up the trunk. The summer foliage hid her well, at least from a distance. She only dared climb down to relieve herself once, shortly after the Forester had ridden out.

Eventually when the sun was a hand's breadth from the western hill, the Forester and his men came back, their saddles draped with conies. The Forester's orders were perfunctory; he went up the stairs to the hall. One of the men took the horses, and Destrey took the carcasses. The courtyard filled with noise. A fine looking grey horse wheeled and kicked as one of the men tried to examine its hooves. Swearing, he gave up and dragged it away to the stable. After some time the men climbed the steps, and the hall door slammed behind them.

Illesa made herself wait until the shadows were long and deep. She crept and ran until she was under the southern gaol windows. The men were talking loudly, enjoying their ale. She could hear nothing from inside the cells.

Staying close to the rough wall, she peered round the back of the prison and stopped short. Light from the hall windows illuminated the whole of the west side of the building. The smell of cooked meat hung in the air. A large woman was struggling up the outer stairs carrying a heavy platter. She balanced it against her waist and opened the thick door. A snatch of a rude song was muffled as the door closed behind her.

Illesa breathed out. She chose the darkest part of the courtyard and ran, heading for the kitchen. At the threshold, the only sound was the crackling of wood. She risked a look round the doorframe, keeping her body in shadow. There was only a guttering lamp and the fire in the hearth for light. A sweet milk pudding and several jugs of ale stood on the serving table. Illesa dipped her finger in the ale. It was strong enough to hide the smell.

The moon was dappling the orchard behind the kitchen. Illesa crouched behind a barrel and loosened the thong around the leather packet. Although the powder was wrapped in several thin layers of fabric, the smell was still acrid, catching the back of her throat. She swallowed hard, willing herself not to cough.

The hall door thudded shut as she was tipping powder into the second ale jug. The woman was coming down the stairs slowly, her arms full. Illesa ran into the deep shadows of the room. A trestle table against the back wall was piled with pots and dishes. She crawled under it and pushed herself against the crumbling daub of the wall. Then the room filled with the woman's breathing and her sharp smell. A stool creaked. She was sitting by the hearth, no more than two paces away.

"Well, he's in a good mood tonight," the woman declared. "More of this and more of that as if he was the King himself. Tomorrow I'll tell him, he'll have to get a scullion. I can't be doing it all myself. I'm run off my feet, I am."

Panic rose in Illesa's throat. Who was she talking to?

"That lazy boy has gone to sleep when I told him to clear the tables. Deserves a good hiding."

The woman reached out with her foot and pushed at something in the shadow beyond the fire. It tipped back and forth. A cradle. Illesa let her breath out very slowly. The baby must be asleep. The woman's foot rocked rhythmically and her breathing began to deepen. The hall door swung open with a bang.

"More ale!" a man shouted. The serving woman started awake.

"Coming, my lord."

She bent to look into the cradle, pressed her thick fingers on her thighs, rose and went to the table by the door. Illesa heard the slosh of pouring and several rapid gulps. The woman slapped the leather tankard back on the table. Then with jug in one hand and pudding in the other, she left the kitchen.

Illesa waited for the sound of the door before crawling out and running from the kitchen into the dark. In half an hour the effects should be felt. She sat down against the south wall of the gaol to wait. Soundless bats dropped from the eaves above her into the warm air.

The serving woman went to the hall once more with the last jug of ale, returning slowly to the kitchen and staying there. Eventually the voices from above stopped, replaced by the buzz of sleep. The courtyard was empty, dark and still. If she waited any longer, the strongest effects would have worn off.

Illesa stood listening at the top of the stairs. Three men were snoring. The fourth man would be the guard, probably asleep on a pallet by the cells. The door moved smoothly and silently on its hinges. She thanked God for his mercies and went in.

It reeked. The sleeping draught was not kind to the bowels. In the low light of the fire and a guttering torch, she could make out two men at the table, their heads cradled in their arms, mouths open. Giles de la Mare, the Lord Forester, wearing an embroidered surcoat, was slumped in an ornate chair by the fire. His head had rolled back and his flushed face was twitching and wet with sweat.

He had aged in the four years since she last saw him and his wife at the Whitsunday feast. Whether Giles would have been a gentler lord if his wife and baby had survived the breach birth was the subject of much speculation. But it was his greed that made him merciless. The living Giles had acquired on his marriage was nowhere near as profitable as he'd been led to expect. A whole church full of wives and children was unlikely to have softened his crushing grip on the lands around the Long Forest.

Illesa backed carefully away and surveyed the rest of the room. In the far wall there was a low door. Lifting the latch, she inched it open. A stone staircase spiraled down. She waited at the top for a moment. The hall floor rustled with mice looking for scraps among the rushes, but there were no sounds from below. She closed the door behind her and stepped down into the dark, the stones of the curving wall rough under her fingertips. The only sound was the violent thudding in her chest. After six steps the darkness lessened. A slight movement of air cooled her damp face. She must be near the window.

After two steps there were no more. In a wall bracket, a single flame guttered. To her left on a low bench, the guard was lying on his back, his head to the wall. To the right was a cell, which appeared empty. In front of her was a central aisle between four more cells, and between the two cells on the right was the arch of the gaol door.

As she walked down the aisle between the cells, something streaked along the bottom of the wall. She looked back. The guard hadn't moved. Illesa crouched down by the second cell on the left hand side. She could hardly see anything except a shape of deeper darkness near the wall.

"What in hell's name do you want?"

Illesa nearly screamed with shock.

"Shhhhh! Kit it's me, Illesa," she whispered.

"Lessa! God's wounds, what are you doing here?" Suddenly he was right in front of her, his hands on the bars, his voice sounding thick and deep. "What have you done to your hair?"

"Be as quiet as you can or you'll wake the guard," she whispered.

"You've come past the guard? Are you crazy, girl?"

"Be quiet Kit, for God's sake!" she said, looking towards the other end of the gaol. She could not see if the guard had moved.

"My God," Kit spoke more quietly this time. His breath smelt foul and one of his teeth was missing. "You better get out of here, Illesa. If they find you - "

"If you keep quiet they won't find either of us. I'll be back in a minute."

"Illesa!"

She ignored the angry whisper and went back towards the torchlight. The guard's head had changed position. She stood still, watching him. A thin stream of saliva came from the corner of his open mouth. His jerkin was unbuttoned. The iron chain was wound around his belt and the end hung down behind the bench.

Illesa slowly undid the buckle and loosened the chain, pulling it, link by link, off the leather belt. Gathering the chain in her hand, she pulled it up. There was a dull clang. The guard grunted and shifted on the bench, but his eyes remained closed. The ring holding the keys was caught between the wall and the bench. Illesa held the chain in her left hand and knelt down. She reached under the bench, her arms stretched around the guard, straining not to touch him. Her fingers brushed against the keys, and she let them rest on her palm. Illesa let the chain slip slowly out of her left hand until she held it, and the keys, in her right hand. She got shakily to her feet and ran to the cell door.

"Where is the lock?" she whispered.

"Here, follow my hand."

Illesa saw the vague whiteness of Kit's fingers; she put her own on top of them, feeling for the keyhole with her thumb.

"Got it," she said, fumbling with the larger key.

It slid easily into the hole, but as she turned it there was a terrible screeching sound of metal against metal. Something hit the floor with a loud thump and a gasp of pain.

Kit pushed the door, nearly knocking Illesa over as he ran out of the cell.

"Follow me!"

The guard was kneeling on the floor, shaking his head like a dog with something in its ear. Kit found the latch on the gaol door and yanked it hard. It did not open.

"I'll try the keys, you deal with the guard before he starts shouting for help," Illesa said, pushing Kit away. She ran her hands over the studded edge of the door, and found the box and the keyhole. She tried both keys but could not make them fit. There was a cracking sound behind her. Kit was sitting on top of the guard, punching his face.

"Stop! I didn't say kill him."

"Devil take the bastard, he deserves to die," he said, punching him again.

"He might, but you don't. If you kill him, they will hang you." Illesa pulled at Kit's arm and he half stood up, looking down at the unconscious guard. "He isn't going to be waking up for a while, by the look of him. Get him in the cell and we'll lock him in."

"I'm as good as dead anyway," Kit muttered. "How are we going to get out of here now?"

"We have to go back up through the hall. The men are asleep. As long as *you* keep quiet, we should make it out through that door." She gave him a meaningful look.

Kit drew the guard's dagger from its sheath and stuck it through his own belt. He grabbed the neck of the guard's jerkin and dragged him to the open cell, rolling him in with a kick like a bundle of dirty linen.

The key made the same noise when they locked the door, and they both winced.

"God almighty, Lessa, you look awful in those clothes," Kit whispered.

"Be quiet, will you! I am trying to get you out of here alive and all you can do is make unnecessary noise."

"My, my, little sister, you've sharpened your tongue!" he grinned. His lost tooth made him look like a little boy again.

Illesa pointed at the dark stair.

"Are you coming or shall I just leave you here to rot?"

"I'm ready," he said, brandishing the guard's dagger. "Let's go, squire."

It felt as if they had been below in the gaol for hours, so Illesa was surprised to see the hall looking exactly as it had before. Kit followed her out of the stairwell, and they stood still for a moment, watching the sleeping men. He had his hand on the dagger and his eyes on the slumped bodies.

"We should slit their throats," he whispered into her ear. "Send them to hell where they belong."

"And yourself along with them!"

He let her pull him away, and they moved carefully across the rush-strewn floor. The door opened smoothly, letting in a gust of fresher air. Outside everything was still. A soft rain had begun to fall, pattering on the broad leaves in the wood. Illesa led the way to the pollard oak and they stood close under it.

"Well, well, my girl, you do look a proper young man. I recognise that old jerkin and the hose." Kit pulled her close to his own hard torso with one arm. The embrace was brief. He pushed her away again and turned her around. "Got a man's chest there too. What is that?" He prodded her abdomen with his finger, and found the hardness of the saint's book. "Quite a disguise."

Illesa stepped away from him frowning. The way Kit was standing looked odd. His left arm was hanging limply and there was a line of pain across his forehead.

"What happened to your arm?"

He moved it slightly and grimaced.

"It wrenched out of the socket. They had me trussed up like a hen, slung sideways over a saddle. They found it very funny when I fell off and started screaming."

"Shall I try to put it into place?"

"No, not here. I may not be able to keep sufficiently quiet. It hurts like hell's arsehole."

She frowned again.

"Sorry. I forgot I'm in the company of a lady, albeit a strange-looking one."

"Would you have me going about the country in my own clothes? Don't you know what happens to maidens without protection these days?"

"It might fool a blind man a mile away, I grant you." He turned away from her, looking back at the quiet buildings. "I've got to go back for my tools, Lessa. They threw my pack into the stable when they got me here. And I'd like to get Greyboy back too. Those bastards don't deserve him." Kit flexed the fingers of his good hand.

"Your horse?"

"Yes, a three-year-old. He was costly, but he's worth every penny."

"But, Kit, the stable boy will be in there. He wasn't drugged like the others. We can't risk going back there now."

"What?"

"He didn't have the drugged ale, so it won't be safe," she said with deliberation.

"You drugged them?"

"Of course I did. How do you think we got out of there just now?"

"Well, you are full of surprises, my girl!" He said with his old, broad smile. "I didn't think you were interested in Mother's physic."

"I had to make the medicines when she got ill, for her and others." She reached out and took Kit's good arm. "You do know she's dead? Did you get my messages?"

"Yes, but only last month. Too late I guess. God rest her." Kit said, his fingers drumming on the dagger hilt.

"She wanted so much to see you before she died." Illesa rubbed her eyes to stop the tears.

"I'm sorry, Sweetheart. I did my best, but they wouldn't let me go. They've had every smith in the land working full tilt to replenish the supplies for the new Welsh castles. I sent word to you."

"I never got any messages," Illesa said. "Mother was so upset at the end, Kit. She told me things about the past - "

"Can we talk about this later, Lessa, when we are somewhere a little less exposed? I'm going back for Greyboy. Are you coming or staying here?"

Illesa looked at him, but he wouldn't meet her eye.

"I'll wait for you here. The sleeping draught will wear off soon, and it'll be light in an hour. Don't get caught."

Sitting back against the trunk of the tree, Illesa watched his long strides moving away and tried to swallow her anger. She shut her eyes and listened. The pigeons were settling back into their roost in the tree. Fat drops of rain fell from leaf to leaf. It felt as if she was far above the tops of the trees, looking over the long line of the forest and the low clouds, and across the dark, wet hills. She jerked awake when a drop of water landed on her head. Her belly felt light and shriveled. She took the skin from her pack and drank the last of the well water with her eyes closed. And she fell backwards, into the black emptiness.

"Illesa!" Kit was shaking her shoulder roughly. "Illesa, wake up, we have to leave now!" She got up, her stomach churning. Kit had his pack over one shoulder, but his face was screwed up with pain.

"What have you done?"

"Nothing, nothing. I got this, but I couldn't get Greyboy. They've locked the stable and someone was moving around inside. Come on, get up! It's only a matter of time before they realise." A shadow streaked across the yard in front of the stable. It was climbing the steps to the hall. The door was flung open. Illesa grabbed Kit's hand as a dog began barking.

"We have to get to a church," she whispered. "Where is the nearest?"

"Eaton I think. This way," he said, heading west into the coppice that stretched up the hill. "Keep off the path."

The wind direction was in their favour, but the roots and branches in the deep shadow of the woods seemed to grab their legs. Illesa measured her length on the ground more than once. The sky was lighter when they reached a clearing at the top of the hill, and the gaol and the crouched outbuildings were just visible. Torches flared in the courtyard.

"They haven't left yet!" Kit said, pulling her after him.

They sped down the long pasture field towards the spur of the forest, with rain running down their faces and necks. Something leaped out of the grass in front of them. For two paces it ran straight, like an arrow pointing the way and then the hare dodged, its back legs stretched out, and it disappeared into the field edge.

They slowed down as they reached the first line of trees. The sun would soon rise. In the pattern of shadows there was just enough light to see a well-trodden track, kicked up by carts and hooves, heading north along the line of the escarpment. On the other side of it, the forest dropped steeply away down into Ape Dale. A path sank into the valley to the west. Illesa turned to Kit. He coughed and spat on the ground.

"That was a bad omen."

They both crossed themselves. Illesa said a quick prayer to the Virgin. The devil used hares as familiars for his witches, but they could also be a holy symbol. The Christian was obliged to flee temptations, like the hare. The devil would certainly be laying traps to prevent them reaching the sanctuary of the church. If they were going to be caught, it would be here, at this junction of paths. Illesa crept onto the track and signaled him to follow, crossing to stand in the lee of a large beech at the head of the western track.

"Which way now?" she asked. It didn't look as though Kit could go another step, but they had to hurry. The sky was already light grey.

"The church is at the bottom of the bank, but that path is too narrow for my liking." Kit said, his breath coming in little gasps. "I won't be able to run it." The track had steeply banked sides held in a net of twisting roots. They would be snared like rabbits.

She heard them before she saw them. Horses approaching from the south. There was no time to run anywhere, only to clamber off the track and press themselves amongst the exposed tree roots and the crumbling earth of the slope. The tools in Kit's pack knocked together as he set it down at his feet, and they exchanged glances. Illesa looked behind at the scrubby cover and the exposed path. They were well enough hidden from the people travelling from the south, but if anyone turned onto the western track, they would be spotted at once.

In front, Illesa could see a small patch of road between the tree trunk and a clump of bracken. She counted ten loud heartbeats until the sounds of horses filled the air. Two palfreys slowed and stopped as they came to the crossing. The men leading them were just out of view, but one of them had a hacking cough.

"Shut your trap, Eadwick. You're drawing attention."

"Shut yours. If you didn't drag me out here in the middle of the night, I wouldn't get a cough. It's unhealthy, that's what I say." There was a pause and the sound of drinking. The palfreys were restless. They shook their heads and pulled on their poor rope bridles, water drops spraying from their manes.

"Put that away; we've got company," the first man said in an urgent whisper.

The sound took another moment to reach Illesa: hooves and barking. She shut her eyes to pray. The noises came closer, then the barking was cut off. Kit touched her arm, and she opened her eyes.

"What's happening?" he mouthed. He was directly behind the tree, unable to see.

The spooked palfreys were kicking up the mud of the track as the men tried to control them. And beyond them, outlined against the eastern sky, two horsemen had stopped on the field edge. One had a crossbow, aimed into the trees. There was a sudden scrambling of leaves, and something bolted towards the track. A hound bounded into the wood after it. One of the riders shouted, and the other loosed the arrow. The hare made two more leaps before it fell just beside the track, the bolt through its stomach. Its feet kicked a few futile paces, and stilled.

The two riders came fast behind it, pulling up on the track in front of the nervous palfreys. Illesa recognised the Lord Forester and Destrey, wide awake and scanning the undergrowth. The Forester wheeled his horse before dismounting. Destrey shouldered his crossbow, slid off his horse and pulled the dog off the carcass wordlessly. It started to bark, and he slapped it hard on the back. The Forester kicked the hare onto the mud of the track.

"Damn skulker hare! It's taken the dog off the scent."

"Gilbert's dog may still be following him, my lord," Destrey said. He unwound a strap of leather from his shoulder and leashed the dog.

"Devil take you, Destrey! You were meant to be controlling it. Now we have lost him," the Forester said. He turned to the men on the track. "What are you looking at?"

"Nothing, my lord," one of the men said. He had moved to calm his horse and Illesa saw his thin, mismatched features and buck teeth. His friend was taller, with a head of very black hair and a face that looked as if it had been flattened in a press.

"You are in the forest without leave. I warned you last time, Jarryd. You and your simple friend will pay if you try to take a single stick from my demesne."

"We were only on the way to church, my lord, to make our confession."

The Lord Forester smiled. He looked at Destrey, and tilted his head towards the two unhappy horses.

"I see. And you have left so early because making your confession will take such a long time."

The two men were silent. Destrey removed the reins from their hands. He pulled the palfreys towards his own mount and tied them on the pommel of his saddle. The black-haired man looked as if he might cry.

"Well, good men," the Forester said, standing in front of them. "You are blessed for your devotion today. I am in need of your help, and when you have provided it, you can claim your reward. An escaped felon, Christopher Arrowsmith, is hiding in these woods." The Forester spat on the ground before continuing. "He is tall, with light brown hair and his arm is injured. I suggest you look for him on your way to be shriven. If you help us track him successfully, you may have your mounts back."

"But my lord, - " Jarryd began.

"You can bring the man to me alive or dead," the Forester interrupted. "Your reward will be the same." He mounted his horse and steered it around the dead hare.

"My lord, the mounts are not ours. We need to return them today to the bailiff." Jarryd looked up in appeal, and then down at his feet.

"You'd better be quick about finding the smith then. We will look to the south. If you catch him, signal us or bring him to the gaol. The guard will take charge of him." He spurred his horse, and the mud flew up from his hooves as he galloped down the track.

Destrey walked over to the dead hare and pulled its neck before removing his bolt and wiping it on the grass. Then he tied the limp body to the saddle, loosed the dog and mounted, setting off after his master with the hound running at his side, barking at the hare as it bounced off the horse's flank. The palfreys were pulled reluctantly behind. Eadwick looked after them, wiping the rain from his mournful face.

"Damn you, Jarryd, now we've lost our mounts. I knew I shouldn't have listened to your stupid ideas." He started coughing again.

"You'd better keep quiet or we'll have no chance of tracking the smith," Jarryd said.

"We've no chance anyway, without any horses," Eadwick said, walking away down the road.

They moved off, arguing. Birds began to call from the thicket.

"They've gone." Kit stood up and clambered onto the track, but Illesa did not move.

"Shhhh." She held her breath, listening.

In the distance she could just hear it; a high, shrill whistle coming from the field they had run through only moments before, and then barking. An answering blast of a horn from the south made them both start.

"The other dog has tracked us. Come on!"

Kit pulled her down onto the steep path. It was winding, and the mud was thick and pungent from horse and mule traffic. After falling and sliding for several minutes, the ground leveled out and they saw the church behind a low wall, surrounded by graves. The village crofts beyond it were still shuttered. Somewhere behind the squatting buildings a pig was squealing, but there was no one in the lane. Smoke drifted above the thatched roofs. There was a smell of wet ashes in the air.

They slowed to a walk at the lych gate. Illesa followed Kit up the path to the south door. It scraped against the floor as she opened it. They took several paces in and stopped, dismayed. No candles, no voices. The church seemed empty of man and God. Illesa shivered, running her hand through her wet hair.

"The Forester will be glad there is no Priest to witness it when he drags me out, " Kit said, leaning against the wall.

"That is not going to happen." Illesa strode up the nave and found a small door leading to the tower. It was locked.

"Is there anything in your bag of tools that will open this door?"

Kit walked over and dropped his pack on the floor. The noise of iron on stone reverberated around the walls.

"Breaking into the church tower is definitely a sin."

"I think the Priest here is likely to be more sympathetic than the Forester if he finds you before you have verified your sanctuary. Get in there and lock the door. I will find the Priest." Before he could argue any more, she was back down the nave and out of the door into the grey morning.

Chapter III
The 14th day of July, 1284
Eaton

"Father Osbert, surely you don't want to impede the King's justice. You are new here. Perhaps the authorities can be more lax in Wenlock, but in this demesne we have to be hard on criminals or they will soon be cutting our throats while we sleep," the Forester said, his hand on the pommel of his sword. "There is no need for you to be involved. We will apprehend the felon and trouble you no further."

Illesa's lungs burned. She was well hidden in the dark corner made by the churchyard wall and the lych gate, but it was so close to the men that she feared they would hear her breathing. The gap made by the hinges provided a restricted view. Father Osbert stood next to the open gate that hid her, unmoving, his hands folded in front of him.

"I understand your concern for the safety of the people, Lord Forester. Nevertheless, I must answer to a higher justice. Sanctuary must be granted when it is sought, no matter what the sin. God's mercy must be offered." The Priest had the low and powerful voice of a younger man. The slowness of his speech was all that gave away his age.

"You talk of mercy for the merciless," the Forester said, pointing at the church. "The man is brutal and cunning. He will break into your homes and take what he likes, killing those who stand in his way. I must return him to gaol where he won't do any more harm." The Forester took a step towards the open gate. "Now let me do my job, Father, or I fear you will regret it."

He was so close that Illesa could see his cracked lips and smell the wet leather of his jerkin. Destrey stood to the left of him, a bolt ready in his bow. A thrush was singing in the branches of the yew tree. Father Osbert cleared his throat, taking his time to answer.

"God knows I am no friend of those the devil has used to do his work, but Church law must not be broken. If he is here, he is under that law's protection." The Priest paused again. Each second of silence was long, like the slip of the mind when sleep takes hold. "But I think that is very unlikely," Father Osbert continued. "He is probably still hiding in the forest. Surely he couldn't outrun you on your horses?"

"Do you doubt my judgment?" the Forester shouted. "The man has been tracked here, and he is in your church as we speak, stealing the chalice and paten! You may be happy to give away the church treasure to a blatant thief, but I will not stand for it." He cracked his gloves on his palm like a whip.

There was another lengthy pause, as if the Priest were listening to someone else. Illesa held still. The smallest twig snapping under her foot would be enough.

"My lord, you will have to leave him to God for forty days. Whatever the man's sin, God is stronger," Father Osbert said. "Now, I must say Mass. You will attend? We cannot fight against the forces of evil in this world without the strength of our Lord in heaven."

"I don't have the leisure to worship with criminals." The Forester stepped closer to the Priest. Illesa could not see what he was doing, but the fury in his voice was clear. "You do your job, Father, and I'll do mine. After Mass I *will* search your church, and then we will see what protection you provide." The Forester's spurs rang as he turned back to where the horses stood in the lane.

Father Osbert made the sign of blessing in the air after him. He pulled his cowl over his head and walked up the path to the church without looking at her. A horse was approaching from the village track. The rider drew up next to Destrey, beardless, with shoulder-length red hair that hung around his face in wet strands. He sneezed loudly and wiped his nose with the back of his hand. His dogs ran towards the churchyard, but he called them back.

"No sign of him in the village, my lord," the rider said.

"Take the dogs back to the crossroads and keep watch on the forest track," the Forester ordered.

"I need a piss," the man muttered, starting to dismount.

"Go, you lazy bastard!" the Forester shouted, smacking the horse on its rump with his gloves. It shot forward up the track with the man half off, hanging on the horse's mane, his leg swinging. The Forester kicked his boot against the wall, knocking off clumps of mud.

"That Priest is in it up to his stinking nose," he said under his breath, examining his boots.

Destrey was adjusting the straps securing the hare to his saddle.

"Stop messing about with that and tie them up properly," the Forester barked. "Keep watch on the church. If that Priest tries to slip Arrowsmith out, shoot him. I'll be in the tavern." He strode down the lane, his sword swinging by his side.

Destrey took both sets of reins and turned the horses round, walking them towards a large oak across the track. It was the only chance she had. Illesa ran, up the slope of the churchyard and behind the church's south wall. She flattened herself against the grey limestone and breathed. Water dripped from the roof on her neck. Illesa did not turn round to see if Destrey was coming up the path to shoot her; she sprinted to the porch. But the rough boards of the south door did not move when she lifted the latch. It was locked.

"Father," she whispered.

The skin on her back crawled. After a moment there was the click of iron lifting, and the door opened slightly. Illesa slipped inside, her sodden boots marking the stone floor.

"Come, quickly."

The Priest took her arm and led her towards the red covered altar. His face was anxious and solemn, quite changed from when she found him striding through the village and begged for his help.

"The churchwarden will come soon, and then the Forester. I will try to protect you both, but it would be best to make your confession now, just in case. Give me your pack."

Startled, she looked at him, but only his thin set mouth was visible in the deep shadow of the cowl over his head.

"Father, my brother is hurt. Please let me go to him."

"We will keep you apart for now," he said, walking up the nave. "If they connect you two, they may take you prisoner as well. You must be hidden elsewhere. Kneel here." Illesa gave him the pack and knelt on the cold stone. He left her in front of the altar and went through the low door to the vestry. After a moment, he returned with a black habit similar to his own.

"Put this on. You should remain here by the altar throughout the Mass. Do not face the congregation and do not speak to them. I will explain that you are a novice from Wenlock who is bound by a silent fast. Keep your cowl over your head in prayer," he said. His voice was so low it seemed to send a vibration through her, as if a deep bell had just stopped ringing.

Illesa pulled the rough cloth over her head, and the Priest tied the knotted cord low across her hips. She had to haul her mind away from the men outside to say the prayers prescribed. When she had finished, the Priest made the sign of the cross over her.

"What is your name?"

"Illesa."

"Illesa," he looked at her closely. "You are a maiden." He paused for several moments. "I believe I knew your mother, Ursula."

Illesa stared, unable to speak.

"I cannot approve of your disguise, but it is necessary to prolong it for a time to preserve your life. We will call you Brother Benedict. God's blessings be upon you."

Illesa knelt where he left her, light-headed and close to tears. She bent down and laid her forehead on the cold flagstone. If only her mother were here in body not just in name, she would get them out of this trap. But that was a silly, childish thought. God was here. He had guided them to this place where they were known. That should be enough.

The church door scraped on the stone lintel.

"Ah, Warden Lyttle, come in out of the rain. A bit late today."

"Sorry, Holy Father," the man yawned and went into the vestry.

Moments later he came out and approached the altar, carrying the chalice and paten. He stopped short when he saw Illesa.

"Oh, God's greetings, Holy Brother."

Illesa stayed as still as she could, her eyes closed and head down.

"That is Brother Benedict," Father Osbert said, walking towards the altar. "He will not answer you, as he is committed to a silent fast until the end of the Sabbath."

"You are welcome, Brother Benedict, in the Lord's name," the churchwarden shouted at Illesa's back.

"He is not deaf, Warden, just silent for a time." Father Osbert sounded amused.

Illesa's throat tightened against rising hysteria. She squeezed her hands together until her fingers turned white and observed the Mass from a hinterland between sleep and terror. The swell of voices in the church came and went like clouds overhead.

Gradually she became aware that the worshippers were gone. The voice of the Forester, close at hand, roused her fully.

"I have been very patient with you, Father. Now give me your keys."

"Ah yes, Lord Forester," Father Osbert replied, coming out from behind the altar. "I have found the man you are pursuing. He has claimed sanctuary and has made his confession. You may place a guard on him, if you so wish. I will provide him with food from the poor alms, unless you would like to take charge of his care?"

The Forester barked a laugh.

"You must take me for a fool."

Illesa only heard two footsteps on the stones and then a blow on the side of her face knocked her down. Her cowl slipped to one side. She pushed herself up, blinking away the tears. The Forester was staring at her. He lowered his sword.

"Stop!" Father Osbert grabbed his arm and pushed him away. "You have struck Brother Benedict."

The Forester sheathed his sword, his face reddening.

"This is a brother of your house is it? He looks half dead. Is this how you treat your novices? Starve them to death?"

"His health will not be improved by your fist. He is nearing the end of a silent fast." Father Osbert helped Illesa up. "You dishonour this place, my lord. If there is anymore violence, I will be forced to request your excommunication."

Illesa pulled the cowl back over her head and knelt in her place by the altar. Her whole body was shaking.

"The devil will take you first!" the Forester replied.

"This is God's house." Father Osbert said each word slowly and deliberately. "The Prior will hear of any attacks on Holy Mother Church."

"And do what? The Church is not outside the law. I assure you Father, that if anyone so much as bends the smallest rule of sanctuary here, I will have it declared invalid. And there will be nothing the Prior can do about it," the Forester's said, imitating the Priest's deliberation.

Silence fell. Father Osbert's habit brushed her arm as he moved away, his sandals slapping on the flagstones.

"The Church offers mercy to all who seek it, even to those too zealous for justice."

"I have not come here for your piety, Father. Save it for your friend inside. Now let me see him and then we may agree the terms."

"Certainly, my lord, but you must lay down your weapons."

The Forester said something under his breath. His sword and dagger clattered to the floor.

"Brother Benedict, take the weapons to the door," Father Osbert said.

Illesa got to her feet. The two men watched her gather the weapons in her arms and walk down the nave. The sword was long, heavy and awkward to carry. She gripped the handle, and her hands itched to swing it. When she reached the west end of the church, the Priest approached the tower.

"Christopher, come near the door," he called through the keyhole.

"For Christ's sake, open it!" the Forester demanded.

"No, my lord. You may see him this way, but you may not enter the tower."

"I am not a servant to be peering through keyholes. Open the door, I say!"

"My lord, the man you seek is there. You can see him quite clearly by looking through this hole. If that does not satisfy you, then you may see him when we can provide a guard to protect him. He is badly injured."

"Are you questioning my honour?" the Forester demanded. "I would not kill him in the church."

"I did not say you would," Father Osbert said slowly. "But what is to stop you dragging him out?"

The Forester paused, his head raised. He almost smiled.

"You heard that did you? Heard how that fool died outside the church door?" He pointed his finger in Father Osbert's face. "All you brothers are the same, passing gossip around like women. I bring offenders against the King's law to justice, and you should not stand in my way, Priest."

Illesa could barely hear Father Osbert's reply.

"You have allowed your anger to take hold of you, my lord. If you do not confess it, it will lead you into hell."

The Forester hit the door with his fist and whirled round, striding down the church, his face in a rictus of fury.

"Forty days, and then we will drag you through the streets, Arrowsmith! Do you hear me?" he shouted. "Give me my weapons!"

He grabbed the sword and dagger from Illesa's arms and was gone out of the door and into the rain, which poured from the sky as if it were Noah's flood.

"Brother Benedict, come here," Father Osbert called.

Illesa ran up the nave to the tower door, her head throbbing with each step.

"You must hold your brother while I manipulate his shoulder," the Priest said, taking her arm. "I don't know if the technique will work after all this time." He reached inside his habit, pulled out a key on a chain round his neck and unlocked the tower door. Kit was lying on the ground, his head on a pile of sacks. Father Osbert locked the door from the inside and knelt down next to him.

"Now my boy, consider the sufferings of our Lord, and your pain will seem as nothing," he whispered. "Illesa, take off your cord and put it in his mouth. He will need something to bite."

"Illesa?" Kit said, raising his head a little. "By Christ, it's you. Whatever will you dress up in next?"

"Shhhh. They may be listening at the window, Kit. They mustn't know I'm your sister," Illesa whispered, sitting down on his other side.

"Sorry. Of course," he said, lying back. He smiled up at her. "No one will ever believe you are a monk, Sweetheart. Not merry enough."

"Kit, can't you hold your peace?" Illesa shoved the cord between his teeth and heaved him across her lap, pinioning his good arm against his chest. Father Osbert put his foot in Kit's armpit and pulled. She felt the stretch of muscles and tendons and the sobbing in his chest. Father Osbert rotated the arm into position in the shoulder joint and tied it securely in place with his own belt cord.

"We'll find a better way to protect it later," the Priest said, looking at Kit's white face. Illesa took the wet cord out of his mouth, and he coughed painfully. She wiped the beads of sweat from his forehead with the end of her sleeve.

"Now, you must rest," Father Osbert said, getting to his feet. "Brother Benedict and I will return later with some food and drink. There is a bucket in the corner. Don't go near the window."

Kit was uncharacteristically silent. He looked like he was going to be sick. Illesa ran a hand through his hair.

"Sleep now. I'll make you something for the pain," she whispered.

The corners of his mouth twitched, but his eyes were already closed.

Outside, the rain had slowed to a steady drizzle. Eaves dripped on the mud of the quiet lane. They turned left at the end of the tithe barn and the silence in the rest of the village was explained. The tavern three doors along was overflowing with loud men and the malty smell of brewing ale.

"The village has been without a resident Priest for years. I'm afraid the people have developed some bad ways," Father Osbert said.

"How long have you been here?"

"Only half a year. The Prior wishes me to stay but he has not yet ordered lodging to be built, so I am staying in the churchwarden's house. Here we are." They stopped outside a two-storey building, old but well tended. A faint pall of smoke hung over the thatched roof. "Goodwife Lyttle has insisted that I live here alone and has moved in with their son and daughter-in-law. She assures me that her son is grateful to have proper food for a change," he said, his expression neutral. The heavy door was locked.

"Ah ha. The good woman is out. Praise God for small mercies." He unlocked the door and led Illesa inside. One window was un-shuttered, revealing the ample hall strewn with fresh rushes, but underneath their fresh smell there was a residual odour of bacon. Illesa's stomach growled. Embers still glowed in the fire where it had been cooked. Near the bay of service rooms, a narrow stair rose to what must be the sleeping quarters. All seemed tidy, if sparsely furnished.

The Priest went immediately to the lantern and lit it with a taper from the fire. He closed the shutters and indicated a low stool. Illesa sat down.

"Father, my pack is still in the church. I will need to get it back somehow."

"Do not worry about that now. It is safe in the vestry."

"Shall we get some food for Kit? He seemed so weak --" Her voice trailed off as the Priest's eyes turned on her.

"Don't fret about him. He just needs time to rest, as do you. He will sleep a while and then we will make him more comfortable." Father Osbert returned to the fire and began feeding it sticks.

Illesa thought of arguing but she was suddenly so tired that she just sat watching him.

"When you've had some food, you can tell me what has happened."

Father Osbert fetched a pot from the table and set it on the trivet in the fire. The smell of cabbage and parsley began to fill the room, and Illesa felt weak with hunger.

"Goodwife Lyttle leaves me pottage every evening. Sometimes it is so good, I finish it." He found a bowl and scraped the pot out. "You are lucky today, there is quite a lot left. Here you are."

He handed Illesa the wooden bowl and a spoon. She tried to make the food last more than a moment. When she looked up he was just coming through the pantry door, holding a loaf of bread.

"Here," he said, handing her a hunk of the maslin.

The Priest sat on another stool, chewing the heel of the loaf. When she had finished, he got up and went through the door again. He came back holding two horn cups.

"Prior John promised me two barrels of Gascon wine when I came to Eaton," Father Osbert said as he sat down opposite her. "Such generosity is not characteristic of him. I have often wondered whether he wanted me out of the way. But in this case it is a blessing to ease your pain and shock. Here," he said putting the cup into her hand. She finished the dark wine too quickly and felt flushed and lightheaded.

The Priest began to pray in Latin, giving thanks for food and drink. Illesa wondered what to do with the cup in her hand. She finally put it on the floor and sat with her hands in her lap and her eyes closed. The drone of the Priest's voice became a blanket of sound.

Illesa's head jerked forwards and she opened her eyes. Father Osbert was looking at her, frowning.

"Come. This way."

He led her up the stairs to a small chamber. There was a simple truckle bed at the back end and a window that looked out onto the lane.

"Sleep as long as you need. I will check on your brother and take him food."

"Father," she blurted out. "You said you remembered my mother. How did you know her?"

Father Osbert put a finger to his lips. "We will talk later. You must rest now." He went to the window, closed the shutter and left the room.

Illesa sat down on the straw mattress and began untying the wet leather thongs of her boots. The knots were tight and swollen together, and she almost gave up and left them on. As she lay down, the weight of her mother's book pressed on her chest. She folded her hands over it and closed her eyes.

A loud sound broke into Illesa's dream, like the stroke of a hammer on iron. She sat up. A bell was ringing in the church.

"And what do you think you're doing?" said a strident female voice from outside.

"Mind your own business," a man replied.

Illesa crept to the window. She could not see who it was through the narrow gaps of the shutter boards.

"It *is* my business. This is my house and Father Osbert is my tenant. Now get away from the door. You have *ruined* the latch."

"I have my orders, good dame. I have my job to do."

"Not here, you don't. This is my property. You should be ashamed of yourself, breaking into a man of God's house. I don't care *who* you work for, get out of here before I fetch the Father. Go on, get away." The woman's voice had grown louder and louder and soon other voices joined in.

"What's going on, Goodwife Lyttle? Is there trouble?"

It sounded as if a crowd was gathering around the door. Illesa opened the shutter slightly. The tavern had emptied and all the men now congregated around the Forester's hunter, who was in front of the door holding a hammer and chisel.

"Who is he?" someone cried.

"It's bloody John Destrey, that works for the Forester," said one man who was still holding a leather mug.

"What do you think you're doing? You can't go breaking into decent people's houses like that."

"I'm on the Forester's business, looking for a felon. Your tithing has a duty to help me apprehend him."

"We'd be pleased to help you, if you asked," said another man wearing a smith's leather apron, who pushed forward to the centre of the crowd. "But we are not so happy when you simply help yourself. These are from my forge." He stood almost a foot higher than the hunter, and calmly twisted the tools out of his hand.

"If you harbour a known criminal, you'll pay twice the usual fine," Destrey said, loud enough for the whole crowd to hear. "I expect you all have plenty of coin to pay for a thief's life."

"The man you are looking for is in the church and *you* can't do anything about it for forty days. So you have no right to break into anyone's property." The loud woman stood in front of John Destrey and emphasised each point with a finger on his chest. She was short and slight with a clean, straight wimple.

Destrey turned on the crowd.

"He has an accomplice. Someone has been helping him. Sooner or later we will find him, or them." He looked around. "I shall tell the Forester that the people of Eaton are shirking their responsibilities. You will pay at the next court tour, unless someone turns him in," he said, trying to push through the men around him.

"You stay away from our property, you hear?" said one man, grabbing Destrey's jerkin. "If you've something to look for, try looking up your own arse!"

He pushed him hard on the chest, and Destrey fell backwards against the crowd, which parted and let him land in the mud. He picked himself up and walked quickly away up the lane to the sound of their laughter.

"Fart of the devil," one man shouted. Another with a full beard began to sing in falsetto, clutching his privates.

"Thank you, good men. You can go now. The show is over and you should be at home with your wives," the small woman said, pushing them firmly away from the door.

"We're going, we're going."

Illesa watched as the street emptied. Most of the men went back, just a few doors along to the tavern.

Goodwife Lyttle looked up at the window, meeting Illesa's eye through the gap in the shutter. She took a key from her waist and opened the door. Illesa heard her close it firmly and tut-tut about the state of the lock.

"You can come down now."

Illesa looked over the railing. The woman was busying herself with the fire. She went down and stood awkwardly, waiting.

"Well, what a state you are in, goodness me. Queer looking thing. I expect you haven't had a proper meal in weeks. You need feeding up, no question. Father Osbert asked me to look after you for the evening and it's a good thing he did. That knave has ruined my door, and heaven only knows what he would have done to you, poor boy." Goodwife Lyttle spoke loudly, all the while making the fire up, cleaning out the pots and setting water to boil.

"Now then, that will be ready shortly. Let's see to you." Goodwife Lyttle approached Illesa purposefully.

"Goodwife, I am well," Illesa said, backing away.

"Come now, I am not going to hurt you. But if you are going to be Brother Benedict, you are going to need a bit more than a habit and a terrified look. The Cluniac brothers take care of their appearance, to give glory to God. Let's sort out your hair for a start. Sit here." She pulled the stool across to the back window, opened the shutters, sat Illesa down and turned her face to the light.

"By Jesu, that's a nasty bruise. The Lord Forester is a brute. One of these days God will humble him, I've no doubt. Now sit still." Goodwife Lyttle went round Illesa's head with a pair of shears, and after a few minutes she seemed satisfied.

"Cut it yourself did you? I've not given you a tonsure you'll be pleased to know. You don't look much like a monk, even now, but I've done my best."

"Thank you, Goodwife."

"Now I expect you'd like a wash; you certainly need one. The water is nice and hot. I'll take it into the buttery for you." She poured the hot water into a leather bucket, and with a light in the other hand, led Illesa through the door.

"Here you are. There are some linen cloths in the chest. Don't soak the floor, now."

She shut the door and Illesa could hear her talking to herself as she chopped the vegetables at the table. Illesa pulled the habit over her head and started removing the layers of Kit's old clothes, holding the book carefully as she unwrapped the strapping that kept it in place. It was warm from her body but undamaged. Saint Margaret's words deserved a prie-dieu and candles, not this rough treatment. She placed it reverently on a stool.

Illesa was naked and wet from the waist up when she heard the front door open. The Priest greeted and blessed Goodwife Lyttle. Illesa quickly rubbed her body dry with a linen cloth and began strapping the book on to her chest, her eyes on the door. The conversation taking place seemed entirely one-sided. The Priest's replies were so short and quiet that only the woman could be heard.

"Look what that man did to the lock, Father. What he would have done if he'd got in, I don't like to think. How long do you think you can keep this a secret? Not a word. Not even to my son. You know you can trust me, Father. But are you sure this is wise? Well, of course you know what is wise, but is it *sensible*? That man can make life bad for the whole village for much longer than forty days."

Illesa felt as if she ought to knock before re-entering the hall, but settled on tapping the bucket on the floor. Goodwife Lyttle stopped talking mid-sentence as she entered.

"Ah, here you are. Feeling better? The food is almost ready. Sit down. Good. Well, I must be off, Father. Leave it another few minutes over the fire. I'll be back in the morning. God give you good evening!"

The door closed behind her. Father Osbert stood by the hearth, an unreadable expression on his face.

"Well, *are* you feeling better?"

"Yes, thank you, Father. How is Kit?"

"He is still in pain, but not as much. I have given him something that will also help him sleep, and I have heard his confession, which will give rest to his soul. He has even eaten a little. So do not worry about him for now. I've brought your pack. It's there by the stair."

"Oh that's wonderful, Father, thank you!" She couldn't stop herself going to check it. The leather was soaked, but the clothes and herbs inside were dry and untouched.

"What about the Forester's man," Illesa asked as she fastened the straps tightly. "Is he guarding the church?"

"Yes, although he will be retiring soon. The alewife has offered him a bed for the night. Your brother will be safe enough till morning. Now I think we are both ready for our food."

They sat at the table, and neither said a word until every scrap was gone. Again Father Osbert brought a cup of wine for each of them. Illesa sipped it and set it down on the table. The Priest was leaning against the carved back of his chair. He shut his eyes for a moment. When he opened them he regarded Illesa with an intensity that made her look away.

"I have already heard your brother's story. If you are able to tell it, I am ready to listen to yours."

Chapter IV
The Priest's Lodgings

"Pray for the mercy of Our Lady," Ursula said, pulling Illesa down to kneel in front of the statue of the Holy Mother and the infant Christ.

She was eight years old, cold and hungry, and had never travelled so far on foot. They had left home before dawn, walked for hours and eaten nothing. It was Easter Eve, and Wenlock was bursting. Every lane was crammed with people, packhorses and piles of dung. The church was not much better. The flower-covered shrine of Saint Milburgha was surrounded by penitents, and a noisy procession wove towards the altar. Several monks passed close to her, swinging censers, and the incense that rose in small puffs smelled like balm and burnt pine. A woman began shouting. Illesa looked over, but in the press of people she could not see who was cursing the devil and his servants so loudly in public. Ursula did not even open her eyes. Her face was wet, and her lips moved in spasms of prayer.

Someone was standing over her. Illesa glanced up and pulled her mother's sleeve. A monk in a long black habit was lowering his cowl, his eyes on Ursula's face.

"Ursula?" he asked. His voice was deep and gentle but his expression was agitated. Illesa hid from his stare in her mother's mantle. Ursula looked up, pushing Illesa away.

"Osbert!" she cried, as if she was meeting the Lord himself.

***

Illesa realised that she had been staring at the Priest's hand where it rested on the arm of his chair for some time.

"I saw you in Wenlock with Mother, when I was a girl. It was the Feast of the Resurrection."

Father Osbert smiled carefully.

"Yes, you were very young. I thought I might see you again, but the manner of it was quite unexpected." He sipped his wine. "I didn't think you had remembered."

The eight-year-old Illesa had felt jealous of this man who had given her mother such delight by merely speaking to her and pronouncing her shriven. Ursula had never looked so happy

54

before. On their walk home, her mother had explained: Osbert came from her family's village, where they had played together as children. He was her oldest friend. This had only made Illesa's resentment grow.

Father Osbert was watching her.

"You were her confessor that day," Illesa said.

"Was I?" he said, slowly. "I don't recall. I was glad to see her after many years. Did she tell you that we grew up together?"

Illesa nodded, and swallowed hard. What had Ursula said to him in that confession? She would never have revealed any detail of Illesa's parentage to their village priest, whose mouth was an open ditch. But she might have told her old friend. And with Ursula dead, he might break the seal of the confessional and tell her.

"I am grieved to hear of her death." Father Osbert pulled the wide cassock sleeves over his swollen knuckles. His gaze did not leave her face.

Illesa lowered her eyes.

"Your father has gone to the Lord also?"

She looked up. His face betrayed no hypocrisy.

"He fell in the Welsh war two years ago. We do not know what became of his body."

In the long silence, Illesa heard the split and tumble of ash in the fire.

"Your mother was always humbly convinced of her own sin and diligent in her penance. Of your father's soul I know nothing." Osbert paused. "You can reduce their suffering in purgatory through penance and prayer, Illesa. The Lord is merciful. If your mother received the sacrament before she died and confessed in true contrition, her time of suffering will be short."

Illesa picked up the poker and riddled the smoking fire.

"She would not have the Priest at her sickbed. As far as I know she confessed to no one. Ursula was not herself before she died. She told me strange things. I think the pain nearly drove her mad."

Out of the corner of her eye, she saw him wince.

"You should not have given in to her, child. The devil makes the weak and dying say sinful things in order to win their souls. Anointing her with holy water would have driven the evil one away and allowed her to make a full confession."

"Holy Father, if you had been her confessor again perhaps she would have agreed. She did not trust the village priest. He has never been able to hold his tongue if he thought he could gain from the telling."

Illesa heard his intake of breath.

"That is disrespectful, child. I am sure you are mistaken. But you say she spoke of strange things?"

He leant forward, inviting her to begin.

"I do not wish to bring disgrace upon her." Illesa looked at her folded hands.

"You will not bring her disgrace, child, but Grace itself. We can still help her, even now," he said, putting his dry fingers on hers. "The dead are like seeds, sown in God's garden. Care must be taken to prepare the seed for sowing, through confession and affirmation of the faith. If your mother has not had this preparation, the seed of her soul will not grow into life in Heaven. If you confess on her behalf, God will be glorified and Ursula's soul will be relieved of some suffering."

"She told me that the man who fathered me was not her husband. She was unfaithful to Hugh the smith. It would not have glorified God for that to become common knowledge," Illesa said, and finally met his eyes.

Father Osbert pressed his pale lips into a thin line.

"I think I am better placed to know what would glorify God than an unschooled girl in a man's garments." He pointed straight at her chest. "The devil will take you for one of his unnatural servants, dressed as you are."

There it was, the tipping point between sympathy and condemnation. Her mother had told him nothing.

"I beg your mercy, Father. I wear these clothes only because it is not safe for a maiden to travel alone. There are many brutal men on the roads since the war."

"That may be, but if you stray from the role God has ordained for you then you invite sin into your life." His eyes cast around the room. "Imagine a snail harnessed to a wagon and asked to pull, or a hare that takes up a bow and shoots the hunter; it is against the natural order of the creator. Women must not seek to take a man's role, or there will be chaos in the world and the devil will reign on earth."

Illesa remembered the shot hare dying in the mud of the track. If this hare could shoot that hunter, she would.

"It is dangerous to make such reversals," the Priest continued. "A dove dressed in the feathers of a crow will be shunned by her own kind." The wine cup shook as he put it to his lips and drained it.

"But God feeds the young of the raven," Illesa said, leaning forward. "When they are unfledged and their own parents do not recognise their true nature because they are not yet clothed in black feathers. God mercifully feeds them, because he knows that they lack the colour of their kind only for a little while. And you have fed me and given me shelter despite my unsuitable dress. And I too will soon be able to return to my true appearance."

Father Osbert laced his fingers together, looking at her with distaste.

"Your mother has provided your education, I see. She often debated like a man, which may have led her into that sexual sin. Knowledge is not for all. You need to learn the humility of your sex. This time in disguise must be short and followed by a period of contrition and penance. I will help you to leave Eaton and after that you must cover your head and behave like the maiden you profess to be."

In the silence that followed, Father Osbert got up and refilled his cup. She had gone too far. He thought her no better than a whore, born of a harlot.

"I am grateful for your help, Father," Illesa said humbly. "Please let me stay with Kit. I can help keep guard."

"You have done enough." The Priest placed his cup deliberately on the table. "Too much, in fact. If you remain here, you will endanger him and others."

The reply was out of her mouth before Illesa could consider its wisdom, or lack of it.

"You think I should have left Kit in gaol, in the Forester's tender care?"

"You should have gone through the men of your tithing to arrange his release."

"The men of my tithing were glad that Kit was in prison. They wanted him out of the way so that they can claim our land. There was no help to be had from them."

Father Osbert got up from his chair and went to the fire. He spent some time raking the embers. When he sat down, he looked tired and old, his anger spent.

"Listen to yourself, child. This is the sin of disobedience. Now, if you were married, you would be able to keep your land and have someone to act for your brother. Women must submit to authority and to the Lord."

That's what they always said. Women were not supposed to mind if the men in authority were stupid or evil, or had no faith in the Lord.

"I do not wish to be disobedient, Father. I have tried to follow the example of the holy saints who obeyed God alone. But I had to help my brother; he had no one else."

Father Osbert shook his head.

"We must all accept the fate that God has prepared for us."

Illesa gripped her hands between her knees.

"You think I should have left Kit to be hanged? You think that is God's will?" she demanded.

"Your brother has led a dissolute life. He is seeing the consequences of that now."

"You have heard his confession, Father. Can't he hope for forgiveness?"

The Priest's expression stiffened.

"He has been seduced by the pleasures of the flesh. I believe that exile may be the only path that will redeem him. I have advised him to take the road to Compostella once he crosses the sea. He may find salvation in pilgrimage," Father Osbert concluded.

"But he won't be able to return. I will never see him again!"

"That is what happens when you take the law into your own hands, child. If you had left your brother where he was and gone through due process, he may have been released and free to live in Holdgate again. But once he has sought sanctuary, he cannot be put on trial." Father Osbert drained the last of the wine from his cup and shifted in his chair.

"But he would never have made it to trial!" Illesa cried. "You saw him. They were going to beat him or starve him to death long before the court met. There was no profit in keeping him alive, as he couldn't pay. And besides, they wanted his horse."

Father Osbert looked exasperated.

"Well, you may have saved his life, only to put it beyond your reach," he concluded, rising from his chair.

Illesa shivered. The Forester would not be denied his kill.

"Kit won't live to be exiled. As soon as he leaves the church, they will take him," she whispered.

Father Osbert went to the window, unclasped the shutter and looked out on the lane. It seemed a long time before he spoke.

"Illesa, these men are Christians, not savages. They will respect the Church law and the Forester's anger will lessen. That is why God ordained there should be forty days of sanctuary, to induce forgiveness as well as repentance." Father Osbert spoke as if to an overwrought child.

Illesa stood up and felt the book shift under her breasts. Showing it to him would be a terrible risk. He did not trust her. But it might save Kit. She leant towards the Priest, her hands open in appeal.

"Maybe we could bribe the Forester? If I found something of value, would you negotiate it, Father?"

He regarded her wearily.

"You should know that I am forbidden from dealing in money. I have none except paltry alms. Where would you get a sum big enough to buy the life of your brother?"

She opened her mouth to tell him, but he was already standing above her, his hand gripping her shoulder.

"You are a girl. No monk's habit or boy's jerkin will change that fact. I will try to help you for your mother's sake, but I will not keep you here under my roof any longer than necessary. After another good meal you will be recovered enough to go. The colour has come back to your cheeks," he said, forcing a smile.

Illesa swallowed the bile in her throat and kept her eyes down.

"As you wish, but give me leave to speak to my brother in the morning. We have not had the chance to mourn our mother's death together. And if he is going to be exiled, I must say farewell."

"Come with me at matins." She could hear the relief in his voice. "I am usually alone at that hour. You may see him then."

Father Osbert would not stay the night under the same roof with a woman, even one so unsexed. He went to sleep with the Warden Lyttle's family and locked the door behind him. Illesa sat by the hearth, making patterns in the ash with her fingers. Her anger burned too hot for sleep. Eventually she got up, took off her jerkin and tunic and unstrapped the book.

Saint Margaret had defied her father, the pagan priest, as well as the brutal Roman Governor. She'd had more power than either of them. But even so, God had allowed her to be killed, her head struck off her shoulders.

Illesa shook the touch of the blade from her neck and turned to the page of Margaret's baptism in the blue waters of the River Orontes. The gold letters reflected the flame of the lamp. She bent close and whispered the words to the dark room.

Chapter V
AD 303
Antioch-on-the-Orontes

Ever since Marina heard the man proclaiming his strange message in the market, she felt something pecking at her mind, like a sparrow in the dust of the road. The first day she had listened for over an hour, hidden behind a column on the forum steps. The man speaking noticed her and smiled, showing startling white teeth, and then continued shouting at the indifferent crowd.

People were used to proselytizing preachers in Antioch, but this man seemed different to Marina. She had never seen such reckless happiness. Even when the market boys shouted abuse at him, throwing stones or dung, he merely brushed off his garment and continued.

The man was there the next day when Marina arrived with her basket. She lingered nearby as long as she dared. He was talking to a half-blind man who begged on the market steps.

"If you put your trust in the righteous one, you will become his child and share in his eternal inheritance. All are welcome at his table." The man's face was exultant. "Tomorrow at dawn, come to the river by the road to Alexandretta and I will baptise you."

The beggar grinned with all his cracked teeth.

"I could do with a wash."

"It is our souls that must be washed, brother."

"I'm not your brother." The beggar spat on the ground. "Bugger off."

"The end of days is near. Do not refuse the Son of God when he calls!" the man shouted after him, catching Marina's eye. She turned and hurried away to get the fish for Baa.

"Stupid girl! You believe everything you're told, do you?" Baa dropped her knife on the table and looked at Marina, bitter lines drawing her mouth down.

"I just thought you might . . ." Marina began.

"Your father is a priest, or have you forgotten? What do you think he'll do if he finds out that you have been listening to them *and* are witless enough to believe them?" She was breathing hard, her fleshy arms wobbling as she gripped the edge of the table.

"I just thought you might know some of them. You know everyone, Baa."

"Don't try to flatter me, young lady. I don't know any of them and I don't want to. They bring nothing but trouble." Baa fixed her eyes on her, and Marina remembered how afraid she had been of Baa when she was small. She had been afraid of everyone then.

"You've worked out that your father lies with me at night, haven't you? Heard some of it, I don't doubt." Baa picked up her knife and cut off the fish's head with one hard thrust. "Now you think I have some influence over him," she snorted. "You're wasting your breath. He'd be glad to have me killed if he thought I was encouraging you." She threw the fish into a dish and grabbed the mortarium, muttering as she crushed salt into the spices.

Marina picked up a spoon and stirred the pot that steamed over the brazier. She could smell dill. Baa snatched the spoon out of her hand.

"You'd better get those ideas out of your head. If he finds out about it, you'll be beaten within an inch of your life."

"Don't worry, Baa. I'll be careful."

"It's not you I'm worried about, your highness," she sneered. "After he's done with you, he'll use up his rage on me."

Marina did not sleep that night. She got up and sat at her window waiting for the light to return. When she could just see the statue of Fortune in the peristyle, she slipped out into the shadows. She found the kitchen door the slaves used, unlatched it with clumsy fingers and almost fell into the dark alley outside.

The sun rose so fast that Marina was sure she would be too late; he would be gone and there would be no one to explain the strange elation she felt. She stopped running when she saw the faint silver light of the water and the outline of the palm trees by the ford where the oxen carts crossed the shallow summer river. The scrubby bank was in deep shadow, but at last she saw him sitting at the base of a low tree, his hands resting upwards on crossed legs. His head was cocked to one side as if he was listening.

Marina stayed where she was. The birds had started to call from the trees above her. After some time her fear began to lessen, but the sense of interrupting an important conversation stopped her from approaching. She turned to go. Her father would have found her empty bed. He would be waiting for her.

"Don't leave."

The man was walking towards her, holding out his hands. She stepped back involuntarily.

"You have been waiting. Don't go now." He reached out and took one of her hands. "Have you come to be baptised?"

Marina shook her head.

"No." Her throat felt swollen, closed.

"Come and sit down. Don't be afraid. I would never hurt you. I saw you listening in the market and the Lord told me that you would come. Here, sit." He indicated an old striped mat laid out beneath the tree.

She sat down, bringing her shawl up to her mouth in a gesture from her childhood.

"What is your name?"

"Marina," she heard herself say.

"Do you know about the coming of the Christ, Marina?"

"No, I just heard you talking in the market place and it made me feel . . ." Her words petered out.

"His spirit is calling you. Let me tell you about him."

The man talked for a long time.

"You must turn away from worthless idols. It is his blood that makes us clean. The sacrifice of his own flesh gives us life that will never be corrupted."

Marina found she was crying.

"My father is the high priest of Jupiter. I cannot leave him."

"Yes you can. When you are baptised, you will become a child of God and you will have life forever. Abundant life!" The man threw his arms wide, taking in the butterflies by the riverbank, the goats in the scrub and the purple slopes of Mount Silpius.

"I want to." Her voice was a whisper. "Please baptise me."

The man reached out and took her hand again. His was hard, calloused.

"You must go and pray, child. Pray in the name of Jesus for the faith and strength to believe. The antichrist in Rome is persecuting the saints by temptation and torture. If you follow him you must be ready to be killed for his sake."

"But I'm ready now!"

The man let go of her hand and stood up. His smile was gone.

"Many have been martyred. You are young and wealthy. You must count the cost. If you truly want to be baptised, come here tomorrow at dawn."

Marina got to her feet, ashamed. She felt the man watching her as she walked back to the dust and smoke of the city.

Her father was waiting in the atrium wearing his priestly robes. His pale eyes examined her dusty cloak, her muddy feet, and she felt naked.

"Get to your room."

"Yes, Father."

Her bed was overturned, the water jug smashed on the floor. She bent down and began picking up the shards of broken pottery. Her father stood in the open doorway, holding the long knotted leather in his right hand. Marina's stomach turned over. She straightened, all the words dead in her throat.

"Can you really be unaware that people recognise you wherever you go? They know you are of marriageable age. They watch your behaviour, thinking of making an alliance with our family. They see you when you stop in the market, and then they come and tell me what you are doing." The end of the leather jerked on the floor with every word.

"You could have a match with one of the richest families, but this is not enough for you. Instead you chase after the preachers of idiocy!" His voice was suddenly loud enough to be heard at the back of the great temple. He crossed the floor in two strides and took her chin in his hand, lifting it so she had to look into his eyes.

"You know, I begin to wonder if your mother was a whore. Maybe that is why the gods took her. She gave herself to a quack preacher who offered her the love of Jesus and had you." Aedisias barked a laugh, spit flying from his lips. "You should have been my consolation after her death, but no daughter of mine would prostitute herself to a foreign god."

He let go of her chin and struck her hard on the cheek. Marina did not make a sound.

"These tears are a sign of your weakness." He wiped them away with the rough heel of his palm, and gripped her head between both his hands. "If you go to this preacher again or any of those blasphemers, I will throw you out and the slavers can have you. Now take off your filthy cloak."

After ten lashes he stopped and left the room without a word. Marina lay on the floor, her knees tucked into her chest. She stayed in her room all day. By evening, the pain had eased. Kneeling by the window, the cool air on her face became a voice, as gentle as a rain cloud settling on a parched mountain.

When she woke, stiff and sore on the ground, it was light. The birds in the eaves were singing. She wrapped her shawl round her and crept to the kitchen door. Baa was not there. Marina did not allow herself to think of what had happened to the slave who had been her only mother. She stepped out into the shadows of the alley.

The city was already busy with traders and women collecting water. She struggled through the crowd, hiding her face with her shawl. Few people were going out of the gate and down the barren road to the river. When she reached the ford, she saw him straight away. He was knee high in the water, his naked torso glistening in the sun, bones standing out like carved alabaster.

He waded out, shedding drops of light.

"Marina." His smile was almost skeletal.

"Please baptise me now."

"First let us pray together," he said, taking both of her hands in his.

Afterwards she remembered none of his words, only the sensation, as if a warm hand was resting lightly on her head. When she opened her eyes, she felt as if she was observing herself from a high mountain. The man's eyes were staring at nothing; his lips moved, but there was no sound. He got up and led her into the river.

"There is a deep pool, this way," he said, his voice hoarse and strange.

The skin on her arms prickled with cold and fear as they waded in, her skirts dragging on the muddy bank. Flies were alighting on the still water of the pool. Marina could see the fish rising to eat them. Scaly bodies seemed to be all around her, their mouths open and their big flat eyes searching for her. She stumbled on a stone or a root, and cried out.

"Don't be afraid. Devils will flee before you, Marina. Have faith."

He pulled her a few steps further under the shade of the trees where the water was dark and deep to her waist. He took both her hands in one of his, holding them against her chest. With his other hand, he pushed her under the water.

Chapter VI
The 15th day of July, 1284

It was not yet light when the Priest touched Illesa's shoulder, and she started from her huddled sleep on the floor. In the guttering light of the rush lamp, his expression was troubled.

"It is time."

Illesa got up, splashed her face with water from the bucket and pulled up her cowl. Her head throbbed with dream. She did not feel strong enough for the day ahead, and she didn't feel like praying.

The churchyard was a labyrinth of shadows. There was no sign of Destrey or any other soul. Inside the church, Father Osbert lit a lamp on the wall with a taper and went towards the tower door.

"We will see that your brother is well before I pray the office," he said, taking the key from his neck and turning it in the lock. The tower room was cold, and the lamplight only seemed to deepen the darkness.

"Kit!" Illesa whispered.

Father Osbert strode across the room to where Kit had lain.

"He is not here."

"Kit!" Illesa called.

"Shhhh! Listen." Above them there was a muffled ringing, then footsteps in the bell chamber. A darker line appeared in the ceiling and grew wider until it was a black square.

"Is it you, Father?" asked Kit's voice.

"Yes, my boy. What are you doing up there?"

The white blur of Kit's face appeared in the hole.

"You gave me a fright. When you called, I sat up and knocked my head on a bell. Just throwing down the ladder."

A rope ladder tumbled down and Kit descended slowly, holding on with his one good arm.

"What were you doing? We thought you had gone."

"When the man began firing burning arrows at the window, I thought I'd better sleep upstairs."

"By the saints," Father Osbert muttered. He put the lamp on the casket in the corner, and lit a cresset lamp on the wall.

"They were just trying to scare me, and it worked. The small one is a good shot." Kit's face was tired, lined with pain.

"I hope you haven't pulled that shoulder again, climbing up there. How does it feel today?" Father Osbert asked as he untied the sling.

"It is hardly day. You monks keep terrible hours," Kit said, drawing his breath as the Priest manipulated the joint.

"It's more mobile," the Priest said. "The swelling will go down gradually, but you must keep it still."

"Father, by God's thigh, I swear I won't take up smithing in here. I see you still have Brother Benedict with you. Do monks embrace their brothers, eh?" he said, pulling the cowl off Illesa's head and putting his good arm around her shoulders.

"Shhhh Kit," she said wriggling from under his arm. "Someone might be listening."

"Yes, you two must be very quiet," Father Osbert said under his breath. "Stay here. There are things I must arrange before you leave, and I must say matins. The sun will be up soon."

They watched the door shut and the end of the key turning in the lock.

"I've seen that sight too much lately," Kit said quietly. He turned to Illesa and forced a smile. "Now what's this about you leaving? Are you abandoning me here with the holy Father, hoping I'll join up? Don't think I'm suited to that life really, although you seem to have taken to it well enough."

"Be serious for a minute, Kit. We don't have much time. Father Osbert will not let me stay. He is sending me home and he expects you to be exiled."

"I know. He was telling me about my soul's need for pilgrimage."

"Well, he's right about that, but not about the exile. I need you here. Without you we will lose our land."

"What do you mean, Illesa? What's happened?"

Illesa looked at him. He was genuinely perplexed. Could he really have given her so little thought over the past year?

"What's happened is you left us alone to do all the work on the croft and all the boon work ourselves. We were just managing but then Mother became ill, and I had to tend to her as well." Illesa realised her voice was getting louder. She continued in a whisper. "There was no time to do the boon work and no money coming in. We could not pay the rent or the fees."

"Wait, wait. Didn't you get the coin I sent you before the Feast of the Nativity? I got four new groats and sent them to you in a letter. I had to pay a scribe to write it for me. He charged a fortune to write 'Here is some money. God keep you both' as if he were writing the holy book itself."

"No, Kit," Illesa sighed. "We never got the coin. It would have been very welcome."

"Bloody bastard! That thieving fletcher said he was coming this way. Gave me his word he was going to bring it to you. If I ever see him again, I'll rip his lying tongue out!"

"You should have brought it yourself," Illesa hissed. She took a deep breath and continued. "The bailiff has been taking our goods and stock in payment, but he really wants the land. The Templars demand an increased profit or he will lose his position."

Kit was cracking his knuckles, one by one.

"You must come back to the village and pay off our debt, otherwise we will be homeless." It seemed a foolish dream as soon as she said it. Why had she thought that the arrival of Kit would dismiss the line of creditors like a boy scaring crows? It was all just as childish as her silly disguise. By the end of this day, Agatha would be at her father's door, telling him all about the book and how Illesa had stolen it.

"So you haven't got married to a rich merchant since I left home, eh? Mother seemed convinced that was your destiny. It would certainly have solved our problems."

"Without you or Father how could I meet someone like that? I've been stuck in Holdgate for years, and the people there are just the same as when you left." Illesa gestured at him angrily. "You coming home to help would have solved our problems."

Kit said nothing.

"Why didn't you come? Mother was ill, and now she is dead and you weren't there!"

He moistened his lips and turned towards the window, his back tensed.

"I'm sorry Lessa. I couldn't."

"Why not?" she demanded, going to him and pulling at his jerkin, as she had when she was a child. "And don't tell me it was army work. I don't believe it. They would have spared you after your first forty days. They have no right to keep you without leave any longer."

Kit shifted his shoulder and grimaced. He did not meet her eyes.

"I'm paying for it now, that's clear. Look Illesa, I was wrong. I wish I had come sooner and made my peace with her."

He had the same look he wore whenever family conversations became difficult. But she was not an ignorant girl any more. Her mother's silence had been no protection, it had just taken her family away one by one.

"Do you really think that I still haven't worked it out, Kit? I knew why Father left and took you away. You have known what Mother did since that day."

There was no need to say which day. They both remembered it, and all its pain. They'd been in the far wood, to gather fuel and not to play games. But she'd asked and badgered him to play until he chased her, screaming with delight, around an ash copse. When she fell, twisting her ankle in a rabbit hole, Kit had carried her all the way home. He'd told her not to be afraid, promised that he would not tell.

Kit had gone back for the pile of sticks himself and afterwards had taken the beating from Father without a word. He cried silently, his fists bunched in his eyes, bent over with pain. He'd only been ten. And when Father had come for her with the belt, Ursula had stood in front of Illesa and said - *She's not yours, don't touch her.* Neither of them escaped his anger. He had already gone when Illesa crawled out of bed the next morning. Kit too. Her mother had said nothing, just washed her bruised face and went out to the hens.

Kit's good shoulder twitched at the memory.

He turned to her, and then away before she could see his expression.

"So I am not your sister." Illesa's throat thickened around the words.

"I suppose we are half-brother and half-sister," Kit said. "Not that it matters."

Illesa could not speak. The knot of grief that had been tied up in her chest loosened.

"Don't cry, Lessa. Come on, come here. Of course I'm your brother. You're the only family I have left."

He moved closer and put his arm around her. She leant against him and muffled her sobs against his chest.

"But that is why you didn't come back," Illesa blurted out after a while. "You wanted nothing to do with us."

"No, Sweetheart. I was angry with her, not with you. I didn't want to hear any more about that book or your father's family. I want nothing to do with it."

Illesa drew breath.

"You knew about the book?"

"She told me last year, when I came back, after Father died." Kit took his arm from her shoulder, and fiddled with his sling. Illesa sat on the edge of the chest, her stomach churning.

"Did she show it to you? Did she say where it came from?"

He barked a laugh.

"She didn't know I had seen it when I was a little boy. As far as she was concerned, I should not look at it or even touch it. The book was only for you and your family. But she wanted me to take it, wrapped in cloth and wax, all the way to Saint Margaret's Church at Caus. She thought the Saint might be angry with her. I can't imagine why." His face twisted in mock surprise.

"Why to Caus? There are lots of churches of Saint Margaret."

His look told her she was being particularly stupid.

"I suppose that is where your father is from, Illesa my girl. Anyway," he said, running his hand through his lank hair, "I said I wouldn't go. Told her to take it herself, if it was so important. I said plenty of things that I now regret."

"Did she say anything else? Anything about him?"

"No." The anger in his voice was gone. Kit ran a hand through his hair again and scratched his scalp. When he continued, he sounded almost indifferent. "She just stood there with her lips pressed together watching me shout. She told me I was too quick to judge. You know how pious she could be when anyone scolded her."

They sat in silence for a moment, the sound of Father Osbert's low monotone barely audible.

"Did she ever take it to Caus?" he asked, not looking at her.

"No, she was too ill. The pains got worse and worse after you left."

Her voice sounded accusatory, and Kit frowned.

"Well, maybe I should have taken it. Maybe if I had, she would not have died." He gestured around the room. "Maybe none of this would have happened."

"It's not your fault she died Kit, but the rest of it probably is." She shot him a wry look.

Kit fumbled with the cloth sling and winced.

"Even if it isn't Saint Margaret, *someone* certainly isn't very pleased with me right now." Kit began walking round the room as if he was looking for something. "I'd sell my soul for a good tankard of ale. Doesn't this Priest eat or drink?"

"He's saying matins. We need to decide what to do before he comes back," Illesa said, following him to the far end of the room. Kit turned and looked her in the face at last.

"You know, Mother always wanted you to have the best. What would she think of you now, eh Brother Benedict? I doubt you will be marrying well." He drew the dagger he had taken from the guard and tested its edge. "Maybe we *should* go to France."

"We wouldn't make it to the port alive," Illesa said. "They don't want you exiled, they want you dead. The Forester's pride has been pricked. You made a fool of him."

"No, my dear, it was you who made a fool of him." He poked her midriff the way he used to when they were children, and his finger hit the book.

"What *is* that? Armour? You are taking no chances." He stopped talking and traced the outline of it. "Oh no. I see." His face fell. "Illesa, that is suicide." Illesa put her hand protectively over the book. "Don't worry, I'm not going to ask you to take it off. I was hoping my sister didn't have a chest like an ox. But really, if you are caught with that you won't stand a chance."

Illesa crossed her arms over the book and shifted her weight.

"I know, but I couldn't leave it behind for the bailiff. Kit, we need a plan. Even if you stay here for forty days without being dragged out, you will die as soon as you leave the church."

"Isn't there a rule about having to be within a mile of a church and you are still in sanctuary?"

"If you want to try that, go ahead, but you will be shot down within minutes, and there will be witnesses swearing you were nowhere near a church when it happened. Most people would rather perjure themselves than let the Forester take their goods and end up with a cracked head."

"You are probably right," Kit sighed.

"The only thing that might work is bribery. Don't you have anything I could take away and sell? You must have earned enough in all those months with the army."

"I've never been very good at saving, Lessa. The best thing I had was Greyboy."

"That's not going to help us. The Forester has already got him. We will be convicted of theft if we try to sell the book without help. What about your tools?"

"They won't fetch more than a shilling. Especially around here." He paused for a moment. "Richard might help, I suppose."

Illesa chewed her lip.

"You mean Richard Burnel, from Acton? The one you talked about when you were last at home?"

"Yes." Kit paused. "I did him a good turn in Wales and he's got me out of a sticky situation or two since. You know he is related to the Chancellor. He might be willing to lend me some money."

"Where is he now, do you know?"

"At Clun. He was wounded in the war and has been recovering there for a few months." Kit paused. "It might be worth a try."

"You don't sound very sure about him."

Kit looked at her, his expression guarded.

"I'm not. Four years ago I saved him from being hacked to death when he was knocked off his horse at Flint. And after that he was a great friend for a while. But since two of his uncles died in that disaster at Anglesey, his cousin the Chancellor has favoured him. He is busy making alliances with the gentry. That's why he's at Clun with the FitzAlans. When I last saw him, he was all fancy manners." Kit paused, rubbing his nose. "And he lost an eye in Wales and has taken that hard," he finished thoughtfully.

"He is our only chance," Illesa said, getting up.

"Richard's a good man," Kit said. "I'm sure he will help us, he'll just never let me forget it."

"Well, that won't do you any harm. So we need to get a message to him."

Kit was pulling at his beard, looking worried.

"We could send someone from the village."

"No. The last time you sent someone else, it didn't work, and this time it's even more important," Illesa countered. "We don't know who we can trust here."

"Don't tell me. You have a plan," he muttered.

"I will go."

Kit was silent, looking at his feet in their worn boots. Illesa went to the window. The sky was clear and golden. She turned to Kit.

"I am the only one who can really convince him of the situation. And everyone here thinks I'm a monk, so they won't be suspicious when I leave. The villagers would be stopped and questioned by the Forester."

"You've become more stubborn than ever."

"And you've become more foolish than ever. You know it is the best chance we have."

"How are you going to travel all that way on your own? Do you even know how to get there?"

"I'll be fine. I know the way." It was five years since she had been anywhere near there, but there was no point saying that.

"There must be another way to get a message to him." He paced the room, and stopped at the window.

"We haven't got time for other plans, Kit. I will go there and come straight back. You just need to keep quiet and stay out of sight for a couple of days."

He didn't say anything for several moments. Framed against the light from the window, his profile was just like his father's: prominent nose, full lips and hair curling over his forehead. Reaching inside his tunic, Kit drew out a scalloped lead ampulla on a leather thong.

"Take this with you. Richard will know it is from me." He pulled it over his head and handed it to Illesa.

"Holy water?"

"No, even better. Holy oil. He gave it to me. It's from Jerusalem."

"There's still some left," she said, shaking the battered container gently.

"You might need it on the road," Kit whispered.

Illesa pulled the thong over her neck and tucked the ampulla under the habit.

"I was an idiot. You should have left me in gaol, Illesa," Kit said, looking at the floor.

"You haven't even told me what happened yet."

"Suffice it to say I was set up for a fool."

"You weren't drinking were you?"

"Not much."

"Dicing?"

"Only a little."

"Kit!"

"I'll tell you the whole story later."

The key turned in the lock and Father Osbert came in. He put his finger to his lips, turned and locked the door again.

"Now, Brother Benedict, how do you find the patient?" He paused. "Good. I am sending you to Wenlock. I need you to go to the Prior." He handed her two sealed packets of parchment. The wax was still warm. "This letter states that you are travelling on the Prior's business. It should ease your journey a little." He took Illesa's elbow and pulled her towards the far wall.

"The Forester's men have brought door-breaking tools," he whispered. "This letter to the Prior asks for help safeguarding your brother. We need a higher authority to stop them from removing him. The smith and I will keep the guards here busy so they do not follow you. Warden Lyttle will accompany you part of the way."

"Yes, Father. Shall I come back with the men sent by the Prior?"

"No. There is another place you must go. Somewhere safer."

Illesa's heart sank. She turned to Kit.

"Give me a kiss before you go," he said.

Illesa put her arms carefully around him, kissed him on the cheek and whispered in his ear:

"Don't do anything stupid while I'm gone."

Chapter VII
The Overhang

Destrey was leaning against the wall by the tower door. He watched as Father Osbert turned the key in the lock and hid it under his habit.

"Where is the other man who brought the tools?" Father Osbert asked, approaching him.

John Destrey picked his teeth with a sliver of wood and shrugged.

"Listen to me, now. If anyone attempts to break this door I will set in motion the process of excommunication. I trust you understand me?"

"Loud and clear, Father," Destrey said and threw his toothpick over his shoulder.

"This is God's house, not a tavern."

"More's the pity."

Father Osbert looked at him with disgust and signaled for Illesa to follow him to the main church door.

"You carry a lot of goods for a monk who has made a vow of poverty, Brother," Destrey remarked, staring at the pack on Illesa's back. She swallowed her sharp retort and followed the Priest, keeping her head bowed. Father Osbert stopped just inside the church's south door and stood watching Destrey, who wandered over to the tower and bent to look through the keyhole.

"I have sent Warden Lyttle to fetch the smith and his boy," Father Osbert whispered to Illesa. "They will reinforce the door and help me keep watch while the warden accompanies you."

"There is no need, Father. He will just make me more conspicuous."

"We cannot risk the messages being seized by the Forester. Warden Lyttle is not fast, but he will defend you like a bear. Unfortunately, he cannot go all the way to Wenlock, but once you are away from the Forester's demesne you should be safe enough in the habit of our order."

Illesa was about to argue when the warden came through the door, breathing like a bellows.

"They are on their way, Father. Just gathering their tools and they'll be here. What's that man up to? Hey, get away from that door!" The warden started down the aisle, but Father Osbert grabbed his tunic.

"Peace. Let the smith deal with him. You must leave. Have you brought the bread?"

The warden nodded, lifting up a linen parcel in his hand.

"Good. I can see the smith coming through the gate now. Be on your way. God keep you." He laid his hand on Illesa's forehead and then made the sign of the cross over her.

"Thank you, Father," she murmured and followed the warden out of the churchyard.

They trudged up the Jacob's ladder track that she and Kit had skidded down the previous day, and Warden Lyttle was able to keep up a steady stream of comment, despite being short of breath.

"The disrespect they show to a man of God! It's disgusting. When I was a child no one would dare, but the Forester's men have no fear of hell." Warden Lyttle stopped to suck his teeth. "But if you ask me, Father Osbert should just leave the key and let them take that poacher back to gaol, although he would admonish me for saying so. But it's my job to keep the church safe, with God's help, and if the Forester's men damage the church we will have to pay for the repairs."

He made the most of her silence, not running out of complaints until they came to a thickly wooded part of the escarpment. Illesa could hear nothing but the warden's loud breathing and the harsh call of a jay, giving warning. She was sure they were being followed, but every time she looked back the path was empty. It was strangely quiet. They had only passed one man, stave in hand, leading a loaded packhorse heading south.

The sun was high when they reached an unfamiliar crossroads. To the east there would be views towards her home at Holdgate, but that was on the other side of the high cliff. The warden turned and put a finger to his lips. He pointed to the right, and they took the path leading up the hill. After a steep, slow ascent, they reached the base of the cliff, and the warden led her off the path. They made noisy progress across fallen branches and patches of thorn, heading towards a narrow fissure in the cliff face below an overhang.

The warden stopped by a large stone. The opening behind it was too shallow to be called a cave, but it offered some cover from above and below. He gestured for her to sit on the dry, sandy ground, while he stood, red-faced, catching his breath. She very much hoped that he would unpack the bread.

"Here we are," he said at last, running a hand across his wet forehead. "This is where I leave you, Brother. I'm sure you know about the outlaws living in Easthope wood. Devils they are. Robbing and harassing ordinary people going about their business. They don't come down as far as this, I'm told, so you should be safe if you go east, join up with the Ludlow road and head to the Priory through Brockton and Boarton," he said, pointing over the top of the cliff. "You know that road? And you have the document of safe passage with his seal?"

Illesa withdrew it from her pack.

"Good, good. Even the Forester is not coming this far north now, and that's saying something, so the sooner you get out of the forest the better. The Ludlow road is well cleared and they are used to seeing the Wenlock monks travelling. You'll find help there if you need it. Well, I must go back. God speed, Brother."

Illesa sprang to her feet and brought her hand to her mouth, as if eating.

"Of course! I'm sorry. Nearly forgot." He handed her the linen tied parcel.

Illesa smiled, trying not to look at the warden directly. He would be expecting a benediction, so she made the sign of the cross in the air between them. Warden Lyttle seemed satisfied and left without another word, labouring over the uneven ground. The overhang was a good lookout point. Illesa watched him as he rejoined the main path and headed south, his arms swinging. She pulled the black habit over her head, rolled it up and dropped it behind the stone. It was a relief to be rid of the itchy cloth.

The maslin was soft and light. It took all her will to save a third, gulping water from her skin to fill her stomach. The two packets of parchment lay at the top of her pack. They were stained with droplets of wax; sealed in haste. Illesa carefully stowed the one giving her safe passage. The other she turned over in her palm.

The Priest had assumed she could not read. He probably also assumed that she would not read a letter addressed to the Prior. Illesa removed the small steel knife from her belt. The wax was new enough to still have some give. It lifted easily away, and Illesa unfolded the parchment very slowly.

Holy Father, Lord Prior

Blessings upon you in the name of our Lord Jesus Christ.

The person bearing this message to you is a maiden in the habit of a monk. I pray your mercy on her in this disguise as she is in danger of her life. Her brother has claimed sanctuary in Eaton Church, and she has no protector left in this world. She is the daughter of Hugh Arrowsmith, and is a devout follower of our Lord. She would do well as a servant to the Cistercian sisters at Brywodde. Please arrange for her to be taken there with all speed.

The rest of the letter begged for the Prior's assistance in keeping the sanctuary, and, at the bottom, Father Osbert had put his seal and his name. Illesa let the parchment drop into her lap. If she went to deliver the message to the Prior, she would not be able to leave for Clun Castle. They would take her to the White Sisters, a full day's journey away. Illesa doubted they could keep her there against her will, but it would be a significant delay. If she did not take the message, no help would arrive and the Forester would break into the tower and take Kit. Illesa folded the parchment, aligning the wax with the discoloured patch it had made, and held it gently together.

A harness jangled on the path below her. Illesa dropped to the ground, her heart suddenly racing. The rider was pushing his horse hard. He came into view, a bow and quiver slung across his back. Destrey had changed his mount: he rode Kit's horse, the dappled grey stallion. He must have come on the valley track and hoped to cut them off from the western path. Illesa retreated behind the rock and crouched down, watching.

Destrey pulled up short at the crossroads and dismounted, bringing his bow into shooting position. He was examining the marks on the path, but he would have to be an excellent tracker to pick their footprints out of the muddy ruts and holes. He straightened up and slowly turned around, sweeping the area with the bow. The cliff stones were clearly visible from the track; he would be a fool not to look. She waited, holding her breath. Below, the restless horse pawed the ground. Destrey swore as he mounted and whipped Greyboy's haunch.

Illesa grabbed her pack and crept out from the overhang, heading down the steep slope of bracken and brambles. It was impossible to move quietly enough. After about twenty paces, she came to a broad fallen tree lying diagonally across the hill and crawled into the lee of it, lying with her back against the rough bark. It seemed hours before she could quieten her breathing. She was half hidden by bracken, but anyone within ten paces would see her.

The beat of the hooves grew louder and slowed.

Between the leaves and undergrowth, she could just see the limestone overhang. He would go and search it, but perhaps he would not beat the underbrush. If she lay very still he would not see her, and pass on up the track to look elsewhere.

Illesa's stomach turned. She was a fool.

She had left the monk's habit neatly rolled up behind the large stone.

Destrey had already tied Greyboy to a tree by the track. He was picking his way towards the overhang.

Illesa looked up at the cloud-streaked sky, struggling to form a prayer. A blackbird called loudly, startling her. Then, overhead, was the sound of metal drumming on stone. On the cliff edge, three horses came to a halt. A rider, dressed in a long gambeson, levelled his bow, an arrow ready. The other two had drawn their falchions. One of their mounts, a bay mare, whinnied and Greyboy answered, but otherwise there was silence.

"If you wish to live, stay where you are," the rider with the bow ordered. He sounded wellborn.

His men turned their horses sharply, the hooves scraping on the stone. Illesa heard them galloping down the rocky path. Only when they had halted by Destrey did the rider on the cliff lower his bow and turn his horse to follow. Each unhurried step sounded on the steep track.

"Come here, sirrah," demanded the bowman, as he joined his men. "You look familiar. Declare yourself."

"John Destrey in the service of the lord Forester. I know you well, sir."

"Is that so?"

There was a crack, like a stick breaking, and Destrey cried out.

"I would not presume to know your superiors well, if I were you. Are you unaware of my new agreement with your master? We patrol this part of the forest. Your presence here is neither needed nor welcome."

"My master has sent me here, Sir Perkyn." Destrey's voice was a pitch higher and lacked its usual sullen quality. "I hunt a man dressed as a monk heading for the Priory. He is an accomplice of an escaped felon we have trapped in the church at Eaton. If he reaches Wenlock, the Prior will get involved and start interfering in our business."

"Ah, I see. You are sent in pursuit. The quarry must surely be terrified, eh?"

Sir Perkyn's men grunted appreciatively.

"You need not worry. Such a man will not get past us, and when we find him we will deliver him to you for a fee. But your master cannot have it both ways. If he wants his cut of the profits, he cannot send his spies to poach our quarry. If he does, he may not get them back." The bandit sounded almost bored.

"Yes, Sir Perkyn."

"Run back and tell your master that we will take care of your little problem for you. The Prior will not risk involvement after we have dealt with the unholy brother."

There was a long pause and then a horse whickered.

"What are you waiting for, sirrah? Get running! You do not deserve such a mount. It demands a rider of quality, which I can provide. Let us call it your fine for infringing our territory," the man drawled. "A very acceptable offering, you can tell the Forester."

"My master will not bear this ill treatment," Destrey said, sullen again.

"Bear it? Well, let him come and be unburdened of it. We are experts at unburdening people of their problems and their heavy loads. Let him come!"

The sound of arrow feathers being smoothed was just audible.

"Run, Destrey, or you will not give us sport."

She heard him, falling haphazardly down the slope. He came into her field of vision, slipping with arms outstretched, the arrows cutting the air on one side of him. Illesa shut her eyes for two heartbeats and then he was past her, still running headlong. Another arrow blurred by as it spiraled through the leaves of an oak sapling.

The men laughed and shouted after him. Someone was pissing on the ground.

"A good morning's sport, my lord!"

"And a good horse, though the saddle is old and worn."

"He's recently shod."

Greyboy whinnied complainingly. There was a loud smack.

"Yes, a fine courser. He'll serve for a stud. I'll test his nerve on the cliff path. Spread out, men; let's see what that dog was after. There may be some more profit in it. We could do with a prisoner to lever some of the Prior's wealth out from under his arse. Find him and bring him to me at the rock."

The syncopated rhythm of two horses walking up the steep track gradually faded. The remaining men did not seem in any hurry. Swords were being sharpened. A wineskin was un-stoppered. Eventually, one of them mounted heavily.

"You take the north path, I'll go south. Sound your horn if you find him."

"Eh Jack! Give that wineskin back, you whoreson."

"You've had enough, damn you. It's my turn."

The man cursed, mounted the other horse and walked it down the track, the saddle creaking as it tipped forwards. Jack moved heavily through the undergrowth. When he reached the overhang, he unslung the wineskin from his shoulder and drank deeply, wiping the back of his hand across his thick brown beard. He stood there, scratching his neck and belching, for some time. Then he pulled down his hose and disappeared behind the large stone. When he came out again, he was holding the black habit. The cloth was streaked white with limey soil.

"Not a monk now, eh? Where are you, you devil?"

He dropped the habit and peered out across the slope, drawing his falchion. Illesa had to force herself to keep her eyes open and watch him. All her limbs were heavy and senseless, as if they were dead wood. She bit her lip hard. Jack began striding down the hill using his sword to clear the undergrowth, stabbing it into the thick areas of bracken. A robin flew away with a trill of notes. Jack was working his way down methodically, the wine sloshing in the skin across his back.

He stopped ten paces above the log, looking at the broken stems of the bracken where she had rolled. He came forward, falchion raised.

Illesa watched him.

When he was three paces away, she could see his yellowed eyes.

Two paces.

She lunged up and thrust his leg backwards as he was in mid-step. He fell heavily forward against the log. His weapon clattered down and the wineskin slumped over his head. Illesa scrambled to her feet and heaved his legs up and over the log. He crashed to the ground on the other side, face down. She grabbed his falchion, the hilt still warm from his sweaty hand, and flung it away into the thorns, but it was heavier than it looked and didn't go far. It was a steep uphill run across to the track where a bay mare stood, one foot bent, by the tree. She untied and mounted her in a scramble.

"Come on, come on," Illesa begged, whacking the bay's haunches. The horse rolled her eyes and broke into a reluctant trot.

Eventually they reached the hilltop, and Illesa looked over her shoulder. Jack was on the track, his falchion back in his hand. He was searching for something; something he did not find. His horn must have fallen off in the undergrowth.

They were on the high road of the Long Forest, running southwest to northeast, in the bandits' territory. She would have to turn south and look for a track heading east, towards familiar open land in Hope Dale. Illesa kicked the horse's flanks. Its pace did not alter. If she got down to find a stick, it would probably never let her mount again. Ahead, she could see a gap in the tree line to the east. She smacked the horse's shoulder as hard as she could, but it only shook its mane.

A wailing cry came from behind her. Illesa looked over her shoulder, but the track was empty. She pulled the horse to a halt for a moment to listen, and it stamped its hoof impatiently. The rising note of a horn set up all the hairs on her neck.

Illesa squeezed the horse hard with her heels and steered her down the narrow stony path, still at a walk. Her hands were shaking. The mare would not be instructed; kicking it did no good. If the horse had its way, the outlaws would hear her whinnies and find them easily, still ambling along at a moderate walking pace.

"It will have to be stealth rather than speed," she muttered, letting the rein lie loose across the bay's neck.

The mare shook her head violently and cantered down the steep track, out of the trees. Illesa crouched down and gripped its mane. Strips of waving crops stretched across the valley. On the western slope, people were working in the ripening corn. To the east, a long wooded forest rose to a round hill. The old fort. It would be good cover, and she might get through it without being noticed. There were no trails of smoke rising from its centre.

When they reached the eastern slope, Illesa turned the horse north towards the fort, but the mare took offence, slowed again to a walk and tried to crop the tufts of grass and groundsel. The sun falling through the tree branches was making strong patches of light and shadow, and she could not see far. She gripped the reins tight to still her trembling hands. They were on the edge of a densely planted coppice, exposed to the view of the valley. If anyone came down the Long Forest path, they would catch her as easily as a snared rabbit. An arrow was probably already aimed at her throat.

Large flies buzzed, making the horse jump and shake her mane. The mare suddenly broke and galloped forward into the sunny meadow. In the glare Illesa could see the sheen of water. The pond was caught in the low point of the valley, deserted except for a stand of rushes. They drew up at the water's edge.

A cloud of flies droned above it, black like the smoke from old linen. Illesa shivered in her sweat-soaked clothes. The smell hit her next; a stench that hung thick in the air and caught the back of her throat. She covered her mouth, trying not to retch. The horse's neck was twitching as she lifted her head from the foul water. She shook her mane and wheeled round, galloping back towards the wood, her legs kicking out behind her. Illesa put her arms round the mare's neck and held on.

Only when the mare slowed to a trot did Illesa sit up in the saddle, breathing cautiously. They were on a thinly wooded track, and the fort was ahead of them. The branches were moving against a sky full of black clouds, and the wind was whipping west to east. She gulped the air, trying to blow the smell of death out of her mouth and nose. The outlaws must have given many of their victims that water burial, weighed down with cliff stones where their purses had been.

The horse was climbing up a track between steep banks intercut with ditches when the downpour began. To the right and left, the rings of bank and ditch stretched out into a wide twisted circle, hiding the view of the interior. Illesa had no desire to be trapped in the fort, but there seemed to be no other path, or none that she could find in the storm. They needed to keep out of sight until she found a way through. She dismounted and led the mare down into one of the ditches, out of the driving rain and wind. The horse began cropping patchy tufts of grass. Illesa stood in the shelter of its bulk, one hand on the reins, and opened her pack for her jerkin. She tugged it over her wet tunic, leant against the horse's warm shoulder and shut her eyes.

Chapter VIII
The Wenlock Road

The bay mare shook her head, sending spray from her mane, and whinnied restlessly. Steam was rising from her haunches. The rain was lessening.

"Shhhh, girl." Illesa stroked her neck. The horse twisted her head and shook her bridle, ringing the harness loudly.

"Shhhh. Do you want us to get caught? They'll cut my throat and throw me into that pond. I don't suppose you care about that, do you?"

The horse defecated and began browsing for food in the scrub. The clouds were scudding away and each leaf edge shone with reflections. It was unnervingly quiet.

"Come on, we'd better go." Illesa grabbed the reins and swung herself into the saddle. They'd only walked a few paces down the ditch when a cow lowed nearby and startled the horse into a gallop. Illesa fell off, landing on her side and shoulder, with the edge of the book digging into her ribs. She scrambled up, slipping on the fresh mud, fighting to get her breath back.

The sound of galloping hooves was fading. There wasn't a hope of catching the horse when she could only manage a limping run. In front of her, a track cut across the bank and ditch, leading into the fort. A wattle fence blocked the entrance. The lowing was coming from inside. Illesa sped across the track to the ditch on the other side. There was no sound of the horse, but her hoof prints were clearly visible, skidding as she came to the next intersecting track. It was narrower and quite overgrown.

The wattle gate at this entrance was slightly open. Inside, Illesa could see the remains of a poor timber house, its roof just ragged straw and moss. Staying close to the bank edge, she crept up the track to the corner and stopped. A strange high-pitched murmuring came from the ditch. Illesa put her head round the corner. The bay was about twenty paces away and, holding her rein, was a barefoot girl, maybe ten years old, with wet tangled hair. The shift she wore was streaked with mud. She was trying to speak into the horse's ear, but the bay shook her head as if bothered by flies.

Illesa went towards them slowly. When she was still ten paces away, the girl looked up and screamed. The horse wheeled around in fright. Illesa raced forward, caught the reins in one hand and the girl's arm in the other.

"Be quiet, I'm not going to hurt you," Illesa whispered, squeezing the girl's arm. The horse breathed out a cloud of angry breath and pawed the ground against the tight reins. The girl was crying, her whole body shaking with sobs. Illesa squeezed her arm tighter.

"Shut up, will you?"

The girl nodded, trying to keep her mouth closed.

"Now I'm going to let you go. Don't move or make a sound, or you'll regret it."

The girl gulped her sob and nodded again.

Illesa dropped her arm and the girl took a step back, almost falling against the sloping bank. She stood, eyeing Illesa and biting her lip. Illesa loosened the rein slightly and adjusted the halter, which had twisted sideways. She turned back to the girl who was chewing the end of a mat of brown hair.

"Do you live here?"

The girl nodded.

"Whose cattle are they?"

The girl took a shaky breath.

"You know they are Steward's at Brock," she whispered. "Don't take any more, he'll kill my Da."

"Where is your Da?"

"Asleep."

"If you scream or tell anyone I was here, I *will* come back and take them."

"But we gave you one last week," the girl wailed. "You said you wouldn't come back till Michaelmas."

"Well, I won't as long as you are quiet," Illesa said, trying to hide her confusion.

The girl took a step back as Illesa swung into the saddle. Her tears had stopped, and she looked up appraisingly, rubbing her arm.

"You're not one of his men, are you? I thought you were, cause you look so dirty. Who are you? What are you doing here?"

Illesa squeezed the horse's flanks hoping for a quick response, and this time the bay sprang forward into a trot. She looked over her shoulder.

"You've stolen that horse, you dirty vagrant! If you try to steal from us, my Da will cut you open with his pike, so he will." Transformed by her fury, the girl looked like an old crone as she ran after Illesa, almost catching the bay's tail.

"Hey, you filthy bastard, don't come back here or I'll send Perkyn's men after *you*!" the girl shouted, gesturing.

Illesa held on as they went round a sharp bend. Glancing back, she saw the girl was still close but had stopped running. She was bending down to pick something up. Illesa kicked the bay's flank hard as the first handful of mud smacked into her back. The horse broke into a gallop. They lurched down the track out of the ditches and into the tall beech trees, shining with rain. In a moment they reached the eastern edge of the wood and raced out between the strips of wheat and barley woven across the land. She looked behind them, but nothing came out of the wood.

Illesa slowed the horse to a trot and unclenched her hands from the reins. She should not have been so frightened by a slip of a girl, even with her father nearby. She was giving herself away. Rain ran down her face and her hands and clothes were filthy with mud. Before she arrived at the Priory, she would have to repair her appearance.

It didn't take long to reach the broad road that ran to Wenlock. The trees and brush on either side had been cleared of hiding places for thieves. Illesa tried to rein in the horse as they joined the steady flow of people, but the bay bucked and swerved, so Illesa had to let her gallop. They overtook merchants loaded with bales of wool and several pack horses, heads hung low, being whipped up the hills. It was late afternoon when she heard the barking of dogs in the distance. The abbey church was hazy in the rising smoke of the town.

The bay's coat was foaming. She had been galloping for miles, but it was all Illesa could do to hold her back from a heart-stopping, headlong pace. At the crossroads before the town, she stopped at a trough and drank long and deep, the water dripping from her white whiskers. Illesa stood beside her, cupped the water in her hand and scrubbed at her face and hair. Her boots had dried, and most of the mud had come off on the long ride, but she doubted she looked like a messenger, even one who had just endured a long journey on meagre rations.

The bay was skittish, pulling on the reins. There was no point trying to ride her through the town. They could avoid the high street and find a different road to the Priory on foot. She turned down a sparsely inhabited lane which ran in a semicircle to the west. One dwelling exuded the familiar smell of heat and metal, and the bay pulled Illesa towards it. She slapped her on the haunch.

"Come on, girl. You don't need shoes; you're fine. We have to get to the Priory." The horse whinnied and wheeled round as Illesa dragged her past the smithy. After a hundred more paces, they reached a crossroads. The tower of the church was to the right and the Priory roofs below and behind it. A tall black-bearded man carrying a heavy leather pack was coming up the lane from the other direction. He was a fair distance away, but Illesa could see that his pace had quickened. He was staring at her, or the horse, his face set in a frown.

Illesa crossed the road and ran down the lane towards the Priory gatehouse, the horse trotting next to her. She arrived breathless at the porch, hitched the horse to a ring set in the stone of the wall and went through the outer door. A man in a torn, brown tunic and hose sat on one of the benches inside. He did not look up.

"God give you good day," she said. The man's head turned slightly. His slack-mouthed face bore the marks of the pox. Around him was an odour of earth and fetid water. Illesa went quickly past and pulled on the bell fixed above the iron-studded inner door.

Nothing happened for several minutes. Illesa looked out of the doorway. The bay was still there, tied and standing calmly. The strange man began rocking forward and back, droning part of a high-pitched chant.

Illesa was just reaching for the bell again, when she heard the slap of feet on stones and the door opened.

"God's blessings upon you, Brother."

"And on you, my son." The monk was young and well fleshed, but his eyes were wary.

"I come with an urgent message. I have been asked to deliver this to the Prior and ensure he sees it today. It is a matter of great importance," Illesa said, taking the parchment from her pack, and trying not to spill the contents on the ground.

"Indeed?" said the monk, watching her fumble with the pack. "And you are?"

"William in the service of Richard Burnel. I was riding north from Clun on an errand for my master, but when I stopped to water the horse near Rushbury, a wool merchant there asked me to deliver this message as I was bound for Wenlock. He said he had been charged to ensure it reached the Prior today. He could not reach here in time with his packhorse, so he asked me to bring it. It is from a Father Osbert in Eaton, I think," Illesa said, pressing the seal down with her thumb as she showed him the parchment.

"There is a Father Osbert in Eaton, that much I believe. Did the merchant have a name?" the monk asked, shifting his weight onto his other foot.

"He did not say. He seemed respectable enough, but worried about the message being delayed."

"I see. An interesting tale. Shall I take that now?" the monk asked, holding out his hand. Illesa gave him the parchment, seal faced down.

"Wait here." The monk turned to go.

Illesa caught the door before it closed.

"I cannot wait, Brother; my master's errand was also urgent. Now I must attend to his affairs."

"Very well, I shall see to it that the Prior has it today."

"God reward you. I believe it is a matter of life and death." A noise behind her made her turn. The man on the bench was banging the back of his head on the wall. Illesa called out through the closing door.

"Brother, this man is in some distress."

"He's just a simpleton," the monk interrupted. "He's had his food, but that swine is always wanting more."

"Is there food left, Holy Brother?" Illesa regretted the words even as she spoke them.

The monk looked exasperated. He stepped forward and looked her up and down.

"Doesn't your master provide for you, but expects us to feed his messengers?"

"Forgive me, Brother, my hunger leads me into sin," she said, stepping back, her hand over her growling stomach.

"Any surplus food is distributed to beggars at the hospitaler's door. You have missed it today. You will have to come back tomorrow, if you are not too busy on your master's service." The monk shut the door firmly, and fastened the latch.

Illesa heard his unhurried footsteps retreating.

The man had stopped banging his head and resumed staring at the wall. His eyes looked old, but something about his mouth had the fullness of youth. He held his hand out in a practised gesture as she moved past him towards the outer door.

"I have nothing for you," she said, but almost immediately remembered the piece of bread saved from the morning. She unpacked it, divided it into two pieces and held one out to the man. He snatched it, and they both ate quickly, like wolves. When he finished, the man grabbed her jerkin, his face twisting in appeal.

"Let go of me! There isn't any more." Illesa pulled sharply away from him and ran out, into the last of the sunlight.

The horse was just a shadow by the wall. She hurried over to it and began to work the knotted rein loose with clumsy fingers. If she hurried she could get out of the town gate before it closed, then perhaps she could find a sheltered place to sleep by a small church. She had passed a few on the Ludlow road. Quiet places where she could conceal herself and a horse for a few hours before riding on to Clun. Pray God the dogs would be locked up.

The shadow behind the horse grew taller and wider. Illesa lurched back, but a large hand came down on hers and gripped it so hard that she gasped in pain.

"I believe you have something that belongs to me." The voice was deep, but it held no anger. The tall black-bearded man stood on the other side of the bay's shoulder. His strong fingers worked the leather rein out of her hand. It dropped to the ground. The bay was nuzzling him. He held Illesa's wrist tightly, and she looked at him in dismay.

"Is she your horse, sir?"

"Indeed she is. My Jezebel. I've missed her for many weeks. Now, perhaps you would like to explain how you come to be in possession of her, before I raise the hue and cry against you."

"Yes, sir. I swear I will, but may we speak privately, away from this place?"

"What game are you playing? Passing secret messages to the monks on a stolen horse?" He looked at Illesa for a moment, absently stroking Jezebel's nose. "Well, I'll hear your story. You don't look capable of harm, but if you try to escape you will certainly come to some."

He twisted Illesa's arm behind her and led her up the quiet lane, with Jezebel trotting along behind him like a dog.

The tall man said nothing more until they reached the smithy. He hitched the horse to a ring by the stable, opened the door to the living quarters and pushed Illesa inside. The light was very dim. There was a strong smell of leeks and butter, but no pot on the fire. He had already eaten.

The man let go of her, and Illesa stood where she was, rubbing her arm. He brought a stool close to the fire, sat down and nodded towards another one by the hearth.

Illesa sat gingerly, her legs and buttocks stiff from riding all afternoon.

"Tell your tale, boy," the smith said, "and mind you make it the truth."

"I've only had the horse a day, master. I didn't know who it belonged to except the outlaws. They were hunting me in the Long Forest, but I managed to get to your horse and escape from them. I had an urgent message to deliver to the Prior, so I came straight here. I will swear this is true, by the Holy Virgin and all the saints."

The smith watched her for several long, silent moments, while Illesa gripped her hands together between her thighs.

"Perkyn's men had the horse?"

"Yes, master."

"How many men were there?"

"I saw three, including Perkyn."

"And you are the fourth; I've heard that there are four or more of them."

"No sir, I swear I am nothing to do with them. I am a freeman's son from Holdgate."

"Holdgate, eh? Well, I must admit you don't look like an outlaw. But I don't believe your story; how could you escape them when so many others haven't?"

Illesa kept her eyes lowered. The events of the day were about to come down on her like hungry crows.

"The outlaws split up to look for me. I was hiding by a fallen tree, and when the man came for me I kicked his leg and he fell down the hill. I ran away from him, and, by God's grace, your horse was tethered to a tree nearby."

He looked at her and chewed his lip.

"She kept you on her back did she? That's quite something. She don't take to strangers generally."

Illesa just nodded. She felt sick with anxiety and the smell of food. The smith was sitting forward, his great hands on his knees, watching her.

"By rights I should turn you in. I'll be held accountable if you go on to commit crimes here, you know." The smith got up from the stool. He was taller than Kit, and probably ten years older. There was no sign of a woman's presence in the house. He lit a lamp with a taper and filled a tankard with ale from a barrel by the door before sitting down opposite her again.

"You are a strange one, that's clear. I've never seen you before in Wenlock, and I've seen most from round here."

"I am not a criminal or a vagrant, master, I swear." Illesa felt tears coming behind her eyes. "I have the seal of Father Osbert at Eaton, given to me this morning when he sent me with his message. I must go on to Clun as soon as I can; a man's life is at stake. Please don't have me locked up."

The smith did not touch the parchment she held out to him. He looked at her severely and folded his arms across his chest.

"So who have you been lying to, me or Brother Jonas?"

"You heard me talking to the Brother doorkeeper?" Illesa whispered, cradling the parchment.

"Yes, every word, my lad, so you better start telling the truth."

Illesa swallowed, but her throat was still tight with panic.

"It is a long tale, but I will gladly tell it and pray you believe me," Illesa managed, her voice breaking.

The smith held her gaze for a moment and then stood up suddenly.

"A long tale you say. Well, we best see to the horse first. She will be hungry and thirsty. You come with me. You won't outrun me, lad. I will catch you if you try to get away and then you will be straight in the gaol, and no question. I'll have my eyes on you all the time."

"Yes, master."

They went out into the cobbled yard. Jezebel whickered and pulled on the ring.

"Stay where I can see you, lad. Into the stable there."

He nodded her into the dark building and led the horse into the far stall, next to a small grey donkey. He took off the bay's harness and saddle and began brushing her down.

"She's a good horse," Illesa offered, piling hay into Jezebel's manger.

"Good is not the word, but she's strong and fast."

Jezebel ate enthusiastically, and they watched her in silence.

"Where did you get her?" Illesa asked.

"She doesn't look like a horse for a smith, does she?" he said, gruffly. "It is also a long story." He was combing out her tail and didn't speak for several minutes. Illesa regretted her question. He was already suspicious of her; asking questions would only make him more so.

"I did a job for Roger Montgomery, about a year and a half ago, it was," the smith said, eventually. "We were down in Ludlow, with the army. He wanted a special presentation dagger. It was to be of very fine workmanship on the hilt, and he wanted the blade to be of equal quality. He had Jezebel there, training her for the hunt, but she obviously didn't like him. Did everything she could to throw him off. He is a determined man, though. He brought her to me to be fitted for a special bit to help control her, but then she made her feelings known. She would do anything I asked." The smith bent over and picked up her hoof, cleaning it out with a bent nail. "Give him credit; Sir Roger saw when he was really beaten. He let me have her. Said it was payment for my work, but he was really just happy to be rid of her. She's never given me any trouble." He straightened up and looked at Illesa, who was standing at Jezebel's head watching her eat. "She must have liked you well enough not to throw you."

"I couldn't get her to go faster than a walk to start with, and then I couldn't make her slow down."

"Best to let her have her way. I'm sure she was only captured because her rider reined her in. She can outrun most mounts; most arrows even." He ran his hand down the horse's back, and she turned her head to him, breathing in his ear.

"All right girl, all right, you're home now. Get some sleep." He looked at Illesa and his sternness returned. "I've got to lock up. Stay in front of me."

Illesa crossed the yard towards the dim glow of the embers in the forge. She looked out over the hill in the direction she had ridden that day, fighting the urge to disappear into the dark wood and hide. The first stars were visible in a deep blue sky. The smith got a lantern down from the wall and lit it from the remains of the fire.

"My father was a smith," Illesa said, looking at the half-finished hinges on the anvil.

"Was he? What was his name?"

"Hugh, the smith at Holdgate."

"Ah. Big man, blond hair? Spoke French when he was angry. Did he once live in Acton?"

"Yes, when I was a baby, I believe."

"I knew him when I was a boy, just starting my apprenticeship. He was a good smith, but what a temper."

"Yes," Illesa said. "He was." There had been no one to equal him in either regard.

"He has died then?" the smith asked, picking up his hammers and fitting them in their places on the wall.

"Two years ago in Wales, with King Edward's forces." The feeling of relief Illesa had felt the day they'd heard the news still made her hot with shame. Grief had swiftly followed, and now the mixing of these emotions blurred her memory of him, like well water strewn with soapwort.

"God give him rest. You have not followed his trade?"

"No."

The smith made no comment. He replaced the irons in the corner and raked the fire. Illesa stayed by the anvil, even when the smith's back was turned. He was more likely to be sympathetic than the town reeve; that was certain. Finally the smith picked up the lantern again and went to the door.

"Come, I'll hear your story now. Inside."

The retelling was not easy. With every word it became clearer how little chance there was of saving Kit, or herself. She had been forced to lie again and again, and now even the truth sounded false.

"So you are not a lad, then," the smith said.

"No."

"No, you don't particularly look like one. What is your name?"

"Illesa."

There was a long uncomfortable silence.

"Well, Illesa, your story is too strange to be invented. I've had some dealings with the Forester myself and I don't envy your brother. I don't know anyone who has been released without paying with their life or half their worth. But to escape from his gaol, well that is something new." Under his thick beard, the smith might have been smiling. "Nor do I know anyone who has been taken by the Perkyn gang and lived to tell the tale. Jezebel was stolen when I lent her to a friend travelling to market late in the month of May. He was attacked on the forest road, but he was not as young or as fast as you, God rest his soul. You are lucky to be alive."

"Yes, master," Illesa said. By some miracle he seemed to believe her.

"But now we have a problem." The smith rubbed his hand across his beard several times. "What am I going to do with you? You are a girl in boy's clothes and that is improper, according to the Law and the Church." He paused, and then looked up at her. "Who has seen you here in the town? Have you spoken to anyone other than the doorkeeper and me?"

"No, master. No one else," she said, sure that the simpleton in the porch would not be able to give an account of her.

"If you are discovered here, you and I will both be arrested. You know that, don't you?"

"I can leave now. Is there a way to get past the town guards?"

"No, no. You're not going anywhere tonight. Sit down," the smith said. "I am not going to send you out to be killed when you have escaped death once today already. God would judge me harshly for that, indeed." He seemed agitated, his fingers lacing and unlacing on his lap. He cleared his throat with a deep cough. "I must ask you. This impropriety is not a sign of something worse is it? You aren't going out there to look for trade?" he asked, his voice harsh.

"No, master. I swear by the blessed Virgin, I am not a whore."

There was a long pause.

"Good." His face was still agitated and flushed. "I had to ask, you understand."

Illesa did not like the way he was staring at her, as if she was a holy image illuminated by candles. She fingered the strap of her pack and started to get up again.

"You can't go," the smith said quickly, putting his hand out and taking hold of her wrist. "I will not try to take you by force. God knows I would not. No. I will sleep in the stable and you will stay here by the fire. I'll lock the door. Tomorrow I will decide what to do for the best."

"Yes, master," Illesa whispered, trying not to pull away from his hand. "You have been very kind to me. I don't want to make trouble for you."

He let go of her arm, and went to the table to get the lamp.

"No trouble, really," he said, not looking at her. "In fact you have done me a service by bringing my horse back, haven't you. And you have given me a good tale to tell. Perkyn is not usually the butt of the joke." The lamplight made his face look sad and drawn.

"It was God's providence at work," Illesa said, standing very still next to the stool.

"Indeed. You are right. God is always watching us and working for our good." He went towards the door, but didn't open it. He paused there and then turned, going back to the table by the hearth. The smith held the lamp over a pot and looked inside it. "I am not good at keeping the house since my wife died, but there is a little pottage in here, if you are hungry. And some ale in the barrel. Shall I get you some?"

"I can manage. Thank you, master," Illesa said, trying to smile.

"Yes, help yourself. Good. I'll come and wake you before dawn." He covered the width of the room in two strides, and closed the door behind him.

Illesa sat down on the stool and listened to the thumping in her chest. What if he let himself back in while she slept? She should escape in the night; find a way out, but first she would eat and drink and maybe that would stop the sick feeling and trembling in her gut.

She ate the pottage standing by the table straight from the pot with a wooden spoon. Then she let the ale fill a tankard and downed half of it in two gulps. With the tankard in her hand, she went round the rest of the room and the sleeping area above the hearth, reached by a ladder. The windows had bars in front of their shutters. There was only one door, which was locked as he had promised. She sat down by the fire and rubbed her eyes, trying to scare up a plan from her marshy mind. But her head sank into the cradle of her hands, and sleep came, sudden and dreamless.

Chapter IX
AD 304
Antioch-on-the-Orontes

There was nowhere to hide from his gaze. Marina drew her shawl across her face and turned back to the flock, but she knew he was still assessing her from his saddle. At that point she understood who he was. This devil would test her, but he would not break her. She turned and faced him. His breastplate armour shone like scales.

"Take her," he said, wheeling his horse to prevent her escape.

Two of his guards dismounted and approached her. She did not run or resist. They lifted her onto a horse, and one of the soldiers mounted behind her. He held the reins in one hand and the other fondled her breast, laughing hot breath on her neck.

The man in armour came towards them, his sword drawn. He set the tip of it against the soldier's neck.

"Dismount."

The soldier dropped from the horse, and the man in armour took the reins, drawing the horse close to his.

"If you try to escape, I will let them have you," he said.

"I will not flee," Marina said.

He kicked his horse into a trot, and they began the slow descent from the slope of the mountain, the disgraced soldier running behind. Marina could see the city below in all its detail, the smoke from countless fires clouding the sky. The cliff of the Charonion blazed in the sun. In the distance Daphne was a green oasis, and beyond it, the glittering face of the sea.

Marina had not returned to her father's house after her baptism. Sometimes she watched the door, hoping to see Baa coming out, and hiding in the alley if her father emerged. But the slave did not appear. After a week she heard in the market what had happened, and where Baa's body was buried. She slept in the scrub by the river, but there was no sign of the preacher. He was not in the market or anywhere in the town.

After almost two weeks, as she was sheltering from the rain under the eaves of a house, a woman approached her and whispered in her ear. Marina followed her through a maze of streets to the Jewish quarter.

Sincletica was older than she looked, with many grandchildren, but her faith was young and energetic. She organised the converts, fed them, and even led the prayers. But her house was full of young male Christians with hungry eyes. Soon Sincletica was arranging Marina's journey to the mountain. One cold dawn, she had pressed a circle of bread into Marina's hand.

"Give this to old Rebekha from us, in the Lord's name," she'd said, leading Marina to the door and shutting it behind her.

One of her grandsons took Marina to the far side of Mount Silpius. Rebekha watched their approach from her goat pen, leaning on the makeshift fence. She did not speak, but took Marina's hand in hers, rubbing the smooth skin with her cracked fingers. It took Marina several days to realise that Rebekha couldn't or wouldn't ever speak.

They lived on the milk of the goats, the cheese made by the old woman and the herbs on the mountain, praying silently at dawn and dusk. No words were necessary. Marina had been there for six months when the riders came to view the western territory from the summit of the mountain. She was herding the goats across the narrow tracks on the southern slope. The wind was whipping her skirts across her body and her hair from her neck, and Olymbrius, the Governor of Antioch, decided to pluck her as he would a mountain berry.

The ride to the Governor's palace took very little time, but coming from the mountain it seemed to Marina that she had travelled to the other side of the world. Soldiers in Roman imperial armour were everywhere, lining the bridge leading to the island in the river, and at every door of the palace. The sun on their armour was piercing. Marina shut her eyes.

She was pulled from the horse by one of the soldiers and led through the large atrium, where a fountain gurgled above flowers and vines conjured in jewel-like stones. They stopped at a door in the right hand wall and the soldier knocked. After a moment it opened. A thin woman in a frayed tunic stepped back as Marina was pushed through the gap. She could hardly see in the sudden darkness.

It was a small, windowless room with benches all around the walls and a brazier in the corner. The woman bent over the coals, stirring. There was a smell of strong wine and something else, sharp and unfamiliar.

"Sit."

Marina sat on the nearest bench. After a moment, the woman approached her with an earthenware cup.

"Here." She handed it to Marina, who took it. The cup was warm in her hands. "Drink."

"No, Mother. I do not need it."

The woman looked at her and shrugged.

"You'll wish you had. It dulls the pain and helps you sleep afterwards."

"My Lord will save me from corruption."

The woman spat, and turned away.

"No one can save you here, girl. There is no god that cares for the likes of you. But have it your way." She went through the door and slammed it shut behind her. Marina put the cup down and the rounded base toppled over, spilling the untouched wine across the stone in a dark stain.

When they came for her, they found her sitting on the bench, hands turned up on her lap, eyes closed. The guards led her through many interconnecting rooms, one set for a banquet, others with only a bed and ewer. The last room was full of light coming through the tall arches. In the centre was a large bed on a dais. The floor mosaic depicted the Judgment of Paris.

Olymbrius was sitting on a gilt chair, a small table beside him set with a glass goblet full of wine, still dressed in his breastplate with his helmet on the floor beside the chair. He dismissed the guards with one gesture, and they marched out, leaving the door open. Olymbrius looked at Marina and reached for his wine. She saw his throat working as he swallowed.

"Put it on," he gestured to the bed. A white gown lay on it, trimmed with gold. She went to the bed and picked up the fine, smooth cloth. It was as soft as water. She slipped it over her head and drew the golden cord tight around her waist. Olymbrius poured more wine in his cup. His eyes were dark, almost without colour, and bloodshot.

"Lie on the bed."

Marina did not move.

"I said lie on the bed!" he shouted, standing up. She stepped back involuntarily, but moved no further.

He banged his fist on the table.

"Guard!"

A soldier entered.

"Bring me rope."

Olymbrius stood gripping the glass goblet in one hand, his other fist clenched.

"You'll regret that disobedience."

He put his goblet down with deliberation and strode towards her.

"If you will not submit willingly you will be subdued by force, let Mars bear witness!" His breath was hot, stale wine. The Governor was only slightly taller than her, but his physical force was like a wave breaking. He grabbed her chin, twisting her skin.

"You are merely a vessel. You are worth less than this cup, and easily broken."

"My father is the Priest, Aedisias."

"I know." Olymbrius smiled.

The soldier entered the room with a salute, one arm holding a ring of rope. He stepped forward and handed it to Olymbrius, who took it and began pulling out its length.

"Your father is the Priest in *my* temple. We have spoken of you. You are worthless to him. He told me of your corruption, your denial of familial obedience."

"I obey the one who saves." The words came out in a whisper, but he heard them nevertheless. The blow was so hard, she staggered. She pressed the stinging skin on her cheek. He stood, breathing deeply, watching her.

"I will break you like they break the horses from the plains, with ropes and whips." He took her hand suddenly and whirled her around, winding the rope quickly around her wrists behind her back. Holding the rope in his hand, he turned her round to face him. His face was flushed almost purple.

"I told Aedisias that I would bring you here and put you into service if I found you. Those who deny the law and the gods must be corrected, not left to corrupt others and fill the air with their lies." He jerked the rope suddenly so that she fell against his breastplate, and he gripped her waist before she could regain her balance. His other hand gathered up the white fabric and reached underneath.

"Your father said he would be glad if I killed you," his hot breath said in her ear. "The shame you have brought on him is great. It will only be assuaged if you renounce your faith in this false god. The true religion of the Roman Empire will not share loyalty. You can be taught obedience by Venus or Mars. If you learn quickly, torture will not be necessary. But if you persist, you will beg for death before you receive it."

Marina strained away from his hand, but the rope kept her within his reach.

"I will not renounce him," she said, but her voice was only a croak. The room was spinning around her. If she fainted, the Governor would take her.

She called out the name.

"Shut up," Olymbrius shouted, suddenly letting go of the rope so she fell to the floor. "You will not address him here." He put his knee on her back and pushed her chest into the stone floor, pulling the rope tight. Her arms wrenched backwards.

She opened her mouth to shout again.

"Shut up, I said!" He was fumbling with his clothes. She squirmed from under him on the marble floor, kicking out with her feet and scrambling away. But he brought her down again and her head hit the marble. She felt warm blood pooling on the floor under her. Olymbrius pushed her down with both hands and she felt his weight on her back. Then he made a sound as if he'd been struck. He fell forward on top of her.

"Guard," he gasped, "Guard!"

Marina's lips moved silently. Olymbrius' body grew heavier, pressing the breath from her chest. The guards knelt by him, loosening the straps of his breastplate.

"Get it off," he groaned. He was lifted off her as they removed the breastplate. She crawled as far away from him as she could. Olymbrius knelt on the floor, holding himself up with both hands. His breathing was fast and shallow, his face pale as flour from the quern.

"Get me to the bed."

The guards heaved him up and managed to lift him onto the dais. Marina watched them from a crouched position. Olymbrius did not move. He looked like a body laid out for funeral rites. She sat back on her knees.

"Praise the righteous one. He will not let his servant be corrupted. In his hands he holds the keys to life and death!"

Olymbrius turned his head and stared at her. The blood was dripping on the white robe, and her ecstatic face was raised to the sky. She looked like a god herself, ready for the next sacrifice. He could not lift himself from the bed. The guard bent over him, holding the cup of wine to his lips.

"Take her to the cells," he whispered.

Chapter X
The 16th day of July, 1284

The smith was bending over her, holding a smoking lamp. Illesa sat up quickly and brushed the sleep from her eyes.

"Is it prime?"

"No, the bells haven't rung yet. I thought it was best to send you on your way before the town woke. You don't need anyone following you."

Illesa got up and felt around for her belongings in the dark. The smith watched her, his face just lines and shadows, as she pulled on her jerkin and boots. Outside the air was cool, and the stars were spread across the sky like flowers in a meadow. He went to the stable door.

"Come, I've got her ready for you."

"What?"

"Jezebel. She's ready to go. She's had a good feed and I've put on a better saddle. She'll carry you there and back." He went inside the stable.

"No, I can't take her," Illesa protested, following him. "You've only just got her back."

"My mind is made up, girl," he said, untying the rope across her stall. "I can't let you go on such a journey on foot, at the mercy of thieves. What kind of man would let you go like that?" He only looked at Jezebel, stroking her nose. "I've done without her for nearly two months, another week won't hurt. But you must bring her back to me when you've finished what you need to do."

Illesa put her hand on Jezebel's back.

"I really can't take her," she managed. "What if she was stolen again?"

"We must do what is right and let the Lord look after the rest. Now, let's get you on your way," the smith said, briskly.

"I will come back as soon as I can, master. God willing."

"Aye, I don't doubt it," he said, glancing at her. "I've put bread in your pack and I've given Jezebel a good talking to. She understands that she's to take you as fast as possible. Let her drink regular. She won't need to eat till tonight." Jezebel's eyes were shining with reflected lamplight. He backed her out of the stall and led her into the dark yard. The horse shook her mane and stamped her hoof.

"She wants to be off. Up you go." He gave Illesa a hand to mount and stood back as she adjusted the stirrups. "I went to look, and the guards are asleep. If they wake when you unlatch the gate, just tell them you're on John the smith's business." He smacked Jezebel on the haunch and went inside. Illesa held Jezebel's reins, not believing what had just happened. But the smith did not re-emerge, and no one stopped her as she guided the horse at a quiet walk out of the yard.

The journey down the dale road was quick. After the first hour, Illesa's stiffness dissipated. She felt light and free, like the just-milked cows that broke into a trot as they reached the water meadows.

The road became rutted and broken as it curved west, with thick undergrowth on either side. There were few travellers. Although the sun was not yet high, the day was hot. Illesa could not expect the horse to go any further without a rest. She needed water. They passed through a small village, but everyone was working their strips and paid her no attention. At its outer boundary a track led south, towards a low hill, half-covered in young trees. It was empty except for birdsong. Jezebel walked slowly, snuffling the ground, but the grazing was sparse. Illesa led her to the far side of the plantation and into a meadow leading down to the eastern bank of the Onny. A boy with a stick was herding a scattering of cows. His shouts rose up, calling each one by name, and they followed him along the river towards a distant croft. Illesa stooped on the bank next to the horse, doused her head and drank.

Before midday she glimpsed the keep at Clun between the trees, and all around it unfamiliar hills. A band of archers, walking east with their bows across their backs, shouted as she cantered past them. They wore no insignia. But for their comradely banter, she would have taken them for outlaws.

The town gate was open. A lone guard gave the seal on her parchment a cursory look, before waving her through. The castle stood on the far side, its grey stone walls rising in a clear sky. Illesa dismounted and walked through the busy streets, trying to ignore the ragged boys offering a room and stabling for the night. One lad with a cracked front tooth followed her when all the others had given up in favour of the next traveller.

"Lovely horse."

"She'll give you a kick if you get in her way."

"Oh, no. Horses like me. I know all about them."

"Really?" Illesa tried to put some scorn into her voice, but his optimism dampened it. She stopped and turned around.

"I don't have money for you. You'd be better off finding someone else to fleece. Get lost."

He looked up at her and an astonished smile spread across his face. He knew.

She grabbed his arm and pulled him into an alley, Jezebel skittish behind her.

"If you say a word, you'll regret it," she whispered in his face, smelling hay and horseshit. He was still smiling.

"Yes, m'lady," he whispered back. "Why are you disguised?"

"Be quiet! There is no point trying to use this against me, I don't have any money to pay you off."

"I wouldn't. Honest." The smile was gone, replaced by a thoughtful expression, as if he was trying to remember something. "Are you going to the keep?"

"None of your business." Illesa let go of his arm. He was a disturbing child; too self-assured. She wished she had not started a conversation with him. It was going to be hard to end it.

"I could help you." He was stroking Jezebel's nose, and she was letting him.

"I don't need your help. I just want you to go away."

"I promise I will, if you let me ride your horse."

Illesa laughed in surprise.

"You want to ride this horse? How old are you?"

"I dunno. More than ten maybe. I've ridden lots of horses, but yours looks fast. I bet she goes like the wind." He blew on Jezebel's nose, and she nuzzled his hollow chest.

"You want me to trust you with my horse? I don't think so."

"Your horse trusts me," the boy said matter-of-factly. "What's her name?"

"Jezebel."

He kept on stroking her nose and started whistling softly through his teeth.

"God's wounds," Illesa said, under her breath. "All right but I must go to the keep first. I'm on urgent business."

"Don't you want to know my name?"

Illesa did not reply. She took Jezebel's rein and started leading her down the dusty street, dodging the traders and piles of rotting straw.

"I'm William," he said, trotting along on the other side of Jezebel's head. "My father died last year. He was the innkeeper of the White Hart. I know this place back to front."

Illesa almost said something, but decided against it.

"I don't have a home any more. The new innkeeper lets me sleep in the stables and feeds me if I bring him some trade. I know all about horses. This one is a beauty."

"She's got a temper though," Illesa said, without looking at him.

"That's why she goes fast; she's got fire in her. She drinks a lot I bet."

Illesa gave him a look, but he had eyes only for Jezebel. They were already approaching the bailey gate. People were glancing at her as they walked past. William was making her even more conspicuous.

"Go away. I can't have you along if they let me in."

He looked downcast for the first time.

Illesa sighed.

"I'll meet you by the river meadow at vespers if I can. That's the best I can say."

William nodded, as if he'd known all along and leant towards her.

"You need to speak differently, my lady," he whispered loudly. "You have to try to talk like a man."

"I will. Now will you go away? You're making me nervous."

She hoped the guard at the castle would be just as uninterested in her as the one at the town gate. But this one was dressed in a clean tabard bearing the FitzAlan arms, and he scanned her scruffy clothes with obvious contempt.

"Name?"

Illesa hesitated. William had distracted her and she hadn't prepared a lie.

"Name, I said!"

"William, of Wenlock." Her voice was breaking, like a lad's.

"What is your business here?"

She handed her parchment over, and he scrutinized it.

"What does this have to do with you?"

"Father Osbert sent me with a message for Richard Burnel."

"This scroll is for safe passage for a Brother Benedict," the guard said, and squashed it in his large hand before slapping it back on her palm.

Illesa's stomach dropped. Another guard, sitting just inside the gatehouse barked with laughter.

"He fell ill and they sent me instead. It is very urgent," she said, her voice much too high.

"You have a message for whom?"

"Richard Burnel."

"Do you mean Sir Richard Burnel?"

"Yes."

"This Father Osbert has sent *you*, a slovenly boy? He must have been desperate. What business does he have with Sir Richard?"

Illesa swallowed.

"I have been travelling long and hard. I apologise for my appearance, but I need to speak to Sir Richard urgently."

"Is that so?" the guard said, looking bored. "Sir Richard does not want to see anyone. Those are his orders. You may leave a message, and I can see that it reaches him," the guard drawled, "or not." He looked up at her and smirked. But she had no bribe to offer.

"I cannot do that sir. I must speak to him in person." Illesa pleaded, but the guard had moved away and was now standing by his friend inside the gatehouse, cradling a pair of dice.

"Please master, I must speak to Sir Richard. It is extremely important," Illesa called. Jezebel pranced in a semicircle, shaking her head and pulling hard on the rein.

"I have my orders. No visitors. Now either leave a message or get out. You and your horse are blocking the gate." The guard had sat down at a small table. He didn't even look up.

Illesa moved to the side. Out of the corner of her eye she saw William, leaning against a wall watching her. She beckoned him. He ran across the street, almost colliding with a dray horse, and stopped in front of her, smiling.

"Hold Jezebel. She's nervous." She handed him the reins. "Don't move from this spot."

Illesa reached inside the tunic for the leather cord and pulled out Kit's lead ampulla. She approached the guardhouse again and spoke over the clatter of dice.

"Master, give this to Sir Richard and say I carry a message from Christopher Arrowsmith which must be delivered in person."

The guard looked up at her, and then away.

"You'll have to wait, I'm busy." He carried on with his throw, while his friend sneered at her.

"Does your lord allow his guard to dice while they are on duty?"

"Don't tell me how to do my job, boy."

"If the man who sent this message dies because of your game of dice, Sir Richard will not be pleased," Illesa said, holding out the ampulla.

The guard's friend sat back, grinning.

"Go and do it, you lazy sod, before I win your hose as well as your coin," he said. "There is no profit to be got out of that one."

The guard got up and snatched it from her hand.

"Give it here."

"Tell him I will await his attention." She stood in the gateway as the guard spoke to a page and heard the instructions he gave him. William was having some trouble keeping Jezebel still, so Illesa ran over to them.

"Take her for a drink at the river and then bring her straight back. No riding," she said, her voice stern.

"Yes," he said with a smile that displayed a whole mouthful of cracked teeth, "master." She watched them weaving through the street towards the Watergate.

The sun was hot and her throat was dry. She found the water skin in her pack and drank the last of it. The guard was eyeing her. She pretended to be looking at the hawkers on the street, glancing back after a minute. He was still staring at her. Illesa folded her arms and looked at her boots.

"Boy, you are called for." A young page stood at her elbow. She followed him through the gate, past the steep banks topped with wooden stakes. They passed the kitchens, the farrier's forge and the practice yard, where squires were training with the sword. A racket of hammering and cursing followed them. Banners showing the arms of FitzAlan were everywhere. The page hurried past it all.

"Where are we going?" she asked, half running to keep up with him.

He did not turn around.

"To the mews."

They went through a guarded gate and onto a bridge. Below was a deep ditch between the walled outer bailey and the inner bailey on its high mound. The great keep rose four storeys to their right, a massive square tower with crenellated turrets. Several soldiers at its top were scanning the wide valley and the hills to the west. Even from where she stood, the view was impressive.

The mews were tucked close to the inner wall, a long low building on the quiet side of the yard. The page led her to the doorway and went to wait by the opposite wall, within hailing distance. Illesa peered into the shadows and took a step inside.

"Sir?"

"Here."

He was alone, standing by the perches, putting a hood on a peregrine falcon. She could not see his face, which was bent to his task. The air seemed muffled with feathers; the only sound was tethered falcons flapping their wings. Illesa waited, standing as still as possible. He did not turn to face her until he was finished.

"You come with a message from Christopher Arrowsmith." He had a patch over one eye, and below it a livid scar ran down his cheek to his mouth, twisting it into a grimace. His voice was level, but there was some quality about it that made her uneasy.

Illesa nodded.

"Yes, Sir Richard."

"I expect he is in trouble and needs my help."

"Yes, sir." Her voice broke with embarrassment.

"Well, get on with the tale of woe. Whatever it is, I won't be surprised." Sir Richard was putting on a thick glove. With the jesses in his hand, he brought the falcon on to the glove. The bird's sharp talons gripped the leather fiercely as he adjusted the straps and bells.

"Yes, sir. He was imprisoned by the Lord Forester of the Long Forest on the charge of poaching. He escaped and is now in the church of Eaton, seeking sanctuary. The Forester and his men are trying to break in to re-arrest him. He has no family able to bribe the gaolers, so he sends to you, hoping that his past service for you will incline you to help him. If you do not, I fear he will be dragged out and killed very soon, or at the end of his period of sanctuary."

Illesa looked up when she finished speaking. Sir Richard was watching her closely, his expression unreadable. He held the falcon still and did not speak.

"Sir Richard, I beg for your help. Kit is in a desperate situation." She met his eye, and then lowered her gaze again.

"And who is the person he has trusted with this message?"

Illesa hesitated.

"I am his sister." She did not look up until she couldn't bear the silence any more. He was smiling. The first unambiguous expression she had seen. It made his face younger, almost boyish.

"I said I would not be surprised and I am not. Ha! You and your brother are two of a kind." He spoke in an undertone, but he had taken a step towards her and was still smiling. "He talked much of you, but this was four years ago, and you were still a girl. He always said you were bright and stubborn. Not girlish at all. I never thought I would meet you myself. But here you are dressed as an impoverished messenger boy. Wonderful! And speaking French as well as your brother does."

"Our father came from France. He made us learn to speak well," she gabbled. "Sir, I am sorry for appearing in this manner. It was the only way I could travel. Our parents are dead, and we have no one else to turn to."

"Yes, I dare say. You can tell me all about it, but not here. Anyone could come in. We will go to the forest. I need to fly my falcon, and we can talk there. Page!" Sir Richard shouted out of the open doorway. The boy ran over.

"Have my horse saddled."

"Yes, Sir Richard." He ran back in the direction they had come.

"Now what was your name? Something unusual. I've forgotten," Sir Richard asked, walking slowly, the falcon on his wrist.

"Illesa."

"Ah yes. That was it."

They walked past several groups of soldiers. Sir Richard said nothing else until they had crossed over the bridge and reached the stable block.

"Now you best go back out of the gate." He pointed across the practice yard. "Have you a horse?"

"Yes, sir."

"Good. Meet me by the church. We can go into the southeast forest from there. The hunting is better," he said, striding away.

"Thank you, sir."

He was already in the crowd of grooms by the stable entrance.

Illesa walked quickly towards the outer gate, appealing to all the saints that William and Jezebel would be waiting outside.

Chapter XI
Black Hill

At the back of the White Hart, William had attracted a small crowd of grubby friends. Jezebel was enjoying a manger full of oats and the attention of William's grooming brush. Illesa held back her anger. William, on his haunches, looked up from his work, smiled at her and continued brushing down Jezebel's hocks.

"Get lost everyone!" he said cheerfully, and the other children scattered. She heard the innkeeper shout from inside. A serving girl walked past with a slop bucket, heading for the pigsty behind the stable.

"William, I need to take her now," Illesa said, under her breath. "I didn't ask you to bring her here. You know I can't pay for her stabling or her food."

"Don't worry about that, master." William stood up. "Are you going right now? Can I come with you?"

"No, I have to go alone." Illesa began loosening the reins. "She's eaten a lot. How are you going to sort that out with the innkeeper?"

"She was really hungry. She needs a lot of food, you know. What about the ride you promised me?" William stood by Jezebel's head, stroking her.

Illesa picked up the saddle and sighed.

"Look, I don't know how long I will be, but I will come and find you if I can."

"Promise?" He held Jezebel still as Illesa threw the saddle on to her back.

"You are too bold." Illesa tightened the girth and took the leading rein from William, who managed to look very sad.

"I'll wait for you by the bridge," he said, giving Jezebel a last stroke.

Illesa wound her way out of the close press of buildings and people and finally saw the church on the hill past the lines of burgage plots across the river. Each strip was dotted with crouching figures under wide straw hats.

She walked Jezebel to the Watergate, over the arched bridge and up a street lined with larger crofts towards the church. It had a fine, long nave and a high tower with a shingled roof. On the east side of the churchyard, several mourners were grouped around a small narrow hole; a child's grave. The Priest held a branch of hyssop and was flicking water on the shrouded corpse when the tower bells began tolling. Startled, Illesa had to wheel Jezebel round hard to stop her from bolting. She smoothed the soft hair of the horse's neck and steered her up the path at a walk. Bells and holy water would have scared the devils away from Ursula's grave, if only she'd had the coin to pay for them.

Richard was mounted on a chestnut courser and waiting in the shade of a yew. The hooded falcon was still calmly balanced on one gloved hand. His face was in shadow.

"You have kept me waiting."

She could barely hear him above the ringing coming from the tower.

"I am very sorry, Sir Richard," she began, but he drew his hand across his neck in an unambiguous gesture and steered his mount onto the steep path to the forest, where the branches quickly muffled the raucous bells. Jezebel scented the other horse and caught up with it in moments. They quickly reached the summit of the hill where the trees were sparser, and Richard pulled his horse to a stop. The rocky outcrop at the summit was bare, with an excellent view of the wood below.

"It would be best if you acted like a groom, and didn't draw attention to yourself," he said, dismounting. "Take the horses while I fly Bess. We can talk easily enough."

He handed her his rein, and she stood in front of the two skittish horses that were trying to circle each other. Richard climbed up the rock and faced east, with the light at his back. He took the hood off the falcon, talking to her quietly. The bells on her jesses chimed as she flapped her wings.

"It might be too hot for her, but we'll see." He lifted his gloved hand, loosened his grip on the jesses and launched her into the air. They watched her circle back over their heads, the bands of feathers on her wings a blur. From a bag at his waist, Richard took out a strip of red meat. More beef than Illesa had eaten since the Feast of the Nativity.

"I'm sure you have an exciting tale to tell, judging by your disguise and the quality of your mount, but perhaps just tell me how your brother comes to be in trouble again."

"Jezebel's not mine, sir. I'm only borrowing her. I didn't steal her."

"I didn't think you did, but it is unusual to see someone dressed like you on so fine a mount. I see Buskins has taken a liking to her." The horses were already nibbling each other's necks.

"I'll struggle to hold them apart much longer." The leather tightened around her palms as they kicked out, trying to prance round each other's haunches.

Richard hit his glove with the meat, and the falcon suddenly dropped from the sky to his hand. He held the end of the strip in his fist while the falcon began tearing it with her beak.

"Perhaps we should talk on horseback and keep these two lovers moving." He mounted easily, the falcon still eating. Sir Richard took charge of Buskins with a firm hand, and they walked down the track side by side. Illesa was glad that she did not have to try to control Jezebel, and fail, in front of such an accomplished rider. He turned his good eye to her.

"So, your brother has been misbehaving again, has he? I expect he is never going to change, but there is a limit to the number of times I'm prepared to help him."

Illesa kept her eyes on the track ahead, tired of carrying Kit's shame for him.

"Sir, Kit told me how grateful he is to you for assisting him in the past. He didn't want to have to ask again."

"I'm sure he didn't. I gave him an earful last time."

They didn't speak for several paces.

"Kit told me that he remembered you from when he lived at Acton, when he was a young boy," Illesa said, hoping to put the conversation on a better footing.

"It seems so. We were both with the King's company in the first war in Wales. He was still working at the forge alongside his father then. I was sent to him with a commission. We got talking and realised that we must have seen each other as children, before we both moved away from Acton. Kit is a bit younger than me. I am sure he was one of the children I was forbidden to play with. I have a vivid memory of a little boy who used to climb up to the top of the wall and throw acorns at me as I was practising in the yard."

"That sounds like him."

"So what's he done this time? You said poaching?"

"That is what the Forester claims. But I'm sure it was a set-up."

"Hmm." Richard frowned. "Which Forester did you say it was?"

"Giles, of the Long Forest. He has many men in his pay all over the area."

"I have heard of him. He is diligent in keeping the Forest Law, they say, and popular with the King."

"No doubt," Illesa said, under her breath.

Richard turned to her.

"You think he will take a bribe?"

"I pray so, although he seems determined to kill him."

"Kit will have provoked him. He would not make a good prisoner," Richard said, and swatted a fly dead on Buskins' neck. "How did he escape?"

"I think that is the other reason they want to kill him. They didn't like their prisoner locking up their guard and walking out while they slept."

Richard turned to look at her again.

"Ah. I see," he said. "Broke him out with your bare hands, did you?"

"No, sir, I put a sleeping draught in their ale and got the keys."

"Was that all?" he said, a half-smile pulling his scar. "Your brother is certainly fortunate in his sister, although many may say otherwise to look at you."

"Yes sir, thank you."

They had come to a clearing shaded by a large oak. Richard pulled to a halt and dismounted.

"Tie up the horses. No one should disturb us here."

They sat on the mossy bank. Bess, the falcon, was tied to a narrow branch by her jesses. The horses stood quietly, side by side. Illesa tucked her legs under her, smelling the broken bracken and crushed moss. The gravity of Kit's situation seemed to be fading in the bright sun.

"Sir Richard, it has been two days since I left my brother. The Forester's men were trying to break into the tower when I left. Father Osbert asked for help from the Priory in Wenlock, but I don't know whether they have sent anyone or not. Kit may already be dead. I must leave tonight with whatever help you can give me. I will be forever in your debt." She took a deep breath and waited, looking at the ground.

He took his time to reply.

"Sometimes I wonder if it is good for such people to be helped or if they should face the consequences of their actions like the rest of us." Richard's tone was almost bitter.

"Such people, sir?"

"He goes through life as if it's a game and takes no care with others or himself. And when things go wrong, it is never his fault. I've seen it before."

"He said you would not like him to ask again."

"At least he has that insight." Richard rose to his feet and went to the horses. Illesa got up hesitantly, and stood by Jezebel's side.

"Sir, he is the only family I have left. My father died in Wales and my mother was taken this year. I am sorry to involve you in this trouble, but you are our last hope. Without Kit, I will lose my home and land." Illesa tried to keep her tone neutral. But when she looked up there was pity in his face.

"You have no husband?"

"No."

"How old are you?"

"Eighteen before Michaelmas."

"Old enough. Well, I can't solve that problem for you. Kit will have to if he gets the chance, although I'd advise you to change your mode of dress if you want to make any kind of match." Richard paused, lacing the rein through his fingers. "Do you know why I keep helping your brother against my better judgment?"

"He said that he had saved your life," Illesa whispered.

"That is true. Kit should not have been fighting, but he was talented so they let him join the infantry at Flint. I was patrolling the forest road in front of the foot soldiers and was ambushed. Kit heard the attack and charged three Welsh guards to pull me out." He turned to look at her. "I could have done with him at Moel-y-don. Maybe he would have saved my eye."

Illesa looked down, her mouth dry. Even she had heard of that disastrous battle, when the Gascon commander, Luke de Tany, without taking into account the advancing tide, had sent his division of men across the Menai straits into a trap of Welsh spears. De Tany had ignored the King's order causing his own death and many others, including two of the Chancellor's brothers.

The accounts she had overheard had made vivid pictures in her mind: the water choked with armed men and panicked horses, drowning in a deep-filled cauldron. Despite Kit's attempts to describe the sea to her, she could not picture it. It sounded like the very dwelling place of the devil.

Richard untied Bess.

"I will go with you to Eaton. That is the only way. You cannot negotiate with the Forester. He would enjoy taking your money and locking you up anyway. We will leave at first light tomorrow." He mounted Buskins and wheeled him round onto the track.

"Thank you, sir. May God reward you," Illesa said, trying to hold Jezebel still enough to mount.

"Questions will be asked if you come to the keep or follow me out of the forest. You'll have to stay in the town." Richard leant over and put four silver pennies in her palm. "That should be enough for a bed and stabling. Meet me at matins by the Watergate." He set off at a canter down the track ahead.

Illesa watched him ride away in dismay. The forest stretched around her on every side. Jezebel did not want to go a different way from Buskins; she would be no help in retracing their steps. It was a slow ride back. Illesa was relieved when she finally saw the church tower below, the smoke rising from the town and William waiting on the bridge.

He led her on to the water meadow where half a dozen sheep were grazing. The sun was low on the horizon, the air hazy with light and insects. William stood at Jezebel's head, looking at her with devotion.

"Three laps, no more. She has gone far enough today," Illesa said, dismounting.

"Yes, m'lady."

She stood in the middle of the meadow and watched as they flew by in the golden light: the boy leaning over the horse's neck, her mane and tail flowing, the grass kicking up behind her hooves. Finally they slowed and walked to her, Jezebel flicking the flies from her ears. William slid to the ground, still smiling.

"Come on, I've some money now," Illesa said, taking the rein. "Take me to the White Hart. We both need feeding."

The innkeeper was brusque, but his rates were reasonable. She had enough for a private room, a good meal and stabling for Jezebel with some left over.

"Wake me before matins, and you will have a farthing," she said to William when she left him in charge of the horse by the dark stables.

"I'll knock your window; the doors will still be locked then."

"You'll keep Jezebel safe? She isn't mine, and I must return her." Illesa gripped William's shoulder. He looked away, chewing his lip.

"Don't worry, there's a guard. See?" He pointed to a stool on the other side of the courtyard. A pike was propped up next to it.

"An absent guard isn't going to be much help."

"He's just having a piss. He's awake most of the time. Anyway, I'll sleep right by her, so you needn't worry."

But Illesa went into the tavern with a feeling of misgiving. She gobbled a large eel pie in her chamber, glad there was no one to see her. For the first time in weeks she felt full. After a tankard of ale, she took off her boots and lay on top of the bedclothes. It seemed she'd only slept a few seconds when the sound of something hitting the shutters woke her with a jolt. Her head felt thick and stupid. She opened the shutter to a night lit by the full moon, and below, William's shadow beckoning urgently.

Illesa gathered her pack, pulled on her boots and slowly opened her door. There was no one in the passage and only one lantern burning by the stairs. In the hall, several guests were sprawled on the benches, and the smell was fetid. She fumbled with the back door, finally pulling out the stop and stepping into the yard of shining cobbles. William was standing in front of the stable door, fingering the latch.

"The guard went for a piss and hasn't come back, and I heard someone trying the gate. They've gone now, to get a crowbar or something. You'd better go while I try to rouse the master."

"Here's your money, William," she said passing him the farthing. He took it without a word, showing her into the stable. Jezebel was already saddled.

"Where does she belong?" he asked, stroking her between the eyes.

"Wenlock. A smith there owns her."

He smiled.

"Perhaps he needs a groom."

"Don't be a fool. You will only be locked up as a vagrant. Stay here where you have a living," she said, following Jezebel out of the stall. William whispered something in the horse's ear as he took her into the yard. He stopped by the stable door.

"Get out of town quick, before they find you." He was standing in the shadow, his face hidden. Illesa raised her hand and led Jezebel out into the empty street.

She hurried down the lanes towards the river, hoping Sir Richard would be there, so she wouldn't have to wait alone. As she approached the dark shape of the timber gatehouse, two figures formed out of the shadows. Illesa grabbed the pommel of the saddle, ready to mount, when one of the men began to unlatch the gate. Jezebel whinnied and another horse answered. Sir Richard came forward with Buskins, snorting on a tight rein. Without a word he went through the gate, and Illesa followed.

Chapter XII
The 17th day of July, 1284

The horses raced each other, their hooves churning up the meandering path that followed the river. Illesa was glad of their speed, the way the ground disappeared behind their hooves. Every stride was a prayer that they would arrive in time, that Kit would be alive. The sky was a clear, light blue directly above, while the track remained shadowed by the hills. Richard did not speak, but Illesa saw the flash of his teeth as Buskins shot past Jezebel on a turn. When the sun had finally risen above the hills, he called a halt.

"The horses should rest and drink," he said, dismounting. A path led off the track and down to a clearing by a beech tree which overhung a wide turn in the river. The bank had eroded into a gentle slope, perfect for watering horses and cattle. They walked the panting horses down to the water's edge. Richard stood beside Buskins, pulling on the buckle of one of the tooled leather panniers strapped behind his saddle. Illesa watched Jezebel as she lowered her muzzle to the clear water. She was as dependent as the horses on Sir Richard for food and drink.

"Come, we can rest for a moment," Richard said, sitting on a rock by the bank. Illesa found a log nearby. He tossed her a small loaf of bread, still slightly warm. The light brown crust came off in flakes, and inside it was soft, white and airy, like down. It would have been easy to eat a dozen such loaves. She licked the crumbs from her fingers, and when she looked up, Richard was watching her with an amused expression.

"There is another loaf," he said, "but I thought we should save it for later. Here." He handed her a small wineskin. She held it inexpertly. The wine sloshed into her mouth and over her chin. Richard had risen and was standing by Buskins. Illesa wiped her face on her sleeve, not risking another swig of the rich wine. She took the skin over to Richard, who was adjusting the saddlebags.

"Where are we, sir?"

"About three miles from the start of the forest. We will have to slow down now, but we might make it to Eaton before tierce."

"Do you really think so?" she asked.

He looked at her and raised his eyebrow.

"As long as we go steadily. No more racing. That pace will ruin them."

"Yes, sir."

The sound of hooves nearby startled them both. Two riders pulled to a halt on the track and regarded them. Richard turned Buskins and led him away from the river. Illesa pulled Jezebel around, but the horse was reluctant to leave the water. The men were talking to one another in an undertone. The horses they rode were work-a-day mares, foaming and panting. They had been ridden too hard. The men dismounted at the same time, their swords clanging on the stirrups. One took both sets of reins and tied the mares to a tree branch. The other came down the path to the river with a confident stride. He took off his cap and bowed.

"God give you good day, sir. May we water our horses here?" He was a handsome, heavy young man, not a noble, but well spoken, wearing a bright blue surcoat, elaborately stitched and generously cut. "We have come far and they are suffering in the heat."

Richard's face was impassive. He made a slight bow.

"Take the horses," he said, handing Buskins' reins to Illesa. She led them a few paces away to the beech tree and turned to watch.

"I thank you, good sir," the man said with an exaggerated bow.

Richard stepped towards him, his hands hanging by his sides.

"Where have you come from and what is your name?"

The young man smiled, showing large white teeth.

"Peter of Hopton, at your service. We have been riding from the north bearing a message for my master." He walked over to where Illesa was holding the restless horses.

"It must be an urgent message for you to drive your horses so. Who is your master?" Richard asked quietly, but his hand was now on his sword hilt. The other man had left their horses and was making his way quickly down the path.

"Yes. It is very urgent." Peter reached out to Jezebel's nose, and Illesa realised he was holding something. He turned it over and held it out. Jezebel snuffled up the apple and crunched it round in her mouth. Illesa breathed out with relief.

"My master is one of the lords of Billings Ring," Peter said, reaching across the horse's neck. Illesa heard the hiss of Richard's sword being drawn a second before a sharp blade pressed into her stomach. She dropped the reins as she tried to lunge away, but

Peter grabbed her by the arm and pulled her sharply against his chest, the dagger now on her throat. The other man, sword drawn, lunged at Richard. Jezebel and Buskins wheeled round in alarm and trotted away about a hundred paces.

"Now what have we here? Not armed?" Peter's free hand was exploring inside Illesa's jerkin. She tried to push him away but the dagger cut every time she moved. Blood already dripped down her neck.

"That's right," he hissed, "if you move you will regret it." His hand moved across her chest, lingering on the strapping over her breasts, and moving down to the outline of the book.

"God's wounds, you're a strange groom; body armour and breasts. Oh, and a little knife," he said, taking it out of the sheath and throwing it wide. He lifted her chin up with the flat of his blade, grasped her jerkin and ripped it off. "Jacques! This groom will provide some unexpected sport."

Jacques did not reply; Richard was keeping him busy. Their swords rang as they tested their strength; lunge and parry, like a harsh change of bells. The two men were matched in weapons, but the horse thief had the advantage, being considerably taller.

"Come on, man," shouted Peter. "Can't you better a one-eyed opponent?" He started moving Illesa away, one step at a time, from where Richard was fighting, holding her face close to his, his breath intimate on her cheek.

"When I saw you at the White Hart last night I had no idea, or I would have taken more advantage of the situation. I suppose I only had eyes for your horse's lovely haunches, not yours, eh?" he laughed in her ear. She tried to twist away, but his grip was brutal. The dagger pressed harder. Illesa's arms felt stiff with the effort of not reaching up to her throat. Her mind could not form a prayer. They had almost reached the tall ash tree where the horses stood, twitching their ears in alarm. Peter pulled her left arm behind her and moved the dagger swiftly to her back.

"Get the horses, wench, or I will stick this through your spine."

Illesa inched towards Jezebel. Was it sweat or blood that was running down her back? Behind her, the clash of swords sounded frenzied. Illesa forced herself to breathe out. She held her free arm out towards the horse.

"Come girl, come," she tried to call, but her voice rasped with fear and Jezebel galloped away shaking her bridle, followed by Buskins. The horses stopped when they reached the track, pawing the ground and looking at the men.

Peter swore loudly. He twisted Illesa's arm against her back, and she cried out. Before she understood what he was doing, he'd taken a length of rope from his belt and looped it round her neck. Illesa ducked her head and lurched forwards, falling on her knees, but he held her arm fast and pinned her on the ground, tying the loop of rope into a noose and pulling it tight. Coiling the rest of the rope around his hand, he pulled her up to a kneeling position, and then to her feet.

"Get that horse or I will hang you by your pretty throat," he said in her ear.

"She won't come when you are here," Illesa whispered. Every word was painful, and the cord felt tighter with each breath, but her mind had cleared, as if she'd been dunked in the cold river. She tried to turn her head. Perhaps there would be a stick within reach.

Peter was staring at her, breathing fast. He twitched the rope playfully.

"Well, if you cannot catch your own mount, we will have to find another use for you and track down the horses later. They won't go far, and I have plenty of apples." His dagger rested on the top of her breastbone for one heartbeat.

"Let's get a closer look."

The dagger went through the old worn cloth of the tunic like air. The book was still held to her chest, but covered only with the thin straps of cloth, which also hid her breasts. She pushed at his probing hands, but all her limbs felt weak. The effort made her cough and the cord squeezed tighter. She was suffocating.

"Don't," she gasped.

"What's this?" he said, pulling at the strapping around the book. Illesa lashed out with her fist but he sliced it down with his dagger.

"No fighting or I will carve you up."

Keeping hold of the rope in one hand, Peter inserted his dagger under the straps of cloth between her breasts and jerked it upwards. Illesa clasped the book as the cloth fell away. Peter slashed down the side of her breast, cutting deep, and she let go. Her scream was barely audible.

"Shut up," he said, giving her a shove.

Bending down he picked up the book, thumbing the pale leather and gold lettering. Illesa lay on the ground. She put her hand to her neck and tried to loosen the noose. Blackness was creeping across her eyes.

"What is a book of this quality doing in such poor company?" Peter said, turning the pages. He looked over at her and tugged the rope tight again.

"Put it down." Richard's voice was just behind her. "Now, or I will run you through."

Peter placed the book on the ground.

"Kneel down or I will behead you now!"

Peter did not move. He stood with his head bent forward, the point of Richard's sword pressed on the back of his neck. His dagger was in one of his hands now, and the rope in the other.

"Wait, sir. I have money," he said. "I'm sure you would like to see how much."

"The devil take your money and you!" Richard swung his sword, but the horse thief dropped to the ground and wheeled round in a crouch. He pulled the rope tight and held the dagger in a throwing posture.

"You need to be quicker than that, Cyclops. I can easily break your groom's neck and bury this in your heart before you have moved one finger. But why don't we negotiate instead and then we can all walk away alive."

Richard lunged to the left and brought his sword down on the rope, cutting it through so that Illesa's head hit the ground. The dagger flashed in the air, but she didn't see where it landed. She rolled on her side, gasping and coughing. Her whole chest was red with blood. She pushed herself to her knees. Richard, his sword raised, was running towards the river five paces behind Peter. The horse thief had reached the steep bank on the other side and started to scramble up the protruding tree roots when Richard caught up with him. He grabbed the blue surcoat with his left hand and ran his sword into Peter's back with his right.

Illesa shut her eyes. When she opened them, an old man was standing five paces away, watching her warily.

"Master, help," she croaked. The rope was still around her neck. She pulled at it and managed to loosen it enough to bring it over her head. The man came two more paces and then stopped.

Richard was walking towards them, wiping his sword. His white face made the scar under his eye look more livid.

"Goodman, we need three more men from your village to take these bodies away. Bring the head of your tithing and inform him there has been an attempted robbery and two are dead. Do you understand?"

The man nodded, the lines of his face deepening. He walked slowly up the path to the track. When he was out of sight, Richard came and stood over her, frowning.

"Can you walk?"

She nodded, not looking at him.

"Go and wash. I have a tunic you can wear." He turned away.

Illesa got up slowly, covering her breasts with her arms, and stumbled towards the river. Richard had dragged Peter's body just out of the water. Blood had soaked through his fine white tunic and his blue coat. His mouth was open and red. Illesa circled away from him and found a low rock a few yards up stream. She sat with her head in her hands, struggling to control the sobs that shook her chest. The voices of several men grew louder as they approached the clearing. Keeping her back to them, she took off the ruined tunic and used it to wipe the blood from her chest and hands. The deep cut by her left breast still bled freely. She made a pad of some of the cleaner pieces of cloth and held it on with her upper arm.

"Here." His voice made her whole body jerk. Richard was holding out a tunic, pure white linen with a yellow braid. The book was in his other hand.

"It will be ruined," she said, her breath juddering.

"It's all I have." He threw it on the stone next to her.

"Can you find my pack?" Illesa stuttered.

Richard nodded and turned away. She began tearing strips from her tunic to hold the bandage in place, but her numb fingers could barely grip the fabric. They were wet with blood. She tied the first strip round the oozing cut on her hand. Several villagers were waiting in the clearing, looking at the body of Jacques. Some were estimating the value of the thieves' clothes and horses.

Richard walked stiffly towards her and placed the pack on the rock. He straightened up slowly. Peter's dagger was hanging from his belt.

"Cover yourself and stay here until I come back," he said, and went over to the body. She heard him giving orders to the men, who obeyed him without comment.

The valerian ointment was at the bottom of the pack. Illesa scraped a good amount from the leather pouch onto her finger and smeared it on the blood-soaked pad. Holding her breath, she strapped it on the cut as firmly as she could and pulled Richard's tunic carefully over her head. It helped little. She still felt naked without the book. It was lost to her now, and Saint Margaret's blessing with it.

Illesa got slowly to her feet. She needed to look for her mother's knife, but the men were still at work, lifting Peter's body, and cursing under his weight as they dragged him up the path. Blood dripped from his back and ran down the crease of his neck from his open mouth. They heaved him on the back of his own horse, which rolled its eyes and wheeled round unhappily.

Illesa knelt down behind a tree and retched on the ground, spitting out bile. After a while, the shaking stopped enough for her to stand. She slid down the bank and washed her mouth out in the river. When she looked up, Richard was watching her from several paces away.

"Come with me."

He led the way up the track and pointed to a cottage just visible, about half a mile away.

"Go to that croft. They will tend you while I find the horses."

She nodded, the tears still dripping down her cheeks.

"And when I get back, you will tell me how you come to have this book, which could have ransomed your brother a hundred times." He toiled up the track and Illesa heard him whistling for Buskins. The sound faded into the distance, superseded by the flow of the river and the cry of a hawk circling high above.

Finding the knife did not take long. It was near one of the dark stains on the ground. She had returned it to her belt and bent down to get her jerkin, when a wave of dizziness forced her to her knees. No prayers would come.

It was some time before she was able to start walking.

Chapter XIII
AD 304
Antioch-on-the-Orontes

The cells were under the soldiers' barracks. There were no windows and the smell was overwhelming. The gaoler opened an iron-barred door with a key and the guard pushed her inside.

"Who's this then?"

"One of the apostates to be executed," the guard said, under his breath. "She's a dangerous one. Don't touch her till I return."

"Don't look dangerous to me." The gaoler ran his tongue across his lips as he slammed the iron bars closed. After he had let the guard out, the gaoler went back to her cell, the key ring swinging on his thick finger. Torch smoke hung in the still air. Marina was kneeling on the floor in the darkness. Her hair was matted. Blood had dried on her face, and the white robe was torn and dirty.

The gaoler shoved his torch into the bracket and began to turn the key in the lock.

"You will be cut down."

He stopped and looked behind him. There was no one else there.

"Shut up you!" he shouted into the cell.

"The Lord will return and claim his children. Those who have persecuted him will perish, burnt in a fire." Marina's mouth moved, but the words seemed to come from the air and rain down like stones.

The gaoler grabbed the torch and threw it at her through the bars. It fell to the floor by her robe.

"You'll be the one who burns, bitch!"

Marina did not move. The gaoler snatched the keys from the lock, spat on the dirt floor and went back to his post.

An hour later, when the centurion arrived with two auxiliary soldiers, the cell was in darkness. They brought a torch and the gaoler handed them the keys without a word. The soldiers each took one of Marina's arms and pulled her to her feet.

"Tie her arms tighter," the centurion said. They pulled the rope around her wrists, and then turned her to face them.

"Marina, daughter of Aedisias, Olymbrius has declared that if you renounce your Christian faith you will be spared torture. Your death will be quick. We are ready to take you to the yard to be beheaded." The centurion's voice was loud enough for the parade ground, but in the cell it sounded muffled. "If you do not renounce your apostasy, you will be tortured until death."

She said nothing. She was not looking at them. The centurion slapped her hard across the mouth.

"Did you hear me? Olymbrius, Governor of Antioch, is granting you mercy if you turn away from your false god and sacrifice to the true gods of Rome."

For several seconds there was no sound but Marina's quickened breathing. She swallowed the sobbing that was rising in her chest and looked the centurion in the eye.

"His mercy is worthless. Let him do what he will," she whispered.

The centurion stood still for a moment, then he grabbed her hair in his fist and pulled her towards him.

"As you do not want mercy, none will be granted," he barked, and let go of her hair so she fell backwards.

"March." The soldiers lined up behind the centurion and left the cell.

It was night when the centurion and soldiers returned. They all carried staves. Marina was lying on her front along the rear wall of the cell, her arms still tied behind her back.

"It won't take long," the centurion said quietly as they stood outside the cell. "If we go at her too hard, she'll die, and the Governor doesn't want that. He wants her in agony."

"Break her arms then; that won't kill her."

"Or her fingers," said the other. They stood for a while, watching her sleeping body.

"I know what I want to do to her," said one.

"Olymbrius will cut it off if you do," said the centurion. "If he can't have her, no one can."

"The selfish prick," the first soldier mumbled.

"You'll do double latrine duty for that," the centurion said, and opened the cell. The soldiers followed him inside. When his first blow fell, her body coiled and she cried out.

"Stand!"

They pulled her up by the arms. After they had all struck her once, she could not stay upright, so two of them held her while the other struck her from behind. They left her lying on her front. Blood dripped down her neck from a gash on the back of her head. Her right arm and three fingers were broken. Blood and urine pooled in the dust of the floor.

It might have been hours later or days when the cell bars squealed open. The guards came in and tried to raise Marina by her arms, but she screamed so suddenly and so unexpectedly they dropped her back to the ground. Her breath was ragged and shallow.

"Get up or we will do it again," the centurion said, standing over her. She pulled her knees under her, slumping to the side.

One of the guards reached under her arms and pulled her to a standing position. They took her out of the cell and down the dark corridor.

"Open up!"

The gaoler unlocked the door and pushed it open. The burning sunlight on the other side of the door blinded Marina.

"Bring her here."

She remembered the voice. Olymbrius. She opened her eyes a slit. He was sitting on a gold chair on a dais, shaded by a canopy. There were four soldiers flanking him. The rest of the training ground was empty. Only dust and heat. Someone took her forward a few paces and pushed her down to her knees. Her eyes were adjusting. Behind the Governor's chair under the canopy, her father stood, watching.

"Are you ready to recant your false faith and sacrifice to Jupiter?"

Marina opened her mouth but no sound came out.

"Answer the Governor," said the centurion, hitting her across the face.

Marina instinctively moved her arm as she fell and screamed with pain. She writhed on the ground until the guard lifted her back on her feet. There was dust in her nose and mouth. She spat to try to clear it.

"No, I won't," she breathed out.

Olymbrius stared at her, his face reddening. He picked up his silver goblet from the table and drank, letting the wine flow down his chin. Then he got up and walked towards her. A sob of fear escaped from her mouth. He stopped in front of her and grabbed the top of her robe.

"So you think your Galilean is more powerful than Jupiter? You think that he can save you? You will soon realise your error." He ran his hand down her neck and breasts to her waist. "I will make you an example to the people of Antioch. The fools who follow this crucified god think they can do as they choose." He pulled her very close and pressed her against him, so she could feel his heat. "They think he is a match for Rome. But they will see," he whispered in her ear. "Yes, they will know the truth before they die." He let go of her suddenly and stepped back.

When he hit her across the face with his right fist, she fell like a tree. The guards tried to get her up again, but she was as limp as a dead cat.

"Don't waste time! Carry her. Prepare the fire and the cage!" the Governor ordered.

They laid her in the cell, and, after a few moments, she stirred. She coughed and it set her whole body shaking with pain. When the fit stopped, she heard a hissing sound moving along the ground by her ear. A snake coiled and uncoiled itself in her mind.

"Marina," a voice said, far away. "Marina, wake up."

She opened her eyes but she could not see where the voice came from.

"Father?" she whispered.

"Marina, the Governor has promised me he will still grant you mercy if you recant now, for my sake. He has given me a moment to speak to you. Although you have betrayed me time and again, you are still my daughter! Imagine what it will be like to watch you being burnt before the Governor." His breath caught in his throat. "Your mother gave her life to bring you into the world. Will you throw this life back in her face? Will you bring disgrace on the family name forever? Return to the true gods and earn an honourable death!"

She could not see him from where she lay, but the snake slid into her vision; grass green with a bright yellow forked tongue.

"I am glad you are here, Father." She tried to move onto her side but could only turn her head a few inches towards the cell door.

"Look at you," he said, bending down. "You brought this on yourself, you stupid girl. I have been sacrificing to the gods for you day and night, asking why they have sent you to punish me in my old age with this disgrace. What more honour did you want? The Governor would have had you for his wife, but this was not good enough for you? You would rather stay on the mountainside with the goats, living in their filth?"

"I must tell you something," she whispered.

"Let us hope it is not too late. I hear the guards coming. Do you recant?" he asked, bending down towards her.

The snake coiled its body and reared its head. The inside of its mouth was blood red.

"I forgive you," Marina breathed.

"What did you say to me?"

Marina was silent.

"What did you say?" Aedisias shouted. "Don't you dare!"

Marina shut her eyes and watched the snake spitting its venom and fire.

"In the name of Jesus, I cast you out."

Chapter XIV
The 17th day of July, 1284
Stoke de Say

The lane was very quiet. A blackbird flying across her path startled Illesa out of the vivid bloody scene in her mind. She was almost at the croft. It was a small, squat building. The cobs were showing where the daub and lime wash had crumbled away, and inside a baby was crying with hunger. Illesa knocked on the door.

After a moment, a woman opened it. Her rough russet wimple was pulled back, giving her a startled look. Over her shoulder was the baby, about five months old, pulling on the cloth of the wimple and mouthing it.

"Come in." The woman's voice was high, questioning.

"Thank you, Goodwife." Illesa followed her through the low door.

"Gentleman sent word I was to look after you." She crossed the room and swung the baby down to her breast in a practised movement. "I'll get you some ale." She went out the back door.

The croft smelled of animal droppings and mould. Illesa went to the stool by the hearth and sat down by the low fire. Small brown barley cakes were cooking on the stone in the middle.

"Here." The woman set a wooden cup down next to Illesa. "When you've had that, you can lie down. Gentleman said you were injured."

Illesa nodded, close to tears.

"Well, just look at your hands and your neck!" The woman took hold of Illesa's hand and peered at it.

"It's not so bad, Goodwife," Illesa said, pulling out of her grip.

"I can bring you a poultice if you like." The woman was standing too close to her, looking at her face while the infant sucked enthusiastically.

Illesa took a sip of the ale. It was sour.

"Don't go to any trouble." She certainly knew more about the treatment of wounds than this slattern.

"As you wish." The woman began to turn the cakes over expertly with one hand.

"How old is your babe?"

"Six months, he is. Little Henry. The fever devil tried to take him in the spring. We prayed and prayed and Our Lady saved him, so she did."

"God be thanked," Illesa said, automatically. The baby had fallen asleep, and the woman slung him over her shoulder again as she straightened up.

"Eats like a whole army, he does."

"That's good. He'll be strong."

"You know a lot about it for a groom," the woman said, looking at Illesa suspiciously.

"My mother helped birth many babies."

"One of them was she? Well she shouldn't have been telling tales about it to a boy," the woman grunted. "You from around here?"

"No."

"Where you from?"

"Goodwife, I'm very tired. May I lie down?"

The woman waved her hand at the sleeping platform.

"I swept it out today, I did," she said.

A small boy ran through the back door, his hands caked in mud.

"Mama! Look!"

"What are you doing getting yourself filthy, you little pig. Come on, we shall have to throw you in the river!" She shooed him out the door and closed it behind her. The boy's voice was still audible through the wall.

"That's where I was, Mama. I caught a frog!"

"Come here, you. No more mud. I have to wash those clothes you know."

Illesa lay on the bed, trying not to breathe in the smell of the family. If she hadn't felt so weak, she would have left for Eaton alone so she would not have to try to explain the inexplicable to Sir Richard. But she couldn't even do that now. She had nothing at all: no book, no horse and no hope of help for Kit. Her tears dripped onto the coarse wool blanket. Every heave of her chest made her throat burn.

Illesa heard the door open and rolled on to her uninjured side. The woman went to the hearth and had begun turning over the burning cakes, when they both heard the sound of hooves outside. Illesa sat up. The woman stood in the open doorway.

"He wants you," she called.

Illesa picked up her pack and went out into the bright sun. Richard was on Buskins holding Jezebel on a tight rein. He jerked his head, indicating that she should mount.

"Here is something for your trouble, woman." He threw a coin on the step, and she stooped to pick it up.

"God save you, sir," she said, looking at it curiously.

Richard was already trotting away. Jezebel didn't need instruction; she followed as soon as Illesa had struggled into the saddle.

After a mile, Richard slowed the horses. There were no dwellings nearby. He led them off the track for fifty paces or more into a neglected coppice. Some trees had been allowed to grow, and they stopped under the shade of them. Richard watched Illesa as she dismounted and tied Jezebel to a branch. He went a few paces away, limping slightly. When he turned round, he had his hand on his sword hilt and his face was pale.

"I should have left you there for the bandits to take when they saw fit," he said, pointing at her. "You have been lying to me all along. You have this horse, which is like honey for thieves, and a sacred book of Saint Margaret, worth many pounds, and yet you claim to be too poor to secure your brother's release." He sounded disgusted. "It's nothing but a confidence trick. You aren't who you say you are. You look nothing like Kit. The thieves are using you to carry their stolen goods and to make traps so they can steal horses and money from dead men. Using you as their whore as well, no doubt. You told the thieves where to find me, and they promised you a cut of the takings." His face was twisted with distaste. Her father had looked at her in the same way, the last time she saw him.

"No sir, that's not true." Illesa's voice cracked and she coughed painfully. "I didn't know those men. They would have raped me if you hadn't killed them." Illesa looked at the ground. An ant was crawling over her boot. It stopped to investigate the spots of blood on the worn leather. "I swear by the blessed Virgin, I am Kit's sister and he is in Eaton church. He gave me the ampulla with oil from the Holy Land. He said you would know it was from him, sir, because you gave it to him after Flint. All I have told you about Kit is true. The horse belongs to a smith in Wenlock who lent it to me for the sake of my father whom he once knew. I swear by all the saints in heaven, I have not betrayed you, Sir Richard."

He did not say anything for a moment. She risked looking up at him. He was leaning against the tree, frowning.

"Those thieves did not come across us by chance. They knew exactly where to find us," Richard insisted, but his voice was less angry.

"The stable boy woke me saying men were trying to break in. I didn't see them, but they must have followed us. The thief said he had been watching me at the inn." Illesa remembered the sleeping figures on the benches as she had slipped out of the door.

"Which inn? Tell me it wasn't the White Hart."

She nodded, miserably. Richard looked heavenward.

"Of all the places, you had to choose the actual headquarters of the bandits. That stable boy is a notorious informant. He will hang soon, mark my words."

"William? But he was the one who warned me."

"A standard trick. They don't want their premises broken into; it would be too obvious that they were in on the deal. So the stable boy tells the traveller to get the horse out, and if he is foolish enough to remove it from the secure stable, the thieves ambush him and steal the horse. The boys are experts in identifying inexperienced travellers, like you, who haven't any common sense," Richard said.

Illesa bit her lip. Being thought naïve was better than being considered a thief. She could easily have been on a gallows next to William's thin body while the birds landed for their share. Throwing money around and drawing attention to herself had been very foolish. She and Jezebel were conspicuous enough as it was.

"He must do it to get a share of the food," she whispered.

Richard was examining one of Buskins' hooves, and she could only see the side of his face that was always pulled into a frown.

"The horse thieves follow the outlaws at Billings Ring. Some of the people who so kindly helped us dispose of their bodies will be in their pay, although they claimed not to know them," he said, straightening up. "We should leave now."

Illesa went towards Jezebel, wiping her face with the back of her hand. Richard stopped her as she walked past him.

"You have not yet explained the book," he said. He had taken it out of his saddlebag and was holding it on his open palm.

It looked vulnerable without its cloth covering, lying on his hand in the open air.

"I cannot explain it, sir. I know I should not have such a book, but it belonged to my mother and it is all I have from her. I cannot sell it, as I cannot explain it. Nor do I wish to if another way is still open to me."

"Your mother? How did she come to have a book like this? It must have been made for a wealthy lady." His eyes were caught by the illustration on the first page. "It is fine workmanship. The best I have seen in such a small book."

"I do not know, sir. My mother said it came from my father's family." Illesa's hand twitched with the urge to reach out for it.

Richard said nothing for what seemed a long time.

"She did not mean the smith, I take it," he said, dryly.

Illesa looked at her hands.

"No. Kit and I had different fathers."

"That would explain your lack of resemblance," he said, after a pause. "These things do go on, you know. So who was he then? Someone of standing, evidently."

"I am glad to tell you what I know, sir, but shouldn't we leave now, as you said?"

He glanced up from the book.

"Ah. Yes. I'll keep it in the pack for now. It will be safer there, and a more suitable place for a holy book."

Illesa said nothing. Without the book, she felt as fragile as a moth, easily crushed in the hand. As she mounted, the wound opened wider. She pressed her side, hoping they would come to a place where she could dress it properly before the bandage was completely saturated.

Richard got into the saddle heavily, his breath hissing across his teeth.

"Are you injured, Sir Richard?"

"Yes. When we stop, you may bind it up," he said, walking Buskins out of the clearing. "We will be safe when we come into the demesne of Stoke de Say. They keep the roads clear and have guards." Richard urged Buskins into a gallop as the track straightened out. "I know a short cut."

Richard's path took them past a spring and up a pastured hill, intersected by the old Roman road, the stones now jumbled and cracked with neglect. From the hill, they could see smoke rising from the roofs of Stoke de Say, and beyond, the hills and encampments to the east. The manor was partly built in timber, but there were new walls being assembled of stone. It was large and surely full of people who would stare at her, people who would guess.

Illesa thought of the familiar rise and fall of field and coppice that she could see from her own croft. She stroked Jezebel's mane, concentrating on the rhythm of her stride, trying to stop the homesickness and grief that was welling up in her throat. Year upon year of sweeping, planting, weeding, chopping, tilling, and brewing had woven her into that place, but now the bonds were cut, just as her mother's soul had been cleaved from her body. Without a doubt, Agatha had accused her by now. Word of Kit's escape would also have reached the village. They were both outlaws, and there would be no mercy unless they could pay for it. The Forester had many powerful friends. The lord of Stoke de Say might be one of them.

"Sir Richard, we might be delayed in the manor. Can't we stop somewhere more private?"

"The horses need attention and so do I," he replied, not turning his head.

They took the horses down the hill at a slow trot, which jarred Illesa's chest at every step. The track came past the fishponds and alongside the newly cut timber fence of the bailey. Inside there was a racket of hammering.

"Dismount and lead us in." Richard pointed ahead to where the fence turned and heightened, leading up to the gatehouse. Illesa slid to the ground and took the lead reins of the horses. They were sweating, twitching with the flies that rose from the shit ditch by the road.

The gatehouse was modest. The guards straightened up as they approached, dropping the stones they had been about to throw in the moat. They looked younger than her. Richard did not give them time for their challenge.

"Here, guard! Send to your master that Sir Richard Burnel is at the gate in need of succour, and be quick about it!"

They heard the page inside running across the cobbled yard.

The guards had grown tired of staring at Illesa and Sir Richard by the time the page returned.

"The Steward is coming," he panted.

Richard's frown deepened, but it was not long before a well-dressed man, brushing sawdust from his supertunic, opened the small door in the gate. Sir Richard dismounted as he approached.

"Welcome, Sir Richard." The Steward bowed. "God give you good day. I am sorry to keep you waiting. Lord Laurence is away but you may, of course, come in. He knows the Chancellor well, does he not? Lord Laurence is building a new hall and private rooms, so please excuse the disarray." He held the gate open and they walked the horses into a small bailey. Stacks of timber were piled on one side, stone on the other. Behind the well there was a sizeable stable. Richard stopped near it and fixed his eye on the Steward.

"Our needs are simple. We were on urgent business when thieves attacked us. Our horses want rest and food, and I require a room where my wounds can be dressed. After that we will continue on our way."

"Of course, Sir Richard. I will send a serving boy to attend you."

"That will not be necessary. My groom will attend me; I need no other."

The Steward looked Illesa up and down, but she busied herself removing the saddles.

"Very well. I will have water and towels brought to your room."

"Good. Refreshment would also be welcome."

"Very good, sir. I will see to it." But he was frowning as he walked away.

The stable was well stocked, and the groom there seemed capable. They left the horses in his care and reemerged into the bailey. Richard's face was grey in the sunlight. The Steward beckoned them from a door in the north tower. He led them up a flight of stairs to a large chamber with windows of glass. Illesa had never been inside such a room. She stared, open-mouthed.

"I hope you will find all you need here, Sir Richard. Lord Laurence has not started rebuilding this tower yet, I'm afraid, so it will not be as comfortable as you are used to. But there is hot water," he said, pointing to a brass ewer on a finely carved table, "and the bandages will arrive shortly. I will bring you refreshment myself."

"God reward you. Leave the cloths and food outside the door. We are not to be disturbed."

"Very well, sir." The Steward looked disapproving. He shut the door behind him. Richard did not move till they heard his footfall on the bottom stair.

"Now girl, don't just stand there." He pulled a cushioned chair away from the window and turned it round, sitting down heavily. He took off his surcoat and tunic, dropping them to the floor. His pale skin looked like carved stone and his hands were shaking.

"I saw how you dressed your own wound. You know how to make a poultice like the army doctors or better. This wound is worse than I thought." He pulled down the top of his cloth chausses. Just above his pelvic bone there was a blood soaked pad of cloth, secured with his belt. He unbuckled it and pulled the pad slowly off with an indrawn breath. Blood welled out. The cut was deep, but not wide. This was where the dagger had landed. If it had severed his gut, he would not have long to live.

Illesa knelt down in front of him, took off her pack and opened it.

In the end, she chose to cover the wound with vervain, placing layers of soft cloth over it for a dressing. She held out a long piece of wool, thinly woven.

"Stand up, sir. It must be secured properly." She wound the cloth round his hips, tying it tightly. "Your belt will also help it stay. You should move as little as possible."

"That is going to be difficult," Richard said.

"It is a deep wound. If you do not rest, it will reopen again and again. And every time you will risk illness from it."

"There is no need to lecture me, girl. I have had many wounds in my time."

Illesa moved to the table and poured some wine from the jug into a cup. She sipped it. It was untainted. The roots and herbs would work better if the wine were hot. She went to the fireplace, loaded the brazier with embers and warmed the jug over it, pouring in the freshly crushed leaves and powder. It was the same physic her mother had made for her father when he'd been stabbed in a fight with Edgar the cooper, and should work even better mixed with wine. Her father had recovered well enough to get his revenge on the cooper the following week.

When the wine was steaming, she poured it into a goblet and took it to Richard, who had not moved. His eyes were closed. She touched his hand, and he started.

"Drink it quickly," she said, putting the goblet into his hand.

He lifted the wine to his nose and looked at it suspiciously.

"It will help bring back your blood."

He downed it, and pulled a face.

"You ruined a fine vintage there."

"No doubt," she said, frowning at him. She would soon know about the state of his gut.

"And now you must tend your own wound; you are ruining my tunic."

Illesa looked down. A red stain was blooming across the linen on her left side.

"Yes, sir. I will summon the page to bring more bandages."

Eventually she found the page in the bailey, leaning heavily against a wall, picking a pustule on his cheek.

"Sir Richard needs more bandages. And bring wine and meat."

The page said nothing. He pushed his body away from the wall and walked towards the kitchen, head down. Illesa went back inside and up the stairs. Her legs were weak, and she had to stop and catch her breath before opening the door. Richard was sleeping where she had left him, his head resting on the back of the chair.

She took her pack to the far corner of the room and sat on the window seat looking east. Below the window, a dog was stalking the ducks in the fishpond. The hill that stretched to the northeast was the very end of the Long Forest. She was still many miles away from Eaton. Illesa brought out the pack of herbs and the ointment pouch. Only a little vervain was left. It should be saved for dire need. She crushed the valerian into a small pile of fragrant powder instead.

There was a knock on the door. When Illesa opened it, the Steward himself was there, carrying a tray.

"How fares Sir Richard?"

"Ill, master," Illesa said in an undertone. She took the heavy tray, trying not to grimace at the pain. "He needs rest and refreshment."

"God save him. He is welcome to stay as long as his need requires."

Illesa nodded. The Steward stayed in the doorway, looking past her shoulder.

"Where were you going on your business?"

"I cannot say, master."

"Ah. Well. Tell Sir Richard I am at his service, should he need anything."

"I will."

Illesa backed into the room with the tray; the Steward stood watching her, unmoving.

"Thank you, master." Illesa put the tray on the table by the window.

The Steward nodded.

"We have fed and watered your horses."

"God reward you for your kindness," Illesa said, closing the door.

"Lord Laurence has sent word that he returns tonight," the Steward called up from the stair. Illesa slid the latch across the door.

"He is suspicious." Richard's voice startled her. He was sitting up in the chair, sweat on his brow. "He wants us gone."

"What is Lord Laurence like?" Illesa asked, returning to the tray. There was only one plate. She loaded it with sliced meat and bread and took it to Sir Richard.

"I don't know him well, but my uncle does. He is a merchant who has made a fortune in wool. He bought this house from the Verdun family in coin." Richard chewed his meat thoughtfully. "Uncle Robert has recently overtaken him in wealth, and I am sure Lord Laurence would relish showing off his hospitality. I imagine he will make sure my uncle knows all about his generosity, down to the last farthing of cost. What did you put in that wine? The pain has gone and my head feels clear."

Illesa smiled.

"Good."

"You are full of secrets," he said, pushing the plate away from him.

"It was only root of Solomon's seal and comfrey, sir. Nothing secret."

Sir Richard grunted as he shifted position.

"I will rest here while you dress your wound and eat. They say sleep finishes the cure."

142

"Why don't you lie on the bed? You will be more comfortable surely." It was a fine pedestal bed with a beautiful coverlet, embroidered with flowers; Illesa would have loved to lie upon it herself and feel the softness of the full cushions.

"No, the chair will do for me. If I lie down, I may never rise."

"As you wish."

He settled back in the chair in a practised soldier's slump and was asleep in seconds.

An empty stomach would be better for treating her wound. She could eat afterwards, if she felt well enough. Illesa returned to the bright window seat and pulled the tunic over her head, the fabric catching on her calloused hands. The bandage was stuck to the wound and pulling it off started the blood flowing again. She had to push her breast to the side to see the extent of the cut. Although it was long, her ribs had stopped the dagger going any deeper, and it would heal well if it was clean.

Illesa soaked a pad of the fresh linen in wine, laid the crushed herbs on it and pressed it on the wound. There was still a book shaped mark on her abdomen; she had strapped it on so tightly that it had almost become part of her body. After winding lengths of cloth around her breasts and chest to secure the dressing, Illesa washed her other cuts and bandaged her hand against the friction of the reins. As she had nothing else, she put on the stained tunic and eased the jerkin over it.

The food was not generous for two, but after she had finished the bread and half a cup of wine, her mind felt clearer. Illesa put everything away carefully in her pack and went over to the sleeping figure in the chair. The late afternoon sun was low, streaking golden light across his hair.

"Sir Richard," she said, putting her hand gently on his shoulder.

His head jerked forward, and he opened his eye, looking into hers for a moment.

"Illesa. What is the hour?"

"I don't know, but the vespers bell has not yet rung."

"You look ready to ride," he said, stretching gingerly.

"Yes, sir."

"Well, let me visit the privy before you drag me off again."

"Sir Richard, you must stay here. Your wound is too serious for you to go any further. I will barter Kit's life for the book. It was wrong of me to ask you for money. I'm sure Father Osbert will help me with the negotiations."

"Illesa, I am in desperate need of the privy. Stay here. You mustn't go yet." He got to his feet stiffly. When he returned, he gestured her to sit in one of the chairs. His colour was good, his gut intact.

"The book in question must be explained before you take it anywhere," he said lifting it from the leather bag by his chair.

She took in a shallow breath and let it out slowly.

"I am glad to tell you what I know of it, which is very little, but you must not come with me any further. Kit was a fool to end up where he did, and you are right; no one else should suffer for him. You must rest and recover."

"You are not used to treating soldiers and knights, are you? Villeins may die of such things, but not us. I feel well. You have performed some unholy magic on me and I am revived," he said, stretching out his arms in front of him and swinging his sword arm.

"Long may God keep you so, sir, but you must rest. All the good will be undone if you ride."

"Well, leave that for now. Tell me what you know of this," he said opening the cover.

Illesa reached out a hand for it, and he gave it to her. She turned the pages carefully to the middle; the illustration of the fiery dragon.

"Read this," she said, pointing to the ornate letter 'S' at the top of the page.

"Sancta Margareta sic orante et dicente, draco apperuit os suum super caput beate Margarete et lingua eius pertingens usque ad calcaneum beate Margarete et deglutivit eam. Sed facto signo crucis draco ille terribilis permedium est divisus et ipsa exivit de utero eius illesa sine dolore aliquot," * he chanted.

His reading voice was resonant and melodious, but when he finished, he slowly translated the text under his breath.

"Saint Margaret prayed and chanted in this manner. The dragon opened its mouth above the saint's head and stretching out its tongue as far as Saint Margaret's heel, it swallowed her. But once the sign of the cross had made, that fearful dragon split open in the middle and she came forth from its womb unharmed and without any pain." *

He stopped reading and looked up.

"You think that your name comes from this book?"

She nodded, watching him as he examined the pen strokes of flower and birdwing in the margin.

"It can hardly be said to have kept you from harm, my girl. Quite the reverse, in fact. And having a name mentioned in the book does not give you rights of ownership," Richard said, bending close. "Look at this."

He was pointing to one of the trees that decorated the border of the page. In the fork of a branch was a nest holding three small white birds, their black beaks wide open. Above it, a cloud rained a shower of gold drops on the nest. On another branch of the tree sat a raven, looking away towards the world beyond the book.

It was one of the first illustrations that Ursula had explained to Illesa and was still one of her favourites, for the delicacy of the small birds and the lightness of the brush strokes indicating their feathers. Although the adult raven was meant to be a careless and indifferent parent in scripture, the illuminator had painted this bird in an attitude of attentiveness. Illesa had always imagined it as a guard, keeping watch to ensure that nothing disturbed the miraculous feeding of its young.

"There are many birds in the book which reveal the holy life of the Saint and God's favour," Illesa began. "This shows the young of the ravens, which tells us that like the ravens, Saint Margaret was abandoned by her father, but God was faithful and gave her the heavenly food of grace and a home with Him in heaven."

Richard did not look up. He was turning the pages carefully, not reading the words but examining the marginal illustrations.

"You have had some erudite instruction. However, I think it may mean something else, in fact," he said after several minutes. He closed the book and looked at her.

"Are you sure you don't know any more about it?"

Illesa's heart began hammering in her chest. The silence stretched out between them.

"Just before I left, Kit told me something that might be true," Illesa whispered.

"You'd better tell me then," he said, raising his eyebrow.

"Kit said that last year Ursula asked him to return it to the church at Caus, the seat of the Corbets. She had become fearful of it."

Richard smiled. He picked up the book and opened it.

"I was right then. Look, it is on almost every page." He turned them quickly, pointing to each raven in the margins. "The Corbet arms may not be on this book, but their bird is and their motto: *God feeds the Ravens.*"

"You know the Corbet family?" Illesa whispered. He was holding the book as if it was a newborn child.

"My grandmother was Rose Corbet, before she married William Burnel."

"Oh."

"Rose Corbet had a book of the Apocalypse which also had many finely drawn birds. My mother sometimes let me look at it."

Illesa kept her eyes lowered so he would not see her fear.

"So now we have a mystery, do we not?"

"Yes, sir."

"The book does not belong to you; that is clear enough. Your mother either stole it or was given it by someone in the Corbet family and then came to believe that it should be returned to them. But why did she become fearful of it when she had had it for so many years?" He was looking at her, expecting an explanation.

"I think she knew she was dying, sir."

He waited for more.

"My father had been killed and she was very ill. Perhaps she thought the Saint was angry at being kept hidden all those years and she wanted to make it right before she died."

"Hmm. She realised the gravity of her sin, maybe."

"But sir, for years she used the words of the book to help women in the village. Saint Margaret would not have given her help if my mother had stolen the book."

"She might have been helped by the devil instead. You said she was an adulteress. Would a holy saint help someone like that?"

"Our Lord did. He was merciful to the woman taken in adultery. My mother was a faithful and devout woman, Sir Richard. I swear to you, she shunned the devil." The words choked in her swollen throat.

Richard looked at her impassively.

"In any case, you cannot take the book to be traded for your brother's life. The Forester is not a man to appreciate such a thing. He would sell it for half its worth and it would be lost again," Richard said, pushing himself up from his chair. He took some tentative steps towards the fire. "No, I'm afraid I cannot let it go."

She could not look at him. Her eyes were full. He was quiet for several moments, standing in the warmth of the flames.

"People often become fearful of curses when they are ill. We don't know the circumstance by which it came to be in your mother's hands. So I suppose it could have been a gift for services rendered. Your mother used to live near Acton, my family seat," he said, sitting down again carefully.

She nodded.

"The resemblance to the Apocalypse book is striking. They may have been the work of the same scribe. I will take it to my mother. She may well know something about it, and about your mother," he said quietly, and then looked up at Illesa. "I will give you money for the book, and you can negotiate your brother's release. I have enough coin with me."

Illesa looked away in dismay. Ursula had kept it hidden and safe for years, and now she had managed to lose it and expose her mother's secrets in only a matter of days.

"I pray your mother will not think ill of her, sir."

"If she has sinned, then she does not deserve anyone's good opinion. But you needn't fear the story will be widely told. My mother is not in a position to spread gossip."

"Does she still live at Acton?" Illesa asked.

"She was at Langley for many years, after Uncle Robert bought the estate from our branch of the family. Then he let her become an anchoress at the new church he built at Acton. She was enclosed as soon as the roof went on." He looked at the book cradled in his lap. "But this may be something that will make her speak again." He ran his fingers down the spine. "It might bring her some comfort."

Richard seemed lost in thought. When he eventually moved, his forehead creased with pain.

"I'm afraid you are right. I should not ride yet. I shall have to impose on the kindness of Laurence for a night at least." He reached for his bag and rummaged at the bottom of it, bringing out a large leather pouch. "I set aside one pound against your brother's ransom, but I expect you can get him out for considerably less. If we find that your mother did not steal the book, I may owe you more money for it."

"Thank you, sir." She took the heavy purse and packed it under her cloak.

"I must be at Nefyn by the end of the month for the Round Table tournament. My uncle has arranged for me to assist with the royal entertainment," he said. "Where is your land? If I have any news when I return, I may seek you out."

"Holdgate, sir. But I don't think I can go back there now," she said. To return without the book after all these days would be suicidal, even if she did have any coin left over. "May I hold the book before I go?"

"Here," he said, holding it out to her. "Don't try to make off with it. I may be injured but I can still outrun you."

"I wouldn't do that, sir."

She took it, went towards the east window and knelt in front of the window seat. The book seemed to open itself to the last page where the saint stood, her arms raised in blessing. Illesa lifted the book to her lips.

Richard watched her as she walked back towards him.

"You should stay off the road with that horse."

"Thank you, sir," she said, as she put the book in his open palm. "Kit owes you a debt. I pray he will one day repay it."

"Perhaps he already has," said Richard as she closed the door.

Chapter XV
Nightfall

Jezebel did not slow from a gallop until they came to the first steep climb past the coppices that fringed the Long Forest. The last rays of sunlight were touching the leaves of the beech so that they glowed like stained glass. Illesa passed only one man limping west with a hoe on his shoulder. Most good people were already at their hearths and their board. And the bad, pray God, were on foot.

Illesa drifted in and out of semi-sleep, jerking awake if she started to slip forward across the horse's neck. The bells for compline rang, but which church was it? Across the valley she could make out little. Smoke rose in the last glow of the western sky. She would have to trust to guess work. It would be unwise to stop and ask the way.

Father Osbert would certainly not be pleased to see her; he had meant her to be at the White Sisters convent by now. What if he punished her disobedience by refusing to help Kit, and she had come through all those dangers only to fail? Saint Margaret had been close to her, protecting her, had even saved her from being raped by Peter the thief, just as God had saved the Saint herself from Olymbrius. But she had lost the book now. Without Saint Margaret near her, how would she save Kit or herself from the Forester's anger? His men would take pleasure in her pain. Saint Margaret had bravely submitted to torture, but Illesa's faith was not strong enough to defeat her fear. She rubbed her eyes, trying to push the thoughts aside and concentrate on looking for the turning.

After a while, the pattern of plantation and elevation became familiar. Within a hundred paces they reached the crossroads where, nearly four days before, she and Kit had hidden in the undergrowth and watched the hare dying in the mud. She turned left down the steep path towards Eaton.

Thick foliage shadowed the sunken track. The trees that lined it and held the bank in their roots enclosed it as closely as the stone of a tomb. Illesa gripped Jezebel's mane, winding the coarse hair through her fingers, and crouched over the horse's neck. The air all around her was cold and still. Nothing moved, not even a breath of wind. Overhanging branches fingered her hair. It seemed that everything living, except her and the horse, had been snatched from that place. There was no noise but hooves scraping on stone and the rasp of breathing. Illesa opened her mouth to urge Jezebel faster, but no sound came out. Perhaps this was a taste of purgatory. It seemed to stretch on forever.

The spell was broken by a distant man's voice, a snatch of a song, then the slamming of a door. They came out from the canopy of branches into the lesser darkness. The church was a chiselled shadow on her left. Illesa straightened up and breathed in the smell of pigs and wood smoke. In front of her, the low village buildings emerged. Light trembled in the gaps of their shutters. She dismounted and stood by Jezebel's side, stroking her twitching muscles, until the tightness in her own chest subsided. There was no sign of the Forester's men or horses, and no light in the church windows.

"Wait here, girl," Illesa whispered, looping the rein over the lych gate. She circled the whole church, hurrying from shadow to shadow, and stopped underneath the tower window.

"Kit!" she called.

Silence.

She tried the church door, anticipating the scrape of it on the stone. Moonlight came through the lancet windows in narrow shafts. There was no other light or sound. With her hands in front of her, she walked to the tower door. It was locked.

"Let me in. It's Illesa!"

She banged on the door with the flat of her palm.

"Kit!"

Her voice echoed across the stone space. She waited as long as she could make herself, then ran blind down the nave and out of the door into the starry night.

Jezebel was not at the gate. Illesa looked all around for her familiar silhouette, but every shadow seemed shaped like Peter and his rope. She could see his dead body seeping blood as if she were still in the clearing by the river. Her legs started running away from the church along the lane, the noose of panic tightening around her throat.

She did not stop running until she reached the village strips, stretching to the south with row after row of nodding heads of barley. There were no shadows, just the bright, indifferent face of the moon. As her breath quietened, she heard the unmistakable chime of running water. The stream was only fifty paces further on, and there, at the ford, was the outline of a horse, its lips on the black water.

Illesa went to Jezebel and buried her face in the warm mane. When the horse had drunk her fill, they walked slowly towards the Priest's house. No light was showing. Illesa stood unmoving on the step. Waking the Priest to be told of Kit's death seemed unbearable, but eventually she forced herself to rap on the door. There was no answer. She knocked again.

The shutter on the second floor opened.

"Who is it and what do you mean disturbing people at this hour?" The loud voice sounded familiar.

"Goodwife Lyttle?"

"Yes, and who are you?" the woman demanded.

"I was Brother Benedict. I need to see Father Osbert. Please let me in."

"By the saints!" Goodwife Lyttle's face was a white oval peering through the wooden window bars. "I'll come down now."

There was the sound of furniture scraping and a footfall on the stairs. A light glowed through the gap in the shutter, and then the door opened.

"Come in, and shut that door. Don't let the bad night air in. Oh, you have a horse!"

"Yes. Do you have somewhere I can stable her?"

"She's a big one, isn't she?" Goodwife Lyttle said, staring accusingly at Jezebel. "She'll scare the life out of my little Blinker. Go round the house, I'll meet you at the back."

The stable was home to an old pony, which did indeed have a frightened look. There was another stall and Jezebel was soon working her way through the hay in the manger. Illesa unsaddled her, and covered her with a rough blanket. She was wet and there was lather where the girth had rubbed.

"Come along now," Goodwife Lyttle chided from the door. Illesa followed her into the house.

"Sit down, I'll stoke the fire. You'll want refreshment, no doubt."

"Goodwife, first please tell me what has happened to the man who was in the tower."

The woman stopped, ladle in hand.

"Your brother, isn't he?"

"Yes. Where is he? And where is Father Osbert?"

"He's gone, my girl." Illesa could see little of the Goodwife's face in the firelight; but it was obvious she was not sorry. "Been gone a day by now."

"Gone where? Did they take him away?"

"Now sit down and calm down. You don't want to wake up Warden Lyttle. He's a heavy sleeper, but there are limits. I'll tell you as much as I know but keep quiet."

"I am sorry, Goodwife. I am just very frightened for him."

"You should be, girl, and for yourself gadding about in boy's clothes in the middle of the night. I thought you were a victim of the criminal, not part of his family. The two of you are nothing but trouble. If it weren't for Father Osbert, I wouldn't have anything to do with either of you. And that's the truth." The ladle splashed back into the pot with a clatter.

Illesa sat down on the stool and pressed her hands between her knees.

"Please tell me what has happened. Did the Prior send any help?"

Goodwife Lyttle sat down on a stool opposite and handed the bowl to Illesa.

"There, it's not very warm but it's better than nothing. No, no one came from the Priory until sext on Tuesday, and that was not to help your brother. A messenger came with a summons. Father Osbert was to go back to Wenlock straight away." Goodwife Lyttle put her hands on her knees and looked at Illesa severely. "The whole town is in uproar. All the Abbey's wool fees have been taken." There was a minute of silence in which Illesa heard a snore from the sleeping chamber. "I hope your brother was not involved with it."

"Kit hasn't been anywhere near Wenlock, Goodwife. He's been locked up for more than a week."

"Well, I don't like it. Father Osbert having to get involved and the Prior gone to Bermondsey Abbey. He will have an awful shock when they get word to him." Goodwife Lyttle tugged a loose thread from the sleeve of her shift and broke it between her finger and thumb.

Perhaps Father Osbert had negotiated some truce with the Forester. He might be in the Abbey now, and safe.

"Did my brother travel with Father Osbert?" Illesa asked.

"No, no. The Forester is not a man to let anyone go. Your brother went off by himself, cocky as you like." Goodwife Lyttle shook her head in time to her words.

"Master Lyttle was doing his best to keep those villains out of the church, but it's a busy time of year, there is work in the fields and work in the croft. He couldn't be there all day. They were lighting fires against the tower wall and all sorts. That brother of yours started thinking that he would be better off on the run. Talked Warden Lyttle into letting him out, I'm sure, although he denies it. Middle of last night, he left, when Destrey was asleep."

"You don't know where he's gone?" Illesa put the bowl down untouched.

"Don't you like it, girl? You look as though you could use it." Goodwife Lyttle sounded cross.

"I am sorry, it's just the shock. I need to find my brother. Do you have any idea where he went?"

"No I don't. Nor do I want to know. Be glad to see the back of both of you, I would. It's disturbing the peace, that's what, and putting Father Osbert in a very awkward position." She stared accusingly at Illesa.

"Do you think your husband may know? You say he spoke to him?"

"Maybe. Ask him yourself in the morning. You may stay the night here, but you are to go tomorrow. We've had enough." Goodwife Lyttle took the lamp and, hitching up her skirt, climbed the stairs without another word.

Despite her tiredness, Illesa found it hard to sleep. She lay by the hearth, her head resting on her pack, and anger consumed her. How could Kit abandon her again? He spared not a thought for her safety, even after she had risked her life to free him from gaol. But he had always been selfish and thoughtless. She could think of countless examples.

Illesa rubbed her eyes impatiently. She needed a plan, not tears. Her hand went to the place on her chest where the book had been, and then to her throat. The skin there was abraded and sore, but there was warmth and breath. Her stomach dropped; she had forgotten to pray her thanks to Saint Margaret for saving her life. Nor had she thanked Sir Richard. She tried to steer her mind away from him, but the image of his sword plunging into Peter's back and the sound of it being pulled out through gut and bone came, nonetheless.

Illesa rose to her knees and began prayers to the Saint and the Holy Virgin, but her mind was skittish. Without a home or family, she would be at the mercy of the devil and his followers on earth. Even the money she had would not help her; it would be assumed that she had stolen it. If she had gone to the White Sisters, at least she would have had four walls and a roof. Illesa put her head on her knees and shut her eyes. Tomorrow she would return Jezebel, and maybe the saints would move the smith to help her again.

When Goodwife Lyttle came back from milking and slammed the door behind her, Illesa sat up. It was fully light, but the bleak country of her dream would not fade. Her mother had been there, barefoot, in a torn tunic. There was no sun in the grey sky, but her mother's thin fingers scraped at the dry soil, making a hollow into which she dropped a black seed. Ursula spat on each one and then covered them with a layer of dust. She did not hear Illesa's calls nor look up when she touched her shoulder.

"Warden will be down in a minute. It is past prime," the Goodwife said, her voice flat with disapproval. She dropped a ladle into the bucket at her feet. "There's milk for you." She went out again, carrying a pair of shears.

Illesa found a cup on the shelf and poured the warm milk into it. It was rich and sweet. She refilled the cup and swallowed fast. The desert of her dream had left her thirsty and troubled. She must find a Priest to ease Ursula's sufferings in that dread place. Whatever Ursula had been trying to grow would need watering, and the only way was through prayer and holy water.

In the yard, Illesa washed her face in the water butt and checked her bandage. It was still intact. The wound hurt when she raised her arm, but otherwise was without pain. When she went back through the door, Warden Lyttle was coming down the stairs.

"My wife said you were here." He looked sheepish.

"Thank you for watching over my brother, Warden. I am sorry for the trouble it has caused you."

"No, no trouble," he paused, "Mistress."

"My name is Illesa."

"Ah. Here come and sit by the hearth for a bit." The stool squeaked under his weight. "Well, your brother isn't here any more, as you heard. He went off the night before last. By God's heart, those men tried everything to get him out, and then he walked out right past them without them knowing a thing about it. Ha! You should have seen the face on that man, Destrey. The Forester has threatened all of us, of course, but there is no law against a man leaving sanctuary before time."

Illesa chewed her lip.

"My brother likes doing the unexpected."

"Yes," Lyttle grinned. "He's quite a character, yes indeed. Well, what else can I tell you?"

"Did he say where he was going? I need to find him."

"No, I'm sorry, he didn't say nothing about that."

"Did he give you anything to give to me?"

"No." Lyttle scratched his head, his desire to please and his honest nature at odds. "He took everything with him, all his tools and such like. The only thing he said was that he was going to try to branch out, make some money, try something new."

"Sounds like him."

"He seemed confident enough. Quite happy, like. He even said he'd see me again soon, shook my hand and all."

"Oh, did he?"

"Went off with a spring in his step, he did. I kept an eye from the road, and saw him tiptoe right round that Destrey fella. Full of drink he was and didn't notice a thing!"

"Which direction did he head?"

"He went up into the Long Forest again, said he would keep in the cover at first."

"But that is just where they will be looking for him!"

"No, they won't find him, my girl." He looked at Illesa's expression and patted her knee. "Don't you worry, he'll be alright." He got up from his stool and rummaged in the pile of tools by the back door. "Are you going to come to the fair with us, eh? I'm getting all the jobs done today, as it starts tomorrow."

"What fair?" asked Illesa, as she tightened her pack and lifted it gingerly onto her back.

"The fair at Rushbury, for the Feast of Saint Margaret. The King only granted it to the Manor last year, but it's got everything, plenty of merchants and entertainers. There's one man turns up on huge stilts and scares all the kiddies. It's not far away. You should come. It'll take your mind off things, it will."

"I'd forgotten it was the Feast of Saint Margaret," Illesa said, quietly.

"You come with us, it'll do you good. There is a pie seller there and his wares are worth tasting," Warden Lyttle said, testing the edge of a small axe.

"You are very kind, but I don't think your wife wants me to stay."

"Now, don't mind her. She just takes on a bit when it comes to Father Osbert. She thinks it will be her that keeps him safe rather than God almighty. Likes to protect him from the worries of the world."

"She's a good woman," Illesa said as she got to her feet. "I think I'd better be on my way. I don't want to cause you any more trouble."

"No trouble at all. None at all. But you should go to the fair, really. It's a great event. Even your brother was impressed when I told him about it."

"You told Kit about the fair?"

"Oh yes. We had a lot of time to talk you see. Told him all about it. He said it reminded him of a fair he went to as a child, somewhere." He scratched his head. "I know. Acton. Said your father had taken him and he'd got lost in the crowd. They found him by the pie seller, looking sick," the Warden chortled.

Illesa smiled back.

"I'll be going now. Might see you at the fair after all. I'm sure you're right, it would do me good."

"Right you are."

"Thank you for the stabling and the bed for the night."

"Hardly a bed, but you're young. You can sleep anywhere at your age."

He went out the back door into the yard, whistling.

Chapter XVI
The 19th day of July, 1284
Rushbury

"I knew you would find me and you have straight away." Kit's smile was as big as the whole world. He let go of Illesa, who staggered before she regained her balance.

"Why didn't you leave word for me, Kit? I was sick with worry," she asked, standing at his shoulder. Kit had picked up his hammer again and was flattening a strip of metal to a fine thin edge.

"That Lyttle fellow would tell anyone anything. Couldn't keep a secret to save his life. I didn't want the whole countryside to know I was here, thank you. And besides the good Father Osbert told me you were on your way to a nunnery. I couldn't hang around waiting; it was suicide in that tower."

"But Kit, here you are in full view of the population of the shire, and you think you are safe? Have you lost the few wits you were born with?"

"Now, now. There is no need for that," Kit said, gesturing at her with his hammer. "Strictly speaking, I'm still in sanctuary. The mile around Eaton Church and Rushbury Church overlap, so I am still under their protection."

"Have you seen the Priest here and told him?"

"No, not yet, but as soon as I see him, I will."

"Kit, if the Forester finds you here, he won't care if you are in sanctuary or not. He hasn't stopped wanting to kill you."

"The bastard will be searching for me in the forest. This is the last place he'll look. Besides I'm disguised."

"Oh yes?" Illesa said, looking him up and down. "How so?"

"You think they will recognise me?"

He stood there smiling uncertainly. It was unbelievable.

"I think they will, somehow, by Christ! Shaving your head and wearing a borrowed oversized tunic is not going to fool anyone."

"You always think the worst," he said shaking his head.

"You never think at all."

Kit sighed and looked at the heavens.

"Look, Illesa. I'm glad you found me, but I need to get on with these clasps if I am going to make any money at this fair. We can talk about it later, right?" He bent his head over his work.

"I don't believe it," Illesa said in a vicious whisper. "I have been across the county risking my life to get money for a bribe and here you are making trinkets for ladies at the fair, not two miles from where you were in fear of your life." Her voice became so loud that the smith at the next forge looked up from his fire curiously.

"Would you keep quiet, woman?" Kit said in her ear.

"I am a boy. Remember?"

"Yes, well it's about time you changed back." He took a deep breath. "I know it hasn't been easy for you, Sweetheart, but it will all be different now. You and I can travel around from fair to fair. We'll make good money; people love these trinkets. And you can do the cooking and make your simples. We'll have a fine life!"

"I don't want to travel all over the country with you, Kit. You will end up in trouble wherever you go."

"Well, Mistress of the Fountain of Wisdom, have you got a better idea?"

"Yes, I do. We bribe the Forester, go back to Holdgate, pay our debts and live there." She knew it was impossible; their croft was in other hands now, but really, Kit should at least try to save their home. Without it, they were no better than vagrants.

He put down his hammer and sighed.

"Lessa, I need to be in a place where I can get commissions for the King's forces or the nobility, not in Holdgate." He put a hand on her shoulder and bent to her ear. "We can talk about this when we are alone. Everyone is staring at us."

He was right. Illesa turned round, and everyone in that row of stalls had stopped their work and was looking at them.

"Go through to the back. There's some ale in the jug and some cheese. Help yourself." Kit picked up his hammer, smiled broadly at the other stallholders and set to work on the shaft of a clasp.

"Maybe later."

Illesa stomped away in the direction of the livestock field, not looking back.

Kit had been easy enough to find. She knew he would not be able to resist a fair. The difficulty had been finding somewhere safe from the Forester and his men until the fair started. The Forester might recognise her, even without the monk's habit, and there was no one to stop him killing her on the spot as Kit's accomplice. By the time Jezebel was brushed and fed, she had made up her mind. The message of her dream was clear. If Father Osbert had still been there, she might have stayed in the church tower and paid him for prayers and the sprinkling of holy water. But as it was, she had to find another Priest, another church. A place where they knew nothing about Kit.

The people of Eaton had been weeding the crops before the harvest. No one seemed interested in her departure. She kept Jezebel to a moderate pace heading west, so as not to draw attention. Her plan was to stop in the first church she came to with a resident Priest, and her prayers were answered after only an hour's ride. Hope Boullers was stitched to the hem of a steep hill, and its church, dedicated to Saint Andrew, was open.

The Priest was old and quite deaf, but he understood what she wanted when she took one of the pennies from Sir Richard's purse. The rest of the coins were unfamiliar new groats, with a cross covering the reverse. Illesa tied the leather thongs of the purse tight and pushed it to the bottom of her pack. She had to shout Ursula's name in the Priest's ear. Finally, he unlocked the font, found his aspergillum and began the prayers, liberally spraying the holy water on Illesa's bowed head. Afterwards, he put an unsteady hand on her shoulder and looked at her with watery eyes.

"*Peregrinus?*" he asked.

Illesa nodded, hoping that pretending to be a pilgrim would not counteract the efficacy of her prayers for Ursula. One day it may be true. The Priest beckoned her into the centre of the nave and gestured to the highly coloured painting on the north wall showing Saint Andrew. His brother Simon was by his side in their boat, hauling in a net bursting with fish.

"*Quae inpossibilia sunt apud homines, possibilia sunt apud Deum*" the Priest said, and laughed so loudly that Illesa's heart jolted with surprise. He went about his work, taking no more notice of her and sleeping through the middle of the day.

From the church door, Illesa was able to see Jezebel's head where she was tethered to the gate. The hours flowed into each other in half-sleep, half-wakefulness. After vespers, when the old

Priest left for his hearth and bed, she followed him, leading Jezebel. He pointed his crooked finger at the last croft on the lane.

"*Benedicte*," he said, and waved her on.

The widow who lived there looked at Illesa suspiciously, but let her sleep by Jezebel in the empty cowshed and gave her a hunk of bread. She left before dawn, heading back up the road, before anyone could see the strange route the pilgrim was taking.

When she'd arrived at Rushbury, merchants and craftsmen were everywhere struggling with trestles and lengths of wagon cloth, but it was obvious where the smiths were set up from the sound of hammering. How Kit had wangled a stall and a forge was a mystery, but then, he quickly made friends and inspired trust until you got to know him better. He had not even asked her if she had found Richard Burnel, or where she had been. There he was, clear as day, just pretending that nothing had happened.

Illesa approached the rails where several indifferent nags were tethered next to Jezebel. There was no sign of the boy who had promised to guard her. Three men were examining Jezebel's legs. One of them straightened up when she cleared her throat. He was large, not tall, with a rough, cratered face and a patchy beard. The other men drifted off, but not far.

"This your horse?"

"Yes." Illesa ran her hand down Jezebel's neck as the horse nudged her shoulder.

"You're having a laugh." He was looking her up and down. Illesa ignored him and un-tethered Jezebel.

"I'm taking her now. The security here is somewhat lacking." She started to walk past him, Jezebel shaking her head and rattling her bridle.

"You want to watch your tongue. I am the security here," the man shouted at her.

"I've paid, and I'm going. If you want to stop me you'll have to answer to my master." The man swore at her back but did not come after her.

She walked Jezebel down the lane, against the prevailing flow of people arriving for the fair. Children were running zigzag along the street, spooking the other horses and mules. Illesa held the rein tightly, whispering to Jezebel, and soon they came to the brook and the stone bridge. A muddy track led down to the water's edge. She let Jezebel drink in the clear water, watching the steady stream of excited people pass over the bridge.

The horse lifted her head eventually.

"You're hungry too, aren't you?" she whispered in Jezebel's ear. "The sooner we get you back home the better. Though what I'm going to do after that, I don't know," she muttered as they walked up the bank on to the lane.

"Well, here you are after all!" Warden Lyttle exclaimed, stopping in front of them. "God save you." He looked so cheerful, Illesa couldn't help an answering smile.

"God keep you, master. Yes, I decided to come and see your fair."

"Have you been in yet?" Warden Lyttle was alone and dressed in a fresh tunic, looking as excited as a small boy.

"Only briefly. I am worried about leaving my horse," Illesa said. "Goodwife Lyttle is not here?"

"No, she don't hold with fairs. She's got something against them," he said happily. "Now, if you need a place to stable your horse, I know a man here that will take her in for you."

"Is it someone you know well? I'm so worried she will be stolen, and I must take her back to the smith in Wenlock. She belongs to him."

"Ah, I've heard of him. A good man, so they say." Lyttle scratched his head. "Well, how long you staying? You need stabling overnight?"

"I think so, yes."

"Follow me. It's just down the lane. He takes in plenty of horses during the fair as people don't want to leave their fancier mounts out in the open."

She followed Lyttle to the other side of the Manor.

"When the lord is here, Tom manages his stable, but the new lord ain't been here for a good few months now. You can trust Tom. His family's been here for ever, and he's the warden of the church, like me."

They neared the back end of the manor enclosure, and Lyttle knocked on a door in the wide gate with his fist. After a minute or so, a tall man with a shock of brown hair opened it. He shook hands with Lyttle, smiling.

"Brought me some trade, have you Warden Lyttle? Good man."

"Here now, how much you charging this year, eh? Give us a good rate, Tom. This horse belongs to John of Wenlock. He's the smith to sort out your needs good and proper, ain't he?"

"Well, well." He opened the gate and watched as Illesa led Jezebel into the stable yard. "She's a beauty. I'm sure we can agree a reasonable rate," and he winked at Illesa. "Let's get her settled before we talk money."

"This here is the groom, um, or messenger . . ." Lyttle ran out of ideas and looked worriedly at Illesa.

"William of Wenlock, Master. I have been sent on an errand for the smith."

"He must be Hephaestus himself to have such a horse, and a groom." Tom looked at her curiously, but his expression was calm.

"He is a good master." Illesa kept her eyes on Jezebel, stroking her neck.

"I can believe it," he said, and took the rein from her hand. "Come with me. Warden Lyttle may be released to go to the fair. I know you only get a few hours away from your good lady wife. Might as well enjoy yourself."

"Right you are! See you tonight, Tom."

"You will," Tom said, waving him off.

Illesa saw Jezebel well settled into a manger of oats in a clean stable. There were only two other horses, a roan and a black. She took one of the groats from her pouch, slung her pack over her shoulder and went to look for Tom. He was lifting down a broken shutter on the other side of the stable.

"Got everything you need?"

"Yes, she's wolfing down your oats."

"Ah, one of those is she. How long you staying?"

"I'm not certain. Can I pay you for a day at a time?"

"Yes, it's a penny a day, all in."

Illesa held out the groat. Tom took it, turned it over and gave it back.

"Pay when you go. I can't make change for that now."

"Sorry, it's all I've got."

"I'm sure the clerk will make change for you. But keep it safe. There are more thieves at a fair than in all the country's gaols." Tom bent down to lift the new shutter into place. "I tell you," he said smiling, "I wish I'd taken up smithing. I had no idea it was so well paid."

"It's a long story," said Illesa, pushing the coin back into her pack. When she looked up he was watching her.

"If you've the time and leave one day, come and tell me. I love a good story." And he went back to his work.

The food stalls were at the heart of the fair, but Illesa could not use her coins there. She would have to get them changed first. She wandered towards the keep gate, watching the stallholders setting out their stock. The clerk was sitting just inside the gatehouse, while outside there was a queue of people, fingering their purses, who looked as if they had been waiting since the dawn of time. Illesa was hungry, thirsty and tired by the time she came before the clerk. He had a sheet of parchment in front of him as well as a wax tablet.

"Name."

"I'm not a stall holder, master, I'm a messenger for Sir Richard Burnel. He would like coin in change for this." She laid five groats on the rough table in front of him.

The clerk looked up at her.

"Richard Burnel?"

"Yes."

"What relation is he of the Lord of the Manor?"

"What?"

"I haven't got time for idiot messengers! Have you seen the crowd of people outside? What relation is Sir Richard Burnel to Sir Hugh Burnel?"

Illesa swallowed. She would have to guess.

"They are cousins, I believe."

"Why does he send you? Is he coming to the Manor?"

"No, master, he sent me to buy for him. He has been away with the King's forces."

The clerk muttered something Illesa could not hear. He began marking down on his wax tablet Richard's name and the amount. He opened the coffer on the floor behind him, a heavy carved wooden box with an iron latch, guarded by two men in livery. The clerk opened it and spent some time examining the contents. He lined up two rows of pennies and farthings in small deliberate movements on the table between them. Illesa picked them up one at a time, hoping she was not being cheated.

"What will you carry it in?" he said crossly. "You can't just hold it like that."

"I'll put it away," Illesa said, putting the coin back on the table and opening the pouch.

The clerk sighed heavily.

"You'll need a guard, boy. You can't go out like that. The cutpurses will have you within a minute."

"Yes, master." Illesa fumbled the pouch into her pack and went out, clutching it awkwardly.

"They send any fool servant to change their money for them and expect to receive it intact," he was saying as she stopped outside to secure the straps. "He'll lose all that coin, mark my words!"

Illesa inched through the crowd outside the clerk's office. An excited group was gathering round a tall pole with a glove on the top. The boys at the back of the crowd were throwing stones at it. Church bells started ringing, followed by loud cheers. The fair had officially begun.

It was impossible to tell what was in the pie she bought, but it tasted good. A full stomach and a tankard of ale went a long way to cheering her. There was no reason not to look around before going back to Kit's stall, she decided, as long as she was careful to avoid the crush of people where the cutpurses worked.

Down a less crowded row were the cloth merchants, selling woven wool and lengths of finely made stuff from other lands. At the end she turned left. Baskets of every shape and size hung from poles and were piled on the ground, and everywhere there was the sweet earthy smell of straw and reed. It was intoxicating to see the bounty for sale and to know she had coin enough to buy. After more than an hour, Illesa found herself in front of a stall selling beautifully embroidered clothes. There was a well-made tunic, trimmed with green like verdigris, but she walked away. There was no telling what she would need the money for. A new tunic would not save anyone's life. One thing was certain, she would not be telling Kit about the coin.

Illesa was turning into the row of iron merchants, when a man she recognised passed her, setting her heart kicking. She followed him at a distance of ten paces. He was one of the riders she and Kit had seen in the forest, who'd lost their mounts to the Forester; the small, sharp looking one called Jarryd. His hose was caked with mud and he was eyeing the people not the goods, looking for someone.

Jarryd worked his way down the iron row, stopping at each forge in turn. Illesa managed to get past while he was talking. She could be inconspicuous when necessary, but Kit was another matter. His stall was three quarters of the way down on the left, but she could hear his voice from where she was, finishing a joke and laughing. Kit's neighbour was leaning over the post and rail between their two stalls listening as Kit launched into another tale.

"Master!" she said, as she drew up. Her face must have communicated enough; he stopped mid-sentence and listened as she whispered in his ear.

"Don't worry," he whispered back. "He's never seen me, so how can he tell who I am?"

The neighbour looked her over.

"This your lad, Kit?"

"Yessir. Lazy bag of bones."

Illesa glared at him and whispered again.

"You told them your name? What are you, a simpleton?"

Jarryd was standing in front of the stall. He picked up a few of the hooks and rush light holders displayed at the front. Illesa bent down and started fiddling with the forge bellows.

"You've got some fine stuff."

"Thank you, good man. What can I interest you in?"

"You from around here?"

"Ludlow."

"Ludlow. Now that's a coincidence." Jarryd stared at Kit. "My kin are from there. What's your name?"

"Thomas."

"I thought I heard them call you something else."

"People call me all sorts of names and hardly any of them are pleasant."

A smile crept up Jarryd's face.

"You got a funny looking lad there."

"Are you going to buy or just insult me?" Kit's face was reddening with anger.

"No need to take offence. I'm not buying, just looking," he said and sauntered away, glancing back from time to time. When he finally moved out of sight, Illesa grabbed Kit's arm.

"You and I need to talk!"

"Hey Reg," Kit called, "mind my stall, I'll do the same for you later."

"You got trouble, Kit?"

"Naw, no trouble."

He and Illesa went round to the back of the stall, where several pack mules were grazing on the trodden grass between the lines of colourful canvas. Kit picked up the jug and drank straight from it. He held it out to Illesa who shook her head. Kit put a finger to his lips.

"Don't shout at me, Lessa."

She managed to condense her anger into a whisper.

"He is going straight to the Forester to turn you in and claim his horse back! You know that don't you?"

"Now don't overreact. He doesn't know who I am. He's just an arsehole anyway. I bet he wound up every smith in the row."

"He didn't talk to the rest of the smiths after he spoke to you. He knows exactly who you are."

"But I'm one step ahead of them this time. It's going to take him a few hours to get to the Forester and back. Reckon we're safe enough here for a bit," he said, taking another swig from the jug.

Illesa stared at him, disbelief and anger fighting for ascendancy.

"What?" he asked, with an uncertain smile.

"I give up with you, Kit! I have risked my life and my honour trying to save you, and you throw your life away without a second thought! At least for my sake try to save yourself from the gallows."

"Shhhh, you're shouting."

Illesa covered her eyes with her hands and groaned with rage. Kit put his arms around her shoulders.

"Did something happen to you? What are these marks on your neck?"

"I was nearly raped and murdered, and your good friend Sir Richard with me, not that you care."

"What? Who attacked you?"

"Horse thieves. Sir Richard killed them, but not before they hurt us both. He was coming with me to pay the bribe and get you out, but he was wounded on the hip and couldn't ride any further. He is at Stoke de Say. I bandaged him well. If he rests for long enough, he should fully recover."

Kit's face crumpled.

"It's all right. He really should be fine," Illesa said, abruptly.

"What about you? Did they . . ."

"No. But I've been cut here," she said, pointing to her left side. "It's not too bad now that I've got it bandaged properly."

Kit did not say anything for what seemed a long time.

"God, I am such an idiot!"

"Kit -"

"No, I am. I should never have fallen for that trick; I was a bit drunk. Anyway it was foolish and now you've been hurt. God forgive me!"

"You can take time over your repentance later. We've got to get away from here now," Illesa said. "Through God's mercy I have a fast horse. She belongs to a smith in Wenlock who will give us a meal and a bed for the night. I bet she could carry us both if we didn't push her too much."

"How did you get a horse?"

"I'll tell you later. Let's get your things packed."

"No, Lessa, if we disappear now it will just draw attention to us. Let's pack up quietly after dark and then we can really disappear. Everyone coming and going from the fair will see which way we go if we leave now."

"But what if he comes back before dark?"

"He won't. It will be vespers soon. He won't make it here till gone compline, and we'll be well away by then."

"That is assuming the Forester is at his lodge and not up there," Illesa pointed to the nearby stretch of the forest.

"Hey, Kit!" Reg called.

"Come on, Sweetheart, don't worry." Kit squeezed her hand and went back to the front of the stall. She heard him start up his banter with a man wanting a spit handle.

Illesa sat down with her back to the stall and put her throbbing head on her knees. Her hands were shaking. It was like a labyrinth; at every turn she seemed to face a wall. If she stayed with Kit she would end up gaoled with him, but if she left him she would fare no better. Closing her eyes, she traced the swirls of the letters in the book of Saint Margaret. The noises around her grew distant as the pen strokes formed each word, each tendril. In that world the battle was already won, the danger past and all was peace.

When she eventually lifted her head, there was only evening light in the sky.

A crier came down the row, his voice heavily accented.

"You will be astounded at the mercy of God! Watch the defeat of the dragon Satan by the pure virgin, Margaret. See the fires of Hell!"

Kit stuck his head round the back of the stall.

"Go and see it! You ought to have some fun in your life. It might be your only chance," he said, grinning like a devil.

Illesa had run out of energy to argue with him. She got slowly to her feet, shouldered her pack and followed the pull of the crowd. She was glad all the coin was tucked far down under layers of cloth as she wove through throngs of people gathered in the open in front of a circle of thick rope on the ground.

A large wagon covered in painted cloth made up the back of the stage. Illesa found a spot with a decent view. A man with a black eye and half a front tooth took centre stage and started juggling with skittles, letting them drop directly on his head while he contorted his face into fantastic grimaces. One skittle almost hit a child sitting at the front, prompting loud cheers. When he finished, a man dressed in a white tunic and golden armour came forward. The crowd booed enthusiastically. They had seen this one before.

"Good folk of Rushbury, we welcome you to our humble play, a recreation of the marvellous Passion of the glorious virgin Margaret." His deep voice sounded hoarse. The man coughed meaningfully. "We pray that you will pardon our rude manners when we play the part of the infidel followers of the false gods of Rome and the awful demons of Hell." The crowd was obedient enough and booed again.

The orator of the prologue turned out to be the Governor of Antioch. With a centurion by his side, he declared his state.

"Life and limb and goodness all be at my request,
so of all sovereigns, I am most mightiest."

Saint Margaret was disappointing at first: a pockmarked boy in a wig that kept slipping over his eyes whenever he was tortured. But when they came to the scene with the dragon, he was transfigured in the flames. Fire glowed golden on his wig. His earnest face and hands, which were always pressed together in prayer, affected the crowd, which hushed to hear his words. When the centurion beheaded him, the crowd moaned and booed for so long it prevented the next speaker, the Governor, from being heard.

Illesa left before the end. The sun was setting and she was exhausted. She wound her way back through the sellers of cloth and coal. Most of the people were congregating round the ale and food stalls, leaving the craftsmen's rows almost empty. One of the fair guards walked past the end of the row, his lantern lighting his fleshy face and the red of his livery. The pole star was out, and a cool wind flapped loose cloth and rope.

The smiths' stalls were all tied up, their fires doused. Illesa couldn't see a soul.

The canvas of Kit's stall was still hanging open, but all the wares were gone. Illesa felt her way around the trestle table, straining her eyes.

"Kit," she hissed.

A sudden movement by the canvas made her stumble backward.

He reached her fast, before she got her balance. The fist hit her cheek, but glanced off. She dropped to the ground and rolled sideways under the table, knocking against the tools in Kit's pack. The man kicked at her, swearing. She scrambled out into the row, Kit's large hammer in her hand. Her breath was tight and painful, but she got to her feet before he had rounded the table, and there the moonlight lit upon Destrey's face. He lunged at her with a falchion, but it scraped over the arm of her jerkin. She sidestepped and swung at him with the hammer, missing him as he ducked. He swore and lunged again.

Illesa tried to shout, but her voice was weak and breathless. The noise of the fair in the distance was unchanged. There was no sign of patrolling guards. They circled round each other.

"You," Destrey spat. "Wherever you are, Arrowsmith is not far away."

"He's not here," Illesa said, keeping her eyes on him. He was feinting towards her, his frame small and agile. She didn't dare run; he looked too fast.

"Oh yes he is. He's been seen, in broad daylight, selling his wares. He must think we are fools."

"He knows you are."

That brought on another lunge, and Illesa had to spring sideways. The hammer was very heavy. It was hard to swing it fast and high enough. Destrey was much quicker, slashing his blade and darting out of reach.

"The others will have found him by now."

Illesa swallowed but didn't answer. She changed her grip on the hammer, keeping her eyes on Destrey's broad blade.

"Yes, the Forester is here to make sure justice is done this time," Destrey said, circling round her. "Arrowsmith will pay, right enough, but you will pay first."

He lunged again. She paused a fraction of a second, letting him come closer, pulled to the right and swung the hammer full circle. It hit the back of his head with a cracking sound. He fell forward, balanced on his knees and hands briefly and then fell to the ground. The breath came out of his mouth in short, high cries, like a motherless kitten. Illesa stood away from him, struggling to breathe. Everything seemed bright and clear, but her hands could not hold the hammer handle. Destrey was motionless, apart from a twitching leg. She did not want to look any closer at his head.

Behind the trestle, she felt around on the ground for Kit's tools and threw the hammer in the bag. The slumped shape of Destrey made a black patch amongst the wet straw. She would not go that way. At the back of the stalls she started running towards the light of the torches, the tools clanging with every pace.

The noise and smell of burnt meat grew stronger, rising above the raucous crowd. Illesa dodged in and out, searching frantically around her. She found a barrel and climbed on it, looking over the heads of the crowd. At the second from last ale tent on the right the large frame of Warden Lyttle, his mouth open in laughter, had a tankard in his hand. To his left she saw the back of a shaved head, and a hand gesticulating in a way that was very familiar.

She jumped off the barrel and collided with a man carrying two tankards. He swore but moved on. Progress down the row was painfully slow; the crowd blocked her view all the way. But as she drew near, a familiar voice could be heard.

"Get your hands off him. I'll have you!" shouted Warden Lyttle.

"Fight! Fight! Fight!" Several men took up the chant. The crowd pressed in so much she could not move. The voice of the Forester was easily audible above the shouting.

"This man has fled justice twice. He is wanted for a felony against the Forest Law. If you want to share in his fate, by all means attack an officer of the King. I would advise against it myself, warden." The Forester paused. "My men can administer justice here and now. It will be an added entertainment for the fair."

The crowd buzzed threateningly.

"I beg your pardon, but you have no jurisdiction here, my lord." The new voice was not loud, but the crowd grew quieter. Illesa couldn't place the speaker. A bell rang and guards surged forward, pushing people out of the way. Behind them was a broad man in a bright blue surcoat, a chain of office round his neck and a staff in his hand.

Illesa took advantage of the confusion to push to the front of the crowd. Kit was standing very still; the Forester's sword was resting against the veins of his neck. Tom from the stables had Lyttle's arm behind his back and was whispering urgently in his ear.

"What is disturbing the peace of this holy fair?" the Steward shouted, coming to a stop in front of the Forester. "Account for yourselves!"

Chapter XVII
Compline

The Steward's arrival was greeted by grumbling from the crowd. They expected to see bloodshed at the fair, and a summary execution would have been even better.

"Sheathe your weapon, man, and declare yourself," bellowed the Steward. He signalled to the guards, who marched forward and stood around the men.

"I am the King's Forester. Your master, Sir Hugh, knows me well enough," Giles Forester said as the hilt of his sword hit the sheath.

"Your presence here does us all honour," the Steward blustered, surprised. "I know you only by reputation, of course." The Forester bowed almost imperceptibly. The Steward bobbed his head a few times before he remembered the matter in hand.

"And you, man? Declare yourself."

"Christopher Arrowsmith. A stall holder at your estimable fair." Kit even managed to smile.

"Warden Lyttle and Warden Tom, hold your peace." The Steward waved them away, and they retreated a pace.

"What is your grievance with this man, Lord Forester?" The Steward was speaking with slow deliberation, sweat shining on his face.

"I am apprehending him as a felon. I will execute him here or take him with me in chains. You need not be involved in the matter any further."

"And he is the felon?" the Steward said, gesturing at Kit.

The Forester sighed loudly.

"Christopher Arrowsmith is guilty of poaching a hind and evading the King's justice. He left the sanctuary he claimed at Eaton Church and has used his cunning to deceive you into hiring him a stall while he prepares to make off with your fees, Steward."

"That is a lie," Kit burst out.

"Hold your peace!" shouted the Steward. "Are you implying that our fair is improperly run?" he said, turning back to the Forester.

"The man is a liar; he deceives many," he said, adjusting his scabbard so it hung straight on his belt. "Now, I would like to conclude this matter as quickly as possible. Order your men to seize him, Steward, or I will do the job myself."

"Wait just a minute, if you please, my lord," the Steward said slowly, rubbing his full beard. "The pole is raised with the glove still in place. You have no authority here until the fair is done. It is the Pie Powder Court that must decide on this matter."

The Forester's look of disbelief might have been amusing if he'd been a different man. His fury was only just in check.

"You know this business is nothing to do with the fair, man. The crime was committed two weeks ago in the Long Forest. We arrested and gaoled him, there and then. His violent escape makes him an outlaw. So do not waste my time with your Pie Powder Court, Steward!" He punctuated each last word with a finger on the Steward's chest.

"That is as may be," said the Steward, shifting his weight backwards and swaying slightly. "I am sorry for your trouble, my lord, but if you want to arrest him at this fair you need the approval of the court; no other authority is valid."

The Forester's anger settled around his handsome mouth. He bent over and spoke in the Steward's ear. In the distance a loud bell was ringing. The Steward put a consoling hand on the Forester's shoulder. He obviously didn't know his reputation well enough.

"I cannot help you, my lord. The law of the fair forbids it, and there are many witnesses," he said, indicating the crowd with a sweep of his be-robed arm. "We will take the man into custody, and in the morning after we have celebrated the Mass for the Feast of Saint Margaret, the court will convene in the manor. I beg you to stay the night. Sir Hugh would want you to have a warm welcome."

"I have business to attend to," the Forester grunted and pushed his way through the crowd, towards the village. Illesa dropped her gaze as he passed. A guard was wading through the people from the opposite direction. He broke out of the crowd and bowed before the Steward. From his expression, the news was bad.

"You two take Arrowsmith to the cell, the rest follow me," the Steward shouted, making the most of his expanded authority. The Steward and three guards set off towards the iron row. Illesa skirted them, heading towards Kit, who was having a whispered conversation with Warden Lyttle. Tom was keeping the guards on either side of him talking. Illesa got there just as they took Kit by the arms and began to lead him away.

"Kit!"

He looked round, saw her, and shook his head. Master Lyttle took her elbow and pulled her behind the ale tent, Tom by his side.

"Come here out of the way. We don't know who is watching." They went behind a pile of barrels that stank of piss. Illesa could just see their faces in the dark.

"Now don't look so upset. The Steward's got him safe for the night. Anyway, Tom here is part of the court. He'll see you right, ain't that so, Tom?"

"I'll do my best," the stable master said, looking doubtful. "Kit's your brother, is he?"

"Yes, sir." Illesa's head was pounding. She rubbed her eyes. There was no sense in crying in front of these men.

"I will need to know the truth if I am going to help him. Is he guilty of poaching?" Tom asked quietly, standing in the shadow. Illesa was rubbing her arms to stop them trembling.

"Kit can be an idiot, but he isn't a criminal. He is always getting into scrapes and out of them somehow." She couldn't help the bitterness in her voice.

"I hope he gets out of this one," Tom said. "He has made himself popular with the stall holders, helping people out and sharing new jokes. And I think he made quite a few friends last night assisting the Lord of the Taps in sampling the ale. I will ask around. We may be able to swing it in his favour, but the Forester is a rich man. He has already offered the Steward a bribe, and the good man is not above such incentives, when there isn't a crowd watching."

Illesa swallowed the lump in her throat.

"Where is the cell? Can I get close enough to talk to him?"

"No. It's below the tower and there is no window. Kit said you were to take this and go; get away as soon as possible and make a start somewhere else." Tom put a pouch in her hand. She could feel the coins through the thin leather. "He said he would find you."

"That's all he said?"

"There wasn't much time before they took him."

"He'll be cleared, mark my words," slurred Master Lyttle. "That bastard Forester won't have the satisfaction. We'll hang *him* first."

"Quiet, friend!" Tom said, sharply. He turned to Illesa and his voice softened a little. "You can't leave in the dark. Sleep in the stables tonight; there is a spare bed. Then you can leave at first light when these drunkards are still snoring."

"I'm not drunk," Master Lyttle said. "I'm going to get some food for you." He put his hand on Illesa's shoulder, his face very close to hers. "That's what Kit was going to do before we saw him, and made him stop for a drink. We must fulfil that obligation now, you poor girl. Can't have you starving, can we?" Without waiting for a reply, he lurched away.

Tom shrugged.

"I've never had a lady in the stables before. Do you mind if I speak to you as a boy?"

"It seems a long time since I was anything else."

Tom led her wordlessly through the crowd. They came out of the crush of people and into the lane. The night was clear and the moon rode high above the chaos below. A loud crack behind her made Illesa jump. Just someone breaking up sticks for a brazier, but it was the same sound the hammer had made as it hit Destrey's head. The Steward and the guards would have found him by now. They'd be looking for the culprit.

Tom took the key from his belt at the stable yard gate. The fair was just a murmur in the distance.

"This way," he said, walking across the yard.

"I'll check my horse, if I may?"

Tom nodded and unlocked the stable building. He took a lantern from a hook outside the door and gave it to her without a word. Just inside on a small pallet, the stable boy was curled up asleep with his mouth open. Illesa found Jezebel, who whickered gently. Her warm breath smelt of hay. Illesa put her face into the wiry tangle of Jezebel's mane and took a deep breath of horse.

"Tomorrow, I'll take you home," she whispered in her ear. And after that? The possibilities jostled with each other. Without Kit, wherever she went would be hard.

Illesa found Tom outside, trimming another lantern by moonlight.

"Here, give me a light," he said reaching for her lantern. He lit it expertly and returned the first lantern to its hook by the stable door. "This way," he said.

In the small room at the back of the stable was a truckle bed with a chest at its end and a bucket of water by the window. The bed was obviously Tom's.

"It's not luxury, but I daresay you have slept in worse recently."

"Where will you sleep?"

"Oh, I only use this when the stable is full, and I don't trust the stable boy to manage. I have a room in the Manor. If Warden Lyttle has remembered that he intended to get you some food, I'll bring it to you," he said. "But I wouldn't hold your breath."

"I don't feel much like eating anyway." Illesa un-slung her pack and put it by the bed.

"Are you well? You seem to be bleeding."

Illesa looked down in dismay and took off her jerkin. Blood had seeped through the dressing of her wound and was re-staining the linen tunic with a fresh cloud of red.

"It must have reopened when he kicked me," she said without thinking.

"When who kicked you?" Tom asked, putting the lantern on the shelf over the window and turning round.

"One of the Forester's men found me in Kit's stall. He kicked me before I could get out of the way."

"When was this?"

"Just before Kit was arrested. I told Kit we should leave as soon as I saw the first of the Forester's men, but he wanted to wait until dark," Illesa said. "He never thinks anything bad is going to happen. Not to him anyway."

Tom's face was impassive.

"He should have listened to you; that is clear enough. I'll go and fetch some bandages. You can wash in the water while I'm gone."

Illesa took off the tunic and unwound the bandages gingerly. The wound still looked clean, but blood flowed from it persistently. She put on her jerkin, made a pad of the bandage and pressed down on the cut.

Tom knocked on the door and walked in with some linen bandages, which he draped on the bed.

"How does it look?"

"It will heal once I've strapped it up again."

Tom stood silent for a moment.

"I don't know what to call you. What is your real name?"

"Illesa."

"That's unusual. Illesa, does your escape from one of the Forester's men have anything to do with the finding of a man in the iron row, insensible from a blow to the head?"

Illesa nodded and looked down.

"He came after me with a falchion, and I grabbed the nearest thing, which was one of Kit's hammers. I was afraid I'd killed him." Tears fell onto her lap, and she wiped her face quickly.

"He's not dead, but I don't think he will ever talk sense again, which from your point of view is a good thing."

"You aren't going to tell them it was me?"

"Do you want me to?" he asked with a wry expression.

"No. I'll end up hanged with Kit."

"I will not tell them, but you must be gone at first light. Even if they only discover you are a woman in man's clothing, they will arrest you. I will wake you before prime." He stood at the door, his hand on the latch. "We will do our best for your brother, but you must pray for him. It may be that he is God's fool, and God will always keep him safe." Tom paused. "You, on the other hand, seem to be able to look after yourself."

Illesa couldn't look him in the eye.

"You have been kinder than I deserve."

"I would guess you've had precious little kindness of late," he said and shut the door.

Illesa finished the bandaging, washed her hands of blood and managed to pray only two words before exhaustion laid her out on the bed.

Chapter XVIII
AD 304
Antioch-on-the-Orontes

Marina kept her eyes closed. The demons walked over her body and clung to her arms and legs. They tried to open her eyes. One had his claws gripped on the sides of her head like a vice and his tail wrapped loosely round her neck. She squeezed her eyes shut, trying to remember the face of the man who had been speaking in her sleep, but she could not. There was only pain and stench.

The demons dug their talons in for balance as Marina was lifted in rough hands. The light coming through her eyelids was bright, and she smelled heat and smoke. There was rustling and then a blast of wind. It grew louder and stronger until she heard branches cracking in the heat and the great breath of fire.

The hands put her down; there was cool metal against her skin. Marina almost opened her eyes, but the man from her dream spoke and brushed his fingers over her face, closing her eyelids. The metal clanged and shook. She felt weightless; she was swinging.

The dragon demon on her head roared hot air around her ears. He was growing, bursting with heat. He took all the air, and her lungs burned. His girth pushed her against the searing metal. His scales were iridescent, his eyes were huge plates of mirrors reflecting the world. The long tail wrapped around her neck tightly. He was magnificent.

"Worship me," he roared in a rush of air.

His mouth drew closer; his breath was sweet, like roses.

"Worship me!"

His mouth opened and his tail lifted her by the neck. His black mouth grew even wider and deeper. A long tongue of fire wrapped around her body. She could see down his throat, ringed with gold ribs, to the fire in his belly. The dragon's throat juddered, and the muscles squeezed. Marina moved her right finger down and sideways, to bless.

After she was removed from the fire cage, Marina was dropped into a huge bronze bath of cold water. Steam rose from the surface as she sank, unmoving, to the bottom. Olymbrius started shouting.

"You left her in the fire too long. She's dead! Get in there and lift her out!"

Two guards got in gingerly, not wanting to touch her. They had to heave her up from the bottom of the tank. The centurion, Malchus, looked at the sky for an omen. Clouds were converging around Mount Silpius. He took the body from the guards as they climbed out of the water. Olymbrius was shouting from a safe distance, spit flying from his mouth.

"Keep her alive! We must bring her to the amphitheatre. It won't be a deterrent if the public don't see her."

"Does she live?" whispered one of the auxiliary guards as Olymbrius strode off, flanked by soldiers.

"How could she? He wants her to be roasted like a lamb and then he is surprised when she dies. He has completely lost his reason," the centurion muttered, holding her in his arms as water streamed from the shreds of her clothes. He felt a convulsion in her chest.

"Quick!" he said. The other soldier took her feet, and they laid her down on the ground, pushing her onto her side. She coughed out water and bile, and then retched up blood. The soldiers backed away from her.

"She should have died," the auxiliary said.

"Your life or mine would have been forfeit," said the centurion.

"Why didn't he give the signal earlier?" The young auxiliary sounded as if he was going to cry. He was no more than seventeen, the centurion estimated. He should be killing soldiers not burning virgins.

"How can we lift her?" the boy asked. "Her skin is coming off."

The centurion pulled away the charred remains of her tunic. Marina's head listed sideways.

"No, she is burnt on her front, where she was lying on the fire cage. Her back and her arms are whole," he said, cutting the rope from her wrists and moving her fingers carefully apart. The skin there was clean and undamaged. "Get a stretcher."

They carried her to a room in the main part of the palace and placed her on a soft bed, covering her body in wet cloths. There was only a small patch of her long hair left on the back of her head. It was cut off so it would not stick to her red, oozing skin. Her eyes would not open. She twitched and moaned in delirium for three days.

The room shutters were closed and pungent incense was burnt on a brazier in the corner. Smoke gathered below the ceiling, deadening the sound. The centurion detailed to guard her and the old nurse barely spoke, listening for her every breath. They knew what would happen if she died in their care. By the fourth day, the centurion could only breathe as Marina did, and when she spoke, the relief he felt was drowned by shame.

Olymbrius was informed as soon as she woke. He was pleased she would be conscious for the final torture, the public humiliation and death in the amphitheatre. He had something special in mind for it. The crowds would be entertained, but they would also learn the price to be paid for apostasy. The little gang of troublemakers who were hiding in the Jewish quarter would know that very well. His soldiers were already moving through the city.

Chapter XIX
The 20th day of July, 1284
The Feast of Saint Margaret the Virgin

Illesa must have slept, but she woke when the night was still black and could not sleep again. She opened the shutters and waited for the sky to lighten, while her mind went round and round like a donkey in a mill.

When the eastern horizon had turned deep blue, she put on her boots and took the bucket outside to rinse it. Horses were moving restlessly in the stable. Illesa packed the bandages and checked the purse and other coin. In Kit's pouch there was more than enough to pay the stabling.

Tom was outside the stable door, and the bleary eyed stable boy was pouring water into the trough.

"Thank you for the bed." Illesa held out the coins and Tom took them without a word. She went into Jezebel's stall, untethered her and led her into the yard.

"Warden Lyttle did remember about the food," Tom said, pointing to a parcel on the bench by the stable. Illesa smiled.

"Please send him my thanks. I have money to pay for it." She fumbled with Kit's purse.

"Oh no, he would be terribly insulted. He was determined to buy you all sorts of things last night. He's obviously taken a liking to you. Perhaps you remind him of his daughter," he paused, "or his son."

Illesa looked up at him, but his face was impassive. She stood next to Jezebel, hesitating.

"I should not be leaving Kit," she said.

"You cannot help him, and if you stay you may cause him more trouble. He must live or die by another's word," Tom said, as he buckled the stirrups and checked the saddle. "Whatever happens, I believe you will be better off leading your own life. He is not the kind who looks after others, nor enjoys being looked after."

"You seem to know him well already," Illesa said, taking her anger out on the girth strap.

"I'm used to judging horses. Men are not dissimilar," Tom said, holding Jezebel steady while Illesa mounted.

Someone rapped on the gate.

"Go round the back of the stables and stay there until I call," Tom whispered. He waited till she was out of sight before going to the gate. Illesa heard a well-shod horse enter the yard. The rider dismounted, and spurs sounded on the cobbles. A knight.

Jezebel scented the air excitedly. She started to whinny and wheel around. Illesa pulled hard on the reins, but the horse broke loose and galloped into the yard. In the grey light, she saw a familiar silhouette, confirmed when she dismounted and let Jezebel free to nuzzle Buskins. Sir Richard came towards her.

"Illesa," he said, holding her by the shoulders. "I did not expect to find you here!"

"How do you fare, Sir Richard? You should not be riding so soon." She was breathless, and a sick feeling crawled in her stomach.

"I am well. Whatever you gave me has worked. I bandaged it again and it is healing quickly." He paused, taking in her anxiety. "Is something wrong? I went to Eaton and was told that Kit had escaped from the church tower. Is he still in danger?"

"Sir, let me take your mount," Tom said, separating the two excited horses. "Illesa, you must go, it is almost fully light."

"You are the stable master, are you?" Richard asked.

"Yes, sir, and the church warden. I can tell you the news of Christopher Arrowsmith, but his sister must leave now. Her life is in grave danger."

"You need not concern yourself. I will look after her. You will look after my horse."

"Yes, sir," said Tom. He glanced at Illesa and led Buskins away.

When he was out of earshot in the stable, Illesa turned to Sir Richard, controlling the tone of her voice.

"Sir, Tom is doing his best to help. He has been very kind."

"I am sure he has," Richard said, "and received payment for it, no doubt. This manor belongs to one of my cousins, and you are under my protection now. My authority should be enough. Now tell me what has happened."

"Yes, sir." Illesa took a deep breath. "Kit is under arrest and the Forester is here, waiting for the verdict of the Pie Powder

Court today which will decide whether or not he will hang. The Forester stayed in the manor last night, and we think he has bribed the Steward to ensure Kit's conviction."

"The Steward's favour is for sale, is it?"

"We think so."

"I don't know this Steward, but I will make sure he knows me before the day is out. Now Illesa, take your beautiful horse back to the stable. You are not going anywhere."

"Yes, sir," Illesa said, unhappily, "but I mustn't go back into the fair. Many people saw me with Kit, and I injured one of the Forester's men who attacked me. If they find me there, I will be arrested."

Richard stood, his hand on his saddlebag, looking at her with a wide smile on his face. He took off his gloves and slapped them into his palm.

"You remind me more and more of the wonderful tale of Silence, the maiden knight. Have you heard it?"

Illesa shook her head.

"It is a tale I heard when I was in London. It takes place at a time when the King had decided that only male heirs could inherit their parent's wealth and lands. Silence is born a girl, but her noble parents decide that she must be raised as a boy so that she will be able to inherit. They have her trained in every way as a boy and isolated from the world in a forest castle. Eventually, she escapes and goes to France with two minstrels, then she becomes a knight in service of the King, winning many battles, and finally she captures the sorcerer Merlin, before he unmasks her as a woman."

"What happens to her then?"

"She marries the King."

"Oh," Illesa said, disappointed. "I don't understand what you mean. I am not a minstrel or a knight or a queen."

"In the tale, Silence is caught in a battle between Nurture and Nature. They both want to have their own way, but she becomes the best of both men and women."

"But she was called Silence presumably because she had to keep her true nature a secret."

"Yes, in that way she is like you."

"Sir, I am dressed this way to escape rape and murder on the roads and to try to save my home, not to inherit a fortune or become a queen. It is nothing like me."

Tom came out of the stable and took the reins from Illesa's hands. He led Jezebel back into her stall without a word.

"Perhaps I should not expect you to understand these courtly tales. They are about things outside of your experience," Richard said, crossly.

Illesa stopped the retort in her throat. She mustn't antagonize him when there was so much at stake.

"Sir, my appearance is well known at the fair. Even if I go in with you, they will still have the power to arrest me."

"That will not be a problem. I have some fresh clothes. You can change and act as my page, that way you can accompany me to the court. People won't recognise you in fine garments, and no one will question me about a servant."

The plan contained too many assumptions, but Illesa could see no alternative now that he had taken charge.

"As you wish, but I am not going to become a knight, no matter what you give me to wear."

Richard smiled.

"Groom!"

Tom reappeared from the stable, holding Richard's two saddlebags.

"Ah. That's what I wanted. Is there somewhere to change clothes without going into the manor? We have need for discretion, as I'm sure you are aware."

"Illesa knows where," Tom said, without expression. "I'll get back to the horses. The stable boy will bring you water."

Illesa led the way to the room where she had spent the night. It seemed small and dusty in the daylight. She was almost embarrassed by it. Richard looked around and put the saddlebags on the bed. She stood with her arms folded while he unpacked one of them and laid the clothes out.

"I will look like a lord, not a page."

"I think I know more about it than you," Richard said. "You will look just right. I'll leave you to change."

"Sir Richard."

"Yes?" he said, his hand on the door.

"Do you still have my book with you?"

"Yes, in the other bag. Take it out if you wish. I have decided that you should accompany me to Acton to speak to my mother. You should be there to hear the truth about it."

Illesa's stomach lurched. She could only hope that through God's mercy she could avoid that journey.

"Now tidy yourself up. I don't employ scruffy pages," he said, shutting the door.

Eventually she emerged, feeling self-conscious. It was not easy to tame the wild-haired, grubby lad she had become. The clothes felt so strange and stiff that she kept looking down at herself.

"Don't do that," Richard's voice came from the shadow of the yard wall, "you'll look like a girl dressed up as a boy!" He came over to her. "What took you so long?"

Illesa frowned at him.

"Sir, this is not going to work."

"Yes it is, but you have to try to walk as if you are the page of an important man, not an infant in her brother's borrowed jerkin. Now, try to walk with your head up, attentively. You walk before me and clear the way."

"I know that," Illesa said, crossly. "I was comfortable in my old clothes. I knew how to move in them."

"You cannot be my page in those old rags, you idiot."

Illesa breathed out slowly.

"Let's go, if we are going."

"You can't talk to your master like that," Richard admonished, wagging his finger. "You must be deferential."

"God's blood," Illesa said, almost inaudibly.

Richard smiled again.

"I need to change myself. Wait here and practise," he said shutting the door of the room behind him.

Sir Richard and his new page arrived at the fair just as the mass for the Feast of Saint Margaret finished. People streamed out of the churchyard heading for the manor grounds. Illesa wondered how many would attend the court. Those who had been there at the ale tents the night before might, but what they wanted from the proceedings was a good hanging, or at the very least, a man in the pillory.

Sir Richard, wearing a feathered hat and carrying his saddlebag, followed her through the crowd, past the food tents and up to the office of the clerk. The pole with its glove cast a long shadow in the morning sunshine.

"Sir Richard Burnel has come to attend the court," Illesa declared with a small bow, displaying Richard's seal ring. The clerk, who had only just arrived at his desk, looked flustered.

"Where's my boy?" he shouted. A minute later the boy arrived, pulling on a tabard, and the clerk cuffed him on the ear.

"Here, go straight to the Steward and tell him Sir Richard Burnel is here. Follow me, sir," the clerk said with a bow. He locked his office and pushed past the small group of curious onlookers who had already gathered outside. They went through the gate leading into the courtyard. It was bustling with people setting up benches, chairs and tables.

Eventually the large frame of the Steward emerged from the solar wing, following the boy. The deep creases around his mouth gave him the look of a hound. He bowed to Richard, trying to hide his obvious dismay.

"Sir Richard, what an honour to have a member of the family here for the fair. I am Gerald, Steward to Sir Hugh Burnel."

"Thank you, Steward, I am glad to be here for the Feast. I would have sent word, but circumstances prevented it."

"No trouble at all," he said licking his dry lips. "We will soon find you a room and some refreshment." He clapped his hands.

"Don't trouble yourself; I am refreshed. I believe the Pie Powder Court is about to sit, and I would be pleased to watch. I have never been present at one before. I understand they can be most entertaining."

The Steward frowned.

"Sir Richard, the matter to be decided is very serious indeed. The man is accused of a grave crime and perhaps more than one. I will make sure justice is done, even though the common traders have their say," the Steward said, his colour high.

"Of course, of course. Well done!" Richard slapped the Steward on the back. "Where shall I sit to get the best view?"

"Sir, are you sure you want to sit down here with the people? I can set up a seat in the solar by a window so that you may see perfectly well from the comfort of your own room."

"No, no, I want to be in the thick of it, so to speak. I can sit there, next to the table." He went and sat on the large chair set at the head of the table. "Do get your cellarer to open the wine. I don't care for ale today."

"Yes, Sir Richard," the Steward said, and went away looking crestfallen.

"There, that should shake him up a bit," said Richard, under his breath.

Illesa's hands were cold and clammy. The stiff clothes rustled whenever she moved. People were coming through the gate in a steady stream. The benches had already been filled when she saw Master Lyttle and Tom arrive. She kept her eyes lowered. When she looked up, Tom was talking to a large man with a florid face, bound to be the Lord of the Taps.

The men apportioned to the court sat on the benches, making a square with the table at the head. All the other spectators, including Master Lyttle, stood behind. Two more chairs, a tray with a flagon of wine and three fine glass goblets were brought to the table. Illesa did her best to pour it, but her hands were shaking and the wine spilt.

"Steady yourself," he whispered. "Here comes someone I think you know."

The Forester was approaching the table, followed by the hurrying figure of the Steward.

"Sir Richard Burnel, may I present Giles the Lord Forester of the Long Forest. Perhaps you've met?" The Steward's face was shining and anxious. Richard rose and made a slight bow; the Forester's was even slighter.

"Please excuse me, my lords," the Steward said, removing himself quickly.

"Never met, have we, my lord? It is a pleasure," Richard said jovially, and sat back down indicating the seat next to him. "Do have some Gascon wine. It's very good and quite cool for this hot day."

The Forester nodded curtly and took the proffered goblet. The Steward was talking to the court members in turn, whispering in their ears. Illesa saw him slip one a coin. Richard snapped his fingers for more wine. The Forester placed his cup down on the table, holding on to the rim.

"What brings you to the fair, Sir Richard? I did not know the Burnel family had time to take an interest in such small events."

"Oh, I love fairs. My cousin is indeed too busy to visit all his holdings, but as I have been released from my military duties, I am at leisure to see the country." Richard put his feet up on the table.

"I am looking forward to this very much. I have never seen a Pie Powder Court in session before. Do you think the commoners can put on a good show?"

"So you are just here by chance?" said the Forester, watching the Steward, who had got half way round the court members.

"Indeed, I was on my way to another of our estates, when I heard there was a fair. I did want to see the wares for sale; it is a weakness of mine, I fear. And you, my lord, are here on serious business?"

"I came here to apprehend a felon; a smith who has shown contempt for the law. The court will convict him, though his own conscience does not."

"He sounds a bad sort. Is this him now?"

Four guards approached with Kit in their midst, his hands chained together. His face was swollen, and one of his eyes was closed and black.

The Forester nodded, as two guards led Kit into the centre of the square and stood on either side of him. The remaining two went behind the head table and stood to attention close to Sir Richard. Illesa wondered if Kit could see Richard, or anyone, through the puffy flesh around his eyes. The Steward lumbered across to the chair on Sir Richard's left and sat down.

"Silence! The court is now in session. We will hear the plaintiff's case first."

The Lord Forester rose to his feet, and the crowd quieted. His complexion was bright red, but he seemed in control of his fury. Richard signalled for more wine and Illesa refilled the goblets.

"On the Monday before the Feast of Saint Veronica, my men and I apprehended this man Christopher Arrowsmith in the Long Forest near Wolverton. He had shot and killed a hind with a broadhead arrow of his own making. He resisted arrest and injured two of my men before we gaoled him. He later overpowered the guard and unlocked his cell."

Muted cheers rose from somewhere in the crowd. The Forester slammed his fist on the table and glared at the audience before continuing.

"He fled to the church of Saint Milburgha in Eaton where he took sanctuary and remained for three days, damaging the church tower all the while. He then left sanctuary and last evening we found him here, brazenly selling his wares, having duped someone into hiring him a stall." The Forester cast his eyes over the men on the benches. "Resisting his second arrest last night, he knocked one of my men senseless with his hammer. By law he may hang for the first offence of poaching, how much more for the bodily harm he has inflicted on men in the service of the King? Justice must be done. A felon who has put himself beyond the law, must die by the law." The Forester's face was mottled with emotion. He drained his goblet before sitting down.

The Steward nodded at him.

"Are there any other witnesses in the case against the defendant?"

"He owes me a drink!" someone shouted from the crowd.

"Silence! This court is in session, if anyone disrupts the proceedings I will have the guards take them to the pillory." The Steward wiped his forehead. The Forester gestured at someone near the front of the crowd, who came forward. It was Jarryd. He stood to the left of Kit, his hands twitching at his sides.

"What is your name?" the Steward asked.

"Jarryd of Longville."

"Your father?"

"A villein."

"And what do you have to say in this case?"

"I saw this man shoot the hind," Jarryd said, his voice flat.

"Jarryd of Longville, you identify this man standing next to you as the one who shot the King's deer in the Long Forest, as described by the Lord Forester?"

"Yes, Steward."

The Steward signalled him to retire.

"Now, if there are no other accusations, the defendant may speak."

Kit stepped forward.

"My Lord Forester and Master Steward," Kit bowed to each in turn, "and my good sir," he said turning to Sir Richard. "My thanks for the excellent accommodation afforded me last night and the men you sent to keep me company."

There were several catcalls at this.

"Speak to the accusations against you, or you will be hanged without delay," the Steward shouted over the noise.

"I beg your pardon, my lords. I will begin," he said, turning to the men on the benches. He stood straight, at his full height, and spoke as if he were selling his wares to an indifferent crowd.

"Regarding the first crime I have been accused of, I must admit that the deer was shot by one of my arrows, the Lord Forester is right about that. But it was not shot by me." Kit cleared his throat and took on a conspiratorial tone.

"I was travelling from Stoke de Say, where I had delivered a consignment of arrowheads, northeast towards my family home. At a tavern by the Corve, I struck up a conversation with an archer. We had a common interest and talked a fair while. He said he worked for the Lord Forester, this very man before you. He was interested in my work, especially in the broadhead arrows, saying they were needed by his master. I asked him what they would pay, and the man said that would depend on their quality. He could give me the best price if they were good enough. I asked how he would test their quality. He proposed that the next day we ride together into the forest to a place where they practised with the bow. If the arrows were satisfactory, I would have the commission for fifty at a penny each."

The crowd muttered at the price.

"What was the man's name?"

"He said his name was John Destrey." Illesa jerked the ewer in her hand, and Richard looked up suddenly, meeting her eyes.

"May I trouble you for a drink? My throat is parched," Kit croaked.

"Here, let the man have some wine. It may be his last after all!" Sir Richard pushed the Steward's half-full glass towards Kit with a smile.

Kit bowed to him.

"Thank you, good sir."

One of the guards picked up the cup. Kit took it in his chained hands and swallowed it in one gulp.

The Steward, frowning, gestured for the cup to be replaced and Illesa filled it. The Forester was staring at her. She went back to her place and kept her eyes lowered.

"Get on with it, Arrowsmith. The court has other business today. Keep your story brief."

"Yes, Steward. The next day we did as Destrey had proposed. I was eager for a commission as the army was no longer in need of

190

my services, thanks to the routing of the Welsh by our brave knights." Kit paused while the crowd cheered enthusiastically. "We reached the place after a short ride. It was a clearing with a mature coppice on the west, and a plantation on the right of beech and birch. Destrey strung his long bow. My broadhead arrows soon proved their worth and split the saplings even at a hundred paces."

"What else will you split with your broad head?" a woman's voice called, provoking more laughter.

"All offers happily considered!" Kit replied. "As I was saying, the arrows did their job, and then I heard hooves approaching. Two riders were driving a herd of deer into the clearing. Destrey fitted an arrow to his bow and shot a hind as it ran past, straight in the belly. The rest of the herd scattered. I shouted at Destrey, asking in the strongest terms whether he was aware of the law he was meant to be enforcing. I ran over to the deer, to pull my arrow from its body, and then I felt a blade on my neck. I turned to see it was Destrey himself, and behind him, two other mounted men, who had driven the deer through the clearing. I had seen them at the tavern as well, but I didn't know they were together. They had me good and proper. I put up a fight, but they soon had me tied and thrown over my own horse, the deer on the front of another, and they rode me like a piece of baggage all the way to their gaol at Myllichope, where they accused me to the Lord Forester, showing the arrow as evidence and confiscating my tools and horse."

The Forester stood up, his hands on the table.

"This man is a liar as well as a dangerous felon. We are the servants of the King, and we keep his law faithfully."

"My lord, you have had your say," the Steward said. "Continue, Arrowsmith."

"Everything else that has happened is as he said. I escaped because if I had remained in the gaol, I would soon have died. Despite my innocence, the guard beat me every day and fed me nothing. I left the sanctuary of the church because Destrey and the Forester's other men were trying to break in to take me, against the law of the Church. I have not put myself outside of the law. On the contrary, I am a great respecter of the law, and the King." Kit lifted his head. "I have risked my life serving him. But your men, my lord Forester, are not respecters of the law, and they do not preserve the King's rights. Instead they loot his goods from under his nose, and put the blame on those who are innocent."

Even on his wreck of a face, Illesa could see that Kit was moved by his own rhetoric.

"The other witness in their case is also lying. I happened to see Jarryd of Longville when I was hiding in the forest on my way to Eaton Church. The Forester found him and his companion by the track to the village and confiscated their mounts. He told them they could only have them back if they brought me in. Jarryd never saw me in his life until he came to the fair posing as a customer. He is a false witness coerced to perjure himself."

A sound between a growl and a cheer came from the crowd.

"Silence!" shouted the Steward. "And what of the final charge: that you rendered one of the Forester's men insensible with one of your hammers?"

"I don't know anything about that. I didn't see any of his men, other than Jarryd, until I felt my lord's blade on my neck by the ale tent. I was with my fellow stall holders and the esteemed officials of the fair all the time." Kit winked at the Lord of the Taps as much as he could with his swollen eye.

"He has an accomplice," the Forester stated coldly, looking at Illesa. "And I know where to find him."

"My lord?" the Steward said, looking bemused.

"Take control of this court, Steward, or I will do it for you. Make your judgment. This is not a mummers' play for entertainment of the crowd, man!"

"My lord, there are procedures to be gone through," the Steward said in an undertone. "Please be patient. The members of the court must have their say." He stood up and raised his voice.

"Men of the court, the man who stands before you is accused of a serious crime, the penalty is death by hanging. Will all those who find Christopher Arrowsmith guilty of poaching and bodily harm of the King's men say 'Aye'."

Six members of the court raised their voices. Illesa recognised one from the ale tent and another was the fair clerk, the rest were unknown to her.

The Steward looked pleased.

"I have the casting vote and I too find Christopher Arrowsmith guilty. Step forward, man."

"Forgive me, Steward." Richard rose to his feet. "Would it be permitted for me to speak? Is it not so that in the case of poaching, the accused can either be hanged or, if they are able to find twelve bondsmen, they may be released subject to not being found in the King's Forests again? I have been in hundred courts where this was done. The man is entitled to enquire for bondsmen as the law permits."

The noise from the crowd grew, as the Steward struggled to speak.

"Yes, Sir Richard, that is so. This man is not known in these parts, and I assumed that he would not have twelve bondsmen to call upon."

Richard bowed slightly to the Steward.

"Of course that is a fair assumption, but perhaps I should have mentioned that this man is known to me. Indeed we were serving in the King's forces together on numerous occasions."

"What is this?" The Forester rose to his feet. "What game are you playing, Burnel?"

"I am not playing any game, my lord," he said, looking at him with his head cocked to one side. "Although, I could ask you the same thing. I am sure my cousin Robert, the King's closest adviser, the Chancellor and Bishop of Bath and Wells, would be interested in hearing the accusations made against you." He paused. "But perhaps at another time. I am here to speak on behalf of Christopher Arrowsmith, who I know to be brave on the battlefield and faithful to his lord. His word can be trusted."

"What took you so long?" Kit mouthed at Richard.

The Forester leant over and whispered angrily in the Steward's ear. The Steward stood up and addressed the crowd.

"The defendant has been found guilty by a majority of the court. But he also has one who would vouch for him. Eleven more men must come forward and swear a bond for the defendant if he is to be released from the penalty of death. The bond is set at four shillings from each man."

Kit's face fell.

A great noise went up. Lyttle and Tom were on their feet with the rest of the court, and the crowd surged forward.

"Four shillings? That's more like a king's ransom, Steward," Richard said over the noise.

"It is the plaintiff's prerogative to set the bond, within reason of course."

"Of course. I should have remembered that."

"Silence!" the Steward roared. This had little effect. Illesa saw Tom gathering a group of men around him. Lyttle was red faced with the effect of his outrage. Kit was looking around the crowd desperately trying to catch the eye of his new friends. Illesa gripped the back of Richard's chair. He beckoned and she knelt by his side.

"It's not over yet," he said, seeing her white face.

"What can we do? The price is too high. I only have enough coin to pay for five men."

"Quick, go round and find as many men as you can, guarantee them the payment of four shillings as soon as court ends, if they will swear the bond. I will stand the rest of the cost."

"Yes, sir." She went into the crowd looking for familiar faces. The Steward was calling for the guards.

"Master, Sir Richard guarantees you four shillings if you will swear for Arrowsmith," she whispered in the ear of one of the iron row smiths she recognised. He turned in incomprehension, and then saw her and smiled, nodding.

"Tell the others!" she said, moving to the next group. But she had only just spoken to the first man in that group, when the guards from the tower rushed into the courtyard and began advancing on the crowd. One drunken man who didn't notice them was knocked on the head with the hilt of a sword. There was an almost immediate hush.

"You will all be ejected from this court if anyone disrupts proceedings again!" shouted the Steward, his jowls shaking.

Illesa wove back towards the table, while the crowd was pushed away from the benches by the line of armed guards.

"Anyone willing to swear a bond for Christopher Arrowsmith for the amount of four shillings is to come forward to the bench now!" the Steward bellowed. "Let them through, guards."

Illesa craned her neck for any movement in the crowd. Lyttle came through the line of guards, and Tom stood up from the court bench with the Lord of the Taps beside him.

"Only four including you," she whispered.

Two more men pushed forward, the ones she had spoken to and promised money, and Reg came out from the other side of the crowd, making seven. There were cries of more names, and two young men were pushed forward.

"You have nine men, are there any more?" cried the Steward.

Tom's voice seemed to answer.

"Walter, come here!"

A man eventually came through the crowd, his face caught between embarrassment and anger.

"Swear for him and I will write off what you owe to me," Tom said to him.

"You still have only ten," the Steward said.

Sir Richard bent close to the Steward's ear.

"But Steward, there is you as well. You are in the employ of the Burnel family. You want to keep your job, don't you? If you swear for this man, I will give you a large Christmas donation and recommend to Sir Hugh that you are a man of integrity and one he can trust with his estate."

"Yes, Sir Richard, but . . . " the Steward began, looking sideways at the Forester.

"Don't worry about him. I will take care of it."

The Steward nodded assent, sweating and pale.

"But there is one more needed, sir. You only have eleven."

Sir Richard stood up.

"Men of Rushbury, if you wish to swear a bond for this innocent man come forward! His life is at stake." He looked intently round the crowd and the court, but no one would meet his eye. They didn't want to face the punishment afterwards that the Forester would most certainly mete out. A low murmur started that got louder and louder.

"Hang him, hang him, hang him."

The Forester stood up, a thin smile stretching his lips. He opened his mouth to speak.

"I will swear," Illesa shouted.

The noise from the crowd continued. No one had heard her.

"I will swear!" Illesa shouted again. "I am the twelfth!"

"Silence!" the Steward shouted. "Guards arrest the first one to speak!" He took a big gulp of wine and turned to Illesa who was standing by Richard's chair. "You are a page, unless you are of your majority, you cannot swear. State your age and your name."

"This is William Burnel, nephew to my cousin, Philip," Sir Richard interjected. "He has been in my employ for a year. I will guarantee that he is past his majority and free to swear if it is his will to do so."

"It is, sir," said Illesa.

"Guards, eject the crowd!" the Steward ordered, banging on the table. "We have our twelfth man." The crowd screamed and swore as the guards crushed them through the small gateway.

"Steward, you are being taken for a fool," said the Forester through his teeth. "I have seen this boy before. He is not Sir Richard's page; he is an accomplice of the accused."

"Are you calling me a liar?" asked Sir Richard, his voice light, almost casual, as he got up from his chair and took two paces towards the Forester.

The Forester reached forward to grab Illesa's arm.

"If this is the quality of servant you employ, I pity you. He doesn't even look like a page," he said squeezing her arm tightly. "I saw him dressed as a monk at the church in Eaton, pretending to be a holy brother. I saw this same boy yesterday dressed in rags at the fair. He is an outlaw like Arrowsmith and cannot swear a bond, and you, Sir Richard, are a liar!"

"Take your hands off my servant," Sir Richard said, fingering his sword hilt.

The Forester pushed Illesa to the ground, releasing her arm, and drew his sword from its sheath. Lyttle, Tom and Reg drew their daggers.

"My lord," Sir Richard said, drawing his sword, "let us conclude this legally. It would be a shame if you lost your life over such a small matter."

The Forester looked around, but his man Jarryd had been ejected with the rest of the crowd. He sheathed his weapon.

"Steward, perform the bond," said Sir Richard, sheathing his own sword. The Steward, who had backed away from the fray, now came forward.

"We must have a holy book to swear on," he said, breathing hard.

"A bond not sworn on a holy book would be neither legal nor binding," said the Forester, staring at Sir Richard. "I will not accept it."

"Of course not, my lord," Sir Richard said, smiling back at him. "God and Saint Margaret provide what is needed for those who have faith. I have a book with me, by chance. William, bring my bag." It took Illesa a moment to understand. She went to his chair and returned with the tooled leather saddlebag.

"Here, come and see." Sir Richard removed the book and unwrapped its cloth covering. The men crowded forward around the table. Sir Richard held it up, showing the image of the saint on the final page, and Kit's face went white. Every man, but the Forester, crossed himself.

"We will swear the bond by Saint Margaret on her Feast Day, and that will certainly be both legal and binding," Richard said, with some satisfaction.

Chapter XX
Rushbury Manor

Never was a bond sworn with more fervour. The propitious appearance of the book of Saint Margaret at the fair in her honour affected both men and officers. The clerk was ordered to bring forward a sheet of parchment and record the conditions of the bond. The twelve men were herded in front of it to make their mark. Illesa managed to imitate Sir Richard's letters, the quill slippery in her hand. Coin was counted and handed over. She stood behind Sir Richard feeling dizzy. It was too strange.

Lyttle looked like a boy at the feast table.

"That's it done! You're a free man now," he said, grinning at Kit.

The Steward held the parchment up for all to see and prepared to speak.

"Christopher Arrowsmith, you are forbidden from entering the King's demesne, known as the Long Forest, on any business. If you are found there, you will be hanged and your bondsmen will be liable again for this debt. Do you understand the restrictions placed upon you?"

"Yes, Master Steward. I will never knowingly set foot in the Lord Forester's demesne again, upon my word," Kit said, keeping his eyes lowered.

"There is another case for the court to hear, good sirs," said the Steward, sitting down heavily. "A minor matter of incorrect weights being used by one of the merchants. Of course you may stay, if you so choose." The men of the court were standing in small groups. Someone had brought them leather mugs of ale, and several people were laughing loudly.

"I doubt that any more business will be concluded today, Steward," said Sir Richard slapping him on the back. "Order Master Arrowsmith to be released and we will entertain the Lord Forester handsomely in the hall," he said bowing towards him. "There is plenty more of this fine wine, is there not?" Sir Richard raised a cup and drained it, nodding Illesa toward the flagon.

The Forester looked at Sir Richard with naked hatred, while a guard unchained Kit's wrists. Giles Forester picked up his wine goblet and threw it at the manor wall. The sound of glass on stone

198

silenced the crowd of drinkers. He covered the three paces to Kit quickly and pulled him close to his face by the neck of his tunic. Illesa shot forward, but her arm was wrenched as Sir Richard held it tight.

"Be still," he whispered through his teeth. The Forester was speaking, his dagger in its sheath. Illesa tried to hear over the blood rushing in her ears.

"I will never lose track of you, boy. I keep the borders of my demesne, and I will know if you ever set one foot inside it. Did you know that your fine courser is in the hands of Sir Perkyn, the outlaw? I wonder how you are going to get him back." He spat on the ground by Kit's feet and pushed his way through the silent men and out of the yard.

Kit pulled a face and straightened his tunic. He managed a smile as he approached Sir Richard.

"I owe you my life and my thanks," he said, bowing.

"Stop being so careless with it then. Anyone would think you were confident of your place in heaven." Richard clapped him on the back. "Come, let's leave the Steward to his burden of justice and go inside. You could do with some of William's physic."

"Who?" asked Kit.

"My page, he is a master of healing."

"Ah yes, of course. I remember," he said, as she held the hall door open for them. "Good old William."

The shutters were open and motes of dust floated across the sunlight. Richard looked around at the bare walls, the dusty tables and benches. He clapped his hands together and shouted for a servant.

"I think we will be more comfortable in the solar," he said in an undertone. "And we will not be overheard." A kitchen boy appeared at the door, his apron stained with blood.

"Yes sir?"

"Instruct the solar to be prepared, boy. We need food and drink, and wine for wounds."

Eventually they were admitted to the solar, the door was shut and there was food, including a whole roast chicken. The table had only been set for two with pewter plates. Kit brought a chair from the other side of the room and sat Illesa down in it.

"Here we are, my girl. You can be yourself for a while, and not before time. You make the most appalling pageboy I have ever seen; much too tall, and you get distracted from your duties by the least little drama."

Illesa swiped at him, but she couldn't stop smiling, and he bent over and kissed her cheek.

"You're the first page I've ever kissed!"

"Stop it, Kit. Someone might hear. We don't need more trouble."

"There won't be any trouble now that we have our great protector!" Kit proclaimed, slapping Richard on the back. He sat down next to her, still smiling. "So when are you going to return to the womanly sex? I think it would be wise, although you make a fine boy in many ways: valiant, a good horseman, faithful messenger of diverse uses to all apparently," he said, looking at Sir Richard as he counted on his fingers.

"Yes, she does," said Richard thoughtfully. "But I think before we tease her any more, we should give thanks for your life and our food and eat. No sense can be spoken on an empty stomach."

"Yes, sir," Kit said, winking his swollen eye at Illesa. They said very little until the plates were clean, the chicken a carcass and the flagon of wine almost empty. Her limbs were heavy, but Illesa was so happy she did not want to sleep. She held out her hand on the table to Kit and he took it in his big palm.

"Mother would be so glad we are here together," she said with difficulty. She was only used to ale, and the wine was strong. "I'm sure this will ease her suffering in purgatory."

"Now Illesa, let's not talk about that," Kit said, removing his hand. "You will only get upset again. I want to know how you came to be here, Sir Richard. Illesa told me you were injured by thieves and had to recover at Stoke de Say."

"Even the roads near the towns are no longer safe," Sir Richard said, stabbing his knife into the oak board of the table. "Illesa's horse was the bait. Have you seen it? It's a rare beauty."

"No, I don't even know how she came to have it."

"Well, if you took time to ask me instead of constantly getting arrested, I would gladly tell the tale," Illesa said, banging the plates as she stacked them in front of her.

"I'm not arrested now, am I? It has all turned out well, except my face may never be the same. We must make a sight! Illesa and I make you look handsome for a change, Sir Richard," Kit said with a mock bow.

"You have Sir Richard to thank for your life, Kit. He has been badly hurt on your account," Illesa broke in. "And there are lots of other people who have put themselves out for you like Master Lyttle and Tom the stable master. You should not be so insolent."

Richard's face was amused. Kit bit his lip.

"You are right of course. I have been a fool and should not insult my betters. Sir Richard, you have always been, and always will be, as handsome as Lancelot and twice as good under the covers." They were barely controlling their laughter.

"God has tried to teach you humility, Kit. If you haven't learnt the lesson, you will be taught it again. If I were you, I would be grateful you still have your life and a chance to repent." She regretted the words as soon as she finished. Her cheeks burned. In her own clothes, she would not feel so ridiculous.

"Father Osbert was right, the nunnery is the best place for you, Illesa, old girl. But you'll have to change your dress first," Kit said, giggling. "What do I have to repent about anyway, dear sister? Tell me that? I was imprisoned under a false charge. It is the Forester and his men who deserve the fires of hell, not me."

"I can think of a few things, actually," said Sir Richard. "The daughter of that tavern keeper, for example."

"I didn't hear her complaining," Kit grinned.

"She did the next day when she tried me."

"You two are disgusting," Illesa said, getting up from the table and going to the window seat.

It was a few moments before either man was able to speak.

"You are right again, Illesa," Richard said. "We have been too long with only soldiers and ruffians for company. Kit, you need to change your ways and try to find a suitable husband for your fine looking sister. She deserves better than you."

"Yes, Sir Richard, I shall begin the search immediately." He assumed a town crier's pose. "Anyone want this beautiful girl, all decked in silks and pearls?"

"Hold your peace, Kit," Illesa said. Tears were threatening to spill down her cheeks. "Can't you be serious for one minute."

"This is serious, actually," remarked Sir Richard. "We will need to acquire some suitable clothes for you. I don't think we can risk you appearing as a boy again. You were far too much in the public eye, and someone will go to the Forester and try to win his favour by turning you in for the wounding of his man."

Kit looked at her, the chicken leg bone half way to his mouth.

"That was you, was it? I'll have to watch my step obviously, now I know what to expect when you get angry."

"You left me alone and went off drinking with your friends," Illesa said. "Destrey came after me with a falchion. I was lucky not to be gutted. Now will you stop joking for one minute and think about someone other than yourself?"

There was a long, awkward silence. Sir Richard filled the cups with the last of the wine.

"Sorry, Sweetheart. I'm no good, I know," Kit said quietly, looking at his hands. She did not reply.

Sir Richard crossed his feet on the table.

"Stick to the forge, Kit. You're no good at bantering with the ladies."

Kit's swollen face tried to smile.

"Come on, I'll treat your wounds before your face gets stuck that way," Illesa said, picking up the jug of vinegar and reaching for her pack. While she was working on Kit, Sir Richard summoned a servant and ordered more Gascon wine. He sat with his feet on the table, idly playing with the stem of his empty goblet.

Kit did not make a good patient. She finished treating his injuries as quickly as possible, ignoring his groans. He got up fast and almost ran to the privy. The room was silent. Sir Richard was watching her as she folded the cloths. His face was slack, and the scar stood out white against his red cheek, but his eye was sharply focused.

"Would you like me to dress your wound, sir?" she asked.

"I'd be glad of your attention," he said and pulled his belt loose from the buckle.

The servant returned carrying a flagon of wine and a jug of ale. Illesa waited for him to shut the door behind him and then poured wine in Sir Richard's cup. He would need something to dull the pain. The late afternoon sun was shining through the windows, reflecting on the glass and glazed jugs. It caught the silk threads of Richard's surcoat and the even profile of his nose and mouth.

She knelt by the chair and began removing the bandage. It was stiff with blood, but there was no sign of pus.

"It is healing well," she said. "Is it giving you much pain?"

"Only when you prod it like that," he said, wincing.

"Sorry, sir." She covered the wound with the vervain ointment and pressed a new bandage pad over it. Then taking the long strips of cloth, she began to secure it. Richard put his hand over hers.

"Illesa."

She looked up and met his gaze, and looked quickly down again. He did not release her hand.

"Have I tied it too tight, sir?"

He moved her hand until it was on the bare skin by his hipbone.

"I am in need of your company," he said.

"Sir, I cannot," she said, pulling her hand away and sitting back on her haunches. Her breathing was stifled and she felt very hot. He reached out and took her hand again, playing with the fingers, putting them to his lips.

"I cannot," she said, getting up suddenly. She grabbed the pack of herbs and went over to the window seat.

He reached for his cup and drank it dry.

"That is not the gratitude I was expecting."

"Kit will be coming back," she whispered.

"Is that all that is worrying you? It is easily remedied."

"No, sir."

"You think it would be a sin."

"It is."

"It is a very common sin, and one that could make your life much more comfortable," he said, as he pulled his belt tight around his hips.

"But you do not want to marry me, sir," Illesa said, looking out of the window.

"I cannot marry you even if I wanted to, girl! My marriage or lack thereof is something decided by Uncle Robert." He took his knife from the table and began cleaning his fingernails. "My cousin Philip was married to Maud FitzAlan last year. They paid my uncle two thousand marks, which should have been a warning to anyone. I had to keep court with them this summer at Clun, so I know her very well. They will find me someone with less money, and possibly less charm, as I have very few virtues left. However," he said, putting his knife down with deliberation, "I would like your regular company. You would have a comfortable home, enough to eat every day and fine clothes. Your beauty would be given a proper setting."

The door opened and Kit came in, looking better. He sat down at the table and poured some more wine in his cup.

"I'm starving, let's get some more food."

"Call the boy yourself. I have been bandaged and need to stay put; so says the physic," Sir Richard said, smiling wickedly at Illesa.

"You could make some money that way, you know," Kit said, going to the door. "Start making the salves like Mother did and sell them at the fairs."

"Tomorrow I have to take the horse back to the smith in Wenlock," Illesa said rubbing her temple. Her head was aching and her mouth was dry. "I cannot think about doing anything else until she is returned."

"You can't go alone," Richard and Kit said in unison.

Chapter XXI
The 21st day of July, 1284

"You don't owe me anything. Sir Richard has paid," Tom said when Illesa held out the coin.

She put the money back in her pack as Tom led Jezebel to the gate. The strong morning sun was playing on the horse's well-brushed coat. Illesa followed them, slowly. Everything was so complicated today. The joy she'd felt when Kit was freed had been short lived. He had not even got out of bed to see her off, whereas Sir Richard had obviously been busy since prime. Illesa took the rein from Tom's hand. He stood, waiting for her to mount.

"You don't like Sir Richard," she said, rubbing Jezebel's nose.

Tom pulled on the saddle, and ran his hands along the straps of the girth. "This one's about worn through. Mind it when you are at a gallop." He smoothed it against Jezebel's glossy coat. "It is not my place to like him or not. But you should be careful." He looked at her, one hand resting lightly on the horse's shoulder. "He has seen something he wants in you."

The blood rushed to her cheeks, and Illesa looked at the ground.

"We owe him so much now," she said. Sir Richard was accompanying her to Wenlock. He had insisted upon it. Illesa's head had been too thick to think of viable alternatives. After all the flagons of wine, Kit would have gone with her just so he could try to raid Sir Perkyn's camp for his horse. But in the end, they had convinced him that his life had cost them enough already, and he should stay out of the Forester's demesne. She and Sir Richard had developed an uneasy alliance in that regard.

"All the more reason to be wary," Tom said. "He is used to wealth and what it can buy."

Jezebel nudged Illesa's shoulder and stamped her hoof.

"Always wanting to get going, that one." Tom gave Jezebel a slap on the rump. "Be careful, though. I saw that Forester's man, the witness, hanging around. Probably been told to follow you and Kit."

Jarryd. Of course. The Forester would never let Kit go that easily. He would have a plan to get him, somehow.

"But I believe I am to have the pleasure of your brother's company for a while longer," Tom said.

"It's too risky for him to come to Wenlock. Can you keep him out of trouble for me?" Illesa asked.

"It would take a heaven full of saints to do that, but I'll try to keep him busy and too tired for trouble. There is plenty of clearing up to do."

She led Jezebel through the gate and put her foot in the stirrup.

"When do you return?" he asked, giving her a practised push into the saddle.

"I don't know. I have to go somewhere else first." Illesa adjusted the reins and pulled Jezebel round. Her stomach was turning somersaults, either from too much wine or the fear that had been growing in her gut since Richard's insistence that she go to Acton, and his proposition.

Tom stood in shadow by the gate.

"Don't let Kit leave before I get back," Illesa said, trying to smile.

Tom raised his eyebrows and ran his hand through his hair.

"I will do my best."

"God keep you," she called, and urged Jezebel into a trot, eastwards down the empty track. In only a few moments, she had crossed the bridge and drawn to a halt beside Sir Richard on Buskins.

"What took you so long? That stable master is slow, eh? Didn't have her ready in time?" Richard adjusted his scabbard. He was wearing a new surcoat, and his beard was freshly trimmed. Her own appearance was the same as, if not worse than, the day before. By the time she had been woken, there was no time to wash.

"No, it was me," Illesa said.

"Come on, girl, let's do your duty. Such a shame to have to take this horse back."

"You don't have to come with me, sir."

He glanced at her, his expression amused.

"Forgive me if I don't trust you to the outlaws and robbers of the forest. Besides, we are going on to Acton afterwards, or had you forgotten? You had a bit too much wine, perhaps?" They trotted side by side for a while. "We can get you a nice palfrey in Wenlock so we can ride on to Acton; something more suited to a respectable woman. They have a good horse trader there, or so I've been told."

"Sir Richard, thank you for paying for Jezebel's stabling, but I have the money and I wish you would let me pay you for it," Illesa said, without looking at him.

"What, have my own money back? Don't be a fool. It was nothing." He sounded almost angry.

They spoke no more for almost an hour, the beat of hooves filling the silence. When they came to the point where the path diverged, they stopped to water the horses at a shallow stream. Richard dismounted, grimacing.

"How is your wound?" she asked, and immediately regretted the choice of topic.

"That second bandage you put on yesterday is much better," he said, fumbling in his saddlebag for the wineskin. He held it out to her but she shook her head. "The people at Stoke de Say were useless. I'd take you into battle with me and my men any day, you'd be better than even the King's surgeon and much nicer to look at."

Illesa was silent. Her mind was full of the feel of his skin.

"Would you like that?" he asked, laughing. The horses were side by side at the edge of the stream, shaking their heads against the flies. Illesa walked away from him. She found a stone and sat down.

"I should hate it," she said, keeping her eyes on the water. "You might enjoy bloodshed, but I do not. My mother cursed your Welsh war. You invade our neighbours and bring grief to so many, and all for meaningless treaties that are broken over and over." She drew breath. "Anyway, I would think that you would want to stay out of battle, Sir Richard, before someone takes out your other eye."

Her heart was racing. She did not look up until he spoke.

"You should watch your tongue." The anger was just beginning to inflame his cheeks. He grabbed Buskins' reins and backed him away from the stream.

"Someone has to talk sense to you. I am not a squire or a knight or a surgeon, and I never want to be."

Sir Richard stood by his horse, staring at her. The silence was terrible. She was almost grateful when he spoke.

"If I didn't go to war, what should I do, in your opinion? You are quick with your judgments, and your experience of the world is obviously profound, so do tell me of all the choices open to me," he said, standing rigid by his horse. "I am a son of the impoverished elder branch of the family. I was deemed unsuited to the brotherhood of the Church, for which I am grateful. But with little land of my own and insufficient funds to pay for others to attend battle for me, tell me how I am to conduct myself properly when the King calls us to fight. I have been trained to do nothing else." He paused. "I must fulfil my duties as a knight, even if they destroy my body and endanger my soul."

The colour had drained from his face, as if he had been bled. Perhaps the insult had been enough to bring him to his senses.

"I spoke foolishly. Forgive me," Illesa said.

The air was full of running water and the drone of flies. Richard stared at the stream.

"Your brother has the best life of all, in a way. He can earn his keep honestly, when he chooses to. He is not obliged to go to war."

"But he loves it. And you say he is good at it," Illesa said. "No one will stop him from going back."

Richard was silent for several moments. When he spoke again, he kept his face turned away.

"I don't know why you are angry with me, girl. I've done my best to help you and your brother, at considerable personal expense. And I've offered you honour and security. You could have a future of good food and comfort. Do you think your parents would have rather seen you starve or labour in the fields behind the plough than be the consort of a knight?"

Illesa watched the drops of water falling from Jezebel's mouth catch the sunlight. She knew her mother still watched her from purgatory. Perhaps Illesa's real father had offered Ursula a similar situation. But it was not worth pointing this out to Sir Richard, he would only turn it to his advantage.

"Sir, I am grateful for your interest and will pray to God to bless you for your help, but your regard for me will soon pass. You will tire of me quickly and I will be left with nothing."

Sir Richard sighed impatiently.

"Don't be silly, girl."

"You don't know me. You have never even seen me as a woman."

208

"You are young and pretty and you have spirit. That is enough for me to know for now. I think we are well matched. I have a comfortable manor at Langley where you may await me. I will be gone perhaps two weeks at the Tournament. Now, will you accept that or do you want a simpering lover from a courtly tale?"

His face was vulnerable. She looked away.

"I am very grateful to you, sir," Illesa said, steadying her voice. "But I cannot take what you are offering."

She kept her eyes on his feet. He did not move or speak for an eternity. When he put his foot in the stirrup, the tension broke, leaving her with shaking hands.

"Very well, I will not force you," he said swinging into his saddle. "If you think starvation or gaol is preferable to what I offer you."

She mounted Jezebel and followed him back to the track. The path they took meandered along the valley: to the right the bristling Long Forest, to the left the hills of the west, in front of them Mount Gilbert reared up and a thin line of black smoke rose from the woodland.

"Do you know this road?" Illesa asked, after a while.

"Yes, it is safe enough," Richard replied, curtly.

After another uncomfortable silence, he turned in his saddle.

"I would keep you well, Illesa. I thought you would believe that after all the things I have done to help your brother."

"I'm sure you are an honourable man, sir."

"So what is the matter? We both know that the proscriptions of the church are flexible in this regard. Do you find me ugly?"

"No, Sir Richard."

"I have done nothing but expend effort and coin on your behalf since you arrived in Clun," he reproached. "You have given me many reasons to suspect you of theft, but I have not taken you to the bailiff." He was winding the rein tightly around his knuckles.

He could still do that, and worse, if he so chose. They both knew it.

"You have been restrained as the best of knights should be. I understand why Kit trusts you," Illesa said, keeping her eyes on the road. "You have shared the trial of battle and fought for each other. Despite your wealth and his poverty, you are equals in that regard." She could not look at him and speak. Her words had to be carefully chosen. "When we were attacked by the thieves and you found the book, you accused me of trying to trick you and treated me like a felon. You did not trust me, and why should you? You don't know me. If I were dressed as an ordinary woman from my village, you would want none of me." Illesa cleared her throat. She could feel his eyes on her. "I am unnatural dressed as I am, and that is why you are fascinated. But all I want is to go back to what I was. I am not a criminal or a whore or a lady from a story. What you desire is not what I am. You would tire of me after a week," Illesa finished. She was short of breath, as if she had just climbed a steep hill.

"You are wrong." His voice was softer than before.

"Men do not see the future as women do. We look into the next generation. Men see only tomorrow," Illesa said and met his gaze.

He smiled then, his broad smile of recognition. He jerked the reins and pulled Buskins up next to Jezebel.

"Leaving aside your slander of men, which may contain a grain of truth, you are claiming that you will be happy to put on the clothes of a villager and return to your plot of land, and the ploughing and bearing. Is that what you really think you are?"

She did not answer.

"I think we both know that is not the case. You do not know what a different life is open to you because you have never seen it. I can show it to you, and then, my girl, you will find that you are less eager to return to the custom of the earth."

Dry-mouthed, she followed him along the broadening track. His words and her responses chased each other in her head. Buskins was already fifty paces away when she realised he was galloping. She urged Jezebel after him, concentrating only on staying in the saddle.

When they came into Wenlock around nones, Illesa's head was throbbing with tension. Jezebel's excitement was obvious as they approached the forge. She whinnied when they came into the yard, and the smith looked up from his anvil, a smile on his fire-reddened face. He put his hammer down and came out to meet them.

"God save you! You've made it back, my girl." He pulled her down from Jezebel's back. "I've been that worried for you, I have."

She looked up at him, unable to return his grin.

"Yes, master. This is Sir Richard Burnel."

John made an adequate bow, considering Jezebel was nosing his ear.

"God save you, sir," he laughed, holding his wide palm under the horse's nose. "Please come in. I must hear all about your journey. And your brother, Illesa, I hope he is free now?"

Sir Richard made a slight bow.

"I give you thanks, but I have business in the town. Illesa will tell you the tale." He turned to her, frowning. "I will bring women's garments and collect you at prime."

"Yes, sir."

They watched him mount, his face set, as he trotted down the lane towards the noise of the town church bells.

"You've had a few adventures, I'll warrant," the smith said when Richard was gone. "Get some water for the horse and we'll sit and talk by the wall."

Illesa took the bucket and went to the well. When Jezebel was comfortable in her stall, she sat on the bench and leant back against the warm stone of the cottage. The smith sat down a short distance away from her.

"So, before you tell me the story, perhaps you can explain this strange thing to me. Yesterday evening, I was locking up the forge, when a boy, no more than ten or so, skinny as a snake and road worn, walked up to me. Greeted me most politely and asked me if I happened to be the smith of Wenlock. I said yes I was and what did he want with me. He begged my pardon, and said could he enquire as to whether I owned a horse; a bay called Jezebel. I said yes, what's it to you boy, and he said thank you sir, I will come back when she does. Then he disappeared off into nowhere and I haven't seen him since. So I wasn't a bit surprised when you rode up just now. I thought you'd be on your way, if you were still in possession of her. But who is this boy and what's he want, eh? Someone you know?"

Illesa looked at her palms. They were lined with grime.

"Yes, I'm afraid I do know him. I shouldn't have told him about you, but I never thought he would come all this way."

"Well, who is he, girl? Spit it out. What have you gone and done?" John the smith said, but there was no malice in his voice.

"His name is William. He's an orphan I met in Clun, the son of the former brewer at the White Hart Inn. He has worked in the stables there since his father died and earns some extra betraying travellers to the horse thieves working for the masters of Billings Ring."

John's breath whistled across his teeth.

"Oh, I see. But he can't be expecting to bring that gang over here. Their base is in the west. We have our own robbers here, and I expect they'd give the competition a good hiding."

I don't think he'll be working for them any more. Two of them followed us to steal Jezebel when we left Clun, but Sir Richard fought and killed them both. William is out of work now."

"So why is he here? What does he want with me?"

"He loves horses. He has a gift for looking after them, and he's a good rider. He took a liking to Jezebel. I suppose he had nothing left to lose, so he thought he would come here to find her."

"What does he think he's going to do, marry her? Is he a fool?"

"No," Illesa laughed. "He's actually very clever, he found me out in no time. He could make a very good stable boy, or apprentice. But it's a risk. He's mad about horses." She thought for a minute. "And he will do anything to survive."

"I expect he'll turn up any time now. If he came so far, he'll know when she's returned, right enough," he said.

"Yes, I wouldn't be surprised if he were hiding within earshot right now," said Illesa raising her voice slightly.

"Do you think so?" John said, raising his. "If he's messed about with my things, he'll have me and my hand to answer to. Come on, let's find some food."

They were getting up to go in when Jezebel whickered.

"I'll go and look," the smith said.

Illesa waited by the door while he went into the stable. After only a moment, he came out holding William by the arm. He was thinner than ever and seemed to have a broken nose.

"This the boy you met, is it?"

"That's him," she agreed. William smiled uneasily.

After they had eaten and Illesa had told the story of Kit's trial, the smith gestured for her to follow him outside. William had eaten his pottage and bread; the bowl was clean, and they found him back in the stable, brushing Jezebel's already shining coat.

"You've had a good meal and a look at the horse. Be off with you," the smith said.

"Get yourself indoors and get some sleep, you look like death. I'll keep an eye on the new arrival in the stable."

"I don't want to trouble you. I can pay for a bed and food by the way. I've got some coins now," Illesa said, finding her purse.

"Don't be foolish. Save your money. Not only have you brought Jezebel back, but complete with a groom as well. That's worth a few meals."

William opened his eyes wide.

"Master, I am very good with horses, I can look after her r well."

"I only have one horse and a donkey. I can look after th myself."

"I'm willing to do anything, sir, wood chopping, hoei hammering." His eyes had an excited gleam. "I don't eat much. sleep in the stable, keep an eye on things."

"I have heard about the way you keep an eye on things. N be on your way."

"But master, I don't work for them any more. I only help them 'cause they forced me. They had my sister as a servant. Sa I'd got to help them on account of her. The chief said he would u her if I didn't. She was only nine, so I had to do it."

"So, your sister works for outlaws and you are an informe Not the sort of person to trust."

"But sir, you can trust me now. My sister's dead. I went to fin her after the Billings men were killed. I knew the chief would tak it out on her, but they found me outside the wall and beat me up Then they told me she was dead. Died in the spring. They wouldn' say how she died. Don't even know where they buried her.' William's fists were white knuckled by his sides.

The smith regarded him for a long moment in silence.

"What was your sister's name?"

"Alice."

"How old are you?"

"Eleven, I think."

"You can stay for a week. If I'm satisfied with your work, I wil keep you on as an apprentice. Any lying, stealing or other sins and will personally whip you and take you to the bailiff."

"Yes, master." He shot a grin at Illesa.

"You can start by cleaning the pots."

William nodded and headed for the back yard. Illesa strok Jezebel's nose.

"I hope you don't regret that, Master Smith."

"It'll be good to have a child here, even if he is older than looks," he said, rubbing his beard.

"He has a way of winning people round," Illesa said, yawned.

Chapter XXII
The 22nd day of July, 1284

When Sir Richard arrived the next morning, a black palfrey was trotting behind Buskins on a long rein. He nodded to the smith and dismounted, giving Illesa a cursory glance.

"Not what you're used to, but she should carry you well enough. And I found you some decent garments. Go and transform yourself," he said, throwing a bundle of cloth at her. She caught it and opened her mouth to speak, but he was striding towards the forge leading the horse. The bundle was tied with a plaited length of wool. There was no knowing what kind of finery he would have chosen for her. Illesa went inside and closed the shutter. In the wrapping, folded neatly, were a simple linen smock and a plain green tunic of finely woven wool. The headdress and veil were soft and white, with an aroma of sweet woodruff. To her surprise, they fitted her quite well.

When she came out of the house, Sir Richard and the smith were deep in conversation by the stable door. The palfrey's hooves seemed to be the object of interest. Both of them stopped for a moment and looked at her. She tried not to fidget with the veil. The smith coughed.

"You have a good mount here. The shoes will need changing after your ride, but otherwise Sir Richard has chosen well," the smith declared, giving the left hind shoe a final tap. "Now be off, we've detained the good man too long already, he has a Tourney to attend."

Richard bowed his head slightly.

"Not at all."

"You'll come back, won't you," he said shaking Illesa's shoulder. "Come and check up on that boy." He helped her mount the passive horse.

"What is this horse's name?" she asked, when she had sorted out her skirts.

"Nellie," Richard said. "She's less bold than you're used to."

"Well, I can't do much in these skirts, so that's a mercy," Illesa said, under her breath.

The smith had already gone back to his forge and there was no sign of William, thankfully. Sir Richard would probably hang him on sight. They trotted out on the Shrewsbury road, joining a steady stream of people and animals. A brisk wind was blowing from the west and the far hills were covered in dark grey cloud.

"I expect we will have to go at a sedate pace now that I am travelling with a woman."

Illesa did not reply. She kicked Nellie's side, and the palfrey broke into a reluctant canter.

"Fortunately, it's not far to Acton," Richard said, looking at the bank of cloud that reared up like a black wall on the western horizon. They dropped off the steep slope of the Long Forest into wide Ape Dale.

Richard turned slightly and inclined his head.

"You make a very respectable lady, Mistress."

"I can't get used to this veil, its always whipping around in the wind," she said, fighting to get it under control.

"You'll like it even more when it is wet," Richard said, as the first heavy rain began to fall. By the time they got to Acton, they were soaked through and the clouds were blowing away. They dismounted at the manor and the horses shook their manes simultaneously sending off a shower of shining drops.

"Come, we will find out who is at home." Richard took the reins and led them through the gate towards the stables.

Illesa followed, taking off her cloak and shaking the rain from it. She shivered. The manor was made of red stone and covered in a scaffold. Builders seemed to be crawling all over the towers, hammering and manipulating pulleys for lifting the oak beams. Nearby there was an impressive tithe barn on a much larger scale than the one at Holdgate.

"The church is over there. The last time I was here they were still finishing the plastering," Richard said, pointing.

She had not noticed it, being so wide eyed at the manor. The nave, transepts and tower were built in fresh stone. The glass chancel windows were tall and shining with bright sky and white cloud. It was beautiful.

"The stable boy will take the horses." Richard tied their reins to the post in the yard. "We need refreshment."

The Steward was not in, but a servant brought them into the wide hall with large windows and new floor. Inside the hammering was even louder.

"Uncle Robert has been granted a licence to crenellate," Richard shouted. They ate their meal as quickly as possible.

"The family aren't living here during the building work. I expect they are at Langley." Richard pushed his chair away from the long oak table. "Come. We will find out whether Mother will accept visitors."

Illesa got up from the bench and followed him outside, where the wet ground steamed in the hot sun. They went through the churchyard gate and around to the north door. Above it was a freshly painted statue of Our Lady, the Christ child in her arms, his fingers making the sign of blessing. Richard opened the carved door and the air was full of aromatic wood and wax.

"No expense spared," he said, flatly.

Inside was just as impressive: the walls were covered in fine paintings and under their feet were fresh tiles, each one painted in a different design. The rood screen seemed impossibly tall and delicate, with carved leaves and branches winding upward like the Tree of Jesse. Someone was hitting a chisel with a hammer.

"Even here they are at it," Richard muttered under his breath.

"I've never seen anything like it," Illesa whispered.

"No, outside the King's palaces you probably won't. Uncle Robert has been given the King's own artisans as well as material from his forests and lands."

She walked up the nave towards the sound of the hammering. A stonemason was in the north transept, finishing the base of a piscina. He nodded at them and continued his gentle tapping. The Lady Chapel in the south transept was filled with light; the white walls decorated with beautiful red and blue roses. There was a small altar with a statue of the Virgin Mary beside it, her hands outstretched. The tallow candles in front of it had gone out. To the right of it was a tomb effigy, a small niche and, on a bench next to it, a Priest asleep in his alb and cope.

Illesa covered her mouth with her hand. He looked ridiculous, with his head resting against the stone wall, mouth open and a trickle of saliva at its corner. Richard put his finger to his lips and went towards the tomb. It was a carving of a woman, her wimple folded in the style of the older ladies of the village, but she was young and smiling. Her hands were pressed together in prayer, and under one arm she held a book. An inscription ran across the bottom of the tomb, in Latin.

"I see he has brought her here."

"Who is it?" Illesa asked, touching the book with the tip of her finger. The strap across it looked identical to the one on the Saint Margaret book.

"Lady Rose Burnel. She was the Corbet I told you of, an older sister of Thomas Corbet, and my grandmother. She died over twenty years ago, before Uncle Robert bought all these lands from my father's side of the family. She had been buried at Langley, but I see he has had her brought here to lend the place some ancestry."

"What do you know of the book she carries?"

"She was an educated and devout woman."

"It looks just like my book - the book of Saint Margaret," Illesa corrected herself. She traced her finger along the carved stone. Richard was looking at the niche just to the left of the Priest. A candle was burnt out in the socket. Below it was an inscription in French, cut into the stone of the wall.

"Le quer Dame Guiliane de Dax et le cors de s'enfant."

"I don't read French. What does it say?" Illesa asked.

"The heart of Lady Guiliane of Dax and the body of her baby."

"Who was she?"

"I don't know, I've never heard of her," Richard said, running a hand through his hair. "Dax is in Guyenne. But she must have died here to have a heart burial."

"Perhaps the Priest knows something of it? He may have been paid to say prayers for her," Illesa offered.

Sir Richard was looking at the Priest with a strange expression on his face, somewhere between disgust and satisfaction.

"I wasn't expecting to find him here after his disgrace. He attacked a man whilst drunk. Very nearly killed him. I suppose we must wake him, but it is a shame to disturb such a sleep." Richard cleared his throat loudly and shook the Priest's shoulder. The snoring stopped, and the Priest's body jerked suddenly, making Illesa jump. She got a waft of stale wine on his breath. His eyes opened slowly.

"What do you want?" he grunted.

"I am Sir Richard Burnel. You will stand and address me properly."

The Priest pushed himself to his feet slowly and straightened his cope. He was perhaps thirty years, but his hair was already

218

thinning, revealing a flaking scalp. He looked at Richard, licking his dry lips.

"Sir Richard. You were simply Richard when I last saw you, forgive me," he said bowing slightly. "And who is this?" he looked at Illesa with his prominent eyes.

"Thomas," Richard said, ignoring the Priest's question, "I thought you had been returned to the Parish of Cound after that unfortunate brawl. When were you made Vicar of this church?"

Thomas moved past them to the hanging lamp and lit a taper before he spoke.

"Last Michaelmas. I am surprised you were not told. My replacement was deemed not fit for this position." There was a brief pause. "He was lax, very lax. And so Bishop Robert saw fit to bring me back. He is ever merciful."

"In truth?"

"Family has always been important to the Bishop, as you know," the Priest said, lighting the candles in front of the statue of the Virgin.

"I trust you are grateful. You are charged with a church of rare beauty. It demands a careful and sober man of God." Richard's voice was low, but the hand gripping the leather of his belt was a fist.

Thomas coughed.

"Did the blessed Bishop of Bath and Wells send you for some reason? Are you here to pray or have you just come to admire the work?"

"I am here to see the progress of the building. The Bishop is also concerned to know that his money is being used correctly. I see no sign yet of the stones in honour of his brothers who fell at Moel-y-don."

"I see. You and your companion," he coughed again, "are here on behalf of the Bishop. He did not inform me of your visit. However, I will be delighted to help you if I can. Bishop Robert has left the management of the church to me for the past year, but if he now feels it necessary to send his cousin and a woman to investigate my works, of course, I am at your disposal." Thomas bowed.

"It is not your place to question the Bishop's orders. We have also come to speak with the Anchoress, if she is willing. But first show us the accounts and the chantry roll," Richard said.

"Of course, Sir Richard. You wish to see if the prayers have been said for the soul of your grandmother. I must assure you that, although I cannot speak for my predecessor, I have faithfully performed all the masses required." He left the chapel, his sandalled feet slapping against the tiled floor. He squeezed through a narrow door on the south side of the chancel and re-emerged with a vellum roll in his hand. "Come in here. We can spread it out on the table."

They went through the door, Richard ducking his head. The vestry table was under a high window on the far side. Thomas held the top of the scroll and unrolled it, the tremor of his hands causing the parchment to rustle.

"Here is the entry for your grandmother, Rose Burnel. She died on the Tuesday before the Feast of the Assumption. Bishop Robert, then a humble clerk in the Prince's service, paid ten marks for masses to be said for her. These were transferred to this church when her body was moved last year. You know the masses for your father are still performed at Langley, so the only other entry is from the forty-ninth year of King Henry's reign at Michaelmas when Robert Burnel paid for masses for the soul of Guiliane of Dax."

"Who was she?" Richard asked, his voice uninterested.

"Ah." He paused. "You were very young. You certainly would not have been told of it." Thomas looked amused. "I was studying in the abbey by then and Brother Bernard was involved, so I heard the whole sad story. Of course Brother Bernard did as Robert wished and arranged it all, although she was an unrepentant sinner. God is merciful, even to Priests who defy his law."

"What were you told of it?"

Thomas ran his tongue over his bottom lip.

"She was a woman Robert met in France. He brought her to London and she lived with him in his house in Westminster. When she was with child, he thought it best to send her here, to the country, for her health," he said with emphasis.

"And she died in childbirth?" Illesa asked.

The Priest turned his bulging eyes on her.

"I assume so. The baby was baptised by a midwife," he said with distaste. "Father Bernard was against that practice, as am I. Of course the woman's body was taken back to London or France. But Robert would have her heart buried in the wall of the old chapel."

"What was it named?" Illesa asked.

"Was what named?" The Priest looked up at her, frowning. "Oh, you mean the bastard? I don't know. There is no record here and no prayers for it. If the Priest had performed the baptism, it would have been recorded." Brother Thomas's eyes were fixed on the scroll. "What is your interest in this matter?"

"None, Brother. I am merely curious." Illesa smiled with effort.

"I see." He put his head on one side and looked at her, his eyes bright and alert. "A summons has been made for information about a girl your sort of age."

Silence filled the room. Illesa looked at Richard and swallowed.

"Who is the girl you speak of, and what was she summoned for?" Richard demanded.

"I did not mean to imply anything, Sir Richard," the Priest smiled, pushing the suggestion away with his palms, "but the Bailiff was given a message to watch for a vagrant girl, the daughter of a midwife in Holdgate who had fallen into debt and stolen a valuable, sacred book." He pursed his lips. "They don't yet know where the book was taken from, but all the vills have been informed from Ludlow to Shrewsbury."

"Is that so. A strange tale." Richard waved his hand in her direction. "This is Lunette the handmaiden to the Mistress of the manor of Landuc. She is my charge during her journey on her Mistress's business. I know nothing of your vagrant girl, but we will keep watch on the road."

"Landuc," the Priest shook his head. "I have not heard of it."

Richard fixed his eyes on Thomas and cleared his throat.

"I daresay you have not, never having travelled beyond this county. Now show me what payments have been made for the new effigies."

Illesa turned away and pretended to examine the carving on the stone above the doorway, her pricking hands clasped behind her back. The snare was set for her in every village, and there was no return, even to Kit in Rushbury, unless Sir Richard would stand with her in court with the book in hand and clear her name.

Lunette. Where had that name come from? She turned round to look at Richard, but he was bent over the scrolls. The Priest was watching her with his unblinking eyes. Illesa turned back quickly. She could easily have given herself away, showing so much interest in the midwife of Acton, later the midwife of Holdgate. Pray God, he did not know that connection.

Eventually Sir Richard rose, scraping the chair on the flagstones.

"I will report to the Bishop that you have kept thorough records and that the arrangements seem to be in order, Brother Thomas. I look forward to seeing the tombs completed. Just a word of advice; keep your opinions of the Bishop of Bath and Wells to yourself, and do not be quite so free with your information to people you do not know."

Brother Thomas bowed deeply, but she saw a smile twitch the corner of his mouth.

"You are ever wise, Sir Richard, like your blessed mother. Shall I enquire whether she will see you now?"

Richard nodded and the Priest went up to the chancel and pulled a small wooden shutter in the north wall. The opening behind it was only the span of a hand.

"Blessed Dame Alianore, you have visitors who beg your holy wisdom."

There was no response. The Priest called again, louder, and they heard a painful, rasping cough. He bent over and looked in through the squint.

"The Holy Anchoress is at prayer. Go to the public window outside. She may speak with you when she is finished, but she has not been well for many months. Since she sent her servant away, we haven't found a new one she would accept. It is quite possible she will ignore you completely," he said with some satisfaction, and turned his attention to trimming the lamps in the chancel.

As they walked down the nave he called after them.

"I will take my leave of you now. I must go to visit the sick at Ruckley. God be with you."

"God go with you, holy brother," Sir Richard said, inclining his head.

Richard and Illesa went through the north door into the hot afternoon. Under the eaves adjoining the chancel was the anchor hold, a narrow stone cell built against the north wall made of well-dressed stone. A low door at the base of its north wall was only large enough to allow a bucket to be pushed in or out. It was choked with weeds. In the western wall, there was a small shuttered window. Richard unlatched the shutter and the hinges squealed. An iron grille guarded the opening. Illesa stood back, wishing she had remained in the church, even if it meant an interrogation by the suspicious Priest.

"Holy Anchoress, it is your son, Richard, to beg your blessing." The sound of his voice echoed in the cave-like room. It contained only a low slatted bed and an altar with a crucifix by the east wall, illuminated by a lancet window. The black-clad figure kneeling in front of the altar did not move.

"Holy Mother, it is Richard," he called again. The figure jolted and both arms shot straight out to the sides.

"She is finishing her prayers on the five wounds of Christ," whispered Illesa. The Anchoress held her arms out, as if crucified, for several minutes. As she lowered them, her body was contorted with another coughing fit.

"Mother," Richard called out softly when she stopped.

The figure pushed itself upright and turned towards the window. In the movement of air as she limped across the small space, Illesa smelt decay. Her face was very white, almost translucent. Deep lines crossed her forehead below a threadbare wimple. The skin on her cheekbones was stretched thin and her eyes seemed to be covered in a wisp of cloud.

"Richard?"

"Yes, Holy Mother." She held two fingers through the grille, and he kissed them.

"Who has done that to you?" she said, pointing at his face.

"An enemy who died for it."

"Receive the blessing of our Saviour, and repent of your sins," she whispered.

"Through our Lord's mercy, I beg forgiveness," he replied.

"May you be washed in his blood which will save your soul from hell."

"Amen, let it be so."

"Amen," said Illesa.

"Who is that?" the Anchoress demanded, peering through the grille at Illesa. Richard gave her a warning glance.

"A devout woman who has found something that might interest you, Mother," he said, soothingly.

"Don't try to bring any more whore servants here. They are stealing everything I have," she said, and started coughing again.

"She isn't a servant, Mother. Look, I have something to show you."

He unbuckled his saddlebag and took out the book, wrapped in bright red linen. The Anchoress continued to glare at Illesa as Richard removed the coverings and held the book up to the grille.

"What is it? Hold it closer." She screwed her eyes against the light. "Open the cover, boy."

"It is the Passion of Saint Margaret. I think it belonged to the Corbet family."

She put her index finger through the grille and touched the page that was open, showing the beheading of the saint. A tremor contorted her face as she traced the golden halo.

"Show me the last page."

Richard turned to the smudged image of the saint and held it up for her to see.

"Do you know this book, Mother? It looks like the Apocalypse you used to have. The birds were done by the same hand, I'm certain."

The Anchoress turned away without a word. In the light of the narrow window, they could see her genuflecting before the altar and then bending over something that lay in front of the crucifix. Her hand turned a page.

"Those who deny these holy words will be thrown into the lake of fire," the Anchoress whispered, her voice multiplied by the close walls. "The judgment may have come upon us in this world, but the whore will suffer eternal torments for her sin."

Illesa put her hand on Richard's sleeve.

"Should I leave?"

"No, stay here," he whispered. "She knows something about it."

The Anchoress walked back towards them, her face twisted. The skin on Illesa's back crawled. The old woman looked like the tortured souls of the damned.

"Christ told Saint John what would happen to the unchaste. They will never enter his city," she said. Her eyes were not looking at them, but at the darkest part of the cell, the bare corner at the foot of her bed. "The end of days is near. The corruption of the clerics is a sign."

Richard bent forward and interrupted the Anchoress's gaze.

"Mother, did this book of Saint Margaret belong to Grandmother Rose?"

Her eyes moved to his face.

"You will be one of the soldiers of the beast piled up for the birds of the air to eat, if you do not listen and heed the warnings."

"I pray that will never be so," Richard replied, curtly. "I thought you would be glad to see this holy book again, but if it distresses you, I will take it away." He closed it carefully, his mouth set.

His mother gestured angrily at the book.

"Rose gave it to me before she died, and *I* kept it safe until *he* took it to give to his whore," she asserted, regarding her son with a hostile stare. Richard lifted his eyes from the book.

"Who gave it away?" he asked.

"The Bishop who thinks he is above God's law. Your cousin," she retorted. "At that time he was just an ambitious clerk who took his vows lightly. And he has learned nothing since then, despite his positions of honour."

Richard frowned. He looked more bemused than angry.

"Uncle Robert gave the book to Ursula?"

"Robert is not your Uncle, although he may want you to give him that honour along with your childish loyalty. Who is this Ursula you speak of?" the Anchoress snapped. "That wasn't her name."

Richard drew a long breath before speaking.

"This book was found in the croft of a woman called Ursula, after her death. She had once been the midwife of Acton."

"Why are you trying to trick me? His mistress was Guiliane, not Ursula. The little whore lost the book and brought God's wrath on us," she said and crossed herself, like a butcher slitting a carcass.

Richard and Illesa exchanged glances.

"The French woman whose heart is buried in the church?"

The Anchoress looked at Richard accusingly, gripping the iron grille with her white fingers.

"Why do you want to know of these things? You should not look on the devil's work."

"It is only because I recognised the book and wanted to know how it came to be in such hands. Can you remember when it was lost?"

"I still have my wits, boy," the holy woman said angrily. The thin skin around her eyes twitched. "I remember it clearly. Robert came riding up from London before the feast of the Ascension. The Prince had paid him well. Well enough to buy out the land from your father. He was going to enclose the wood and make a hunting park so he could impress his high-born friends."

Richard rubbed at the scar on his face.

"That was long before Edward was crowned, when Father was recovering from his wounds in Acre," he said. "I must have been eight. I remember the men building the fences."

"No," she interrupted. "You were away, learning some manners. They didn't start the fence until the following year."

"He came when I was staying with the Sandfords?"

"It was a blessing that you were. I should have sent your sister with you."

Richard swallowed. Without warning, he looked like a vulnerable little boy.

"You showed me Matilde's grave when I returned. I was so glad to be home until that moment," he whispered.

The Anchoress pressed her lips together, her eyes filling with tears.

"It was Robert's fault. He brought judgment on us. It is not for nothing that lust is a deadly sin."

Richard shifted his weight to his other foot but said nothing. The silence was filled with hammering on stone. A flush of blood coloured his mother's cheeks.

"You enjoy having his riches and favour, but they will corrupt you, boy." Saliva flicked from her pale lips. "He thought he could hide his French whore. Brought her here on a fancy palfrey, wearing enough cloth for three women. She was already in her fifth month."

"You should not slander him, Mother," Richard replied, his own colour high. "Bishop Robert paid off our debts and provided a new manor for us at Langley. He has been very generous."

The gaze she turned on him was appraising and contemptuous.

"Well, he *has* made you into a good lap dog," she began. "Don't believe everything he tells you. His side of the family have always been jealous of our connections and taken advantage of our misfortunes. Robert wanted our manor." Her eyes shifted away from them into the dark room. "He would not wait for your father to return. He had no understanding of the sacrifices necessary to take the cross and go to the East. It costs money and blood." Her breath rasped. Too much emotion would provoke another coughing attack. Illesa touched Richard's arm, and he let out his breath.

"The Lord God will be his judge. But tell me about this book. You said Robert gave it to Guiliane?"

A tremor crossed the holy woman's face.

"Guiliane could read well enough, but she was lazy. If I led her to the prie-dieu for her devotions, she would only kneel a moment and then excuse herself to the privy," the Anchoress muttered. "She was always laughing with the servants behind my back."

"But she did have the book in her chamber when she was in childbirth?" Richard asked.

His mother leant forward, her face almost pressed against the bars, showing the yellowing stumps of her teeth.

"I thought that the virgin Saint Margaret would show her the sin she had committed and bring her to repentance. But I went to her when her time was nearly at hand, and she said she didn't even know where the book was! She had lost it! God's wrath was swift. The fever and her birth pangs came that day."

There was a moment of silence. The old woman's mouth went slack and she shut her eyes.

"We fled to Langley, but Matilde was already burning hot, running with sweat. She cried with evil dreams." The Anchoress put a hand to her mouth. "I couldn't help her."

Richard bowed his head. After a moment, he made the sign of the cross.

"She is with the Lord," he said quietly.

His mother nodded. She wiped her wet cheek with the flat of her palm and turned towards the altar.

"But Guiliane was not left alone, was she? Ursula did come for the birth, despite the fever?" Illesa asked, craning through the bars.

The Anchoress glanced back.

"The midwife was heavy with child herself, but she must have attended Guiliane because she took the dead babe to Father Bernard the next day, claiming she had baptised it." Her hard eyes turned to Richard. "Of course, *cousin* Robert decided they would have a church burial, and paid the Priest handsomely to overlook their state of sin," she sneered.

Richard glanced at Illesa, thumbing the leather cover of the book.

"Ursula must have taken it when everyone was gone, after Guiliane had died."

"But you can't be certain," Illesa whispered. "It could have been given to her before then."

"Who are you, girl? I know your face." The Anchoress pointed at Illesa through the bars.

"Ursula's daughter."

The Anchoress looked blank for a moment. Then her eyes narrowed.

"Your mother was a thief."

Illesa tried to meet the Anchoress's eyes. Ursula had been in terrible pain and close to death when she had told her that the book belonged to her father's family. How could she have been lying?

"She stole it from us and left our demesne, driven away by the knowledge of her sin," the Anchoress declared.

Illesa shook her head.

"But Holy Mother, Saint Margaret would not have helped her deliver babes if she had stolen it," she managed. "I myself saw the Saint working through her hands."

"What do you know of it? You have no right to speak to me! Your mother was a thief and a liar. You ought to be doing penance on your knees for your mother's sins."

"I will, Holy Mother."

"You should go prostrate before the throne of God."

"I accept the penance you require and will do it humbly." Illesa paused before risking a further question. "What was the babe, boy or girl?"

"She would have become a whore like her mother if God had allowed her to live. Robert has not stopped his lechery, you know. The last time he came, I told him where he will be on the Day of Judgment if he does not repent."

Richard bent forward and spoke in an undertone.

"Robert is a powerful man, Mother. You should not condemn him to his face."

"If I see sin and do not speak of it, I share in that sin," the Anchoress asserted, glaring at him.

Illesa stepped forward, keeping her eyes lowered.

"Holy Mother, I repent of my sins and those of my family. Please will you give me your blessing?"

"Kneel, girl."

Illesa knelt on the weeds. The Anchoress intoned a penitential psalm, making a sign of the cross when she had finished. When Illesa got to her feet, the Anchoress was staring at her.

"I have seen you before. You are one of those whore servants they have been sending to me."

"No, Holy Mother, I am not. I swear it, by the Blessed Virgin."

"You have a face I know."

"Perhaps you remember my mother in my face."

"No, you cannot lie to me," she spat.

"Mother," Richard broke in, "I am going to the King's Tournament in Wales. May I beg your blessing for my journey?"

The blessing she gave him was cursory, cut off by an attack of coughing.

"Have they brought you any food today?"

"It is a day of fasting, boy. You should observe the practice with more rigour yourself. I see the signs of lassitude and corruption in your face. You should not keep company with thieves and liars," she said, looking directly at Illesa.

Illesa bit her lip.

"I thank God the book is back in its rightful place now, Holy Mother," she whispered.

Richard held it in front of the grille.

"Open the door and I will pass it to you," he said.

His mother was seized by another fit of coughing. When she recovered she was breathless, bent over.

"What do *I* need with the patron saint of childbirth?" Even as a whisper, her voice burned with scorn. "The next one in the family who is with child should have the book. Give it to your *wife*. Don't let *him* get hold of it."

Richard bowed stiffly.

"Now leave me. I am disturbed and must pray."

He put his fingers through the grille. She kissed them, but her suspicious eyes were on Illesa.

"Don't bring any more of those whore servants here, Richard," she wheezed. His mother turned to the altar, lifted the book of the Apocalypse in front of the crucifix and prostrated herself before it on the floor.

Chapter XXIII
AD 304
Antioch-on-the-Orontes

The day Marina spoke, Olymbrius visited the small room where she lay. He did not go near her, staying in the doorway where the air was fresher.

"You said she was awake; I see no sign of it."

The centurion felt the Governor's loud voice like a lash.

"She spoke earlier, sir, asking for water."

"The traitor can speak, then? Well, she should open her eyes! Why are they shut?"

"They do not open. The fire burnt the skin too severely."

"She must be able to see or the spectacle will not convince her! Call my surgeon; he can cut them open," Olymbrius shouted, stomping away.

The centurion signalled to the auxiliary. The surgeon was called and arrived within an hour.

"The Governor wants her eyes to open," the centurion said to him as he arrived at the door. The surgeon grunted and approached the bed. Marina turned her face to him as he bent over her.

"She's whispering something to me," the surgeon said, crossly. "I can't make it out."

The centurion bent his ear to her mouth.

"She is praying, doctor. She is praying for you."

"She should stop at once; I am trying to examine her eyes. Why is it so dark in here? I need light!" The shades on the windows were removed. He knelt down by the bed and peered at the red, oozing skin, lifting a flap near her eye with the end of his silver knife.

"No. It will do no good," he said, straightening up. "Her eyes are as burnt as the rest of her. She will not see. Tell the Governor I can give her an infusion which will dull the pain, but there is nothing else I can do."

Messengers and criers were dispatched around the city the next morning. They announced a free spectacle in the amphitheatre, generously endowed by the Governor. The city spilled out of the baths and the forum, down the colonnades towards the arched façade that surrounded the arena. It had been many weeks since the last animal hunt, and many weeks before that since the last gladiatorial combat.

Guards scanned the people pushing through the gates; those with swords were turned away. By noon most of the crowd had been in place for two hours in the sun. Many had bought the cheap wine sold by the vendors. They were restless, and slightly drunk.

A division of the second cohort of the guard marched in before the Governor and lined the sides and back of his box. The Priests arrived next: Marina's father, followed by the Priest of Apollo at Daphne and the Priestess of Diana, in full regalia. They stood immediately behind the Governor's throne.

Olymbrius stood at the balustrade, hung with garlands of white and gold cloth. The soldiers around the amphitheatre crashed their spears on their shields for silence.

"Citizens of Rome and people of Antioch, the purity of our great city, one of the jewels of the Roman Empire, has been contaminated by the teachings of a few Jews from the south. Their heresy has been running through our city like a plague of rats, spreading filth and sapping our strength. This pestilence must be driven out, or the gods will see our degradation and punishment will come. We will not let these traitors endanger our city any longer. I bring them before you now; the dogs who would rather worship a crucified man than the great gods of Rome!"

The doors to the undercroft were opened. A phalanx of guards marched into the arena, surrounding a group of huddled people, their arms tied behind their backs. Many were bleeding from blows to their faces. Perhaps there were fifty or more, and from within the group came the sound of children crying. The soldiers brought them to a halt in front of the Governor's box and each seized a prisoner and forced them to their knees. Shouts of anger and recognition rose from the crowd on the stone benches.

On the other side of the arena, another door opened. Malchus, the centurion, marched in first, followed by the auxiliary. Behind them came two more guards carrying a stretcher. They stopped between the Governor's box and the line of kneeling prisoners and slowly lowered the stretcher to the ground. The Governor leant over the balustrade and gestured at the small, motionless figure.

"Lift her to her feet! Let her stand and face the people she has betrayed! This is the daughter of Aedisias, the Priest of Jupiter. Instead of bringing glory to the gods and to Rome, she has chosen to betray us and dishonour herself."

He watched as Malchus and the young auxiliary lifted Marina from the stretcher and made her stand. She gasped when her feet took her weight. The skin on her ankles was cracked and oozing. Her broken right arm hung by her side. Malchus stood on her left.

"Hold on to me," he whispered. He could hear her prayers that were no louder than a breath, when there was a pause in the shouting.

"She has been cast off by her family," the Governor roared, "but still she refuses to renounce her false beliefs. Instead she has tried to spread this infection amongst her guards and even dared speak her lies to me!" He leant further out and surveyed the crowd. "I have heard that some of you are singing a song in the market about her, praising her courage. Anyone who sings it, and anyone who worships this Jew will share her fate. You will all know the consequence of rebellion."

Marina's sightless eyes and oozing face had the effect on the crowd that the Governor had hoped for. The amphitheatre was silent except for the cries of the children. Olymbrius drew his sword and pointed it at the people below him on the sand.

"The other fools who follow this criminal, you see before you. Their betrayal must be paid for." He paused, standing up to his full height. "But first let us show once and for all that a Jew from Galilee is not a god and has no power."

Olymbrius aimed the point of his sword at Marina.

"It is your lies that have corrupted the people of this city, and your disobedience that will bring punishment upon them," the Governor declared. "Behind you are the citizens and their families who would not denounce your Christ. If you let your arm drop lower than your shoulder, the soldiers will cut their throats." He paused. In the hush, the sound of a woman sobbing carried to the furthest benches.

"You say your Jesus is the only god. Pray to him for help, and let's see if he will save his followers. Surely keeping an arm raised will not be too difficult for him. I have read that the god of the Jews did the same for them long ago." He cast his eyes round the crowd, who were staring at the broken, disfigured girl.

"Centurion, raise her arm."

The amphitheatre drew breath like a great beast.

"Higher centurion, higher!" Olymbrius cried as Malchus slowly lifted her right arm straight in front of her. Marina's face was immobile, but a high-pitched moan came from her mouth. Her knees gave way, and she slumped sideways. Malchus caught her by her tunic and put his hand under her shoulder.

"Make her stand! Hold her up!" Olymbrius shouted. The auxiliary put his sword to the back of her neck, as the centurion braced her body and raised her arm. When it was high enough, he let go.

Malchus felt sick. He could hear her words in his head; she seemed to be speaking right into his mind. Her arm began to tremble. The prisoners on their knees lifted their heads, their silent mouths moved. Sweat trickled down their faces. The soldiers held their swords poised, sunlight burning from the blades.

After the first minute, the crowd began to talk again. Some were placing bets. Many thought she would lower her arm after a further minute. In the crowd, someone began to count, and thousands joined in, until a signal from the Governor and the crash of the soldiers' spears.

"Praise God!" one of the prisoners shouted. The soldier behind her looked to the Governor, who nodded. The soldier grasped the prisoner's long black hair and cut her throat. The crowd hushed for a moment. Then there was a volley of cheering that grew louder and louder. Olymbrius smiled. Blood was what they wanted. The crowd began to chant as one voice:

"Death! Death!"

Marina's arm twitched; her face was a red mask without expression.

"Governor, you are losing control of the crowd. Kill them and be done with it," Aedisias shouted over the noise.

"No! They will only be defeated when she gives up. If we kill them now, she will become a martyr."

The sound from the crowd was deafening, a cloud of noise. The sun was shining directly overhead, so no one saw where it came from, but some of the crowd witnessed it alighting on Marina's outstretched arm.

A white dove balanced on her broken fingers.

Olymbrius sat down suddenly on his throne. The sound from the crowd lowered into a deep murmur.

"It's a sign," someone shouted. "She is blessed!"

Several prisoners cried out. All around the amphitheatre people stood up, lifting their hands to the sky, fearful. Marina was holding the dove against her raw face, whispering to it.

"Governor!" shouted Aedisias. The guards in charge of the prisoners were looking at the Governor's box. The crowd on the stands began pushing forward against the soldiers and their spears. "Governor, order the Christians to be killed!" the Priest cried. "The crowd is breaking through!"

Olymbrius felt his life draining away as he had two weeks before in his chamber. A great hand was squeezing his heart. He lurched to his feet, leant over the balustrade and swept his arm across his neck. The soldiers cut the throats of the prisoners and dropped their bodies to the ground.

Aedisias was standing over the Governor, who had slumped to the floor.

"Get up!" he shouted. "Guards, take him out and revive him. Centurion!" Aedisias bent over the balustrade and shouted in the sudden hush. "Execute the prisoner!"

Malchus saluted.

"I take my orders only from the Governor."

"Do it now! The Governor is ill. Do you want a riot on your hands?"

Malchus felt a touch on his right shoulder. The dove was perching there, its claws gripping his segmented armour. Marina knelt on the sand, her arms raised, palms open to the sky.

"You must do this so that I can go to my Lord," the dove said. Its eyes were as black as obsidian.

"No, I cannot kill you, virgin of God," Malchus whispered. The amphitheatre was a blur around him. He could not feel the sword that he gripped in his hand.

The dove cocked its head.

"Jesus has granted my prayer. When I die, I will become a comfort for many. Grace and forgiveness are freely given. Do not now fear death."

The auxiliary was staring at him, his sword still pressed at the nape of Marina's neck. Malchus saw the fear in his eyes that would make him reckless.

234

"I will do it if you cannot," the boy offered, stepping in front of his commander.

"No," Malchus shouted, pushing him to the side. "I will do it. God forgive me!"

As he raised his arm, the dove flew up into the sunlight. He brought the sword down on her neck.

When the crowd saw her beheaded, they began wailing. The soldiers went forward and killed any who came on to the arena floor. Order was soon restored. People returned to their houses; shops opened for the afternoon. The bodies were counted and flung in a pile. Soldiers patrolled the streets.

The centurion, Malchus, did not return to the Governor's palace. He was never found inside the Empire.

Chapter XXIV
The 22nd day of July, 1284
Acton Burnel

Richard and Illesa passed beneath the impassive chiselled heads that framed the church's western door. Breath caught in her tight throat. Why had the Anchoress called her a whore again and again? Her cropped hair was carefully concealed under the new veil, and there was nothing improper about her clothes. Perhaps the old woman thought there was something depraved about her features.

The Anchoress might know, somehow, what Richard had offered her and know her weakness. She was sure of God's judgment on those who were immoral, calling down his wrath from her dark cell, eagerly anticipating the apocalypse. But what about the judgment on those who did not forgive, who did not show love even to their own son?

Illesa shivered and crossed herself. She would have to do penance for thinking ill of that holy woman, even if she was a foulmouthed old crone. And more penance for her own mother. Ursula got the book that day, when she was at Guiliane's bedside, when she was in her ninth month, carrying Illesa herself. It was hard to see how she had got it honestly. Guiliane was French and probably very wayward. Perhaps to annoy the overbearing, pious Alianore, she had given the precious book away. Perhaps.

Richard was many paces ahead of her. Illesa hitched up her skirts, but could not catch him. He would certainly not be swearing on her behalf in any court in the land. He would not go to any trouble now he thought her whole family thieves and liars. But he might still have her as his whore, as that status was confirmed by his mother's judgment after all. The whole family was quick to blame and slow to forgive.

"Come on!" Richard barked.

He had almost reached the stables. The set of his back told her everything. He would be just like a baited bear, provoked by his mother's indifference to him. Instead of the gratitude he had hoped for, the book had stirred up deep hurts. She tightened her lips against the pity she felt. He would hate pity even more.

"Where are we going?" she called.

Richard stopped and looked back at the church, white-faced. Illesa followed his gaze. A black clad priest was making his way quickly down the path from the church's north door, going in the direction of the village. They could just hear the slap, slapping of his sandals on the stone.

"To the bailiff, of course. Take you there and have done with you." He clapped his gloves into the palm of his hand. "Damn him to hell!"

"Sir -"

"And when they drown you, throw the book in the river as well," Richard growled and flung open the stable door.

Illesa put her hand on his shoulder and turned him round.

"Wait. Sir Richard, you can't condemn me based on what your mother said. Lady Alianore didn't even see my mother that day. She has no proof the book wasn't given to her."

"I can condemn you, if I choose to, as you know. My mother is a holy woman and she has condemned you."

"Your mother is full of hate. She hated that French girl. It is no use listening to what she says. She is not in her right mind."

"You will be damned to hell for saying so."

"You have said worse of my mother and never met her. I have met yours and you cannot deny what I have said."

"Enough!" Richard shouted, raising his hand.

Illesa flinched.

Richard looked up to the sky and ran his raised hand through his hair. He turned away from her and spoke in a low monotone.

"Don't you realise that Thomas, the good Priest of Acton, is going to find the bailiff and report all that he just overheard with his big ass's ears. He was listening at the squint the whole time. Once he has told his tale, neither you nor I will be free to go anywhere until this mess is sorted out. Now, I don't wish to spend hours trying to explain the folly of your mother and establishing the ownership of a book for superstitious women. I have responsibilities at the Round Table Tournament, which I can ill afford to neglect. I will write to the bailiff from Shrewsbury and explain that the book was given long ago to your family and has now been returned."

His shoulders dropped. Behind his anger were years of disappointment. He gestured at the path toward the road.

"In the meantime, what you choose to do with yourself is your own business."

He went through the stable door, and she followed him without thinking, a finger of ice running down her spine. Inside a gangly boy was pretending to muck out. He'd heard every word. Another careless slip. He straightened up, pushing his hair out of his eyes.

"Here boy, stop that. Saddle them up and make quick work of it. Bring them to the hall as soon as you're done."

"Yes, sir," the boy muttered, his face in an agony of embarrassment.

Illesa had to back out of Richard's way as he swept out of the stable again.

He was striding away towards the hall. Illesa hesitated for a moment before following. She could not run; not from this place. She would never find her way through the fields and woods without being caught. They would be brutal to her in gaol, for the humiliation meted out by Kit and Sir Richard. She would be raped at the very least. Even if Richard wrote to the bailiff, it would be weeks or months before he returned to swear on her behalf, and they could keep her imprisoned till then. If she lived that long.

Sir Richard went left past the front door, towards the living quarters of the manor. It was hard to match his pace. When he finally turned to close the side door of the hall behind them, Illesa saw anger had inflamed his scar to a livid red. She put her hand out to him before he could move away.

"Sir, please forgive my mother and me for any wrongs we have done to your family," she gulped, trying to get her breath.

He removed her hand from his sleeve and grasped her shoulder, bending over to whisper in her ear.

"You are not in a court now, Illesa, so save your pleas. As I said, I haven't got time for all the words it would require to tell your sad story to the agents of the law here or anywhere."

"You do not need to, not yet. As you say, you can write from Shrewsbury."

"Then why are you detaining me?" he said through clenched teeth.

"Because, sir, if you leave me here I will be ill-used in gaol, before your message ever reaches the bailiff."

He looked away from her and let out his breath in a long hiss.

"I should have sent you away that day in Clun, without ever setting eyes on you." He pointed his finger an inch from her face. "Follow me, Mistress Lunette, and keep your peace. I will have to be further delayed at Shrewsbury finding a bawdy house to leave you in." Richard began walking down the hall.

"Wait. Who is Lunette?" she called, tripping after him.

"Lunette is a lady in a story about one of Arthur's most famous knights. I am charged with the task of instructing a troupe of travelling players to enact it for the Round Table. I should not have used the name. It made Thomas suspicious, and you have neither her wit nor her manners," he said, without looking round.

"So she is not a real lady?"

"No. She is better than a real lady."

"But she will be played by a man. How can that be better than a real lady?"

Richard shook his head, still striding away.

"You have not met the man. If only there were two like him, then he could play Laudine as well."

Illesa drew a deep breath.

"Sir Richard, let me come with you to the Tournament."

That stopped him. He turned, his hands raised in exasperation.

"You are mad! You cannot just come to a Tourney! Who would we say you were?"

"Hide me in the company of players. I am used to playing a boy. I will not look so strange with others in costume."

He gave a short, mirthless laugh.

"You are blessed by your ignorance!"

"You told me that you could show me the splendour of the world and the comfort of the life you are offering me. Surely the King's court is the best place to find comfort and splendour."

Richard raised an eyebrow. His face became amused, guarded.

"Very well. But if you reveal that you are not a travelling player to anyone, I will not save you. You are nothing to do with me."

She nodded.

"Now move, we must be quick."

He turned on his heel and went down the narrow hallway, panelled with carved wood, and came to a stairway at the end. He took the steps two at a time and was already through a low chamber door by the time she reached the top. The solar was illuminated by small glazed windows and furnished with a prie-dieu, a bed, a cabinet of books with a locked grille and opposite, a fireplace with a carved stone lintel. The settled dust flew up into the shafts of light as they moved through the room.

Sir Richard went to the prie-dieu and began running his hands along the back of the polished bookstand. He straightened up, holding a small bronze key, and went to the cabinet. The lock moved smoothly with barely a sound. The book he took out was small and thick, bound in red cordovan leather with an incised brass clasp. He removed the book of Saint Margaret from his bag, slapped it on to the pile of books, raising more dust, and locked the cabinet. Without a word, he replaced the key in its hiding place and slid the new book into his bag.

Illesa could not see any sign of what kind of book it was, except the richness of the red leather binding. She glanced at the bed with its heavy embroidered hangings and coverlet, wondering if that was where Guiliane had lain, dying, and where her mother had somehow acquired the book. It would stay muffled in that quiet room until Sir Richard's wife was on that bed bearing his child. Then he might regain some of his faith in the saint, for his wife's sake, whoever she may be.

The footfall of boots was already sounding from down the stairs. Illesa shut the door behind her and hurried after him.

Outside the hall, the stable boy stood holding the two horses, looking at the ground, his unruly blond hair hiding his face.

Richard took the reins and waved the boy away.

"Take these," he said handing the reins to Illesa. Holding them, she felt lost. She wanted Jezebel's familiar nose, her soft, strong neck and her speed. With that horse she might stand a chance to flee the bailiff, the Forester and all his men, but not with this fat, complacent pony. Richard was right. Her plan was madness. She would be seen for what she was straight away.

Richard adjusted the bridle, pulled on the girth and mounted Buskins.

"Are you coming or running?" he said, looking back at her. He kicked the horse's flank and headed for the manor gate at a trot.

Nellie's hooves skipped uneasily as she was pulled to follow. Someone was calling out in the village, their voice distant but urgent. Crows were wheeling in the blue sky. A carpenter looked down from the scaffold and spat.

240

She had to run a few paces to catch up and grab Nellie's rein. Richard slowed only slightly, allowing her to get her leg over the saddle before he spurred Buskins out of the gate.

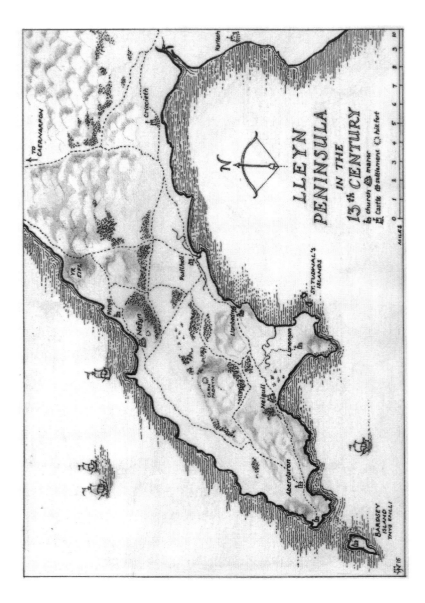

LLEYN
PENINSULA
IN THE
13th CENTURY

church □ manor
□ carte □ settlement □ hafot

MILES 0 1 2 3 4 5 6 7 8 9 10

N

TO CAERNARFON

Harlech

Cricceth

YR EIFL

Nefyn
Ch.

Pwllheli

Llanbedrog

Llangian
PLAS
MAWR

Nefyn Ch.

Llanengan

ST. TUDWAL'S ISLANDS

Aberdaron

BARDSEY ISLAND
YNYS ENLLI

Part Two

Acton Burnel Manor
The 20th day of October, 1266

She had not intended to tell him anything; only what she had said to Lady Alianore and no more. It was his manner that disarmed her, and his obvious grief. The truth escaped from her like a bird released from a net. The babe squirmed unhappily in her arms, and Ursula realised she was squeezing her tightly. Robert Burnel had not moved. His face was very still. Illesa wailed and threw her head back against Ursula's breast. She put one of her fingers in the babe's mouth and rubbed her gums. The man was paralyzed with shock, sitting in his fine hemmed tunic, his handsome features slack and uncomprehending.

"I am very sorry," she added. "I took her just to feed her, but my own baby girl had died the day before and I think I was touched with madness." She shook her head to clear it. Illesa was unhappy with the finger. She wanted milk.

"You are really saying this is the child born to Guiliane?"

"Yes," Ursula whispered.

"And who was the babe that was buried?"

"My baby."

"Unbaptised?"

"Yes." Her reply was barely audible.

"Are you speaking in truth, not to trick me, Goodwife?"

His voice had lost the gentle quality. She knew he was a clerk in the Prince's service, and aiming higher than that, or so the village talk would have it. The authority of the Church and the court formed his every word.

"Sir, I repent of the lies I have told. This is Guiliane's daughter." It was not possible to say 'and yours.' "I swear it, by God's truth."

Robert Burnel laid his hands side by side in the patch of sunlight on the small table in front of him, head lowered. His hands were ink stained but not roughened. He looked up at her. The brightness from the window behind him made it hard to see his face.

"I imagine that someone may have given you the impression that this child was not wanted, and so you took it."

"No sir, it was all my own madness. Lady Guiliane wanted the babe very much. She prayed to Saint Margaret; she called on the Lord to save her and the child."

Robert Burnel leant forward.

"Tell me," he said. Lines of sadness had replaced the anger around his mouth.

Ursula tried to compose herself. The events of that night seemed to have happened at some time when her body was inhabited by another Ursula. A night-time wraith. But she had saved the baby and performed the baptism. She needed the Lord's protection now, from her own folly.

Robert Burnel listened without a sound during her description of the illness and the stalled labour.

"She was too far gone when I got there, sir. The fever had drained all her strength. She'd had no help; no woman had stayed with her."

He waved a hand at her.

"It also killed two servants and Lady Alianore's daughter. I know how fatal the fever is."

Illesa had gone to sleep on her breast.

"They should have called me sooner. No woman should be left labouring alone."

Robert Burnel laced his fingers.

"You say Guiliane called on Saint Margaret," he prompted.

"She told me that she had lost the book of the Saint but it had only fallen under the bed. The image of the Saint gave her great comfort."

"You found the book?"

"Yes, sir."

"Well, where is it, girl? Lady Alianore was sure Guiliane had somehow conjured it to the devil."

"Lady Guiliane told me to take it."

"What?"

"I have kept it with Illesa."

He smiled and then abruptly stopped.

"She gave it to you?"

"Yes sir."

"You know it wasn't hers to give?"

"Sir?"

"The book belongs to Lady Alianore and the other ladies of the Burnel family."

"I am sorry. I thought because -"

Ursula stopped, and lowered her eyes. She gripped Illesa's blanket hard. The tears spilled onto the wool and stayed there, like transparent pearls.

There was silence.

"I know that I should have told Lady Alianore, but she was grieving. She did not leave her chamber for many days. I did not want to - " Ursula could not finish.

"You did not want to what?" His voice was gentle again. He waited until she could speak.

"I could not leave the babe with her. She would not have loved her."

The only sound was the muffled breathing of Illesa and the distant call of a crow. He put his head in his hands.

"Goodwife Ursula, when I called you here for an account of the death of Lady Guiliane and her baby, I did not expect this."

"I will give her to you, sir, or to Lady Alianore as you see fit. I know that I have sinned gravely against you, but I only wanted to look after her."

Robert Burnel rested his chin on his joined hands. His eyes were a deep brown, ringed with black shadows.

"What was the name you called her by? It was strange. Was it chosen by her godparents?"

"Guiliane chose it. It is in the Passion of Saint Margaret. Saint Margaret comes out of the dragon *illesa*, unharmed."

"Illesa."

"Yes, sir."

"She is well?"

"Yes sir, she is a healthy girl." Ursula said stroking the head of the sleeper. "Her mother named her well."

"She has Guiliane's hair."

He turned and looked out of the window.

"You have a husband, I presume?"

"Yes sir, a smith who has been away making arrows for the King's army."

"And other children?"

"A boy of five years."

246

"You cannot read, surely. What did you think you would do with the book?"

"I can sir. Lady Rose showed me the book when she was attending births in the manor with me. She taught me how to read the words." The memory of those hours spent with the older woman in front of the book was still strong. Lady Rose had simply wanted to share the beauty of it. She had been glad of an interested pupil, despite their different estates. "I thought the book belonged with Illesa. She was delivered by the Saint's mercy."

"By the Saint's mercy." He paused. "Mmm."

He stared vacantly at the wall for some time.

Eventually his eyes rested on the babe, and his voice came as if from a great distance.

"You have done well with her. I think it would be best if she remained with you. It would not be wise to disturb Lady Alianore now with this news."

He rose from his seat.

"You should make your act of contrition now." He pointed to the prie-dieu.

Ursula got awkwardly to her feet, holding the sleeping babe.

"I will hold her."

He came towards her and held out his hands. She placed Illesa carefully, cradling her head in the crook of his arm. The confession was brief. She had already made it, after all. The penance he gave her was standard: a brief fast and recitation of the penitential psalms.

"And read her the book. That will also be your penance. Read to her."

Ursula bowed her head, wiping her cheeks.

"I will, sir."

She got up. Robert was looking at the sleeping face.

"She is surprisingly heavy," he said softly.

He held Illesa out and Ursula took her. Robert made the sign of the cross on her forehead and intoned a blessing.

"Thank you, sir."

"It would be best if this was not talked of, to anyone."

"I will not, sir."

"It would also not go well with you if anyone was to find the book."

"No one else will see it."

"Good."

"God go with you, sir."

"You may leave."

He turned away and went to the window as she walked to the door and shut it behind her.

Chapter I
Friday the 26th day of July, 1284
Criccieth Castle, Gwynedd

The chamber was heavy with fumes of burnt chaff. It had been music she'd heard, plucked strings finding the beginning of a familiar tune. Illesa pushed herself up on one elbow and waved her other hand in front of her face, making the smoke whirl lazily. First light was creeping through the shutters.

The harp stopped abruptly as a loud and prolonged bout of coughing came from the corner of the room. It would be the big man who had taken the only available bed. The other one, the boy with blond, almost white, hair was slender enough to be any of the bundles strewn on the floor. Richard had said they would go early. He and the bald leader of the players had been housed in the gatehouse, one of the few places with a complete roof. Perhaps it was the noise of them leaving that had woken her.

Illesa sat up listening. Her neck was stiff and aching. A sack on a wooden floor made a poor bed for the saddle weary. She got quietly to her feet and went into the ruin of the hall. There it was again. A liquid cascade of notes, ending in melancholy. Sir Richard had certainly gone by now, so the figure sitting on the piled up stone in the shadow of the wall with his back to her could not be him, no matter how similar the form and tilt of the head. He was bent over the little harp, strumming notes almost too soft to hear and fingering the wooden pegs.

"Wide the border, strong the wall,
long the waves surrounding me.
My love may come from far away,
my fate will come, my enemy."

"Go to the well, girl. The horses need water."
A woman's voice? It had the tone and cadence.
"We are leaving soon. Hurry up, you!" And then he laughed and turned. It was the boy, wearing a rich cloak and trimmed hat, doubtless from the pack of costumes they had taken off the overloaded cart last night.

"Go on, you! Do as you're told!" he admonished with finger raised, and in Richard's voice this time. The little mimic.

Illesa bit back her reply.

"Your master won't want you to be late," he said in the simpering lady's voice and flounced past her into the chamber.

Illesa stepped out into the remains of the bailey, picking her way through the piles of debris towards the well.

Gaspar, the player of ladies, was going to make a tiresome travelling companion. His skin was soft and beardless. If he shaved, it left no mark. He looked younger than her, but Illesa suspected that he wasn't. It was his slender, graceful body, like the tumblers who performed at fairs, which gave him the appearance of a youth. But his full lips and broad mouth were too knowing, too provocative.

She had only heard some of the negotiations with the players the evening before. A performance in front of the King was a chance any hungry troupe looking for patronage would jump at, she had thought. The payment they would receive for the play seemed generous to her, but Melchior, the leader, had been insulted by the sum. Richard had simply shrugged his shoulders.

"You know the Queen. She will spend pounds on hawks, dogs and books, but nothing on people and entertainment."

"At this rate I will have to write a story on parchment made from my own skin and sell it to her majesty as a book to be paid decently," Melchior had snapped.

"You will be seen by some of the richest dukes on the continent," Richard said, rubbing his thumb and finger together as if testing a coin. "How will they resist Gaspar's charms and your words? Not forgetting Balthazar's voice," he added, glancing at the big man who looked like a bear forced to sit on a small stool. "And there will be opportunities for other performances. Perhaps a chance to play the devil himself being cast out of heaven? I always thought that was your best work."

Melchior accepted the flattery with a slight nod, although his frown remained. The leader and the creator of the plays was a man with a temper. Choler ruled him. He could certainly bring the heights of emotion to his roles. Ursula would have treated him with purslane and sage. As much as it was up to her, Illesa was going to stay out of his way.

The well bucket was attached to a ring in the gatehouse wall with a long iron chain. It looked like a hard, heavy pull, but the water was high and the bucket reached it before the end of the chain. She began to heave. What exactly was going to be expected of her during the Round Table, she had not discovered. All Richard had said was that she would be part of the Arthurian play in front of the King, as she had desired, which was a very contrary interpretation of her actual feelings.

The previous night, he had called her over before he left for the sleeping quarters.

"I know how carefully you guard a book, so look after this one for me," he said, holding out the scarlet leather volume he had taken from the room in Acton. It was warm in her hand, had been kept close to his body. "I don't want it wetted in the sea." Then he turned away, striding towards the door.

"Wait sir," she had called after him. "What is this book?"

Richard looked back, only briefly.

"It is the story you will help perform for the King, the tale of the brave knight Yvain. You will be his wife. Read it as you travel. Melchior and I leave at first light to make arrangements for the performance in Neigull. When I arrive in Nefyn, you may return it to my keeping." He half-smiled. "It will not burn you, girl," and walked out of the door into the dark courtyard.

Gaspar and Balthazar had watched her leave the room without comment, but their laughter was clearly audible as she found a place on the chamber floor to lay her pack. She was too tired to care, just desperate to lie on her back and stretch out her aching muscles. The only book she wanted was her mother's book, the only words, those familiar words of comfort. She had wrapped Richard's book in her spare tunic and hidden it in her pack without opening it.

The covered wagon belonging to the travelling players was near the east gate. On it, in peeling paint, were the figures of three exotic and richly dressed men carrying golden coffers in their outstretched hands: the three wise men, magicians and astronomers: Melchior, Balthazar and Gaspar. In the wreck of the stable behind the wagon, the dun carthorse was standing, its head down as if already harnessed up. She was old to be pulling a big cart. Illesa rubbed her neck and set the bucket down. The horse nosed it, disappointedly.

If they expected the horse to reach Nefyn, the three kings would have to give her more than well water, but there was no fodder in the stable. In the byre Illesa managed to gather an armful of old hay from the manger, then tripped on the rubble on the floor and fell to her knees, her toe throbbing. She brushed the mud from her skirts as much as she could and limped back towards the wagon. Gaspar and Balthazar stood by it, staring at her.

"A fine lady for King Arthur's court!" the boy declared royally. It was amazing what he could do with his voice. "Lady Ragnell indeed!"

Illesa stopped where she was. The name was not familiar but the connotation was plain.

Balthazar made to slap Gaspar with the back of his hand, but the boy dodged the blow and gave a high-pitched squeal like a piglet.

"You do it, Gaspar. And you," Balthazar tipped his head at Illesa, "come with me."

Gaspar made a face like a dried plum as she put the hay into his arms and followed Balthazar into the hall. He looked at her with his legs apart and hands on his hips, the light from the window behind him, making the most of his bulk for dramatic impact.

"Melchior has told me to explain that even though Sir Richard may want you as part of his entertainment, that does not mean you are part of this troupe, you understand?"

"Yes, master."

"While Sir Richard is away, I am your master, and you will do only as you are told. Don't draw attention to yourself because you won't like the attention you get."

"Yes, master."

Balthazar breathed out, having finished his performance, perhaps glad he had remembered the words that Melchior had given him to say.

"So what do you do? Sing, dance, play the citole?"

"No, master."

"Nothing?"

"No," she repeated, shame beginning to heat her face.

"How can you not do anything?" he said, mournfully. "What does he mean to do with you?"

Illesa cleared her throat.

"I can read," she said, hesitantly.

"Well," he huffed, "that is not good for much. We learn by listening to Melchior. He is the only one who reads or writes." He adjusted the thick belt around his belly. "I expect it is because of your face," he said as he passed her on the way to the wagon. "Get your things."

The journey passed quickly. There was the sea to watch whenever it came into view, clawing at the bottom of cliffs and crashing against the land like a battering ram. Its endless movement fascinated her, like a windy day in the forest. Even when it was a fine clear blue-green, it seemed like a giant monster that might immediately turn and swallow her up if she came too near.

And then there was Gaspar, who spent the time lurching from character to song to drollery. He was obviously grateful for a new listener. Balthazar muttered to himself from time to time, but otherwise was silent. They all took turns leading the wagon, riding the black palfrey or bouncing inside with the props and costumes.

Only a very few thin cattle grazed the fields. There were some sheep on the hillsides, but the crofts they found were burnt out or so poorly furnished that they did not knock, thinking there would be no food to spare. At about the hour of sext, they stopped at a stream that ran through a bright green field. The horses ate the lush grass. Balthazar drank from his skin, sharing some with Gaspar, who then lay down on his back, eyes shut, blond hair spread out in the sun. Illesa sat down gingerly. She was very hungry. If only she could be satisfied with grass. The carthorse and the black were tearing up the long blades, barely lifting their heads to chew.

"How did you end up with him, then?"

It had been no more than a whisper. Gaspar had opened one eye and turned towards her. His other eye was screwed up against the bright sunlight.

"With Sir Richard?"

"No, the Queen of Sheba," Gaspar said, pulling the face of an idiot at her.

She smiled despite herself.

"It's too long a story," she said plucking at the grass. Her hands were stained with leather wax from holding the reins, blistered and calloused from the friction of holding on. She laid them flat on the cool ground. "I will be leaving his company after the Round Table. It is just an arrangement of convenience."

"Oh, very convenient, I'm sure," said Gaspar, arching one eyebrow.

"We are not lovers."

"I can tell," Gaspar said. He rolled onto his back again and closed his eyes. "Richard is wound as tight as a nest of adders, and you look like a flower that has just been bitten by the frost." He sighed deeply, and laid his arms across his chest as if an effigy of the dead. "There must be suffering on earth and in hell for the sin of lust," he intoned.

"Do you take it so lightly?" Illesa said, trying to keep her voice from showing her anger. "The teaching of the Church is clear. Would you risk damnation?"

Gaspar sighed again.

"Some of us must rely on God's mercy. We are simply unable to be good when alive, so we must make a good death in full repentance. I am saving my coin for a thousand masses for my soul."

"Life is for indulging
if your purse is bulging –
for it marks the measure
of your paid-up pleasure." [1]

He sang in a high sweet tone, like an angel. Illesa gave up. He was as beautiful and devilish as one of the half-human beasts in the margin of the Saint's book.

After nones, they came through a pass of steep, grey peaks covered in scree and scrub and into green fields, bordered by a long western coastline. It was a further hour till they arrived at the site of the tournament, but the smoke was visible, rising in countless columns, for miles. All around the field, men were at work. Fences, tethering posts, tiers and a hundred tents were being erected.

Not for the first time Illesa wondered why Richard had agreed to bring her this far. He had not conversed with her on the journey except to tell her what to do and where to put herself. When she left the inn at Shrewsbury to send a message to Kit, Richard had not questioned her. Perhaps he had looked momentarily relieved when she got back, but his impatience soon returned as he gave orders to the grooms, the seamstress and the carter, all of whom had arrived from Clun Castle at his order. Richard's squire was not with them. He was ill at Clun; a piece of news that caused Sir Richard to use oaths Illesa had never heard before.

Illesa would rather have been hidden in this large entourage, where she would not have to confront his gaze whenever they halted. But the main body of the servants took the army road to Rhuddlan and would arrive by boat at Nefyn, while she and Sir Richard went overland, through the interior to meet the company of players at Criccieth.

Balthazar wove their wagon amongst the enclosures and tents, occasionally barking out a greeting. Gaspar dismounted the black mare while she still walked, handed the reins to Balthazar and strode, smiling, into the throngs of men. Balthazar cursed after him.

"Gaspar! That bloody boy is as wayward as a cat. Gaspar!"

But Gaspar had disappeared into the labyrinth of poles, canvas and braziers.

"I suppose you don't know how to erect a tent either?" he asked her. "No, of course not. You better stay out of the way then, or I'll hit you with the mallet." Balthazar pulled the dun to a stop and handed the black's reins to Illesa.

"Go on with you. Tie her up to that post and then get out of the way." He glowered at their site and began tossing things out of the back of the wagon.

Illesa tied the horse to the post and took the bucket with her. They would need water, and at least that would give her a job to do. It took her a long time to find a well, and when she did it was almost empty. She would not be slaking her thirst in that muddy water, despite her dry throat, but when she set the bucket down, the horses drank it deeply. Balthazar was still cursing, knotting ropes and wielding his mallet.

Illesa remembered the book and retrieved it from her pack in the wagon. Beyond the next tent, the sea rose and fell, a shining blue in the low sun. She walked towards it. The waves on the pebbles sounded like milk hitting the side of a bucket. The bay was full of boats and barges, some still being unloaded, rocking urgently as baskets and crates were lifted from their hulls and taken to shore. The strong men hauling the loads wore nothing but their braies. A stone wall separated the pavilion area from the fish racks and busy paths along the harbour. Illesa stood by the wall and looked back at the tournament field.

From a pile of sticks and canvas, men were conjuring elegant dwellings. The ground was neither too wet nor too dry. Pegs were driven in with satisfying speed. Hammers flew from one hand to another, never missing their mark. Bands of scarlet and gold, blue and purple and every colour of the earth flew in the breeze. It was a city of cloth so beautiful that it might have been Jerusalem.

The book in her hand was bigger than the Passion of Saint Margaret, and the pages were very white, almost transparent. The first page began with a Q decorated in leaf and flower, but the words had no meaning for her. Page after page was the same. There were two painted scenes, one of a knight holding the hand of a lady dressed in green and wearing a ring. The other showed the same knight, a lion at his side, fighting two warriors in black. She closed the scarlet leather covers and carefully attached the clasp. It was written in French, which she struggled to read. Yet another lesson in humility from Sir Richard. She would have to ask him to tell her the story and hear the unsaid words behind his laughter: 'You are just a foolish girl and you do not belong here.'

Balthazar had set up their tent by the time she returned. He and Gaspar were sitting in front of it at a trestle table, sheltered from the next tent by the bulk of the wagon. They looked up from the food they were eating and Balthazar grunted at her, nodding his head at a trencher at the end of the table. On it was a sopping lot of pottage. In the centre of the table were two fish, almost reduced to bones. Illesa took the knife from her belt, speared a fish head and sat down, reaching to the large jug to fill her cup with ale.

The sun was setting above the sea. Golden clouds floated overhead and the thud and ring of hammers came from all sides. She ate until she was full. Four days' hard riding had left her with trembling, painful thighs, and sitting only seemed to make it worse. She got up stiffly, dragged a straw mattress to the back of the tent, took off her boots and lay down with her back to the canvas and her face to the tent flap. The red sun and its reflection floated towards the shore in liquid flames.

Balthazar sat drinking, his elbows on the table muttering in a voice too deep to hear. Gaspar got up and stretched. He kicked his stool under the table and disappeared from view. Illesa could hear pissing on the other side of the wagon. Someone cursed. Gaspar apologised in his best lady's voice. Then he was in the tent and arranging his pallet next to her. She shifted, trying to keep a space between them. He looked at her with mock astonishment.

"Gaspar will not touch you, fair maiden. Merely worship you from afar." He put his hand under his head, stuck his thumb in his mouth and shut his eyes. Illesa kept her eyes open for a moment longer, until the sun's edge was swallowed by the water.

Chapter II
The 27th day of July, 1284
Nefyn

"You are not attending a burial." It was Sir Richard's voice, his hand just visible at the flap of the tent. "Smile, be merry. You are receiving the King and all his handsome knights, and you have just been married to the boldest and most handsome of all." He stepped forward into the pavilion and took the red book from Melchior's outstretched hand.

Illesa stopped mid-manoeuvre and let go of Melchior's other hand. Sir Richard was scanning the words, his nose burnt from the sun, his riding cloak swung over his back.

"Sir," Melchior began, "we are uncertain of how to position the players and..."

"Yes, my good man, I will show you all, perhaps even on parchment, if it pleases you. Now do it for me from the beginning. No, Illesa, don't hold him like that; he is not a ewe for shearing. Gracefully, delicately place your hand on his arm."

"I don't know why you insist on us using this girl, sir. Gaspar is much better at this sort of thing."

"I require Gaspar for the other role, as I told you, master player. He will be well employed. For this role we require a foreign face, a pretty face. One that is not known to all and sundry as is Gaspar, by now."

Gaspar's expression was one of exaggerated horror. He removed a cloth from the front of his jerkin and made a great show of weeping into it.

"Yes, yes, you old bawd. I will see you later for our discussion. Now on with it, let me see the part with the King."

Illesa felt more self-conscious than ever, stepping in time with her head held high in an impossibly elaborate headdress with his amused eye upon her.

"We will do that again with the knight who is to play Sir Yvain, and maybe you will look happier if it is a comely knight on your arm not a bald old man. Follow me."

He swept out of the tent and Illesa looked at Melchior, uncertain whether Sir Richard had meant her. The bald old man, outrage on his face, swept his arm towards the opening, gesturing her out. She quickly removed the headdress and the heavy ermine mantle.

Gaspar began weeping again.

"Oh cruel knight, leaving me for another." With one hand he held the cloth to his eye, with the other he waved at Illesa with a flourish.

She grimaced at him and hurried out into the low sunlight.

Richard was already past the pavilions of the Queen's retinue. She caught up with him by the noisy tents housing the Earl of Lincoln's men. They came to the spits and hearths where the food for servants and lesser soldiers would be cooked. Richard was walking through the kitchen area, scanning the food. They passed several spits before he found what he was looking for. A large fish, its eyes white from heat, lay steaming on a trestle, while the spit boy struggled to pierce the next fish lengthways on the hot iron.

"Here boy, I am taking this fish."

The boy looked up from his task, startled. He looked behind him. His master was elsewhere.

"Who shall I say took it? I don't want a whipping." He licked his lips nervously.

"Sir Richard Burnel. Tell him I have been at Neigull arranging the entertainment. I am lodged with the King's men." He speared the fish with his knife, helped himself to a platter lying ready by another untended spit, dropped the fish on it and set off.

He was heading towards the large open field where the battle mêlée would be staged. Workmen were finishing the scaffold stands where the King and Queen and all the dignitaries would sit. The other stands stood empty and quiet on the far side of the field, below the keep with its flying banners.

Richard skirted the palisade fence between the stands and the field. He climbed up until he reached the bench at the top of the stands and sat down with the platter on his lap, gesturing for Illesa to hurry up.

Every step made her thighs ache. She sat down a little away from him and looked around. Beyond the pavilions, tents, and columns of smoke, the blue sea shone and swelled, heaving the broad barges coming into the harbour. The sky had begun to lose its harsh brightness. High up, wisps of cloud hung motionless. Everything was being made ready.

"Feeling a bit stiff after your ride?" Richard asked, his mouth full of fish.

He passed the platter to her, and she took some in her fingertips. The white flesh came off in big flakes.

"It is best when freshly cooked. In a few hours when they ask us to table, it will taste like an old boot."

"Thank you, sir."

The fish was already half-bone.

"Tonight the King and Queen and all the earls and foreign dukes will be entertained in the great hall of the keep. But no feasting for us until the play and the hunt in two days time." Richard said licking his fingers. "Do you understand what is to happen?"

Illesa looked up from dissecting the fish.

"Somewhat, sir, yes. The knights will fight, they will capture and injure each other, and there will be feasting afterwards. But as to who I am meant to be, and what I am meant to be doing, no. Definitely not."

Richard put the platter with its pale bones down on the board, and leant forward, his chin on his clasped hands, smiling.

"That is good. It is meant to be a surprise."

"But not a surprise for me, surely."

"For almost everyone except you, and the players. Certainly for the King. He has planned this Round Table himself, except for this one thing. It was the Queen's idea." Richard wiped his knife on the wood of the seat, then on his hose. "She discussed it with my uncle who suggested that I would be a suitable person to arrange it. He knows my interest in the tales of chivalry, and this one is a favourite of mine. It is most important that it goes well. If it does not, the Queen will be very displeased, and she is not forgiving of incompetence. "

He did not seem particularly worried.

"Is your uncle here?"

"No, it seems he has taken himself to Acton, to arrange the building work. I wonder what Thomas the Priest will tell him when he arrives," Richard mused.

Illesa didn't like to think.

"Are you going to explain about the play or not?" Illesa said, attempting to change the subject.

"You understand the need for secrecy? I know I can trust Melchior to discipline his troupe. Their livelihood depends on their loyalty."

"What could I possibly gain from revealing your secret, sir? I am at your mercy entirely."

"We won't go into all the possibilities of gain." He had stopped smiling. "How many people have you spoken to since you arrived?"

"Only the players, and a woman at the well this morning."

"That is plenty. No knights?"

Illesa shook her head.

"That is well. Stay in the tent as much as you can. Do not speak to anyone, especially not the nobles. Don't draw attention to yourself. I will bring Earl Warenne who will play Sir Yvain to the players' tent at first light tomorrow, and you will practise with him."

"But sir, I do not understand what I am meant to be doing with Sir Yvain. Melchior has made me walk with the costume on and shown me a few dance steps and that is all."

"You will welcome my lord the King to his newly conquered kingdom," Richard said, indicating the land all around with a sweep of his arm, "in the person of the Lady of the Well."

"What do you mean?"

"Don't you know the story?"

"The Lady of the Well?"

"No, 'The Knight with the Lion'. But in fact they are the same story, one told in Welsh and one in French."

"No, sir." There was no end to the things she did not know about this kind of life, and these people who could simply go up to a spit and help themselves, and who clothed themselves in cloth so fine she could not see the weft or warp.

"The Knight with the Lion is Yvain, one of King Arthur's best knights. He was cousin to Gawain. Tell me you have heard of him."

"Yes, a little."

"Good. The Welsh also know this Yvain, but they call him Owain, and he is always known as the Knight of Ravens. You see the raven comes in again."

Illesa nodded, bemused. Richard began cleaning his nails with the end of his knife.

"But in this story it is Yvain, and he conquers the land of Landuc by jousting with the Black Knight, who is protector of a magic well, a holy spring."

"Sir -"

"Don't interrupt. I am just coming to the point where you will understand your part. Now, Yvain pursues the injured Black Knight right up to the gates of the castle, and he is trapped inside the portcullis. There he is helped by Lunette, who is the handmaid to Laudine, the Lady of Landuc. Lunette gives him a magic ring that makes him invisible, so even though the men of the castle look everywhere, they cannot find him. When the Black Knight dies of his wounds, Laudine is inconsolable. She tears her clothes with grief. But Lunette convinces her mistress to marry Yvain. He of course is a better knight than her husband because he won the fight, and so will be better at protecting her country, and of course, Yvain has fallen in love with Laudine because she is very beautiful. You are playing Laudine."

"Wait," Illesa interrupted, "you mean that Yvain killed Laudine's first husband, and she knows that he did it?"

"Yes, Yvain poured the water from the well on the stone, and that was a challenge to the Black Knight, Laudine's husband," Richard said, obviously trying to be patient. "So he came to fight Yvain and was killed."

"And then Laudine *marries* Yvain?"

"He is a better knight and will protect the land. That's the legend," Richard said, tapping the book.

"That is ridiculous. No wife who loved her husband would marry the man who killed him. Who wrote that?"

"It is one of the stories about King Arthur's knights, it isn't history chronicled by monks, Illesa."

"But it should at least be true about people. Women aren't as fickle as that."

"Maybe some are," Richard said.

"And men are even worse!"

"Even your own mother was not faithful."

"You don't have any right to talk about her!"

Richard leant back against the seat behind him and looked out over the lists and the distant tents. He pushed the hair from his forehead.

"I'm sorry. I should not have."

Illesa took a deep breath. None of it made any sense, least of all what she was doing in Wales in a company of players acting the part of a mad woman.

"May I continue?" Richard asked. Illesa nodded, not looking at him.

"They are married only a few weeks when King Arthur and his court come to try their luck at the well. The court does not know that Yvain has already won glory by conquering the Black Knight. So Sir Kay jousts with the new Black Knight, who is in fact Yvain, and is unhorsed. Yvain reveals himself to King Arthur and there is great rejoicing as the King of all Britain brings a new land under his rule."

Illesa opened her mouth, then shut it again.

"So we will show this story but with Edward as King Arthur. You will welcome the King into his new kingdom and the crowds will cheer and there will be a joyful procession to a canvas castle, where there will be a feast for the King and Queen. This is the particular story that the Queen wanted to celebrate the victory over Wales. She is hoping for good hunting on that morning, followed by the play of Yvain, music and feasting, and then afterwards a chance for the King to fly his new crane falcon which she has acquired for him. You will be at the feast in your role as Laudine, and so I will need to teach you some etiquette of the court." He turned to look at her appraisingly.

"Sir Richard, this must be a jest."

"Why do you say that?"

"I cannot be a lady and sit at a feast with the King."

"You can, indeed. You will be much better at it than you were at being a page or a vagrant boy. All you need is to hold yourself upright. They will be captivated by your face."

Heat flushed Illesa's cheeks.

"It must be a face they don't recognise, to represent the beautiful, conquered land. Sir Kay will be wearing the arms of Llewelyn and will be defeated. That will certainly provide good entertainment."

Illesa looked at the village just visible between the massed tents and banners.

"Should you be making sport of them, in their own land?"

"Making sport of the people of Wales? No, just their foolish leader who thought he was bigger and stronger than he was. His defeat was a victory for the Welsh people. They will have proper government now, and an end to the fighting amongst their nobles. They will have peace."

"That is the view of the conquering army."

"You know better, do you?"

"I know what it feels like to be hungry and without a home. I know that those people will be blaming the soldiers who burned their houses and ate their livestock, not their leader."

Richard put his face in his hands and spoke through his teeth.

"Illesa, are you going to play this part or are you making your own way home from this place?"

Illesa folded her hands. She could not always stop her thoughts escaping, but she would have to try.

"Sir, I will play Laudine, to repay some of your kindness to me."

He pushed his hands through his tangled hair. His eye was tired, bloodshot.

"Good. Now I will show you the passage that we will be enacting. There is a fine illumination of it in this book."

She moved closer to see the tiny illustration. It was richly painted in deep blue. The lady's mantle had tiny flecks of white representing pearls. The knight by her side was crested with a lion. Before them were a company of knights, behind them an entourage of richly dressed ladies. Somehow she had missed seeing it the day before.

"What does the lion have to do with it?"

"That comes later. You do not need to worry about the lion. There isn't one in this play that will eat you."

"But when will you tell me if not now, sir?"

He leant forward, looking pleased.

"I see you are interested. You may take the book to read again."

She took it in her palm and brushed the smooth, soft leather of the binding with her fingers.

"I do not know how to read French."

"Ah." He paused "I forgot." Richard took the book in his hand. "But it is not hard. I can teach you a little if you wish."

The page he turned was worn, although it had no illumination and only one pretty letter, encircled with vines and flowers. He began to read, his finger moving from word to word.

"Ma tres chiere dame,
vos qui estes mes cuers et m'ame,
mes biens, ma joie, et ma santez,
une chose m'acreantez
por vostre enor e por la moie."
La dame tantost li otroie,
qu'el ne set qu'il vialt demander
et dit: "Biax sire, commander
me poez ce qui boen vos iert." [3]

"My dearest wife, who are my heart, my soul, my treasure, my joy and my health, grant me one favour for your honour and mine,"[4] he continued. "You see this is the part where he asks her leave to go and fight in tournaments with the rest of Arthur's court."

"And she foolishly says 'Yes' without knowing what he asks," Illesa rejoined.

"Indeed. Later he loses her love because he does not return at the agreed time, and he becomes a madman of the woods. After that he helps a lion, and it becomes his faithful companion. Shall I read more?"

Richard was very close to her, bending over the book. The soft hair on his neck moved in the breeze. Over the southern hill, a large moon was rising.

"Sir, I am so tired. If I am to learn dancing and etiquette, I think I should rest."

He shut the book quickly and pulled away.

"As you wish."

Chapter III
June, AD 557
Fortress and Well of Meirchion
North Wales

She saw it from the window, a commotion by the gate, heard shouting and dropped her needle. It was not seemly to run, but she was not able to stop her feet, and saw Gethin's horse, the flanks and back stained bright red. Caron was holding on to his bridle, but the horse wheeled round churning up the dry earth.

"Lady, go in and close the door!" Caron pulled the straining horse towards the tethering post. Lather was mixed with the blood that had soaked its pale grey coat.

"Manon!" He had tied the horse and had her by the shoulders, his eyes wide and black. "Go in, there is nothing you can do." There was fear in his eyes that she did not feel. It had been inevitable, ever since Gethin had dismissed the messenger from Owain. She had seen it in her waking dreams.

"No." Manon shook herself away from his hands and took a step back. "No! We must not leave his body. You will come with me. We will bring him back."

"We cannot. They are coming. Listen!"

Behind the noise of the guard rallying at the gate and swords being sharpened, she heard the beat of hooves, and a long, high cry. The call to follow. He had not let one month go by. But he had a reputation for impatience. She looked around at the people running in panic from one door to another.

"Who else was out?"

"The herd boy, but no other." Caron gripped his spear. He knew as well as she did that they were not prepared. Eluned was there suddenly, tears in her half-blind eyes. Her hands were reaching for Manon's, her mouth was a twisted scream.

"No, sister." Manon pushed her away. "Don't let them hear you."

She looked towards the hall. Someone would have taken her daughter into hiding. Her baby son would sleep even through this: the death of his father, the ruin of his inheritance. There were rules, agreements and these warriors from the north kingdom surely knew them; they were kin after all. The horses and their riders were circling the fence. She could hear their spears scraping the wooden stakes.

Manon gripped the distaff hanging from her belt. The people were unnerved. Some would fight, but they were weak compared to the forces from the north, who were used to battle and had honed their strength on the Angles. Gethin had been too gentle with them. Too gentle. She covered her trembling lips with her hands. When it was time for mourning, she would rend flesh and cloth.

"Come with me," she ordered. Caron looked at her, frowning. He was the best she had, but even he did not want to risk an arrow or a dagger in the neck. "Do not anger me with your cowardice. Come!"

They pushed past the group of guards strapping on shields at the gate. Caron climbed the ladder ahead of her and pulled her up to the viewing platform. Only one guard stood ready, following the circling riders with his head like a skittish calf. Owain, their leader, had been clever to lure her husband to fight alone. If it had been a challenge to his honour, Gethin would not have refused it.

"Give me your spear," she demanded, holding out her hand.

"We will stand on either side of you," he said, as she gripped the ash shaft. "Keep your eyes on the men by the wood," he told the guard. "I will watch the others."

She stepped between them trying to stand upright. Owain, her cousin, was only just clear of the trees, mounted on a white horse, his spear at ease in his hand. All his riders carried spears, and they dragged their points along the wooden stakes. Her eyes followed Owain. The blood of her husband had marked his spear, and him.

He shouted so suddenly that she jerked her head back, as if she had been hit. The riders slowed their dance around the enclosure. They were gathering by the gate, leaving a path clear for their leader. Owain rode slowly forward on his white mare, came to a stop in front of her and rested his spear on the ground. His head was even bare, he was so arrogant, and his tangled golden hair blew around his face. If she had not known him and what he had done, she could have taken him for a youth barely schooled. But she remembered him well, her lust-filled cousin, two years her elder. All was there to see. All his pride and desire. Nothing was hidden from her, or the gods.

He bowed his head to her and the anger boiled over.

"Man of Rheged, since when did the spears of the north turn on their own kin and kill so dishonourably? Have you spent so much time in the company of the raiders that you have taken on their savagery? I will not speak to you until I have my husband brought to his hearth with the honour he deserves."

Owain's eyes did not move from her face as she spoke. She banged the end of the spear down hard, and his horse shook its bridle, the bronze fittings jangling and catching the light.

"My Lady and my cousin," he dropped his gaze before continuing. "It was never my wish to hurt Gethin." He was a good liar, even managing an expression of regret. Manon felt a sneer curl her lip. "But you know the dispute our fathers began years ago. Gethin had no authority to keep our clan from using the spring. My father forgot the slight for a while. He had his other territory to defend. But now the time has come to give us our sacred right."

Manon lowered the spear tip, sighting his throat, the blood that throbbed in his veins. But he was too far away to be taken by surprise. She would have to find another way. A way made by lies, like his.

"Can the men of Rheged not be trusted to keep their vow? Your father was barred from all rituals since he dishonoured and polluted the spring. He cannot have forgotten."

Owain changed his expression to one of rueful resignation.

"You know my father. That happened many years ago, and he feels reparation has been offered and accepted."

"Has the goddess started talking to him? No. She will not speak to one like him. He is nothing but a coward, sending his son to kill where he is afraid to go himself."

Owain jerked his head at that, but when he spoke his voice was even.

"My father ordered that I restore our family rights over the sacred spring, and it could have been accomplished without bloodshed. He believes making offerings to the goddess will help our cause in the north. You have been protected here from the strength of the enemy we face. We are under constant attack, and it is our clan who are bearing the losses."

His clan was also benefiting from all the trade, making alliances, appealing to new gods. Owain's father wanted to rule old and new, and his son was his principal weapon.

"Gethin would not see our need," Owain was saying. "He wanted the spring only for the house of Lot. But you know that one family cannot own the gods, or their favour, even if your wife is the handmaid of the goddess." He smiled at her with white teeth and made a flourish with his hand. "You are a wise woman. You will see the way forward to a union of our families once again. I know this."

"What you know is that no rituals will take place without me. Bring his body with full honour. After the rituals, we will speak."

Manon stepped away from the wall, out of his sight and sank down on the platform. Her husband's blood was still warm, still flowing into the ground and his killer desired her. It was shining out from his eyes. He had stared at her like a stray dog that has been thrown a scrap.

She would bring him to his knees.

"Manon, you should not anger him," Caron whispered anxiously. "He has already taken territory and men from all over the hill and the plain. If you anger him, more will die."

"He is a child."

"What do you mean?" Caron pleaded, taking her hand and pulling her up again. "He is one of the best warriors of the Rheged. They say his sword is magic, unbreakable, that it cuts through stone."

"Do not speak of it. Gethin must be buried; his soul will be unquiet. Stay here and tell me when they bring him." She dropped his spear and left him there on the wall. In one of the buildings her son was crying.

Chapter IV
The 28th day of July, 1284
Nefyn

That evening, Gaspar taught her the dance in a storm of foot stamping and swirling cloth. Illesa had only a vague notion of what her feet were supposed to be doing under her long skirt. Then he had insisted that they refresh themselves after their exertions from a small barrel of strong wine. After her second cup, the whole enterprise seemed extremely funny. She'd had at least two more before falling asleep with her head on a pile of costumes and sacks.

Gaspar, breathing stale wine, woke her and pulled her roughly to her feet, paying no attention to her complaints. It wasn't yet fully light.

"Come on, you old hag. Sir Richard will skin me and turn me into a glove for his own fair hand if I've got you too drunk to dance today."

His cure was to douse her head in cold water. So when Sir Richard and Earl Warenne arrived, she was dripping wet and just drying her hair with a spare tunic. Gaspar had disappeared. She smoothed her hair and clothes as best she could.

"Not ready, Illesa? I told Gaspar to make sure you were." Richard was staring at her anxiously.

"Sir, I will be ready, please excuse me for a moment." She went out of the back of the tent and relieved her full bladder. Already there was sound coming from every part of the field, drowning out the loud birdcall at sunrise. She had hardly dared look at Earl Warenne, who was obviously even wealthier than Richard judging by the embroidery on his tunic. Now she would have to take his hand and attempt to remember the dance that she barely knew with her head feeling like a mill wheel.

She slipped back in through the flap of the tent. The men were standing together, in mid-conversation. Earl Warenne was tall with long arms that hung twitching by his sides. He looked over at her, rested his eyes for a moment, and looked away, with an expression of disgust. Richard seemed to be struggling to explain, turning the red book over and over in his hands.

Illesa sat on the edge of one of the costume chests. Her mouth was dry and foul. She must try not to breathe upon the rich knight playing her husband.

"Mistress Arrowsmith!"

She opened her eyes.

"Yes, sir."

"What has Gaspar been giving you to drink, eh? Come on, get up." He was holding out her costume. She took it from his hands and pulled it over her head. The veil and headdress followed.

"That is a slight improvement."

"It couldn't have got much worse." Earl Warenne was surveying her without enthusiasm.

"You would rather have Gaspar?" Sir Richard asked.

"Very well. What is it you would have me do with this noble beauty?" he asked, mockingly.

He took his position opposite her with averted eyes. The entire rehearsal of the dance was punctuated by Earl Warenne's loud and undisguised sighs.

"Are we finished now, Burnel? May I go back to preparing myself for the actual purpose of this tournament?" He left through the flap without having addressed a single word to Illesa.

"I know," Richard said, seeing her expression. "Warenne has little charm. He is only doing this on sufferance for the Queen. He needs her favour at the moment, but she has never liked him."

"A woman of good taste," Illesa muttered.

"You can't blame him for being disappointed. What were you drinking last night? You look like a cat's arse."

"Gaspar got hold of a barrel. I didn't think I'd had very much."

"That little weasel. You stay here, and don't drink anything he gives you. I will bring you some food."

She crawled back to the pallet, and somehow slept in the midst of the noise and heat all around her. When she woke, her head was no longer spinning, but she felt sick with hunger. Peeking through the tent flap, she could see no one. The sound of drumming and a squealing scream of pain came from the direction of the field. She closed the flap. That must be what had woken her. The mêlée had begun, and men weren't the only ones being harmed. Richard was unlikely to remember to bring her food; there was far too much going on.

It wasn't far to the kitchen area. She might find some unguarded food while everyone was distracted. The veil Richard had bought for her in Wenlock was looking travel stained, but at least it had the effect of making her look less strange. She adjusted it quickly. The noise from the field had subsided. At any time the crowd at the mêlée might disperse.

Illesa stood just outside the tent. The canvas all around caught the gusting breeze, and the ropes smacked against the thick linen. She did not hear the person who came up behind her and gripped her shoulders.

"What are you doing out on your own?"

Illesa turned to see Gaspar, dressed as a rich matron, admonishing her, his face twisted in mock outrage. Illesa shrugged off his hands and put her own on her hips, working on some real anger.

"Have you got a sore head this morning? Oh dear. Now, don't be cross. Come on, I'll help you out. All you need is a good meal and some ale and you'll feel just as virtuous as ever."

He swept her into the tent and pushed her towards the only stool.

"You got me drunk. Then I had to try to dance with Earl Warenne while my head was spinning."

"I know dearie, I was watching! It was most entertaining."

"You were watching? How?"

"No, no, no," he shook his head solemnly. "I'm not going to give up my secrets that easily." He took off his wimple and ran his hand through his wheat-coloured hair. "So let's get you that ale and then we will decide what to do for the best."

"What do you mean?"

"How to beautify you, how to ingratiate you, how to make you irresistible."

"What are you talking about? Earl Warenne thinks I'm a drunken sow after this morning. You made sure of that, didn't you?"

"All part of the plan, my dear, all part of the plan. Lower his expectations so we can deliver the coup de grâce during the actual play. A well known dramatic trick."

Gaspar was rummaging around the tent, looking for something. He stood up suddenly, face victorious, holding a tankard.

"I shall return."

Illesa was still trying to make sense of his motives when he came through the canvas, the ale slopping over his sleeve.

"Do you really go out like that?" was all she could think to say as he handed her the tankard.

"Like what?" Gaspar tipped his head back and his hair stood almost on end. His long, shimmering gown swirled around him in a wide arc, as he posed in the style of a great lady.

"Sir Richard has told me not to drink anything you give me from now on," she said, sipping the ale. It was not sour and felt wonderful on her parched throat.

"He doesn't trust me with his fine lady," Gaspar concluded dolefully. Then he smiled. "Don't pay any attention to him. He asked me to do my best to ensure the success of this little play, and that is exactly what I am doing, though he may not believe it. Warenne is the most boring man. All he cares about is winning honour on the battlefield, showing himself to be the best at all costs. So dull. No sense of humour. He will take it much too seriously. We must shake him up a little. Give him a surprise, otherwise all we will have is a proper little piece of arse licking."

"So that's your game, eh Gaspar." Sir Richard stood in the tent opening, a platter in one hand, a tankard in the other, looking exasperated. "I knew you would have some devious motive for humiliating us this morning."

"Kind sir, do not be angry," Gaspar threw himself on his knees in enthusiastic supplication.

"Get up," Richard said, prodding him with his boot. "Here you are." He gave Illesa the platter. There was coarse bread, cheese and a cake of some kind, perhaps made of curd.

"I see you have been taking my advice." He gestured at Gaspar's tankard, which she had already drained. "You can't trust that boy, you know. Don't believe a word he says." Richard gulped the ale in his own tankard and stared accusingly at Gaspar.

"Yes, sir. I am beginning to see what you mean," Illesa agreed.

Gaspar stopped smoothing his skirts and treated her to his most betrayed look.

"So, you have a plan to make the play more exciting?" Richard snapped. "I expect you would like to sing a rude song and have a lion dance to the music whilst the mummers lead the knights into hell's mouth. You always did lack subtlety."

"No sir." Gaspar stood demurely, shaking his head. "I merely want to add a bit of surprise and romance to a rather boring tale of fighting and conquering."

"You don't seem to understand that the Queen herself has requested this scene, and that a scene from 'The Knight of the Lion' is what we must do," he reached inside his surcoat and touched the red book in its special pocket.

"Ah yes, the Queen. A wonderful woman. Very good at bearing children, but not what I would call an expert in entertainment," Gaspar mused, his head on one side.

"Are you unhappy in the role I have assigned to you, Gaspar? Is that what this is all about?"

"Not at all, by Christ. No, no. Being the handmaiden Lunette will be most agreeable. Indeed, I am taking my role to heart and have already begun to prepare the two lovers to be joined as one." He brought his two hands together in a tight clasp.

Richard's face became stern.

"You are not selling her. She is not for sale."

"Oh, I understand that, Sir Richard. It is all in the service of the play. It is not real, of course. By your leave." He gave a radiant smile and flounced out of the tent.

Richard stood looking after him for several moments. When he turned to Illesa, she was putting the last piece of bread in her mouth.

"You have no idea what he is capable of."

Her mouth was full, so she gave a sympathetic shake of the head.

"Why do you use him?" she mumbled.

"He is the best, the funniest, the most entertaining. But also the most vain, immoral and devious. If he likes you, he will do anything for you. But if he does not, he will find a way to humiliate you without your even realizing. He has fallen out with Earl Warenne, as you heard. Perhaps this is more about him than you."

He paused and looked out of the tent opening.

"The morning mêlée is over. The Earl of Ulster was victorious and some of the Earl of Lincoln's men were captured. One was badly injured. I thought you ought to see him. He is a good friend, and I did not like what I saw of the treatment he received. I will take you to him, but keep your head down. I don't want you noticed."

He was waiting for her to follow him. She cast around for her pack, found it behind the casket containing the players' ointments and dyes, pulled her veil forward, brushed the crumbs from her tunic and followed him out of the tent.

Richard said little as she worked on William de Leyburn. He seemed preoccupied, standing at the tent entrance leafing through his book. Perhaps regretting his choice for Lady Laudine.

As well as a broken arm, which had been treated and set by the physician, the back of the knight's head had suffered either a kick or a hard fall. It took a while to make the infusion for him, and all the time, the sound of the crowd was growing louder. There seemed to be a form to the noise; names she did not recognise being shouted by a thousand lips.

When they left, Richard led the way, but not back to the poor tents of the entertainers and minstrels. They were going to the field and the roar of the crowd. Illesa followed close at Richard's heels as they came into the open. All the colours of meadow flowers adorned the knights, banners and ladies. Most of the knights were not mounted or helmed, but stood to either side of the sandy ground. On the benches on the far side, hung with red cloth embroidered with gold lions, sat a group clad in ermine and velvet, silk, gold and bright jewels. In the centre of this group sat a tall man wearing a crown.

On either side of the field, two mounted knights faced each other, their squires at their sides holding lances. There was a blast of horn from somewhere near the stands, and the lances were passed up.

"It is the Duke of Brabant, in the arms of Sir Gawain, and your friend Earl Warenne armed as Sir Yvain," Richard whispered. "I have never seen the Duke joust, but he is well known for his skill."

Illesa tried to keep her eyes on the two knights, but everywhere there was movement and beauty, symbols and pictures in cloth and thread. She and Sir Richard stood at the rail surrounded by men, probably armourers, wearing leather aprons. All around, there was cloth in colours Illesa had ever seen in nature.

"You can stare at the crowd later," Richard said. "Here they go."

The horn blew, and the cry of "*Laissez aller*" went up. The horses were spurred towards the centre of the field. There was an almighty crack, splinters were flying and the knights were past each other. One of them, the Earl, was leaning back, his lance dropping from his gauntlet.

"Ha!" Richard cried. "Very good!" The Duke of Brabant raised the remains of his shattered lance. "That will give the Earl something to think about." He looked at Illesa. "They will ride again as neither was thrown from his horse. But it is the Duke who is ahead."

"Why do you want him to win? I thought the Earl was your friend."

"He would not call me friend," Richard said quietly. "In any event, it is pleasant to watch a new challenger win for a change. Even the King is pleased." He raised his chin to the stands where the King was leaning forward.

The more she looked at the Queen, the older Illesa thought she was. She did not look at the knights in the lists but only at the boy who sat between her and the King.

"That is the heir to the throne, Alphonso," Sir Richard whispered. "Edmund, the Duke of Lancaster, is sitting on the King's other side."

They were getting ready for the next assault. A passing shadow dulled the tall Duke's armour momentarily, but not the impact of his presence. He laughed with his squire and took hold of his new lance quite casually.

"What if Earl Warenne is injured and cannot play his role?" she whispered in Richard's ear.

"That would be interesting, wouldn't it?" There was a wicked little smile on his lips. "Now who would you prefer to take his place?"

When the horn sounded, the Duke of Brabant spurred his grey stallion. Earl Warenne was bearing down on him, his many tokens streaming out behind him. It was such an elaborate way to be maimed or killed.

Illesa closed her eyes at the moment of impact.

There was no sound of splintering wood. She opened her eyes. The Duke's lance was unbroken, and he was trotting calmly back to his squire. The Earl was intact also. The crowd was muttering

"What happened?"

"What? Didn't you watch? The Earl pulled his horse round intending to catch the Duke on the side, but the Duke evaded him. No points. This is the last pass, so keep your eyes open."

She tried, but at the moment of impact she had to turn her head.

Both men seemed to have been hit. The Duke's head was lolling to the right, and the Earl was slumped forward in his saddle. Their squires rushed forward and led the horses to the edge of the stands. Two broken lances lay on the churned-up sand.

"It is a victory for the Duke, but not by much. I think when they are feeling a bit better we will hear that the Earl has issued a further challenge."

"But they are too hurt!"

Minstrels in the gold and red colours of the King had come on to the field holding their instruments out as if offering them to the royal audience. The King nodded his head slightly and they began to play. The tune was rousing. Richard sang softly along.

"In the tavern, when we're drinking
though the ground be cold and stinking
down we get to join the action
with the dice-controlling faction:
what goes on inside the salon —
where it's strictly cash per gallon —
if you'd like to know, sir, well you
shut your mouth and I shall tell you." [2]

"I doubt those are the words that the King knows," he remarked, smiling, then took her elbow and steered her firmly away from the field. "They are just stunned. A cup of wine and they will be ready for more. Now come away, that is quite enough exposure for one day. People will start noticing you, in spite of your worn-out clothes."

Illesa was feeling particularly self-conscious of the poverty of the cloth she wore compared to the courtiers in their jewels, as bright as sparks from hot iron.

"You will look much better tomorrow once Melchior has tightened the costume and Gaspar has enhanced your features with his paint."

He seemed to be able to read her thoughts like the words in his French romance.

"Let's go round this way, and avoid the knight's quarters," he said picking his way past the armourer's forge and down a quiet path.

"Sir, would you tell me more of the tale of Yvain and Laudine, if you have time. I still find it hard to see the sense of the story."

"That is a humble tone you are employing, Mistress. It is not like you." His glance was amused, but then his head whipped round to the right, and he stopped suddenly at an open tent by the path. In the shadow of the awning were blocks with rings and perches. Not all were occupied. Sir Richard was staring at a large un-hooded white falcon that was tied next to an orange-eyed hawk. Each feather was tipped in black. Its eyes swivelled above a sharp curved beak.

"What a beauty. A gyrfalcon. I am certain this is the bird that you will present tomorrow. You will be one of the few, other than the King, ever to hold it."

The master falconer stepped forward, a slight, stern man with a goshawk on his glove. He did not let Richard approach closer than the rope fence. He had his orders. No one was to touch the bird.

"It is unlikely you will be able to hold it before the play," Richard whispered. "But you are not afraid are you? And you have a strong right arm, I'm sure. You will need to hold the bird whilst you make your speech."

The bird regarded her with fierce eyes.

"I have only held a kestrel once, that Kit found. What do I do with it?" Panic began to stir her fragile stomach.

"I will show you in the morning. The King and Queen will set off early with the lyam hounds to hunt deer, guided by Calogrenant. That is the knight you just treated. He will lead them to the well where the joust will take place."

Illesa thought of the knight lying senseless in his tent.

"I do not think he will be able to ride. Does it have to be him?"

"Well, it should be Calogrenant, because in the story it is he who has the first adventure by the well and tells Yvain, Kay and Guinevere." Richard tapped the book inside his coat for emphasis.

"Can't you ask someone else to wear the arms of Calogrenant?"

"They all have their roles. It was a hard negotiation. Knights of this rank are very possessive of their status." Richard paused and looked towards the sun, estimating the hour. "We must begin the preparations in earnest. So the royal party will arrive at the well and Earl Warenne will joust with Sir L'Estrange who plays your first husband, the Black Knight. After the death of the Black Knight, Gaspar will do his speech, encouraging you to marry Yvain. Then Yvain will be called back to the well where Sir Kay waits to joust. When Kay is defeated you make your speech and present the gyrfalcon to the King, as well as the Spanish horse from the Queen. Then you will all retire to the canvas castle for a feast. After that, the King will fly the falcon on the cranes of the marsh. Don't look like that. It is perfectly straightforward."

Illesa looked at the falcon. Its claws were bright yellow, with long needle talons. She had to master this bird and then present it to the King. She swallowed the nausea rising in her throat.

"You will have a glove, you know," Richard said, as he walked away. "And you will not be required to fly her. It will be fine."

They were all up late with the preparations. Richard spent a long time waiting for an audience with the Queen. She could not see him until after the joust, when the King retired to his chamber in the keep and did not require her. Richard returned to the players' tent in a bad temper.

"Leyburn is still unwell and cannot ride and the Queen has insisted on her choice for the part of Calogrenant."

They all looked up at him, even Balthazar who had been trying to sleep.

"She wants Prince Alphonso to do it."

There was an intake of breath.

"Isn't this complicated enough?" shouted Melchior.

Gaspar was the only one smiling. He was sitting next to Illesa on the chest, wearing only hose and boots, as he had been about to try on the costume of Lunette. It was hard not to stare at his smooth, muscled body.

"I don't know what you are all complaining about. He is perfect," Gaspar trilled.

"No, he isn't," Richard cut in. "He is a child and the heir to the throne, playing the part of an experienced knight of King Arthur's court. If things go wrong the King and Queen will have even more cause to be angry."

"How old is he?" Illesa asked.

"He can't be more than eleven," Richard grumbled. "Although he has a good seat on a horse, I'll admit."

"Very well," declared Melchior in his deepest, most doom-laden voice, "we have no choice but to include him as we have been instructed. But the arms for him must be taken in. He has not Leyburn's height or girth."

"That is the least of our concerns," Richard said, leaning against the chest next to Gaspar.

"I will look after that boy. You, leave him to me."

"You will leave him well alone, Gaspar. You need to spend all your waking minutes instructing our Lady Laudine in the points of court behaviour."

Gaspar pulled a face at her.

"I will talk Alphonso through the part," Richard decided. "Everyone says he is a bright lad and eager to excel at hastiludes, although the Queen always wants him close to her." He fell silent for a moment, scratching his beard.

"She keeps him pinned to her skirts," Gaspar whispered in Illesa's ear. "What he needs is a longer leash."

"You two," Richard said, looking at Gaspar and Illesa, "will remember that the Prince is none of your concern and get to work."

Gaspar tucked his legs up and hugged his knees. He looked like an imp.

"As you wish, Sir Richard."

They did not finish the preparations till after compline, and even then Illesa could not sleep. The noise of men and animals going about as if it were broad daylight did not help. Her speech went through her head and her stomach turned. She could only hope that this play would not offend God or the King, and her inexperience would pass without notice. It had been unwise to eat the strange food set out for the players, especially as she had not kept to any fast since leaving Rushbury. Perhaps there was no fasting for the King and his court, and this was how they always lived: feasting, dressing and watching the fights of their nobles for sport.

Chapter V
The 29th day of July, 1284
Nefyn

The morning sky was grey, and a wind was whipping through the tent. They had not discussed what they would do if the weather turned bad, but when Richard arrived he was unconcerned.

"We need a storm when the knights arrive at the well. There is meant to be thunder and lightning when the knight pours the water on the stone."

"But it will spook the horses and the birds," Illesa said, thinking of the gyrfalcon.

"Maybe. But not everyone is as easily alarmed as you," he said blithely. They packed the wagon and within minutes were ready to go. Richard stood in the tent entrance, blocking the light, while she tried to find her things. Gaspar was complaining bitterly at having to walk with the wagon.

"You are a fit young man, not a delicate lady. Try to remember that, Gaspar," Richard said as he led Illesa away.

She tried not to meet Gaspar's eye as she passed the wagon; his scowl was impressive. At the stable they took Buskins and another horse Illesa had never seen before. The stallion was elegant, well proportioned, and had the colour and sheen of a fresh chestnut.

"Which one would you rather ride? I understand that Maximilian is a bit of a handful, but the sooner you ride him the better as you must handle him during the play."

The stallion was the tallest, most imposing horse she had ever seen.

"Why don't I lead the wagon and let Gaspar ride?" Illesa said.

"You must arrive fresh and beautiful, not road weary."

"I'd like to arrive in one piece."

"I'm surprised at you," Richard said, looking amused. "I didn't think you would be afraid of a horse after riding that Jezebel. Come on. I will lead on Max and Buskins will follow me. You will hardly need to do anything, just hold on."

Once she got used to Buskins' stride it became an enjoyable journey. The rain had stopped, and it was cool. From the high ground she could see the rough sea, dotted with tossing boats.

They came down from the hills, into an area of sparse habitation, reeds and bogs. To the south was a wooded rise, and in the distance to the east the sea crashed at the base of a long steep cliff jutting out into the bay. They joined a track that skirted the marsh, circling around to a large timber manor.

"You see the platform? That is for the celebration tonight. It doesn't look finished. What have they been doing? They've had three days," Richard muttered.

He pulled Maximilian up in front of the wooden structure. It was much bigger and higher than it had looked from a distance. The floor of the platform was above Richard's head, and one man knelt there knocking in a peg with a mallet. Another was sawing off plank ends. The unseasoned wood was wet and pale. On the side near the manor, a set of steps had been erected but not yet secured. The platform above had a raised dais but the steps and the dance floor looked loose and rough.

"Here man, what's this? Why isn't this done? Where is Dafydd?"

The nearest man put his mallet down slowly, came to the edge of the platform and looked at them. Nor was he in any hurry to speak.

"He has gone. He is looking for more wood," the man said in a strong Welsh accent.

"But this must be done before the King arrives this very day!" Richard shouted.

The man shrugged unhappily, looking at Richard as if he were a snail or a beetle in the crop.

"There is little wood to make it. The men are ill and do not work."

"It must be done, man! What there is of it must be hung with cloth and made ready. You must secure the stairs and cut off these rough ends."

The man looked to where Richard was gesturing. His hands hung loose at his sides.

"There is no way to make it ready today."

"Of course there is, man, but you must make haste!"

"This is for the King?"

"Yes," Richard said, exasperated.

"Which one?"

"What do you mean? There is only one King."

"Arthur or Edward?"

"What are you talking about?"

"I hear that King Arthur is coming here to Neigull."

"It is King Edward who comes, in the arms and costume of King Arthur," Richard said speaking slowly and clearly.

The man grunted, spat and picked up his mallet again.

"So you will make it ready, or there will be no pay."

The man ignored him and went over to the steps.

Richard watched him for a moment, then wheeled the stallion round.

"They won't get paid for shoddy work."

"Why do they need that platform?" Illesa asked, looking back at it over her shoulder.

"Tonight there will be dancing, with the finest musicians. They have composed new songs in honour of King Arthur and his knights, who will unite the country under one just law," Richard said rather bitterly.

"But didn't they have dancing last night?"

"No, they played games, which I was lucky to avoid as many of the knights lost more coin than they could afford. This is to be the main dance and feast, just as described in the Tales of the Round Table." Richard felt for the book through his coat. "The Queen especially requested it to be near the hunting grounds, and high enough to provide a good view. Leyburn was put in charge of it. He met the men and explained the requirements, but since his injury, it seems no one has been overseeing it properly. The Steward of the manor should have taken control. The ladies of the court will be very angry if there is no dancing."

"I will not be required to dance, will I? Except with Earl Warenne?"

"I don't know," Richard grumbled. "This is the Queen's entertainment, and we all have to do her will."

They rode up the track in silence. The day seemed impossibly complex and dangerous. The sun had been up almost three hours and everything needed to be ready by midday. The sick feeling she'd had in the night churned in her stomach. And it had been her idea to join the troupe of players. Now she would pay for her folly.

The well was at the base of the woodland, near a tall pine. On rising ground to the west stood the canvas castle, being pegged down by two men.

"Some able bodied souls. Thank God's beard. They can go and help the joiner, at least. So," Richard said, sweeping his arm across the field in front of the well, "this is where the Black Knight will joust with Yvain. The court will wait over there," he said waving his hand to the eastern side of the field. "You will wait at the castle until the Black Knight returns mortally wounded. I imagine you remember the rest," he said, frowning at her as he dismounted. "Now you'd better get up there, I see the wagon coming. Get into your costume and stay out of sight. You lead Maximilian up there. It will give you an idea of how to handle him."

He mounted Buskins and rode over to the wagon, no doubt with more orders to give. Maximilian shook his head as she pulled him towards the castle. He had a way of picking up his hooves that was different, as if he came from a foreign land. Perhaps he was thirsty. She led him to the spring and he followed, eagerly enough. The water filled the square stone-lined well. There was a rough bench on two sides. It was awkward but possible for Maximilian to plant his hooves and drink. When he lifted his nose from the water, he shook all over as if the water had made him shiver. He was a magnificent animal.

Illesa dipped her hand in and drank. It was icy cold with a hard mineral flavour. Surely it was a holy well, but there was no indication of the saint, or any offerings. Perhaps they had been destroyed in the war. The only monument was a smooth flat-topped grey stone nearby.

Illesa made a quick prayer to Our Lady in case she had shown any disrespect. Maximilian was nosing the grass, and she let him graze for a while. There was no sense in rushing to the canvas castle when the wagon had not yet arrived. Richard had read the whole story of Yvain to her last night, and she could understand why the Queen had wanted it enacted and why Richard had chosen this place. It matched the description in the red book very well. The only thing that didn't match was her.

Her speech was not long, thank the saints. Gaspar had three times as much to say. But then, she was meant to represent the conquered land, and they were never encouraged to speak. She led the horse up the gentle slope. The men had finished pegging the sides of the large tent and had lifted the flap at the front up high on poles, as if it were an elevated drawbridge. It was marvellously painted to imitate stone and battlements. There were even sockets for torches. More men were unloading benches and trestles from a wagon at the back of the castle.

Illesa found a tethering post near the entrance and tied Maximilian with enough rein to graze. As she finished, another rider drew up: the master falconer with the gyrfalcon hooded on his wrist. The falconer handed the reins of his black mare to one of the tent men, and stroked the bird's breast. It looked even larger now she saw it on someone's arm. He turned around and gestured her nearer.

"Are you the lady who is to play Laudine?"

Illesa nodded.

"You have handled birds before?"

"No, sir."

The master falconer gave her a sharp look.

"Not at all?"

"Only a kestrel and it was untrained."

"That is a pity." He looked her up and down. "You are not wearing that in the play are you?"

She shook her head.

"There is no point putting the falcon on your wrist now, and then you change your clothes, and there are bright jewels no doubt? Eh? So we will wait until you have transformed yourself and then you and Seraphina will be introduced."

He turned away and went to his pack, taking out and setting up her perch and water dish, entirely one-handed, holding her steady throughout.

The process of getting ready for the play was long and bad tempered. Gaspar and Melchior had fallen out on the journey and would not speak to each other. Gaspar began to paint Illesa's face, while Melchior arranged the headdress, and much later they finally let her move. Her neck was aching from holding still.

"Are you sure this will stay on?" she asked putting a tentative finger up to the jewelled crown on top of the flowing silk veil.

They ignored her. Gaspar was putting the finishing touches to his own beautiful gown and headdress, his slightly turned-up nose twitching excitedly, when they heard voices and hooves from outside.

"Are you ready? The King approaches, led by his own son. Come and see," Richard beckoned. "They have caught a stag and the Duke butchered it properly in the forest, just as in the tales. It is all going well. We might even get that storm. Come and look, all of you, but Illesa, keep out of sight."

She was only allowed to peek through a small gap in the fabric, but it was enough to see the flowing banners of the King's arms being carried at the front of the procession by a small rider on a neat white mare, leading a large party into the clearing. They circled round. The King rode a fine grey stallion in front of the Queen on a matching speckled mare. They drew up by the well.

"I must go. Remember, loud voices, and Gaspar, for God's love, don't say anything to upset the King or the Queen," Richard said, pointing at him.

Gaspar winked.

"Of course not, Sir Richard."

"Come with me, Balthazar."

As Richard strode down the slope brandishing the red book with Balthazar at his side, a knight in bright armour with a black tunic and banner and a black shield rode up, saluting Richard. He drew to a halt to the right of the castle door.

"All well in the land of Landuc, eh? Be kind and nurse me well, for I fear I will die today," shouted the knight.

Gaspar laughed like a girl.

"Good Sir L'Estrange, die in my arms. I will carry you all the way to Paradise."

The clouds were being chased across the sky. A patch of sunlight shone on the water of the well, where Earl Warenne as Yvain, a lion on his helmet, stooped to scoop up the water and pour it on the rock. The musicians at the base of the hill drummed the thunder. The Black Knight hoisted his lance and allowed his horse to gather pace down the hill. The King wheeled his horse to face the approaching knight, and the Queen put her hand out, restraining him, and spoke in his ear, explaining. Illesa could see the age in the King's face, if not his bearing, but he was still ready to fight; any threat, any foe.

Chapter VI
The 29th day of July, 1284
Neigull

There was very little to the contest between Earl Warenne as Yvain and Sir L'Estrange as the Black Knight. The twenty or so mounted courtiers and nobles tried to encourage the Black Knight to more effort, but to no avail. After five passes, Sir L'Estrange slumped in his saddle, spurred his horse and made for the castle moaning and clutching his breast.

"Quick! Now!" Gaspar called. He grabbed her hand and pulled her towards the open flap. "Stand there! When he falls from his horse, weep at his side." He pushed her to the right of the castle.

The Black Knight was nearly at the top of the rise, only paces away. He pulled off his helmet and tossed it to the side, reined in his horse and slid from it, collapsing on the ground at her feet. Sir Yvain was still galloping after him. He did not stop, but galloped straight into the canvas castle, and two tent men brought the flap down behind him.

"Weep! Mourn!" Gaspar said in a loud whisper. He had the black horse's rein in one hand and the Black Knight's helmet in the other as he wheeled round to face the murmuring crowd below.

"My Liege, Your Highness and all nobles here.
All ladies, all knights give me your ears."

Gaspar's voice managed to be loud enough for the nobles below to stop talking, and at the same time it had the air of a husky whisper.

"For now our tale is sorrow unalloyed,
Yet soon all will be light and joy.
I am Lunette – "

Gaspar paused to thrust out his stuffed bosom,

"As round as the moon.
So comely, that I can make a man swoon.

But virtue is mine, as is very fitting.
I don't eat my meal in only one sitting.
I serve my lady, Laudine the fair.
She is like sunlight, with golden hair.
Wedded to a noble as black as night.
What a marriage of dark and light."

Gaspar gestured at her. Illesa began to get up, but Gaspar waved his hand again, as if swatting a fly.

"More of her later," he said with disdain.

"But what of this knight so covered in gore?
What was he so sorely wounded for?
Where is the culprit? That Knight Yvain?
He must die for his sin, that is plain.
Or so says the court, but not Lunette –"

Gaspar struck an attitude of defiance:

"He's not dead, nor captured yet."

Illesa could see Gaspar's face in profile and his smile of anticipation.

"I know this knight."

There was a long meaningful pause.

"He's very good.
He's as upright as a plank of wood."

There were guffaws from below.

"He's brave and strong, and full of passion
the finest knight that nature could fashion.
His lance is strong and long and broad
and many have felt it, upon my word!
He rides so well than none can throw him,"

Gaspar whipped an imaginary horse,

"but he throws off others upon a whim."

He mopped tears from his eyes with the end of his sleeve. Illesa watched him, horrified. The words were not Melchior's. Gaspar was making up his own play.

"He serves the ladies well, I hear.
He served me far too well I fear!
But fain would I see him cold and dead.
I'd rather see him in my bed."

Gaspar reached into his bosom and brought out a glittering thing.

"I have a ring that will make him vanish
and then I can hide him wherever I wish!"

The gesture Gaspar used at this point was not ladylike.

"I will comfort him, and give him joy,
What a lucky maid to find such a boy!"

Gaspar disappeared into the tent. The musicians at the well began to play an interlude on tabor and pipe.

"What do we do now?" Sir L'Estrange asked, opening his eyes.

"I don't know, sir. Gaspar is not playing it as Melchior instructed."

"Oh well. I shall simply have to stay here and gaze into your eyes, for ever," he smirked. Illesa looked away. The courtiers were restless. Some had begun to talk amongst themselves.

"Stand up and let him be carried off!" came a loud whisper from the tent.

Illesa stood up and immediately four servants came with a bier, lifted him onto it and carried him away.

"Mourn! Weep! Rend your clothes!"

Illesa self-consciously began to cry.

Gaspar re-emerged from the tent, a big smile on his face.

"What a man, there's none so fine.

If only I could make him mine.
But he has seen the light of this lady
and all he wants is to make his plea
for her hand, her love and all her treasure.
He has a love that is without measure."

Gaspar stood in profile and measured an enormous member.

"It is up to me to make the match.
And I can do it, just you watch.
Although she hates him for killing her love
Soon her love I'll make to move
and soon she'll breathe, and blush and bite
only to have him by her side all night.
Come my lady, do not mourn!"

Gaspar approached Illesa, put an arm around her shoulder
and rocked her from side to side.

"You are crying more water than a storm.
What is the point of all your woe?
You must find someone to fight your foe.
For who will defend this kingdom when
an enemy comes to the well again?
When they pour the water and bring the thunder,
You must have a knight. But who I wonder?
It must be someone strong and skilled.
I know! The Knight who wasn't killed!
The man who beat the old Black Knight,
who poured the water and won the fight.
He is strong, there's no one stronger.
He will defend all your honour."

Illesa shook her head and continued to cry into her hands. At
least that bit sounded familiar.

"Oh what a fool you are, my lady.
There's none with a better pedigree.
He is one of Arthur's best.
He has been tried –" Gaspar paused: *"and stood the test."*

290

Laughter rippled through the courtiers.

"The Black Knight is lying cold and dead.
He can't keep you warm in bed.
He can't bring you hot desires.
He can't bring you passion's fires.
But this knight loves you with all his soul.
His love for you is beyond control.
Won't you see him? You'll change your mind
Then to him, yourself will bind."

Gaspar reached out and took her hand and led her into the doorway of the tent where Yvain stood. He joined their hands and brought their heads together.

Earl Warenne was pale with fury, his lips thin and white. He would not take his eyes from Gaspar.

"That boy is trying to make a fool of me!" he said, gripping her hand very hard in his mail glove.

Gaspar winked at him and continued.

"So it was I saved his life,
and so it was he got his wife.
And they are happy as sun and flower
They make love at every hour.
But what is this? Another knight
has come to give them all a fright.
It is Sir Kay, that old buffoon
I think he deserves Lunette's full moon."

Gaspar lifted his skirts, turned his back on the courtiers and stuck out his bottom.

Illesa's heart sank. Gaspar smiled at her as he showed his arse to the King.

"Don't worry, girl. I've kept my braies on," he whispered.

The court burst into laughter as Gaspar smoothed his skirts back into order and Sir Kay cantered around the field.

"Sir Kay has come to prove his worth,
but soon he'll be laid out on the earth.
Come Sir Yvain, now leave your love.

You have your prowess to prove."

Earl Warenne stomped into the tent and got his horse. When he returned, he grabbed Gaspar's arm.

"Any more of those jokes and you will answer to my sword," he hissed.

Gaspar gave a gasp of delight and curtsied.

"Oh dear sir, I would love to converse with your sword. Sheathe it with me," he giggled, fluttering his eyelashes.

Earl Warenne looked at him with impotent rage, then he glanced down the slope at Sir Owen de la Pole, wearing the arms of Llywellyn Gruffydd, beside the waiting King and Queen. He mounted his horse and descended the hill at full gallop.

The blow he struck de la Pole on the first pass knocked him out of his saddle. Warenne galloped around the fallen man, until it was clear he was not able to get up. Sir Owen's squire came forward to assist him and the Earl backed away to the side of the well. Eventually de la Pole was helped to his feet, and both knights removed their helms.

Sir Richard was gesticulating wildly behind the King. It was her cue. She picked up her skirts and rounded the corner of the castle. Maximilian was tethered just out of sight, and the master falconer was waiting for her by his side, holding the hooded gyrfalcon.

Balthazar was just audible, speaking in his deepest tones.

"Sir Kay is shown to be a fool.
No longer will his wit be cruel.
No more will he insult his betters,
or else he will end up in fetters.
King Arthur knows of Yvain's strength;
he has taken this land, both width and length."

The falconer fitted the glove over her left hand, lifted Seraphina and pressed her talons to the glove. The gyrfalcon stepped back and gripped the leather. He brought the jesses into Illesa's palm and let go.

"Don't release the jesses until the King's hand is by yours, then press as I have done. He will know what to do."

The falcon was bobbing forward, her black-edged feathers rumpled in the wind.

292

One of the grooms brought Maximilian's lead rein to her. It was going to be a long walk down the slope to the King. Thank the saints she had been allowed to wear her own boots, which did not show under her enormous skirt.

"The land is his, and all is well," Balthazar continued.
"There is a victory to tell.
Here comes the lady of this land
to welcome the king with her fair hand.
She brings to him all he is owed,
in tribute and in honour showed."

Balthazar was standing before the King, his arm raised in the agreed signal.

The musicians began to play. The noise of the citole, drum, and pipes became louder as she descended and Seraphina began to bate, her wings flapping frantically. Balthazar gestured for the musicians to stop, and the crowd stood suddenly hushed and expectant. Illesa continued down the slope, tugging on the rein. The bird was still unhappy, digging her talons in hard and bobbing her head so the feather on her hood wagged comically.

The King was not in his place next to the Queen. He had ridden over to Prince Alphonso, who was dressed in the tunic she had helped sew the previous night. The King was standing, speaking earnestly to the Prince, unaware of his role in the next part of the play. Illesa changed direction pulling the reluctant horse behind her. There was a murmur of laughter. The King looked up, saw her approach and frowned. She probably looked like a stable boy, not the noble lady of a fabled land. The Queen pulled her horse up by his other side and regarded Illesa with a hard enquiring stare. Illesa inclined her head to the King and Queen.

"My King, the liege of my dear lord,
I welcome you by his bright sword.
I welcome you by Christ's true cross
I bid you come without fear of loss.
All that sought to take your crown,
all the foe have been thrown down.
Here take our tribute, sovereign King:
a horse so swift, it feels a'wing,

a bird so strong it strikes its prey
hard as a lance or sword in mêlée.
And now the rightful King has come,
the feast begins with pipe and drum."

The musicians led by Melchior began again. Illesa held out the falcon and the rein with shaking hands. The King tilted his head to the Prince, who smiled warily and took the rein. She lowered her gaze as the King came towards her, tall and broad in a thick red cape.

"A beauty," he said, and placed his hand behind her own. Seraphina stepped onto his glove. Illesa removed her hand as the King took the jesses under his thumb. His person had the scent of leather and aromatic wax. Illesa curtsied.

"Your land awaits you, sovereign lord.
Come in the name of Christ's own blood.
Come to table, in all good faith.
Come to feast, all good men saith."

She went to Maximilian, knelt by his side and held the stirrup.

The King whispered something to the Queen, smiled and strode to the horse's side. He mounted easily, still holding the falcon. Illesa backed away from the horse as the King wheeled it round to face his court.

"A hundred thousand welcomes lord,
and all God's blessings do thee good."

Illesa opened her arm, indicating the canvas castle, and lowered her gaze. The blood pounded in her cheeks. No one moved. She glanced up through her lashes. The King was holding the falcon close to him, examining the detail of her feathers.

The Queen coughed, and the King looked up and around at the assembled nobles, as if surprised to find them there.

"Very good, very good!" he declared, holding Seraphina confidently aloft at arm's length. "A diverting play. I thank you. Let us all go to the feast. Come Knights of the Round Table, come ladies of those Knights, come victors over our foes. We will give thanks and eat in the name of our victorious Lord."

With his other hand the King raised a jewelled reliquary that hung around his neck. The relic inside was set in rock crystal, mounted in gold and adorned with pearls and sapphires. All the courtiers bowed their heads and crossed themselves. Illesa quickly did the same.

The King and Queen urged their mounts up the rise to the canvas castle. Nobles streamed past behind them. Illesa could just see Sir Richard next to a lady wearing a deep blue cape on the other side of the crowd. The knights were taking off their plate and mail. As the King and Queen reached the entrance to the castle the minstrels began an old tune.

"Woods and glades with honey drip, apples gild the trees,
lofty mountains, broad green fields, sheep of golden fleece."

Illesa stood and watched as they entered the canvas castle, feeling the blood draining from her head. If only she could find a quiet place and sit alone. There was no sign of Earl Warenne, her escort. Slowly she began dragging her skirts up the hill.

"Come, my lady, you are supposed to be at the front of this crowd." Sir Richard appeared at her arm and began pulling her along after the last of the courtiers. "You did well. Even Melchior had to admit that you played the part. After Gaspar's folly, he was just grateful you spoke the lines rather than a ribald song."

"Where did Gaspar get those words from?" Illesa said, stumbling on the uneven ground.

Richard sucked his teeth.

"Straight out of hell's mouth."

Chapter VII
July, AD 557
Fortress and Well of Meirchion

"You know my retinue is at the gate. They have been waiting for many days. You have buried Gethin's body and given him his honour. Now we must speak."

Owain stood in her hall, looking the master, but uncertainty twitched his mouth as the morning sun came through the eastern windows. It was a good time to set a vow. Manon sat in her chair, her hands cupped in her lap. The women would all be huddled outside these windows trying to hear what she would say to tame the wolf they had let into the compound. His thirty men were grouped outside the gate, bristling with axes and spears.

"Tell me how he died."

Owain looked at her frowning. He shook his head.

"Blood has been shed at the spring. I must know what was done. Propitiation is needed," she said, not taking her eyes from his face.

Owain glanced down the hall. His hands were clenched by his sides.

"He died bravely, as a warrior. You do not need to know any more than that. The spring was not polluted. Why should propitiation be needed?"

"I am the guide. I know what is needed."

He looked at her warily.

"Many of the elders in the north are submitting to the new priests. The old guides are now ignored."

"Worshipping a dead god. That is not a faith for warriors," she said, cutting him off. "If you wish to fight and live, propitiation must be made. You killed the spring's guardian. You must make that offering."

He laughed, half-turning away from her.

"You may say so."

"You may ask others, if you have no faith in me. But I think even your father would understand that this must be done. He would not want the guilt burden to rest on your family. His plan for earning the goddess's favour would turn and bite him like a snake." She rose and walked to stand in front of him at the table. "When we go to the spring, the ritual will cleanse you of blood guilt."

A cow lowed from the corral. Owain glanced down and fingered his belt. He looked so young, even at close quarters, some of the softness of his features remained. And the hunger he'd had in his eyes seven years before was just as strong.

"I will accept you as my lord," she said, making the gesture of submission with her hands.

The blood drained from his face.

"You accept me?"

"Yes."

"Your husband is not ten days dead and you accept another lord?" He laughed, his relief undisguised. "I did not expect that, Manon. Did you have so little respect for him?"

Manon dug her fingers into her palms to stop herself striking him.

"Gethin had my respect when he lived. He has the honour of his men in death. But my people need a new lord. One that is able to protect them. You have taken our lord away. You must replace him."

Owain shook his head as if there was something in his ear, and leant forward with both hands on the table.

"You do not tell me what I must do."

Manon did not move away from his anger.

"You know this is true, my lord. Gethin's soul will not rest if there is no one to guard the spring. He will still walk, still fight. You must take me as your wife and become the guardian. If this is done, he will rest."

Owain barked a laugh. He straightened up and looked around as if expecting to see Gethin striding towards him, sword ready.

"You want me to take you as a wife?"

Manon stood very still, feeling a wave of nausea in her throat.

"I have seen it," she lied.

He stepped away, suspicion written on his open features.

"What do you mean?"

"The goddess showed me. There must be an oath. Ride with me to the well, and it will be done today." She took his hand, forced herself to hold it, and even to brush the hairs on the back with her thumb. He gripped her fingers hard.

"The goddess showed me to you?"

He wanted to believe it. They must go to the well before he saw the truth.

Around his neck, the finely engraved silver torc reflected the light straight into her eyes. She stood still, feeling the pressure of the hand that sometimes reached into her mind and gave her visions. It was pulling at her skull.

"Manon – "

She pulled her eyes back to meet his.

"You and I will go there, my lord. Bring one of your men. I will bring my witness. The ritual will be accomplished. Then you will have me as a husband has a wife, and Gethin's honour will be yours. Give me your leave to prepare myself."

She stumbled to the chair and sat down just in time as the blue mist came surging upwards, like a waterfall in the sky. And all fear flowed out of her to the centre, the mist of words and power.

When she opened her eyes, feeling the familiar drained exhaustion, he was still there, staring at her.

"My lady –," he began.

She put her hand to her gold torc.

"The preparations have begun. Call your man," she whispered. She looked into his eyes, blue like a hot flame. Lost.

He nodded and left the room. Eluned got up from her hiding place behind Manon's chair, and came forward.

"You had a vision, with him in the room?" she whispered. Her face was still marked by grief, scratched and bloodied from her mourning.

Manon took her hand and got to her feet. The dizziness would pass. It was a good omen.

"Help me to the hearth, sister. The drink will be ready by now."

They walked across the compound arm in arm. She had told the nurse to keep her daughter Nesta out of the way, but her voice could not be contained. It carried all the way from the weaving room, singing the song of the hawk and the hare.

At the hearth Manon dipped the ladle into the bronze pot. The smell was pleasant and aromatic. He would not notice it. Only a little was needed. The wine was good, and he would take it before they rode.

"Go and tell the people what will happen," Manon told Eluned at the door. "Prepare for a feast. It must seem that we rejoice."

Chapter VIII
The 29th day of July, 1284
Neigull

When Illesa arrived at the entrance to the canvas castle, the King and Queen were already at their places on a raised dais. Prince Alphonso sat next to his mother, holding himself erect and looking with interest at the people arriving. The high table was laid with linen and the finest polished dishes, and the seneschal was seating each noble according to his rank. Edmund, Duke of Lancaster and John, Duke of Brabant sat on the King's side. A beautifully dressed girl, probably a Princess, took a place next to the Prince. The second table was filling up with the earls and their consorts.

"Wait here," Richard said. "I will get Yvain to escort you."

"Can't we stop the play yet?" Illesa said. "You know I don't belong here. Earl Warenne despises me."

"That has nothing to do with it," Richard hissed. "The Queen wanted the banquet to take place as if it were the story, and that is what will happen."

"Well, if you want to find Earl Warenne, I would suggest you look for Gaspar. The chivalrous knight promised to kill him," Illesa retorted.

Richard opened his mouth, closed it and strode away without a word. Illesa stood to the side of the entrance, out of the way, and rubbed her neck. It ached from keeping her head erect under the heavy headdress. A richly robed Bishop had risen and was intoning a prayer. When he finished, the King signalled the food to be brought.

"You are requested by the Queen," the seneschal said at her shoulder. Illesa followed him to the high table and stood in front of the Queen's place, her stomach tumbling like an acrobat.

"Ah, the Lady of Landuc," the Queen said, turning away from the Prince. Illesa curtsied. The Queen looked down, unsmiling. The loose olive skin of her face bulged at her cheeks, pressed by the tight wimple under her fine veil. Her dark, staring eyes did not move from Illesa's face.

"Earl Warenne has forgotten his courtesy, but we should not keep the lady of the land standing at her own feast." The Queen's stern voice had laid heavy emphasis on the words "lady" and "land". She gestured to the seat next to the Princess. "Take your place, if you please."

Illesa curtsied and sat down carefully on the chair.

The Princess was eating very little. She pushed the crumbs of her bread across the cloth to her brother, who was paying no attention. Illesa glanced at her out of the corner of her eye. Perhaps she was fourteen years, no more. There were many dishes on the table, meat, roasted and seethed, and steaming sauces. White bread rolls were piled high. Illesa swallowed the saliva pooling in her mouth and pressed on her abdomen under the table to silence the sound of her hunger. The bright sun outside glowed through the canvas, which flapped disconsolately.

She had performed her role without disaster and now she felt utterly drained. Not four paces away from her sat the King and the Queen, their faces turned to the page pouring wine. The King's crown looked like iron and seemed slightly too small for him. It perched on his curling hair like a sparrow in a hawk's nest. He was not smiling, but he seemed disposed to find amusement in his near companion. The lions on his embroidered mantle had fur of gold thread and their open mouths were tight stitches of the deepest red.

She must be staring. Illesa averted her eyes as the King turned to the Queen. Someone had filled her goblet while she had been in that reverie. She sipped it and then took some bread. Her knife was in her pack with her other clothes, and it would be impolite to take any meat without it. Sir l'Estrange, the Black Knight, was sitting at the table in front of her, his neck craned around the head of an elaborately coiffed lady, watching her. When she met his eyes, he winked at her, smiled, and took the meat from the point of his knife in one mouthful.

The Princess shook her head as if a fly had landed on her and reached out to the rolls.

"He likes you," she said, her voice flat. Her eyes were on her plate, so Illesa was uncertain at first who she was addressing.

"Where is that funny boy, who was playing Lunette?" the Princess asked peevishly, still looking at her plate. "He usually sings us songs while we eat. Or there is some entertainment. The music by those minstrels is boring," she sighed. "We at least are having dancing and mummers tonight. What will you be doing?"

"I have only this one role, my lady."

"Oh." The Princess turned to look at Illesa and frowned slightly. "You are a girl. Why are you in the Three Kings?"

"They needed an extra lady for this play. Gaspar couldn't do it all himself."

"Gaspar. That is his name. Where is he? I want him to come and sit here. He is so amusing."

"Shall I go and find him, my lady?"

"Yes, bring him to me. He is much better than those serious minstrels that mother likes." She shot a resentful glance at the Queen. The minstrels were playing quietly on the citole and pipe, gentle music that did not interrupt the conversation. Illesa rose to her feet, looking sadly at all the food she was missing. She curtsied deeply to the Queen.

"Please excuse me, my Queen. I have been sent to find Lunette, for the Princess."

The Queen glanced up, waved her hand and returned to listening to the story the Duke of Brabant was telling about his Flemish falconer. The King laughed out loud at the tale. Wine was being served as generously as the meat, piled up on large platters. Illesa moved carefully past the burdened servants towards the opening, and stopped. A squall of rain had just begun. She had no idea where to look.

Several knights had left their banners impaled in the soft ground of the field and they cracked in the wet wind. The hunting dogs were being allowed to drink from the well, watched by the kenneler. Just visible in the distance, servants were emptying a wagon loaded with barrels by the manor. There were now people crawling all over the platform, and smoke was rising in great wafts from the kitchens.

Illesa took a breath of the cool air and skirted around the outside of the canvas castle. The voices within were only slightly muffled. Someone, probably the Duke of Brabant again, was speaking highly of his armourer. Elsewhere, the barley yield was being discussed. No wonder the Princess was bored.

The servants were gathered under the little shelter offered by an ordinary tent at the back of the castle. Inside they had the rest of the feast laid out on trestles, ready to be served. The seneschal had them well disciplined. They were not speaking or eating, but stood silently arms folded, waiting. Balthazar stood with them, drinking wine from a horn cup.

He looked at her disapprovingly.

"You are meant to be in there looking beautiful, not out here getting wet."

"The Princess sent me to find Gaspar."

Balthazar rolled his eyes, drained his cup, put it in the pouch that hung by his waist and beckoned to her.

"Come with me."

He took her round the back of the service tent, and there was a small church she had not even noticed before. It was of low grey stone with thin lancet windows. Balthazar led her to the west door.

"He's in there, but he is not going to be singing for some time. Your Yvain made sure of that. I hear you are a physic of sorts. Sir Richard has taken your pack and is trying to do Gaspar some good. I shall go and explain to the Princess that he is indisposed and sing to her myself." He frowned at that prospect, pulled his hat over his ears and went out into the rain.

Only one candle was lit by the altar. She went forward slowly into the shadows.

"Sir Richard, where are you?"

"Illesa, get back to the table," he shouted. "You are supposed to be hosting the King and Queen."

She followed his voice and saw them. Gaspar lay by the south wall under the light of a window. Sir Richard knelt at his side.

"I was sent to find Gaspar by the Princess."

"Princess Joan asked for him?"

"Yes. So Balthazar has gone instead. What are you doing? Let me see." Gaspar was lying on his side facing the wall, a small pool of blood around his head. "What has happened to him?"

Gaspar's eyes were shut, his mouth open and blood was seeping from the place where his left ear used to be. Illesa's headdress tilted forward, threatening to fall on to the injured player.

"Sir Richard, get this thing off my head and ask for some water and bandages. We will not know how bad it is until we can see it."

He removed it without a word, went to the door, shouted for a servant and then went out into the rain. Illesa moved Gaspar's head slowly to the side; his other ear was intact. Something else must have caused him to become insensible; it would not be caused by lack of blood. Across his neck was a lightly bleeding scratch, as if someone had drawn a dagger across it. Earl Warenne probably had his squire hold Gaspar while he dealt the blow. Illesa ran her hands lightly over his skull, trying to feel areas of damage through his thick hair.

"You fool," she whispered. "What were you trying to do?"

"He went too far this time," Richard said behind her. He knelt down with the bandages and jug.

Gaspar groaned and spat blood and saliva, then began to retch. At least he was waking up.

Richard got quickly back to his feet, and brushed off his tunic.

"I'll kill you myself if you have ruined this tunic and hose, Gaspar."

Illesa's fingers found it as Gaspar leant sideways to retch again. A large lump, about the size of the hilt of a sword. She could see how the Earl had done it. He had probably cut off the ear after Gaspar fell to the ground.

"The Queen wishes Gaspar well. I have told her that you are caring for him, and she has excused you from the feast."

"What about Earl Warenne? Have they found him?"

"He is sitting in his place by the Duke of Brabant."

"What! Look what he has done. He should be gaoled."

"That cannot happen unless the victim accuses him, or some other witness comes forward. I'm afraid Gaspar is not without enemies. He never was careful."

"Why did he provoke him so much?" she asked, angrily tearing the bandages into thinner strips.

"Perhaps he wanted Warenne to notice him again. He used to be a favourite of his. Now the Earl has found a new companion." Richard looked at her and raised his eyebrow. "I can see I will have to speak plainly. At the last feast where the Three Kings were present, Gaspar became his lover. But he did not know that it was a temporary position. He has been trying to get Warenne's attention ever since."

Illesa swallowed. This kind of thing was obviously not uncommon at the court amongst nobles. It was only the poor who were condemned for such sins.

Richard shrugged.

"That is what they say."

Illesa turned back to Gaspar, feeling betrayed and guilty for feeling so. She began to wash the wound in cold water to lessen the swelling, loosening the mats of congealed blood in his thick hair. She didn't know him at all, this strange, boyish man.

Illesa was so absorbed in her thoughts that Richard's voice at her back made her jump.

"A litter is here. You are to accompany him to the manor and attend him there, on orders of the Queen." Richard made an impatient sweeping gesture. "Come on, make him ready to go. There are more problems than this to meet before the end of the day."

Two of the tent men lifted him on to the wooden planks. It looked like a bier. Gaspar's head lolled to one side, and, in the sudden light in the church doorway, he looked worse, grey as a winter sky and smeared with blood.

"Go gently, don't tip him!" she called. They were striding down the hill as if he were a load of logs for the fire.

Richard put a hand on her arm as she went after them.

"Stay here. The court is going to hunt. You may eat once they have gone. I will settle Gaspar into his quarters and make sure he is not tipped into the well on the way. Come down to the manor when you have finished. I will tell them to expect you." He moved off after them quickly, his tunic flapping behind him, emblazoned with the lion and castle.

The sun shone brightly on the rain dripping from the canvas. Scraping and clanking came from inside. They would all be coming out now, led by the King and Queen. Illesa ducked back so that she could not be seen from the tent entrance when they emerged. She did not want to see Warenne's smug face, or worse still, have to speak to him.

The procession of the court was impressive, nonetheless. It was as if some highly coloured serpent was leaving its hole. In pairs, the robed figures glided slowly down the hill behind their mounted King and Queen, swirled around the open field and dispersed to mount and form a broad new force.

At a blast from a horn, a huddle of men unleashed four hounds, which ran ahead, barking. The King held the gyrfalcon aloft on his left hand and another horn sounded, causing the riders to stream away down the track, like barges towed on a river. The master falconer brought up the rear on horseback, with his servant wearing a large wooden cadge.

Illesa hurried into the tent, trembling with sudden hunger. She circled the room like a rat, picking up scraps, until one of the pages pulled out a chair for her and made her sit.

"It is unseemly for a lady to eat in that way," the boy said, frowning at her.

Illesa ate hastily from a honeyed dish as the feast was disassembled around her, and then slipped from the tent. The sea was now as clear and blue as a gemstone, whispering and hissing along the cliff.

When she arrived at the manor door, it was open. A line of porters carried bundles of cloth and candles through the hall. The large red-faced man sitting at a table in the middle of the hall holding a roll of parchment was probably the Steward. She approached him and waited for him to glance up.

"Good sir, where have they taken Gaspar the player? I am sent to attend him."

The man looked at her testily.

"Gaspar the player," he muttered. "Bloody nuisance. The Princess insists he is accommodated, and now we don't have enough beds for the royal family. I have a carpenter making another one to put in the little solar for him, but right now he is bleeding all over the Prince's bed up there," the man said, pointing impatiently at the steep stair rising from the hall floor on the south side.

"You!" he shouted at a passing servant, carrying a heavy box. "Bring me the butler, he must report his stocks to me before they return."

Illesa hitched up her skirt and climbed the uneven stairs.

Chapter IX
Neigull

Gaspar was enjoying the comfort of a luxurious bed, although by the look of him he did not know it. He was as pallid and limp as before, and the bandage was red through. Richard was standing by the window, his head turned to the door, his expression black.

"For Christ's sweet sake! You have blood all over that dress. Don't you have any idea how much that cost?"

Illesa looked down at herself. He was exaggerating. There were some smears of blood on her sleeves, but none on the embroidered bodice. She ignored him and went to the bed. Gaspar's mouth was open and his breath shuddered across his lips. They had laid him down the wrong way.

"There are bandages and wine," Richard said pointing to the table by the fire, "but please do not do anything in that dress. Here is your pack, and your clothes. Come, I'll unlace you."

She straightened up.

"I can do it myself."

"Not with those hands," he said grimly.

She looked down. Her palms were stained red. Had she really eaten with hands covered in blood? No wonder the servants had stared at her.

Richard was untying the laces of her sleeves with quick fingers. He turned his attention to the bow at her back and let the skirt drop to the floor. Soon she was standing in her shift. Richard gathered up the heavy cloth and draped it carefully over the chair.

"You must wear it again this evening. Try to remove the blood, please, before you appear in front of the King again." He sounded exasperated. "In fact, do that first before you attend to that fool, it will have a better chance of coming out."

Illesa was pulling her kirtle over her head. When it was in place, she saw he was serious.

He returned her look angrily.

"He has ruined the play. The Queen will be furious!"

"How can you blame the one who is lying here bleeding? Isn't it his attacker who is at fault?" Illesa snapped her belt into place and picked up her pack by the strap, nearly knocking over the stool it lay on.

"Steady, girl. You are supposed to be the regal Laudine. Keep your temper!"

"The play is over, Sir Richard," she said, her voice shaking with anger. "Gaspar may not live out the day. I think it is better if I try to do him good, than if I stand calmly by as he bleeds to death."

"It was his own fault. He brought it on himself."

"It was Earl Warenne who cut off his ear and knocked him insensible. Are we supposed to congratulate him for that?"

"Gaspar knows Warenne. Very well indeed. What did he expect would happen if he made a fool of him in public?"

"That doesn't excuse what he did to Gaspar."

"Not to you maybe. But to Warenne and most knights, Gaspar got what he deserved."

"And to you?"

"He was stupid to do what he did," Richard said, not turning from his view of the window. "He promised me he would behave himself."

The door opened without warning, and Melchior stood in the doorway. He tipped his head cursorily to Sir Richard.

"Well?" It was obvious he refused to enter the room by his disgusted look. "Will he be able to dance? If not, I want nothing more to do with him. He is out of my company."

Illesa opened her mouth, but Richard grasped her arm, pushed her towards the bed and went to Melchior. They stood, heads close together, arguing in low voices. Illesa swallowed her invective and collected the bandages. She had no desire for an argument with Melchior.

Gaspar's face was painted with dried blood. As she moved his head, his left eye opened slightly and he whimpered like a kicked dog. One bandage across his head, properly tied, could cover both injuries, but he would have to be sitting for it to be done. She looked across to the doorway. The two men were still locked in conversation.

As soon as she pulled the bandage away from his ear, the blood immediately welled out. There was no sense in bathing it in wine or treating it with ointment until the flow had stopped. She pressed a pad firmly against the torn flesh. Gaspar cried out and his leg jerked up, nearly winding Illesa.

"Sir," she called, whilst trying to hold the pad in place, "I need your help!"

Richard turned around frowning. He said one more thing to Melchior, who shook his head and banged the door shut.

"We must sit him up so I can bind his wound firmly. There is too much blood still flowing," she said, as Richard approached the bed.

Richard grunted and put his arms underneath Gaspar's torso.

"He is ruining this bed as well," he grumbled as he held Gaspar upright in an awkward embrace.

Gaspar groaned, and his head lolled to the side. Richard pulled back as the blood seeped onto his arm.

"Gaspar," Illesa said sharply, "wake up and hold your head up straight!"

His bloodshot eyes could not focus on her face, but he held quite still. She worked as quickly as possible, and by the time she had finished his head looked twice its original size. They laid him down gently. He was breathing in quick, shallow gasps.

Illesa carefully tipped some wine into his mouth and he swallowed. When she looked up, Richard was standing at the window watching her. He turned his eyes away.

"Melchior is very angry."

"He is always angry," Illesa retorted, getting up from the side of the bed and going to the ewer and basin to wash her hands.

Richard left the window and came towards her.

"Actually, he thinks you are also at fault."

"What?" Illesa could not help a mirthless laugh. "Does he think I was trying to get attention as well?"

"No. He thinks you encouraged him in his folly. I did try to explain that you had no idea what he intended to do, but Melchior has decided and he does not readily change his mind."

"I don't care if he throws me out of the company of the Three Kings. I never wanted to be in it in the first place."

"That is not completely true, is it Illesa?"

Richard stood next to her and took her damp hand. She could not look up at him, so she turned to the door.

"You have already seen more of the King's Court than almost anyone in Christendom, but you seem unimpressed."

It was hard to form words. Richard was rubbing the soft centre of her palm.

"It is beautiful, sir. I can see how wonderful it is. But I cannot be part of it. I don't belong."

"You look as if you do. When you wore that dress, you looked like the most beautiful woman in the world. The royal ladies were outshone, as the moon outshines the stars."

"You are speaking words from your book."

"I know," he said, and let go of her hand. He went to the table and placed the red book carefully down. "I need you to act one more time Illesa, and then it will be over."

"I know you wish me to dance tonight, sir, but can't you ask one of the Queen's ladies to play the role? They would be much better suited. I doubt I can be with Earl Warenne without wanting to kick him."

Richard's smile was wan.

"You would be ill advised to try it. The entertainment must continue for the King and Queen after the hunt, the dancing must include the Knights of King Arthur and their ladies. We will have to cancel Gaspar's role, but the rest must be done, as the Queen has instructed."

"What will happen to him?" she whispered, looking at the bed.

"Melchior doesn't want him any more, and as disfigured as he is, I doubt he will find another company. I will see if he will be welcome at the FitzAlans'. Their house certainly could do with some entertainment. But first he must regain his senses. Do your best and then get dressed in your finery. As soon as the royal party returns, you must be there to greet them."

He walked quickly to the door, without turning back, and shut it carefully behind him.

Illesa's heart was beating like a bolting horse. All Richard's anger seemed to have gone, replaced by sadness. She went to the window. The men were still working on the platform, smoothing the rough planks and building a dais for the royal chairs. A pile of trestles waited to be carried up the stairs. Sir Richard was walking towards the kitchen block. His figure looked small and burdened. He had just avoided the Steward, flanked by servants, approaching the platform, shouting orders left and right.

Illesa did not want to listen to his panic. She had enough of her own. That night she was expected to talk to these nobles, to be witty and graceful amongst people whom she could not understand. Their conversation, manners and morals made no sense to her.

An infusion of Solomon's seal might help Gaspar. But before it sent him to sleep, she would ask him what was expected of her this evening. There was something that Richard was not telling her.

She crushed the herbs with the powdered root, flung them into the pitcher of wine and shoved the fine bronze vessel roughly into the embers. It was her own fault, she supposed, as much as it was Gaspar's to be without an ear. She had sought refuge here, an unschooled country girl. Richard might tell her all sorts of lies about her noble bearing, but he would leave her just as quickly as Earl Warenne had left Gaspar. Only she would have a child, no doubt.

Her stomach tumbled again. The wine was too hot already; she had not been watching it. Illesa poured it into her own horn cup, and swirled it round. The fragrant steam rose, conjuring a comforting memory. Her mother would have known what to do, even with the King of England and Wales and his Round Table of overindulged knights.

She went to the bed and took Gaspar's hand.

"What —" he croaked, opening his eyes.

"Shhhh, don't talk yet. Drink this."

His fingers went to his face, his head.

She took his hands away and held the cup to his lips.

"This will help, Gaspar. Drink."

He coughed a little but she got most of it into him. It might make him vomit, but if he kept it down he would sleep for many hours.

"What is it?" he whispered. His face was covered in sweat.

"Just herbs. They will help you sleep."

She wiped his face with her sleeve and adjusted the bandage a little. He breathed out slowly and put his hand up to his head again, pushing her away when she tried to stop him.

"What happened? My head feels like it has been butchered."

"Earl Warenne," she began.

He put his finger on her lips.

"No, I don't want to hear about him. Tell me how I look. Will I be scarred?"

"But Gaspar, we know it was him!"

He tried to shake his head, and the pain made him gasp.

"Stop, don't move like that." Illesa steadied his head on the pillow. "You are like one of Pilate's men. Your ear has been cut off. Oh and a mysterious villain has hit you hard with the pommel of his sword, I think."

Gaspar shut his eyes. After a minute a little smile turned the corners of his mouth.

"That is not surprising. I am lucky I kept my tongue."

Illesa looked away, and bit her own tongue. The boy sounded just like Sir Richard.

"That is stupid. You did nothing worthy of being cut up like an animal."

Gaspar still had his eyes shut. When he spoke, he sounded like someone else.

"All lovers are fools."

It was pointless. Illesa got up, and took a deep breath.

"Gaspar, do you know what I am meant to be doing tonight? Sir Richard says it must carry on, but without you there I won't know what to do." Her voice was shaky. She looked down and brushed angrily at her skirt.

"He didn't want you to know. He said you would panic," Gaspar wheezed.

"It can't get any worse, can it?"

"You must dance with all the knights of the Round Table, and with the King. It is, I believe, symbolic."

"What?"

"I would have been able to turn it into an entertaining joke, Sir Richard said. He wanted me to dance with all the worst knights and leave the civilised ones to you." There was a little bitterness in Gaspar's voice.

"What do you mean it's symbolic?"

"It is the dance of the victor over the victim. You represent the land of Wales. The King and then the knights will dance with you. It is a way of showing that you are theirs."

Illesa felt a sudden twisting in her gut.

"Whose idea was this?"

"The Queen. She wanted it to be the first dance of the evening."

"She wanted me to be symbolically raped?"

Gaspar shook his head slightly, and had to suck his teeth with the pain.

"You put it too crudely," he said after a moment. "She wants you to represent the land of Wales that now gives itself willingly to the King. She does not want you to have intercourse with him, just dance, and look as though you are enjoying it. After that you can sit down and eat the marvellous food that is always presented to the nobles at feasts." Gaspar closed his eyes. "But be careful where you sit," he murmured. "Some of the knights may want to turn the symbol into reality. I would recommend that you sit next to Princess Joan. Her complaints usually manage to keep away even the most amorous of knights."

No wonder Sir Richard had held her hand. No wonder he looked sad. He could probably imagine what she would say to this. Illesa had twisted the fabric of her skirt in her fist so tight that there was no blood in her fingers.

"It wasn't his idea." Gaspar's weak voice came from far away. "He doesn't want to share you with the whole court."

His breath came regularly, to and fro. On the platform, men were hanging red and gold cloth on the dais and putting torches in place around the dance floor. There was no shouting, just the sound of rushing feet and busy hands. If she ran into the marsh as the hunters were coming out, could she get away? Where to?

The sun was in its final quarter. They would light the torches soon.

She touched the embroidery of her dress draped on the chair. On the table, the red book glowed like a painted heart.

Chapter X
Neigull

Balthazar knocked on the door and seemed surprised to find Illesa dressed in her costume, arranging her veil by the window. In his hand was the headdress she had left in the church where they had found Gaspar. He stood looking from the figure on the bed to her without speaking.

"His ear has been cut off," she explained.

"Oh. Will he dance tonight?"

"No. He is too weak. Someone knocked him out with a sword hilt."

"Ah," Balthazar said. He took a couple of steps into the room and held out the headdress as if it were a spider. "Here you are."

"Just put it down there," Illesa said, her hands busy with the silk of the golden veil. Binding her short hair was making her scalp itch. Balthasar did not seem to notice the slight bulge where she had hidden the red book under her dress. He would not have understood. Even she was not certain why she had bound it to her. But doing so had made her more erect. Stronger.

"What are you doing at the feast, Balthazar?"

"What?" Balthazar was still looking at Gaspar on the bed. "Oh. I am watching you," he said, running his hands through his beard and pulling it straight.

"Watching me for what?"

The big man looked almost embarrassed.

"To make sure no one tries to take your virtue. Sir Richard says I am to be your guard."

"Stay with me then, Balthazar. Stay here until I go."

"Yes, my lady."

"What is Melchior doing?"

"Melchior? Why he is the master of the dance. He will announce the dances and the dancers. And he will sing the song that he has composed about the defeat of the Welsh."

"You do not have to sing or dance?"

"No, not unless Melchior decides I should."

"Help me with this headdress," she ordered, holding it above her head.

His hands were not as nimble as Gaspar's, but he managed. Balthazar kept glancing nervously towards the bed where Gaspar lay motionless, breathing lightly. She rose from the chair and checked her hands. There was still some blood under her fingernails.

"Bring me some fresh water."

Balthazar went straightaway, without a grumble. This was what it was like to be a noble. All she needed to do was act like a lady and make it clear that people were there to serve her. If she could simply believe it, then others would.

Richard had given her a guard. God willing, he would stay near her.

Illesa was waiting in front of the high table when the King and Queen ascended the stair. Balthazar stood three paces away, holding a drum. Melchior was next to the musicians, plucking a low melody on his lute. Richard was nowhere to be seen.

When Illesa rose from her curtsey, the nobles were parading on to the platform, unannounced. The King and Queen stood side by side at the head table, and Illesa turned so that she did not have her back to them. Wisps of cloud blew across an otherwise clear sky. The moon was a thin sickle over the sea. The torches smoked in the breeze. One of the ladies in a long red and blue kirtle began to cough, her veil flapping.

Illesa stepped back towards the musicians as more and more people came on to the platform, the ladies in bright heraldic gowns. The platform moved under her feet, as if it were pulled by horses. Earl Warenne was one of the last to ascend. He was speaking to another knight, the one who had played her first husband, Sir L'Estrange. Illesa stood as still as she could make herself, her eyes fixed on the part of the table just below the King and Queen. They strode into the centre of the crowd and bowed briefly to the King, who signalled for the musicians to stop.

The Bishop came forward from his place by the King's side, made the sign of the cross over the assembly and began to pray. The Bishop's voice had a harsh, guttural quality, and she understood little of his heavily accented Latin. While the prayers went on, the Prince Alphonso drew designs on the table with his finger, and the Princess examined the embroidery on her sleeve, fiddling with the seed pearls at her wrist.

Illesa's gown pulled as someone stepped on her skirt. Sir Richard had changed into a deep green tunic and a cape trimmed in soft fur. His face was grim enough to be an old prophet of doom.

"Come with me!" he hissed. He pulled her over to the corner where the musicians stood, holding their instruments, and they squeezed into the gap between the high table and the big man holding the crumphorn.

"You remember the dance?" he whispered.

She only nodded. The Bishop was still reciting what sounded like the litany of saints for the day.

"You will be dancing with many of the knights. It would be better if you did not speak to them."

"Gaspar told me," Illesa said in his ear. She felt him stiffen.

"I have instructed the musicians to make each round very short, and when it is done we will seat you with the Prince and Princess again. I will come with Balthazar to escort you when it is time to leave." He looked preoccupied, worried.

"What kind of trouble are you expecting? " She heard herself laugh nervously, and put her hand to her mouth.

"Knights are not known for their courtesy after a feast such as this. When you dance with the King, do not look at him. He will not dance for long; it is not his pleasure." Richard looked back at the musicians and exchanged a signal. The Bishop had performed the blessing and was retreating to the high table. "Now, take your place next to Yvain." He gave her a small push towards the centre of the dance floor where Earl Warenne stood with a sardonic smile on his face.

The King held his arms wide, came forward, and the crowd fell completely silent.

"Nobles of the realm and of our allies overseas, we are here, as you all know, to celebrate our victory in this country and our work of unification. We have before us the victor, Sir Yvain, and the gladly conquered, the Lady Laudine. Knights of the Round Table, come and seal this victory in a dance. After this we may feast with the victors of war and with the tournament champions, renewing our vows of loyalty."

Earl Warenne grabbed Illesa's hand and held it out. The crumphorn blew and the drums picked up a stately beat. For several seconds she remained still, knees trembling as the King spoke to one of the knights standing by the high table. He clapped the man on the shoulder, turned round, and strode towards her. As he touched her hand and then took it, Melchior began to sing.

She and the King circled the dance floor twice. He performed the steps deftly but without enjoyment, gripping her hand as if it were a sword. When the verse finished, he brought her to the Prince, who stepped forward, his lips pressed together in concentration.

"The Prince Alphonso, as Sir Calogrenant," declared Melchior.

They began the dance slowly, with deliberation. After the first turn, the Prince stepped on Illesa's gown. He flushed red.

"Do not worry, it is not torn," Illesa whispered as they began the second turn.

"I am only used to dancing with my sister, and she is not as tall as you," he whispered back.

"You are doing well, my lord."

"What is your name? I do not know this story we are enacting."

"I am Laudine, the Lady of the Well."

"That is not your real name," he said seriously.

Melchior had almost finished the verse.

"This is where we exchange, my lord," Illesa said, moving across. She saw Sir Richard bringing forward the knights who were to dance with her. Perhaps ten richly dressed men, with heraldic arms picked out in blue and gold.

"I won't tell anyone else if you are keeping it a secret," the Prince said. "I've never seen you before with the Three Kings."

"I am only here for this. I am not part of the troupe."

The Prince furrowed his brow.

"Where is Gaspar?"

"He is injured, my lord, and not able to dance."

"That is a shame. My sister laughs when he dances. It is the only thing she likes at the moment. Everything else bores her."

"But not you, my lord?"

They came to a stop in front of the line of knights. He grinned at her happily.

"No, I am going to be King. I must learn these things," he said, and brought her by the hand to the next knight.

"The Earl of Ulster, Richard Og de Burgh, as Sir Lancelot."

He was a red-haired stocky man, not old, but clumsy. His steps were hindered even more by a limp, and his hands were damp and warm. Melchior had to slow the musicians and his words to keep time with him. He was not a good likeness to the Lancelot of the romances.

Henry de Lacy, the Earl of Lincoln, as Sir Perceval, John the Duke of Brabant, as Sir Gawain, and Roger Bigod the Earl of Norfolk and Earl Marshal, as Sir Bors, all danced quickly and competently, exchanging a bow, but no words, as they passed her hand to the next knight.

After Earl Warenne, the next knight was a stand-in for the injured Sir Kay. He led her in the dance with a grip so tight it was like being manacled. She had not noticed his name, but his face was unforgettably marked with an expression of habitual cruelty.

The King was speaking loudly to Edmund, the Duke of Lancaster, and ignoring the dancing completely, but the Queen and the ladies of the court were still watching her with fixed, hostile eyes.

"Sir Roger L'Estrange, as the Black Knight," Melchior announced and launched once again into a fresh verse of his song.

Sir Roger's feet were shod in fine, tooled leather. He took her hand with a wide, knowing smile.

"Aren't you glad I have returned from Purgatory to dance with you, my wife?"

Illesa shook her head slightly.

Sir Roger laughed lightly and led her into the turn.

"No? You are glad I was killed?" He twisted the skin of her hand as they moved across. "Now you may enjoy your new husband, you perfidious whore," he said sweetly.

Illesa tried to keep her eyes away from his. Melchior had reached the repeated stanza and soon it would be done.

"Now you won't even speak to me. Do I smell like the grave? Am I as fleshless as a skeleton?" He gripped her suddenly, drew her close to him, and she felt his member against her hip.

Her face was burning as they came before the high table.

"No, no, musicians. One more verse." Sir L'Estrange gestured heartily to Melchior to continue. A loud murmur came from the hungry and bored audience.

"Come now, humour a dead man!" he shouted. "We don't have many pleasures left. Give me a last dance with my wife!"

He swept her round so that she was facing the King and Queen.

"Bow, my darling," he said close by her ear. She did.

"I am very angry that you rent your clothes for me only when I died," he scolded. "I might have to tear them myself, now that I'm a ghost." He held her tight as they moved across the floor. The King watched them, unsmiling, gripping the back of his chair. The Queen was directing her children to sit.

At the last repeated verse, several voices joined in. The King clapped his hands and the music stopped.

"Bow to me and to your lord, my beauty," Sir Roger ordered softly. "I may come and haunt your bed later."

Illesa curtsied first to the King and then to Sir L'Estrange, and quickly moved towards Balthazar and the musicians.

"Not even a dead man should deny the monarch his bread," the King remarked with a stern look at Sir Roger. "We are hungry and have bounty from the land to satisfy us. Let the servants bring in the feast."

The next moments were a blur of activity as the high table was laden with dish after dish of steaming delicacies, and other servants brought trestles, benches and dishes for those of lesser rank. The Steward, crimson-faced, instructed the nobles where to sit. Illesa wondered if she was unsteady from all the dancing. She had to grip Balthazar's arm to keep her balance.

Earl Warenne beckoned her impatiently. He was at a table with Sir L'Estrange and many other knights. Illesa fixed her eyes on the musicians. She could not go and sit herself at the head table next to Princess Joan. It would be very improper. Balthazar was looking around the room, eyes flicking back and forth, as if he feared a wolf was about to spring from amongst the guests.

Sir Richard was on the other side of the tables. An older woman wearing a bright fur-trimmed kirtle was talking to him. She smiled at him, as if to solicit his help.

Illesa reached up to speak in Balthazar's ear.

"Will you go to the Earl and tell him that I cannot be seated next to him as I have been requested to sit next to the Princess Joan. Then go to the Princess and ask her if I may entertain her during the meal with some of the stories that Gaspar has told me."

"What are you doing?" Melchior demanded, coming up behind her. "You should sit with Yvain."

319

"It is Sir Richard's order," she said shortly.

"You are ruining this play, girl. First you encourage Gaspar to be a fool - "

"I did not," Illesa retorted. "It was all his own idea. I have done everything demanded of me."

Melchior's cheeks coloured.

"Don't you dare argue with me! You looked like a plank of wood dancing out there. That is not what we are paid for. Now go and make the nobles happy or we will get no coin for this. You are not being paid to sit and eat!"

Richard was suddenly at her elbow with a look that silenced Melchior.

"I am sure that the nobles will be happy to have a glimpse of her beauty as she sits at the high table with the equally beautiful Princess. Lady Laudine, you are requested by Princess Joan and Prince Alphonso. Come with me."

Illesa was seated between the two, and far too close to the Queen for her liking. Some of the stories she had been told by Gaspar were far from polite. She found it very hard to eat, as the stories were long and involved and as soon as one was finished, the Princess expected the next.

"Gaspar told us that one at Rhuddlan," the Princess complained, but listened all the same.

Illesa kept her eyes on the Princess or her food, but it was hard not to see the knights who faced her. Their comments and their raucous laughter were clearly audible.

The last of the courses was finally cleared away, along with the trestles and boards that had covered the dance area. She cast around for Balthazar to lead her away, but he was playing his drum to Melchior's direction.

"Estampie!" a lady cried, as the drumbeat quickened.

The King held his palm out in acceptance.

The music became louder and faster. Princess Joan kept time with one finger on the table. The space filled with lords and ladies holding hands in a circle and they began to stamp in time to the music, their feet crossing at every second step, their arms held high. Illesa's stomach lurched, as the floor shifted again. Prince Alphonso smiled and got to his feet.

Someone cried out from the dance floor. The Prince lurched, falling against his sister's chair. Illesa grasped her, and they crashed against the Prince. The air was full of screams and the crack of wood. She saw the torches on the left of the platform falling and the tables sliding, as the platform collapsed in a wave of bodies and broken planks.

Chapter XI
July, AD 557
The Well of Meirchion

Manon rode in front. She felt his eyes on her back, so she did nothing more than pull the rein, neither speaking nor looking at him. They passed through the start of the forest, the elder trees and the ash. She did not lead him into thorns, but kept to the path. Her husband would have taken the hidden track on his last ride, to keep watch. Perhaps he watched her now.

The witnesses had reached the enclosure first. Caron was there for her, and a tall, dark warrior, older than the rest. Owain's cousin, Gwalchmai. He was easy in his saddle, and his look was amused. He was not a believer.

The tall pine by the spring cast its shadow towards them as they approached. Sweat crawled down Manon's back, making her shiver. She did not dismount until he came next to her on his fey white mare. Her husband's blood was in this ground, soaked into the grass and soil. But the stones of the spring were untainted, and the water flowed calm from the mouth of the stone head into the pool below.

"Come, my lord." She took his hand. "We must make our sacrifice and our vow."

"I am now a Christian," he said without conviction. "I cannot make sacrifices."

She turned to face him. She would use a calm voice, calm words, not to alarm him.

"You did not say. But that is not an impediment. Do the Christians not say that their god Jesus paid the bloodguilt for men? This is the wellspring of the mother. Christians also have a mother who gives birth to a god? You may make a gift to her name, if that is what they say, but it is the same mother. Here you must cover the gift to her in the blood that springs from your head. The gift will take the guilt away and the blood will also seal the vow."

She caressed his hand, which she was about to condemn.

"Does your father also worship the new god?"

"No. He cares only for the fighting and the drink. He will worship any that will give him victory."

"I have brought the sacrifice," she touched her torc, "and the knife. Here." She brought it out from inside her robe, and he flinched. The knife was old, black flint. Now it was warm from her body and ready.

"You know I will not harm you with this knife. It is only to make the small cut, like the cutting of a baby's cord. A new beginning." She took his hand and stroked it again. It was hard to look at his face, it was so young and so feeble, like the boy she had refused when he was fifteen. He had taken the drink that Eluned had given him as a stirrup cup. She could see its effects in his large, staring eyes.

"What will you do?" he said indistinctly, as if his tongue were too big.

"I will cut you here," she touched the soft part of his right ear with her finger. "It will heal well and you will remember the vow whenever you feel it." She let go and he stumbled a little, as if he had been leaning against the weight of her finger. He looked around, caught sight of Gwalchmai watching him.

"I will do it to myself," he said, reaching for the knife.

"No, my lord. I must cut you and you must cut me."

He blinked at her.

"I will do both."

"That will not seal the vow."

"I have made many vows, binding my men in blood. This one is no different."

She lowered the knife and put her head on one side. It would be easy to speak to him as she did to her children.

"You are not seeking brotherhood or fealty. You are seeking propitiation, a surety of future glory." Manon moved close to him. "Is it worth taking the risk that the ritual will not work? Hasn't your father sent you to ensure the help of the goddess?"

If she stayed close enough to him, he would do as she said. The promise of possessing her, and the honour he would receive when he became the successor to the cult land were shining beacons in his eyes. She held out the knife.

"The blood must mix with the water. It must flow." She took his hand and led him to the grey, stained stone.

"I will make the first cut," he said, taking the knife from her hands.

Manon laid her head in the smooth hollow of rock and shut her eyes. Owain would not want her disfigured, would not want to cut too far. But he was not familiar with this knife. His breathing became loud as his hand grasped her hair. She opened her eye a slit. The knife was at her neck, and then she felt the cut, grasped the sides of the stone and bit her lip.

Blood was dripping from her ear, staining her cheek. She pushed herself up. He was pale, the knife stretched out rigid in his hand. She took it by the blade, and he let go.

The red stain was spreading down her neck, over the torc and on her tunic. She would not touch the cut to see how deep it was.

He braced his arms on the stone, would not lay his head down as she had, but his blood would mingle, nonetheless. She grasped his hair. The last cut she had made had been to her son, only a week before the arrival of Owain from the north. She had been very careful with him. Before that stretched a long line of ancestors whose blood had fed the goddess and her eels. This man was not going to join them. His blood would be scattered. Perhaps not today or tomorrow. But he would not be allowed the rule, not allowed the sight of his child following his rule.

She went to the spring, wading into the stone-lined pool, knowing he would follow. The eels slipped in and out between their legs and rose, their bulbous mouths pulling at the red water. That was when she did it.

The lead sheet inscribed with the curse was very warm from lying between her breasts. She had fixed the curse with the correct words, written backwards to ensure their power. Owain was in the water, so the goddess would know him and know his blood, which would be tainted from then on. He would not be victorious. He would not have glory. She had cursed his very blood with shame and disaster. His body would come apart at the seams.

Manon waded to the centre of the spring and dropped the folded lead sheet into the deepest place, while he still watched the eels with his wide eyes. Then she said the prayer of propitiation and dropped in her golden torc. A fitting sacrifice for what she asked.

The fool did not even notice.

Chapter XII
The 30th day of July, 1284
Neigull

Illesa had been pulled out and carried to the side. Time must have passed; the fire was almost extinguished, but there was no sign of dawn. She could not make her body rise from the ground. The dead were lined up on the grass not far from her. The smell of burnt cloth and burnt flesh was thick in the air. She had already been sick twice.

A Priest was walking among the dead, a boy with a lamp at his side, bending to anoint their faces. There were five in all. One lady. Her clothes were charred, stuck to her skin. Richard was not amongst them. Melchior was. He was untouched by the fire, but his head lay at an odd angle. Broken neck.

Balthazar was lifting sections of the wooden platform, while the guards and uninjured household knights worked to clear the area. Water hissed. There was a line of men with buckets. The injured nobles must have been taken inside. In the gaps between the noise of talking and the sounds of falling timber, she heard crying.

Perhaps she had been knocked out, but she remembered landing, on top of the Prince, headfirst on the strut that supported the dais, and the Princess screaming in her ear. A beam had come down on top of them, splintering and pinning them to the ground. Princess Joan had a cut on her arm, but she became quite sensible when she saw that she was not going to die. The Prince had been knocked out, but he was alive. She had heard him breathing.

Illesa put her hand to her throbbing head. The headdress was gone, and there was blood flowing slowly from the back of her skull. The red book was still bound tight to her chest. She pushed herself up onto her knees, but the dizziness made her shut her eyes. She stayed there, hands splayed on the earth for some time.

"Lady?"

"Mmmm."

She looked up at the voice and knew his face but not his name. Large. Bearded. Not kind. She shut her eyes again.

"You must come with me. You are needed." His arms were round her back, pulling her upright under the shoulders. She pushed feebly at him.

"Come on. I will dunk your head in the water butt. That will wake you."

Her feet were being dragged behind her and the wreck of her dress caught on the ground.

"Put me down, I can walk," she muttered.

"You might be able to crawl," he replied.

She began to retch, and he put her down. She spat the bile on his shoe.

"Damn you!" he shouted and backed away.

She wiped her mouth on her sleeve and looked up at him, remembering. One of the dancers. The cruel-faced stand-in for Sir Kay.

She was crouched on the ground by a wagon in the rutted mud, and he stood a pace away, watching her, his face shadowed.

"Get up then, if you think you can walk."

There was torchlight on the other side of the wagon. Men's feet walked past quickly. She gripped the wheel and pushed herself up, freeing her dress from under her feet. The Lady of Landuc had been cast down, along with the King and Queen of England. But she would not let herself be dragged through the mud of the road.

"Who has called for me?" Her voice was hoarse with smoke.

"Your good, dead husband. He might overlook your stink and your hair. I wouldn't. I like my women clean."

Behind his bulk, a shadow appeared, larger and taller.

Balthazar put his hand on the knight's shoulder and pushed him back without a word. In his other hand there was an axe. He had been using it on the fallen timber, but he held it ready to swing. Balthazar put the bulk of his arm around her shoulder and half carried her into the lane.

"Come, I've got you now. I'll take you to him. Not that you'll be of much help," he muttered.

They were very near the manor, but it had been so shrouded in smoke that she had not seen it. Inside, it was almost as dark, and very quiet except for a low murmur of pain. People were sitting or lying on the benches all around the hall, among the darting shadows of servants. Two guards stood at the bottom of the stairs.

Balthazar ignored them all. Still half-carrying Illesa, he went through the door into the small hall, shutting it behind him.

This room held fewer injured, and more lamps. It was possible to see that on the pallet by the fire lay a man, not sleeping, not dead. His face was turned to the door, and on seeing her, it slackened and relaxed. His head rested back on the cushion. Balthazar let go of her and she went to him, knelt beside him and took his outstretched hand.

"You live," Richard breathed. A smile stretched the scar on his lip. His hand was cold. She rubbed it between her own. "What have you done to that dress? You look like a fury, covered in blood and soot." Her eyes searched for the injury that kept him lying so still. Only his hand moved, touching hers, then moving up to her face. "You are bleeding."

"Only a little. Where are you hurt, sir?"

"Is that all you are interested in? Always my injuries. Do not look. It is not worth it."

The sweat stood out on his forehead. She moved the blanket away and ran her hands down his torso. Nothing, but his right foot lay at an angle and his leg looked misshapen, as if it didn't belong to him. His hose and the thin, makeshift bandage were red and wet.

"The Queen may let her Spanish surgeon see me, when he has finished tending the Prince." She put her hand on the leg and pressed lightly. The pain made him shut his eyes and grip her fingers.

Illesa looked round the room. Balthazar was gone. There were no able-bodied people, just the harsh breathing, muttered prayers and curses of the injured. Her pack must still be in Gaspar's chamber. She would need wine and a splint, at the least. His hose would have to be cut from his leg. But her knife was also upstairs. She brought his hand with hers to rest on the blanket and wriggled her fingers.

"Where are you going?" he whispered, his eyes still closed.

"To get my knife. Looks as if we will have to cut off your leg, sir," she said keeping her voice light.

"Cruel girl."

He loosened his grip, and she pushed herself to her feet. The dizziness was not as bad as before. She stood still until it passed, and then went to the door. The other people in the room probably needed her too. She could see two knights with burnt arms covered in wet cloth. But treating them would have to wait.

The guards stopped her at the bottom of the stairs. Under no circumstances was she allowed to enter the upstairs chamber where the royal family was being tended. She stood there, unable to think of how to get past the officious guard, until Balthazar came back through the doorway still holding his axe. They knew him well, allowed him to go, took his axe before he lumbered up the stairs. He reappeared with the pack, holding it out as one would a kicking child.

"I need a long, thin piece of wood for a splint," she said to him. "And I need you to help me."

He nodded, pushing the singed hair from his eyes, and went out into the dawn light. She found a servant and shouted at him until he understood what she wanted. He brought her a flagon of wine and a long length of fine linen, probably a table cover.

The chamber was hot and airless, but Richard was shivering, his teeth chattering behind bloodless lips. She pulled off his wet, perished tunic as carefully as she could. Around Richard's neck, on a leather thong, was the ampulla of holy oil, the token that had gained his trust. Illesa took it in her hand and eased it over his head. There wasn't much left, but holy oil might be the one thing that could help him. She un-stoppered it, turned it on her thumb and made the sign of the cross on his forehead. He did not open his eyes or move. If things went ill, she would have to use the rest for a different purpose. She knelt at his side and squeezed his hand.

"Can you move your legs?"

He nodded his head slightly.

"Only my left," he said between clenched teeth.

"I am going to give you something for the pain."

"Good idea."

The infusion seemed to take hours to work, and Illesa worried that she had not made it strong enough for a man. But his breathing changed finally, becoming regular and deeper. She nodded at Balthazar who was bent over her in a position of grave concentration.

The hose and bandage parted under her knife's blade, revealing the jagged end of Sir Richard's shin bone sticking out from a bloody wound. She swallowed hard. It was possible to treat fractured bone like this. Her mother had splinted the son of the thatcher, who had fallen and broken his leg in much the same place. It had not taken her long to reset, but two grown men had held the boy down while it was done, and the bone had been much smaller and more supple.

She had been right in her jest. It would probably be better to cut it off at the knee. If he had been a horse, someone would have put him out of his misery by now.

Resetting the bone took much longer than it should have because she could not stand his agony. It seemed he would die of it. At the sound of his cries, a Priest came in and flapped around the room denouncing her for torturing a dying man. He began to perform the final sacrament, but Balthazar shouted at him to get out of the way, and he left, slamming the door behind him. Richard had swooned, and at that point Illesa gritted her teeth and pushed and pulled the bone into place.

Her hands were trembling so much with the effort, that she could not tear the linen. She left it to Balthazar who calmly tore it into strips and then went to fetch the honey she wanted from the kitchen. That was one good thing. Wherever the King travelled, there would be plenty of honey. It would be best mixed with vervain and slathered on.

When she had applied the tincture and bound the leg around the splint, she sat back on her haunches and looked at Richard's face. It was slack, and the breath shuddered across his chest. He had wet his braies during the manipulation.

"Will you find him some fresh bedding, Balthazar? He must not grow cold."

He nodded and got up without a word.

She went to the window and opened the shutters. The sun was rising in a blue sky. There was no wind at all. From this room, she could not see the ruins of the platform, but the smoke from it rose like a large dirty cloud. The bells of the small chapel on the hill were ringing, loud in the still air.

Illesa looked around the room at the slumped forms of the injured. Before she started to help the burnt, she must wash. Blood had dried on her scalp, matted in her short hair and covered her hands. Illesa closed the chamber door quietly behind her and slipped out of the manor. She would go to the holy well, where it would be quiet, and wash and pray. Wash and pray.

She saw nothing of the journey, only the leg, the bone and Richard's contorted face. It was a shock to find herself at the well, to see the flow of water just as it had been yesterday, only brighter in the sun. She sat down on the stone bench, legs and hands shaking, then knelt down to the water and dipped her face in, scooping it over her head. The blood was a rusty stain, flowing away into the water. The cold made the shivering worse, but she kept on, feeling the cut sting until the water cleared.

When Illesa finally stopped, she sat back on the bench, dripping. She wiped her face with a clean part of her kirtle and then closed her eyes. Her hand went to the familiar shape of the book on her chest, but the prayer did not come, only strange faces evolved into each other in her mind, through flames or leaves or waves. She was empty of anything to offer, or any request.

Illesa mouthed the *Ave Maria*, but her mind slid away from the words, returned to the horror, became blank. A movement on the Nefyn road drew her gaze. A rider had crested the hill and was walking his black horse down the uneven slope. She could see the man's broad shoulders, his glance left and right along the road to the manor, the angle of his look, the way he sat on a horse. It was all too familiar.

She got up, grabbed her pack and began to run. Her head jolted with pain at every step, but he quickly noticed her, reined in his horse and dismounted, leading it towards her.

"Kit!"

He stood still, holding the reins, while she embraced him.

Illesa looked up. His expression was cold.

"Kit, what are you doing here?" she said, dropping her arms.

"What are *you* doing here, *sister*?" His mouth twisted unpleasantly. She stepped back.

"You got my message?"

"You know I can't read. I had to ask the Priest, so it's no secret now. My sister is a whore. The whole of the Hundred will know it."

"That is not true!"

"You sold yourself, that *is* true," he said jabbing at her chest with his finger. "Riding off with *him* like the whore of Babylon. You have brought nothing but shame on our family. If it weren't for the promise I made to Mother, I would have nothing more to do with you. Instead, I have ridden all this way to find you dressed like a vagrant. Who is going to keep you as their mistress when you dress like that? Look at you!" He grabbed her shoulders and turned her around. "What's that?" His voice changed. "Why are you bleeding? Who has been beating you?"

"Let go of me and listen, Kit!" Illesa took a breath and steadied her spinning head. "No one has been beating me. I have been helping entertain the King by performing the play of 'The Knight with the Lion.' Then last night, there was an accident. The dance platform collapsed," she said pointing to the smoke rising from the manor. "Many were injured. Five people died."

Kit was silent for a moment, looking at her. He licked his dry lips.

"You look and sound like a mad woman."

She took the reins out of his hand.

"If you have so little trust in me, then go and leave me here. I'm sure whoever you stole that horse from would like to see you again." Illesa watched the anger flare in his face. "But if you want to know the truth, then you'd better come with me. It may be your last chance to speak to him."

She had led the black mare just a few steps towards the manor when Kit grabbed her sleeve.

"What do you mean?"

She shook his hand off.

"Sir Richard is gravely injured. If you want to question him about my virtue, you may only have this chance. But if you trust me, you will not mention it, and just give him comfort as a true friend would."

She looked Kit in the eyes and held his gaze until he turned away.

"I don't understand any of this," he muttered.

"Keep your mouth shut and listen, then maybe some of it will sink in."

He said no more until they reached the manor, which was like a hive of angry bees. Carts of supplies were lined up in front of it. Servants were hurrying in and out, and men, bare to the waist, were covering the smouldering timbers with sand. The bodies were covered in palls, watched over by a tonsured Priest. She tied the horse to a tree out of the main thoroughfare. It looked exhausted, but it would have to wait for stabling. Kit looked around him like a little boy.

"Is the King here?" he whispered as they approached the manor door.

"Yes, so behave yourself."

She led him into the chamber and was surprised to see it was almost empty. The walking wounded must have been taken elsewhere for treatment or prayer, leaving Richard lying exactly where she had left him. His eyes were shut, his mouth slack. A figure, its head bound in a stained bandage, sat near him, strumming a small harp.

Gaspar looked up as Illesa touched his shoulder.

"He woke and told me to shut up, so I thought I'd better continue annoying him. It might keep him here and drive off all those devils that are lined up to collect his soul."

Gaspar's bandage needed changing, but his skin was a better colour. There was an uncharacteristic quietness about him. He continued plucking the strings, playing a melancholy little tune.

"You shouldn't be up," she said, pointing at his head.

"I had to get up. There is a Prince in my bed," he said, turning to her with a sudden, wicked smile. The smile widened as he noticed Kit behind her.

Illesa shook her head slightly at him and raised her eyebrows.

"Oh well," Gaspar said. "Suppose I should find some ale. My throat is parched from all the weeping." And he wiped his dry eyes, got to his feet and moved gingerly towards the door.

Illesa caught Kit's gaze following him.

"He is one of the company of players."

"Hmmph." Kit shook his hair out of his eyes. "Looks familiar somehow."

Illesa knelt down by Richard's pallet. His forehead was cold and clammy. Under his blanket he wore only braies. Balthazar had changed the linen, but not found any more clothing. The fire was almost out.

She took Richard's hand, but it lay limp in hers.

"Kit, take off your cloak. We need to warm him."

He was kneeling next to her now, staring at Richard's leg.

"What happened to him?"

"The bone broke the skin. I had to put it back in place and splint it, but it may not work. Try to wake him up. I will make something to warm him," she said, getting to her feet.

There was still wine in the flagon. She poked the fire, cleared away ash from the embers and burrowed it into them.

Kit was whispering Richard's name, looking deeply uncomfortable.

"You will never rouse him that way. Shout at him. Make him wake up."

Illesa went through to the hall, and caught the sleeve of a servant who was carrying a pile of linen. She ordered hot water, more wine and logs for the fire. The boy looked at her in dismay.

"And when you've done that, get a stable boy to see to the black mare tied to the pine tree," she waved a hand at the door. The lad put the piled linen on the hall table and ran towards the kitchen.

She could understand why the nobles liked having servants so much. You shouted at them, and they did what you asked.

Illesa grabbed two blankets from the pile and reentered the chamber. Kit was slapping Richard's hand, calling his name. Steam was rising from the wine jug. She covered him and made the infusion, this time using henbane. Her supplies of herbs were running out. He would certainly need more physic for many days to come. If he didn't die within the hour. She swallowed the black, sick feeling and stirred the wine. It was obvious he should not be left alone. Why hadn't she made sure Balthazar understood that he needed to be kept warm?

Kit had stopped calling his name. She turned around. He put Richard's hand back by his side and got to his feet.

"We should get the Priest."

"No," she almost shouted.

"He won't wake up, Illesa. You can see that."

"He will. You sit there." She pushed him back down by Richard. "When I tell you, spoon the wine into his mouth." She handed him her spoon.

Gaspar was standing in the doorway, Balthazar behind him. The servant squeezed between them and the doorpost, arms full.

Illesa grabbed the water jug from the servant and dipped in a cloth. She squeezed it out and laid the hot cloth on Richard's forehead. Under her breath she began to chant. No matter that it was the prayer for birth. It called the soul forth, and it was Richard's soul that needed to return. She stroked his Adam's apple, nodded at Kit who spooned in wine. Richard swallowed. Kit smiled.

"Again," Illesa said.

Once Richard coughed up the wine, and she thought he would be sick, but he lay back against the cushion again, and his eyelid twitched.

"Now talk to him. I will do the wine," she said. She went to make another hot cloth.

"Sir Richard, it's Christopher."

"Tell him a bawdy tale; stick to what you're good at," Illesa said, as she spooned more wine. It leaked out of the corner of Richard's mouth on to the cushion. He had gone again.

"Sir Richard, wake up!" It was the same tone Ursula would use on her when she slept past milking time.

His eyelid twitched, opened a slit. His lips moved.

"Stop shouting at me," he croaked.

Illesa smiled.

"Very well. Look, you have a visitor. You are on the wrong side, Kit," she said, waving him over, "he can't see you out of that eye."

Kit moved into view and Sir Richard groaned.

"Not again. What is it this time, Arrowsmith?" His voice was barely audible.

"Heard you got yourself in trouble. Thought you might need me," Kit said bravely.

Richard rolled his eye. Gaspar and Balthazar came forward and Balthazar cleared his throat.

"The King asks after you."

"Please tell our lord the King that Sir Richard is gravely injured. He needs a warm, quiet room to make a good recovery." She shooed them out.

"Drink the rest of the wine, Sir Richard," she said, taking his hand.

Kit had turned to the fire and was stoking it so it blazed. It took some time, but Richard managed the rest of the draught and followed her face with his eye by the end.

"You must not go anywhere in your dream," she whispered, her lips close to his. "Do not follow the faces that lead you away. I will be here. Stay with me."

His breathing gradually deepened and slowed. His fingers relaxed. She adjusted her position so she could sit, cross-legged, and keep stroking his hand, her other hand on the shape of the book.

"Get me some food, Kit," she said, keeping her eyes on the rise and fall of Richard's chest.

"You can leave him now, Lessa. He will sleep."

"No. I'll stay with him. He is still in danger. He lost too much blood."

Kit didn't argue, just ran his hand through his hair, and went to the window.

"You care for him," he said quietly.

She did not reply.

"He will only hurt you, Lessa."

She could tell that Kit was watching her, but she did not look up. He left the room quietly, softly sliding down the latch.

Chapter XIII
The 30th day of July, 1284
Neigull

It must have been around the hour of none when she heard the herald. The King was going to make an address. All were to assemble in the field next to the manor, near the wreckage of the dance floor. The walls had been echoing with the sound of hammering for hours. What could they possibly be building now?

Balthazar came in, looking haggard. His clothes and hands were filthy. She noticed for the first time that his cheek was swollen and turning black and blue.

"Come, lady. We have been summoned," he said. His eyes were darting around the room wildly.

"He mustn't be left alone," she objected, pointing at Richard's sleeping form. Richard's face was a better colour, but his hands were still cold, despite the blankets and the fire, and his breathing was shallow.

"It is the King's order," Balthazar shrugged. "I will see if there is a servant who can stay." He kept his foot in the door and shouted into the hall.

"You boy! Come here now!"

The boy who came in was small and sallow, and his expression was wary. She took hold of his thin arm and pointed at Richard's chest.

"You must watch him. Watch his breathing. If it changes, or if he starts to cough or anything else happens you must come and find me in the field. Keep the fire going. If he wakes, give him a drink of the wine."

The boy nodded, his eyes sliding off her face and resting on the figure on the ground. He had probably seen plenty of injured in the war. He was not frightened now that his duties had been explained.

Illesa got to her feet and shook her legs to move her blood. The food Kit had brought had made her feel better, but now there was nausea in her stomach. The gathering ordered by the King would not be for celebration.

She saw it as soon as they rounded the manor. It blotted out the array of bedraggled people around it, and even the mound of smouldering ash and blackened timbers. A gallows. It had not taken long to build. Next to it was a small platform. She looked around it for anyone familiar, for Kit, but the faces blurred into each other. Her gritty eyes hurt with tiredness. Balthazar was leading her round the side of the platform, away from the view of the gallows, avoiding the cluster of knights gathered there.

Illesa stood in the restless, sombre crowd for several minutes before she noticed Gaspar behind her, unsmiling and grey-faced.

"What is going on, Gaspar?" she whispered.

"They have found some goats to sacrifice," he muttered.

"Who?"

He shook his head and raised his eyes to the platform.

"Here they come."

Guards streamed forward from the back of the manor, holding pikes. They lined a path to the platform. The horn sounded.

"King Edward, our Sovereign," the herald shouted. "The blessed regal Queen Eleanor. The most blessed and holy reverend Bishop of St Asaph's."

The King strode forward, the Queen following behind him accompanied by ladies in waiting. They came like a wave of sunlight, dazzling, with banners of the golden lion. A boy walked before the Bishop carrying a tall cross. The King's eyes were hooded, his lips set in an expression of fury. But the Queen looked much worse. Her eyes were swollen and she held herself as if she were in pain.

Kit arrived at Illesa's side without a word.

"I have called you here," the King began, "for two purposes: to mourn and pray for those taken from us, and to punish those responsible for their deaths. We have lost five members of our court and its dependants. Our most beloved knight, Sir John de Bonvillars, a brave man, and a faithful soldier, has fallen. Alongside him, a man not well known to this court but to his master, the honourable Duke of Brabant, Sir Hugo has also perished. And most sadly, my dear consort Eleanor has lost one of her ladies, Dame Berengaria of Castile. The golden throat of Melchior, player and leader of the company of the Three Kings, has been stilled in this world and a servant of this manor also perished."

The King looked past the crowd below him, cleared his throat and seemed to address a large white cloud in the sky. Gaspar and Balthazar followed his gaze, as if expecting to see Melchior floating there.

"We know through the mercy of our Lord and Saviour that these beloved kinsmen and faithful servants will live with God and be comforted, once penance has been completed."

The King made the sign of the cross, and the entire assembly followed. More people had joined the crowd behind her. Illesa cast her eye over the rows of bowed heads. One head, taller than the rest with thatched black hair, seemed familiar. The man was not at prayer; his eyes were scanning the crowd. Wide forehead, flat nose. She could not place him. Behind him, a group of villagers approached from the road, followed by a cordon of guards.

"There are many who are gravely injured, some very beloved of us," the King continued. "But we thank God that he has seen fit to save his monarch and all the royal children. The Prince Alphonso is in the care of a skilled physician and is already stronger. He will remain here to fully recover and not continue on pilgrimage with us. We leave on the morrow. During our time on Holy Bardsey Island, we will give thanks for the Lord's mercy and make supplication for those who suffer."

The King turned to look as the group of villagers, feet bare or bound in rags, was led up to the gallows. They stared at the King without expression, and Illesa wondered if they understood his French. Most likely they knew what to expect even if the words were foreign. Gaspar had slunk away somewhere. Illesa wished she could do the same, but Edward had begun speaking again.

"It is not unusual for those who faithfully serve their King to be asked to sacrifice their lives in the arena of war, and many dear friends have died so in this land. However, it is a heinous act to kill brave knights and innocent revellers while they feast and dance. It is an act contrary to every law of chivalry and courtesy. Three men have been found responsible for sabotage of this royal court; three men who were charged to build it and paid well for their labour. As an act of revenge for our victory, they chose to cause death and destruction in our time of joy."

The King put his hand very deliberately on the pommel of his sword.

"These men will be hanged by the neck until dead."

Four guards marched forward pushing three figures chained at wrist and ankle. When the fettered men were at the base of the scaffold, Illesa could see them clearly. Two were the men who had been making the dance platform the previous morning, the men Richard had told to complete the job as fast as possible, before the arrival of the King. Surly men, perhaps not glad to be working for the English, but not criminals.

"They had them make their own gallows. I saw them at it all morning. That is a final work, by God," Balthazar muttered.

The Steward was now standing on the platform behind the King, his hands interlocked on his belt.

Illesa pulled on Balthazar's sleeve.

"Those men didn't do it on purpose. They were just behind with the work and had to hurry. The structure wasn't strong enough."

Balthazar looked down at her, bemused.

"What?"

"I was here with Sir Richard when they were finishing it." Her voice was shrill as she tried to make him understand over the shouts of the crowd. "He told them to stop working on the struts and do the steps or it wouldn't be ready in time for the King's arrival."

Balthazar put his finger to his lips.

"Don't talk about it, Illesa. You will only get him into trouble."

"But they are going to be hanged for it!"

"Shhh! Listen to your big friend." Kit gripped her by the shoulders. "They are Welshmen and would be glad to knock the King and his knights at the moment of his triumph. The bastards." He spat on the scorched ground.

One of the men was shouting as the noose was hung around his neck, but she could not understand his words.

"What did he say?"

"I don't know," Kit said. "He is probably praying for mercy."

"My lord the King!" Illesa shouted. "Please listen!"

Balthazar clamped his big hand over her face.

The King turned his head in her direction, but quickly returned to observing the preparations on the gallows. Balthazar turned her away from the platform, his strong arms pinning her to his side.

The man that Richard had spoken to directly had begun to shout in words she could understand.

"It is God who has cast the mighty from their thrones and has sent the rich empty away! That is his judgment on you!"

"As good as a confession," said Kit.

Illesa bit Balthazar's hand.

"Stop it, you fool!" He squeezed her head even tighter. "You will get us *all* hanged if you are not careful," he growled.

The hanging had begun, but Balthazar's grip held her out of view, his fingers crushing her lips on her teeth.

She forced her breath in and out swallowing the wet of her own tears, hearing the sobbing and retching as each man was hanged, and the muffled crying of the women standing in their rags.

When it was over, Balthazar loosened his grip on her mouth and pushed her upright.

"Don't shout again or I'll have to gag you," he threatened. His angry look collapsed as he stared at her. "Look what you made me do to your pretty face."

But Illesa had no voice to cry out or complain. Her lips were bleeding, and her neck was wrenched. She paid no attention to Edward's final words or the prayer intoned by the Bishop. She was only roused by Kit's voice, calling out. Illesa looked around her. The King and Queen and all those dressed in gold were gone, leaving a crowd of tattered souls cutting the ropes, taking the dead and cradling their bodies.

Now other men were calling out their names and going forward towards the platform.

"What is he doing?" she mumbled through her swollen lips, but Balthazar did not hear. He was looking around the crowd as he had the night before, alert to threat. Kit was in a group of about ten men at the front. A workman in thick boots had joined the Steward on the platform. He was asking the men questions, looking them up and down. Kit was the tallest of the group, but two others who had the arms of ploughmen were signaled forward with him. One of them, almost as tall as Kit, was the black-haired man she could not place. All the others were dismissed.

The servant boy appeared at her side.

"You must come. The knight wants you," he said, not meeting her eyes.

Kit was listening to the workman, with his back to her. He had his own business, obviously, and was unconcerned with hers.

Balthazar was at her side as she ran back to the manor after the boy. She could not bring herself to tell him to leave, despite what he had just done to her.

Richard simply needed help to relieve himself. Balthazar moved and held him so gently that Illesa almost felt able to forgive him. Even so, Richard was sweating with pain and did not speak or move for several moments after he lay down on his back again. His eye was shut tight and forehead drawn in.

She needed more herbs for pain and wounds. Perhaps she could find the Queen's physician Richard had mentioned. Illesa pressed a spoon of wine to Richard's lips, and he opened his eye as he swallowed it.

"You look very ill," he whispered.

She put a hand to her lips without thinking, then lowered it.

"No sir, I am quite well, and I will be even better when you begin to mend."

He closed his eye. His hand rested lightly on the red book. She had put it on the pallet by him in the night.

"That will be my only care. I promise to give up all other pressing pursuits to address it."

The door opened and Kit looked in.

"It's only Kit," she whispered at Richard's frown. The frown did not lessen.

Illesa got up and intercepted him in the doorway.

"He is a little better," she said to his enquiring eye. "But what are you doing? Why did you go forward?"

"You didn't hear?"

She shook her head and stopped with the pain. Kit was looking pleased with himself again. That couldn't be good.

"They want more men to erect the royal tents on Bardsey Island. The three men who were hanged were due to go to make the camp platforms."

Illesa looked at his face. It was untroubled, even excited.

"How long will you be gone?"

"Now, don't start worrying," he said, shaking her lightly on the shoulder. "Only a few days. It's a job and the King pays. I need coin and so do you, by the look of it. When I get back, I might get a job with the court if they like me. Travelling with the King! That's the way to see the world." He smiled and then caught her gaze. "I know, I know. But it might happen, and you have to agree that I need a job. You could come too. They only allow high-born ladies like you on Bardsey," he said with a sly look.

Illesa ignored his taunt.

"You need to take that horse back to whoever you stole it from before the constables come after you."

"Oh don't worry about that. It's Tom's horse. He won't accuse me. He understands."

"Tom?" she cried. "Is that how you repay friends who go out of their way to help you?"

Kit put his big hands on her shoulders and shook his head.

"Don't take it so seriously, Lessa. I left him a good knife in its place. He will know I will bring her back safe."

"Well, I wouldn't trust you with my worst donkey, never mind a fine palfrey."

Kit raised his eyes to heaven.

"You are just like Mother."

"You make that sound like an insult."

He closed his mouth on whatever he had been about to say and looked out of the window, his fingers restless on his knife hilt.

"You aren't actually. Not like Mother at all."

The sun was shining through the window and hitting the side of his face, throwing half into shadow.

"You have never looked like her. Father saw it too. You might act like her sometimes, but you looked as different as a dove and a crow."

"What do you mean?" This change from the jaunty and infuriating Kit to a quiet and serious one was unnerving.

"Illesa I was five when you were born. I remember the day I first saw you. I have been thinking about it ever since Mother asked me to take that book to Caus. Of course she told me not to be silly when I asked her. She said that I was too little to remember. But I do remember, because I had to lie. It scared me that first time, but I've got used to it," he said, grimly. "I've been trying to make sense of it, trying to decide if it was important."

"Kit, what are you talking about?" Illesa said, taking his hand. Her voice sounded high and nervous.

Kit looked around, but Richard lay silent and motionless, and there was no one else within earshot.

"There were two babies that day. I saw one in the garden. That one was dead," he said softly. "And then there was another one, wrapped in cloth in the linen chest. She told me that the dead baby belonged to the lady from the hall. The living baby was hers; was you."

Kit took his hand out of hers and began pacing the room.

"Mother took the dead baby to the Priest and left you with me. She told me to tell anyone who came to the house that I was ill, so they would not come in. She told me you had to be a secret. You lay there so still that I thought you might be dead too. But I touched you to make sure and you woke up and looked around. I even picked you up. Good thing I didn't drop you, eh?"

Illesa nodded slowly at his smile. Talking about it had made him look like a boy again.

"When an old woman came to the cott to collect something, I stood in the doorway and lied to her, just like Mother told me to. And you didn't make a sound."

Kit came to a halt in front of the window.

"But I have been wondering. Why did I have to lie? Why didn't she want anyone to see you that day?"

Nothing he was saying made any sense.

"It was a long time ago and you were very young," Illesa tried.

He shook his head.

"I remember her exact words. She didn't want anyone to know the baby was there. The next day it was completely different. She made me go to tell the Priest that she'd had the baby, then I had to go on to tell the miller's wife."

"Why would one day make such a difference?" Illesa frowned.

He shrugged.

"I don't know, but under you, under the blanket you were wrapped in, was the book. Maybe it was the book she was hiding, not you."

Illesa shivered.

"Why didn't you tell me this before, when we were at Eaton?"

"I was too busy dodging the arrows there," he said. "I wasn't thinking straight. Now I just can't piece it together. Why she had the book, what she wanted from me. It's all mixed up in my mind with what Father thought. He was sure she had been unfaithful to him."

"I don't understand," Illesa said. "You must have it confused with another time, perhaps when she was looking after someone else's baby."

Kit began to check that all his tools still hung from his belt.

"I don't think so. Anyway, I've told you now and I'd better go. We are to meet in Nefyn and take the tents over to Bardsey by boat. We must get there well before the King. I will come for you when I return, then we can both take that horse back to Tom and pay him for the loan of it. That will make you feel better, won't it Lessa? Then we can make a new start."

And he was his old self again, ready for action.

"I don't know, Kit," she said, turning to look at Richard. "I don't know what to do."

Kit's smile faded.

"Of course. I see. Well." He looked down at Richard. "I won't wake him to say farewell. He wouldn't thank me for it."

He embraced her briefly and walked from the room. She watched him from the window, a solid figure, going forward, unburdened.

Chapter XIV
The 1ˢᵗ day of August, 1284
Neigull

The room where Gaspar had bled and slept had been transformed. The arms of the royal house hung from the bed and the walls. Carpet of a rich red and gold covered the wooden boards. Silver plate and silver cups shone from the table by the window. The floor was strewn with fresh flowers and rushes.

The Prince Alphonso was sitting in a chair, gesturing her forward. Illesa closed the door carefully, curtsied and approached.

"Lady Laudine, how you have changed."

"I am glad to see my lord looking so well," she replied. But he wasn't. His skin was the colour of dust. The Prince had been toppled backward on to his head and impaled by the end of a splintered beam. He should not be out of bed.

"My physician says I am making good progress." He turned his head stiffly, and it was only then she noticed the man sitting at a small table, a hunk of white bread in one hand, a goblet in the other, his head covered in a close fitting, pointed, black cap. Dark-skinned, beardless, not very old. The physician glanced at Illesa, nodded amicably and put the bread in his mouth.

"We must thank the Lord that we were saved from too much harm," the Prince said. He shifted in his seat and winced. His right arm was bandaged, wrist to elbow.

"Yes my lord, but I wish that you had not been injured. I fear I may have caused you harm when I fell on top of you." She tried to smile.

"Not at all," he said with a trace of his former pride. "There may still be a splinter of wood lodged in my arm, but Padre Xavier has put special ointment on the wound to draw it out. I should be well when the pilgrims return from Bardsey, by God's mercy."

The physician continued to sit and eat, paying no attention to the conversation. He refilled his goblet from a beautiful glass jug, decorated with swirls and dots.

Illesa drew her eyes back to the Prince. He was only holding his head up through great effort.

"Forgive me for asking for an audience with you, my lord. I was taught the use of herbs and physic by my mother and have been tending some of the wounded since the accident, particularly Sir Richard Burnel, who has a serious injury. My herbs and ointments are almost gone. Would you allow your physician to give me some of his remedies, if he has some to spare? I would not wish to leave the injured whilst I go in search of all the plants and mixtures I need."

The Prince looked at her blankly.

"You are a physic? I thought you were a lady."

"No, my lord, I am only the daughter of a village midwife."

"That is a strange business. So how did you come to be here with the Three Kings?" The Prince leant forward a little, cradling his wounded arm in his good one.

"Sir Burnel arranged for me to act the part, my lord, as I have lost my family to war and disease. He has been very good to me and my family."

"I see." A knowing smile changed his curious expression. "So you mustn't let your patron die. Indeed, my father the King would not wish it. He is the favourite of the Chancellor, who has already lost heavily in this war."

The Prince gripped the arm of the chair with his good hand. Sweat was beading on his forehead.

"You may ask for what you want from my physician," his voice was harsh with effort. "Do you speak Spanish?"

Illesa looked up from her curtsey of thanks.

"No, my lord. I am sorry."

"Then I will have to ask for what you want."

"Forgive me, my lord, but I have kept you from your bed and rest," she said, putting her hand out to refuse.

"I am well enough," the Prince said shortly. "It will not take long will it?" His stare was glassy eyed and defiant. The boy who had mounted the charger Maximilian without hesitation would not show weakness to a common village girl. He turned his head slightly. "Padre Xavier, ven aquí."

The physician got quickly from his seat and bowed to the Prince, his expression sorrowful.

"Mi Señor?"

Illesa watched the man's face throughout the Prince's explanation. It was clear that the physician knew the Prince was in pain and barely concealed distress. His hands were clasped in front of him, restrained from their work by the obligation to obedience. The Prince was obviously a stubborn patient. If Sir Richard continued to improve, he would be just the same. She caught the man's eyes on her, looking her over with curiosity. The Prince had probably just told him that she was a physic. She had managed to find a plain veil and make her appearance less alarming, but she was obviously not what he expected.

"Sí Señor."

He was bowing again. The stream of Spanish had broken off.

"You may go with him," the Prince said suddenly, sitting forward, his face ashen. He could not wait for them to leave so he could lie down.

"Thank you, my lord."

Illesa curtsied quickly and followed the physician to the door. It was only when she was almost out of the room that she saw the woman, skirt swirling as she went to the Prince, lips pursed in concern under a heavy wimple. She had been sitting so still by the wall that Illesa had taken her to be part of the bed's hangings. Perhaps this woman would put him to bed, bathe his skin with cool cloths soaked in chamomile and give him ground poppy seed. If he would allow her.

The physician, Padre Xavier, led her to a smaller solar at the back of the manor laid out with pallets, some of which were occupied. Two men, one with a bandaged leg, another with both hands and arms wrapped in linen, lay asleep. The physician stepped awkwardly around them in his heavy cloak.

"Aquí, aquí," he beckoned her to the far side of the chamber where there was a casket on a low oak table. The wood was oiled and scented, and inside were rolls of herbs in fine linen.

He went through all the compartments and she pointed out what she required, providing the English name. Her arms were full of linen bundles by the time he closed the lid.

"Vervain, lady's mantle, centaury, sage, cowbane," he repeated, counting the strange syllables on his long fingers. Then he pointed at her. "Fox's clote," he mixed it in an imaginary bowl, "sage."

He went to the table by the window and handed her a small clay pot. She shrugged, unsure of what it was. Padre Xavier pretended to be burnt, jumping back from the imagined flame so quickly it made Illesa start, and then laugh. He mimed the correct way to apply this ointment, and then pushed her gently to the door.

He followed her, murmuring in Spanish as she carefully picked her way out of the room. Illesa understood none of his words, but she knew what she needed to do. It would keep her busy for hours to come. Good to be busy. It kept the anxiety away and stopped her looking out of the window for Kit, when she knew he could not come back for days.

Padre Xavier was still behind her when she reached Sir Richard's door.

"Thank you, Father," she said, bowing her head at him, trying not to drop the parcels.

He smiled, nodded, and followed her into the room.

Afterwards, she realised the Prince must have told him to come and check what she was doing. After all Sir Richard was a favourite of the Chancellor, the King's most trusted official. Behind his benign smile and expressive gesture, Padre Xavier was assessing her and her physic.

He unwrapped Sir Richard's leg, keeping up a quiet stream of Spanish, calm, untroubled and oddly reassuring. Richard stared at the man uncomprehendingly, while his long, gentle fingers pressed and stroked the skin. When he had wrapped the leg again and remarked happily on the honey ointment, he got stiffly to his feet, raised his hand in the air and pronounced a Latin blessing.

Before she could thank him, he had bowed to Sir Richard, turned and was out of the door. Illesa heard his footsteps taking the stairs two at a time. He did not want to be away from his patient for long.

"Who was he?" Richard whispered.

"The Queen's own Spanish physician. I think he is happy with you."

Richard turned his head to her.

"And I am happy with you. You are not going to give up the care of me to that old man are you?"

"No, sir," she said. "But I do expect you to do as you are told and not to fight me when I give you instruction for your own good."

The smile on his lips was that of someone who has won at dice.

"Of course. You will find me very amenable."

"I hope so," she said, pulling his blanket up over his chest. "If you are, you will find me a kind mistress."

His eyebrows shot up.

"I'm looking forward to it."

"Drink this," she said. Whilst Padre Xavier had been examining Richard, Illesa had prepared an infusion of comfrey with honey. Perhaps the physician was doing the same for his patient. The Prince's wound was not as serious as Richard's, but the wood had splintered in his arm, and it might stay there like a serpent's tooth, poisoning him. Alphonso looked as if he had recently been ill. She crossed herself. It was not her place to help him. He needed God's mercy. She must pray for him.

"What are you thinking about, Illesa?"

She was spooning the infusion into Richard's mouth without seeing him at all.

"The Prince Alphonso," she whispered. "Pray for him, sir. He is sorely wounded."

"In truth?" he asked. "Dear God." He paused. "Did the Queen know before she left?"

Illesa nodded. Richard let his head rest back on the pillow. He shut his eye.

"You mustn't blame yourself," she said, almost allowing her hand to smooth the lines of worry on his forehead. "You were only trying to make the scene right for the story in your book."

His eye opened suddenly.

"What do you mean?" he asked sharply.

A cold stone settled in her stomach. She had not told him of the hanging of the men. Could not talk about it. Balthazar had not either, she was sure of it. Richard had not even asked about the accident. The physic he was taking would make it hard for him to concentrate. His memory would be vague. But now she had brought it to his attention.

"Nothing, sir. Drink." But he pushed the spoon away from his lips and grabbed her hand.

"What did you mean?"

"I spoke without thinking, sir. Forgive me." She twisted her hand, but he would not let go.

"I will not have things kept from me, even if I am an invalid," he growled. "What did you mean?"

"I don't want you to blame yourself because you told the men to stop working on the platform struts," she whispered.

There was a long silence during which she did not look at him.

"But you blame me, that is obvious." His voice was thick.

"No, Sir Richard! It was all an accident. No one should be blamed." She felt the tears coming, and wiped her eyes angrily.

"Someone has suffered for this, I can see. Tell me what has happened."

He watched her face carefully as she recounted the hanging.

"Which of the men?" he demanded, pushing himself up on his elbows.

"Sir, I don't know their names." She tried to describe them, but the tears kept returning, and he stopped her with an oath.

"By Christ's five wounds! Must we continue this way and make enemies out of willing subjects? Go, send for the Steward."

She cursed herself for being every kind of fool as she left the room. The only consolation was that Sir Richard seemed more himself when he was shouting and giving orders.

The servant brought the flustered Steward to the door within moments, and shut it behind him.

Illesa went out into the sunshine and sat on a stool. Despite being near the window, she could not hear the words of their conversation, just the angry cadence of Richard's voice. The Steward would not find him easily placated. But the men were dead, and what good could Richard do them now? She opened up a packet of sage that she had hung from her belt and began to pluck the dried leaves from their stems and crush them in the linen bag. The smell was a comfort. She shut her eyes and leant her head back on the warm wall.

That is how Gaspar found her, half asleep with sage spilling on her lap.

"The beauteous Lady of Landuc," he chanted, "may the good Lord give her new robes to wear."

She swatted him as he sat down on his haunches next to her. The bandage on his head was unstained, and, although he was still pale, his face had a vitality she had thought he might never regain.

"Stop it, Gaspar. That play is long over. There won't be any fancy robes for me."

"You never know," he said, wagging his finger. "The world is on the wheel of fortune. It could be your turn to rise to the top. I, on the other hand, know when the wheel is coming to crush me. I have come to bid you farewell."

"Where are you going?" she asked, reaching for his sleeve and feeling the tears starting in her eyes again.

He kissed her hand, and then held it out as if about to take her in the dance.

"To London. Balthazar and I will start again where there are people who will pay up front. The Earl of Lincoln will keep us, he says. At least for now. We will entertain him where and when he wants, and nowhere else. And I will be a good boy and do as Balthazar bids me."

Illesa shook her head, smiling.

"He is never going to be your master, even I can see that much."

He patted her hand.

"You would be surprised how much he has changed, now that Melchior isn't here to bully him. I think he has decided to adopt me as his prodigal son. So, I will bid our lord *adieu* and take my leave," he said very formally, and embraced her. "Don't let him cage you, little bird," he whispered. She heard him singing as he reached the door.

"Ah, lady fair, beware your fate
for prudence always comes too late,
And love will capture you!"

Illesa let the sun make the world red and bright inside her lids, and the tears dry on her cheeks. She did not hear Balthazar's approach at all.

"You should not sit here by yourself, lady." He stood before her, blocking out the sun, as he had when they were at Criccieth.

The sky was bright. Little clouds hung motionless over the sea. There was a hum of talk and activity from the manor and the kitchens behind.

"Why do you say that?"

Balthazar looked around and bent over close to her ear.

"Some of the knights are still here and the King is not. None of those servants will stand up to an armed knight. Sir Richard cannot fight for you. You need to be careful. Don't get caught out by yourself."

"I haven't seen any of those knights since the –" Illesa stopped abruptly.

Balthazar looked uncomfortable. What had happened at the hanging sat between them like a demon. Balthazar cleared his throat.

"They are still coming and going on orders left by the King. You should be wary." He wouldn't quite meet her eyes. "The Earl of Lincoln is leaving now with the rest of the entourage. He is employing us, did Gaspar say?"

She nodded.

"He has a tournament in mind for the feast of the Exaltation of the Cross, while the weather is fine. We have not been paid by the Queen so we must take our meat where we find it."

"But the Queen should pay you!" Illesa exclaimed. "Can't you ask the Prince?"

He grunted his amusement.

"She said it all went wrong, and she would not pay us a penny, never mind our expenses. Richard has promised to give us what he can and to speak to the Chancellor, but considering what happened, it is best not to draw too much attention. The Prince is in no condition to hand out coin, anyway."

He saw her expression and clapped her on the shoulder, shaking his shaggy head.

"Don't worry about us. Gaspar is planning long hair to hide his ear, and soon we will be as good as ever." Balthazar straightened up. "We still have Melchior's songs in here," he said, tapping his head, "and the tongues to sing them." Then he bowed suddenly. "Get yourself inside, and God keep you." His great strides took him around the corner and out of sight before she could raise a voice from her swollen throat.

It was a busy afternoon. Most of the wounded were packed into carts and taken to Nefyn by the King's remaining retinue. He had promised the noble injured the attention of his own physician until they regained strength enough to continue to their homes. She had bandaged several guests before they set off. One of the ladies had lost all her hair when her headdress caught fire. Her scalp was red and weeping and her face tight with pain.

It was a very embarrassing incident for the King in front of the most powerful men in Britain and Europe, gathered to celebrate the victory and strength of the sovereign. Of course he had chosen to believe in sabotage, rather than rushed workmanship on an over-ambitious idea inspired by a romantic story. It would be more acceptable to the nobles to be injured by an enemy than by an unsupported beam.

She turned away from the sight of the slow cavalcade and went inside. Richard had not summoned her for hours. She opened the door slowly and silently. The light in the chamber was low, and she mistook the lumpy pallet for him, before she saw that he was sitting in the chair by the window, his leg raised on a padded stool. He looked pained. Whoever had put him in that position had not considered well.

"Would you like to lie down again, sir?"

"In a moment." He waved his hand at the empty chair near him. "Sit, if you please."

"Who has been tending you?"

"That boy. You know, the surly-faced one."

The boy who had watched him during the hanging.

"He heard me call for you. You were tending the other wounded, apparently."

"They have gone to Nefyn now."

"Yes, I saw." Richard glanced at the window, then gripped the chair and pushed himself up with a grunt of pain. Illesa moved to help, but he waved her back. "Some knights have remained to guard the Prince, but your favourite, Warenne, has gone with the King to Bardsey, for the good of his soul. I do not know whether it was his idea or not."

"God save him," she muttered.

"Indeed," he said flatly. "Well, I expect you would like to know the outcome of my conversation with the Steward." He didn't wait for her reply. "I instructed him to pay a sum of money to each of the families of the hanged men. It is very important that you do not speak of this to anyone. It is a very sensitive issue. Do you understand?"

"Yes, sir."

She got up to make something in the fire, and to hide her welling eyes.

"Come back here, Illesa. There is something else." His voice was impatient. She returned slowly to her seat.

"After the Steward left, I had a visit from Sir L'Estrange. He made a great show of sympathy for me before he came to the business of his visit."

"Was that other man with him, the one who danced with me just before L'Estrange?" It would be welcome news if he had gone.

"You must mean Mortimer. Balthazar told me what he tried to do. Mortimer is a hired sword, just a third son, not a knight. He did well in the Welsh battles, but he lacks discipline. Sir L'Estrange has decided to employ subtler tactics now, and I believe Mortimer has been sent to Caernarfon." Richard looked out of the window again. "I'm afraid that once Sir L'Estrange has decided on his goal, nothing will move him from it but its replacement by another, more desirable one."

Richard's voice sounded strained, with something other than pain. Illesa looked down at her lap.

"He came to me to enquire about your situation. He would like to have you, for a good wage in meat and clothes no doubt, and more besides. He is not a scrimper. You will get enough from him to live comfortably for some time."

The hammering inside her chest made it difficult to speak.

"You have promised me to him?"

"He has several women, and they say he treats them well." Richard turned to the fire. "They have their own chambers and their own servants."

"You have no right," she began, her voice cracking with anger. "I am not yours to give away, even if you don't want me."

There was answering anger in his face, but his voice was controlled.

"I know you are not mine, Illesa. You have told me that often enough. How could I keep you now? I've but one eye and one leg. I merely said I would tell you of his proposal, as he sees me as your patron. I would not force you to go to him. But it is a good chance for living well. A much better chance than staying with your brother, who is as reliable as a will-o'-the-wisp."

There was no denying that.

Illesa gripped the green wool of her skirt in both fists. Why did the people you loved flee, while the ones you hated chased and pursued you like a hound after a hare?

"Kit does not believe he is my brother," she said after a while. "He thinks my mother took me from another woman in childbed and raised me as her own." It was all so strange when put into words that she felt a bubble of foolish laughter about to burst in her throat. She had not let herself think about what Kit had said, or what it meant.

Richard leant forward.

"He said that to you?"

She nodded, taking a shallow breath.

"It doesn't matter anyway. He was never going to save our home or keep us with his work. He has found a new way of life."

Richard shifted on the chair, and had to stifle a curse.

"Let me take you to your bed, sir. It isn't doing you any good to sit like that."

He let her support him to the edge of the bed, and hold his leg as he lowered himself on to the cushions. He was pale and sweaty with the effort just of lying his body down.

She went to the fire and poked it angrily with a stick.

Sir L'Estrange and his arrogant mouth and his wandering hands was so spoiled, he thought that everything before his eyes was his. She looked at the neglected pots of physic and set to work. When she returned to the bed with a cup and a spoon she was surprised to see Richard still awake.

"Do you reject the knight's offer then?" he asked.

She put the pot down on the table by the bed and cocked her head at him.

"I have my hands full here with you. I don't have time to entertain other knights."

He frowned at her.

"Don't make light of it, Illesa. I may die soon, and even if I live, I will be a half-blind, limping wreck. You should take this opportunity."

"Don't tell me what I should do." She found she was looking straight into his eye, dark and gleaming in the firelight. She rubbed her finger along the soft coverlet on his chest; heard his breathing change. His hand covered hers.

"You are very foolish," he said, pulling her close. A delicious dizzy spinning began in her chest.

"No. The Lady of the Well chooses the best knight."

Her eyes were closed when she kissed him and felt the yielding softness of his lips as if she were falling forward.

He did not want to let her up, but she put a firm hand on his chest. His lips were cold.

"Take your physic, sir. Kisses will do you no good without it."

There was his wide smile again.

"Kisses from my physician will do me most good of all."

"No more until you've done what you're told," she said, stirring it and keeping her head averted so he wouldn't see the smile that made it hard to speak.

He swallowed the comfrey quickly, although her hands were not steady with the spoon.

She smoothed his forehead, and laid her cheek on his.

"You will be well," she whispered. His hand was on her head, plucking at the thin wool of her veil. She reached up to take it off and his fingers caressed her hair.

"We will go to Langley when I can travel. We can stay there for months before anyone asks after me. I can be unwell in your care for half a year or more."

"You will be well inside two months, sir."

"No one needs to know that."

She clicked her tongue at him.

"I suppose you were also a truant at your studies."

"No, indeed. The Priest was as strict as a Tartar, and almost as demanding as you. I didn't dare give him an excuse. He had many and various punishments." Richard's hand wandered across her breast, and paused. She took it and placed it firmly by his side.

"So have I. Now go to sleep before I begin."

"I am not afraid of you, Mistress," he said, shutting his eye. "Do your worst."

She freshened the pallet with clean linen and placed it next to his bed, but she was bubbling inside and knew she would not sleep. Besides the song in her head, there was the tread of servants' feet, the changing of the guard outside the Prince's room, the many owls calling for their mates, and behind all that, the beating of the waves on the beach below the cliff, drawing in and breathing out. She was only in the dim hinterland of a dream when she heard the door open. A large man, swathed in a travelling cloak, stood in the opening, a lamp in his hand, while a servant held the door.

Chapter XV
October, AD 557
The Fortress of Meirchion

Owain was making many friends. It was Eluned who showed it most clearly. By the end of the first week of his lordship, he had already given her a pet name: Adar, the bird who calls in the dark. It suited her and she accepted it, and smiled at him with her cloudy eyes.

Eluned had been listening to him when he spoke of his new faith in the dead god as well. There was a way she sat, body bent in his direction, her small hands folded in her lap, which showed her loyalty. And she was Gethin's sister.

Manon raged inside. She had waited for months. The curse should make him ugly and mad, drive the light from his eyes, stop his smile and his disarming laugh. Why had the goddess not blighted him? Manon had done everything as it should be done.

The curse was washing away in Owain's confidence. He was so certain of his place, of his right to be happy. He hovered over her like a bird of prey, mantling its kill.

Each time he came to her at night, her anger burned. When he roused her, she would bite him and that roused him even more. She would drive him to exhaustion. She had to consume him; could not leave him alone. Manon was worn out waiting for the revenge that should have struck long ago. Now she was feeling sick every day.

Owain was out, riding the boundary with Gwalchmai, when Eluned found her in the bedchamber and sat down next to her, holding a steaming cup.

"You are having the sickness again?" she asked.

Manon took the cup and nodded.

Eluned folded her hands in her lap.

"Have you thought that you are making this sickness yourself, my lady?"

"What do you mean?"

"You had none with Gethin's children."

"I had a little, with Nesta."

"But with this child it is very bad. It is because you are rejecting it, as you reject Owain."

Manon turned her head away and did not answer.

"He has made the propitiation, Manon. He is a good leader. I loved my brother, but he could not command the same loyalty from those who have a right to hate him. These men would follow him to death."

"And you too, calling bird," Manon said, spite in her voice.

Eluned sighed.

"Even with my bad eyes I can see that he loves you, my lady. And I can see that he is a good leader of the people. Why can't you see that with your good eyes?"

"So you think that he should take Gethin's place," Manon said, turning to face her. "You think he deserves that?"

"I think you are only harming yourself and the baby by refusing to return his love. You can forgive him and flourish, or wait for your world to fall again. If you lose him, you may get a lord who is cruel. This man will protect us all, if you let him."

Manon hid her tears in her hands. It was a long time before she stopped crying.

When she opened her eyes, Eluned was gone. She felt the stone of anger and spite sitting heavy in her chest. What if she should disgorge the stone and enjoy her new husband? What would the goddess do then? Where would the curse come to rest?

Manon went to bathe in the spring.

Afterward, there were three days when she felt no anger at all, when they made love with slow deliberation. She kept her eyes open to his eyes. She felt every part of his body as he moved in her.

Gwalchmai came into the hall on the fourth day, when she and Owain were eating.

"Your father calls you, my lord. They need your strength."

"He calls me where, cousin?"

"To the battle line, near Catterick. The tribes are gathering there for an assault on the fortress of the Angles."

They began making plans for equipping a force. They were already discussing the horses they would take.

"Gwalchmai, leave us," she commanded.

"My lady?" Gwalchmai looked not at her but at Owain, a smile twisting his mouth.

"Leave us, cousin," she said loudly. "You may have your council of war tomorrow."

"My lord," Gwalchmai bowed to him, "My lady." The bow he gave her was very low. He walked out with a swagger.

"You cannot leave us here unprotected, my lord."

"I have no wish to, but my father has called and so I must answer."

"He has other sons. They have followers."

"They are already there with him, dear lady."

"If I am dear to you, why are you leaving?"

He smiled then.

"I never thought you would mind," he whispered touching her cheek with one finger. He leant over and kissed her salty lips.

"You will be protected. I am leaving plenty of my men. Within a year I will be back. My father will let me return. He wanted this land for our family, so he will not want to lose it to another, and I will not lose you to anyone." He put his hand on the small bulge of her belly. "I will return before our child is half a year old."

She brushed his hand off.

"You may never see our child, if it dies. Or if you die," she spat.

"He will not die, and nor will I."

Manon stood up, feeling her anger like a drink of mead.

"This will remind you of your promise." She loosened the fine silver torc from around her neck, which he had given her as a marriage gift. "Take it and if you do not return, let it weigh you down and crush you."

He did not take the torc she held out. He put his hands on her arms and pushed her slowly down into the chair.

"Wife, do not be upset. All husbands must leave for a time. We must go and prove our worth on the battlefield. You would not want a man who was known to be a coward." He held out his arms, smiling.

"A man knows if he is a coward or not. He does not need fools who run to any battle to tell him."

"Manon, come. You know that the north is being hard hit. If it falls, the Angles will run on, unhindered, into lands far and wide. It is a battle that must be fought."

She knew the Manon of a few days before would not have stopped him, would have pretended to be glad he was going. She had betrayed herself. It enraged her even more.

"Hear what I say, Owain. If you do not return within a year, you will not see your child, or me, again. The goddess hears my vow."

The next day she watched him go, with the best men of the clan streaming after him on the best mounts, taking the best weapons. She saw the silver torc glimmering on his neck, where it had been when she first touched his hand.

Eluned accepted Manon's fury with her usual calm.

"He is conscious of his duty to his family. Isn't that something admirable? Do not judge him harshly because he does what it is common practice to do. Your love for him is so strong because you denied it, that is what is making you angry."

Manon screamed at her until she left the room. But the following day she called her back. The time would not pass without Eluned. She was the only one with a voice that could charm sleep. And sleep would bring relief from the sting of love.

Chapter XVI
The 2nd day of August, 1284
Neigull

Richard could not understand it when he awoke.

"Uncle Robert is here? But I thought he was in Acton, ordering the building work and the timber from the forest."

"The King sent word to him of your injury and the Prince's. He will come to see you and explain today. He did not wish to disturb you last night, just to assure himself that you were alive."

The frown on Richard's face remained.

"There was not time enough for him to come all the way from Acton." Illesa helped him as he pushed himself to a sitting position on the edge of the bed. "Perhaps he can give me one of his men, so that you may be relieved of these menial duties," he muttered.

Illesa shook her head and waggled her finger at him.

"I need to keep my eye on you. Can't trust you to someone else." She made him lie back on the bed, in spite of his objection. "I should examine the wound and change the dressing before your uncle visits you. After that, I think some food would do you good."

"I hope they have left someone here who can cook," Richard said. "Uncle Robert likes his meat."

There was a good deal of noise coming from the hall and footsteps up and down the stairs. It provided a distraction for Richard as she treated his leg. But her mind was still full of the night's dreams: fires running down the field to the sea, Kit taking her to a strange cottage door and thrusting her through it into a dark room. And Kit again, speaking to her, holding her by the chin, telling her something very important.

She should repent. No doubt that is what the dream was saying. Kit would be angry, but there was no other life she could see, nowhere else, but in this room with this man.

The flesh around the wound was stained yellow by the honey, but it felt cool and healthy, the wound itself had scabbed and that needed to be cleaned. Balthazar's strong arms would have been helpful, as Richard struggled to hold himself still. She did not envy the two remaining kings their journey. It was a blessing to be in one place, to see the same trees outside the window today as yesterday, to be at rest after being blown about for weeks like a dry leaf in a storm.

Richard was clean, bandaged, dressed and lying on the bed when she slipped from the room to order victuals. The hall was looking quite different. A rich red carpet lay on the floor, and on it was a large carved wooden chair set behind a polished table, with three smaller chairs on either side of it. The light of a bright morning streamed in through the windows, shining on the wood and the silver plates. A servant she did not recognise entered the hall, his arms around a large tray. He ignored her and began setting out ornate horn cups with great precision on the table.

Illesa went through the back door to the kitchen. There had certainly been a shake up. There were at least eight men working at the hearth, butchering a side of beef, and removing loaves from the oven. Two spits of roasting fowl were being turned. Barrels and crates were piled high. The small plump cook of the manor was at the centre of things, grinding spices in a mortar and looking as if his house was burning down.

"Master, Sir Richard is well enough to eat. He needs pottage and soft bread, and some sliced meat. More wine as well."

He grunted, and wagged his head towards the man at the bread oven.

"Tell him. I must make this concoction for the Chancellor."

It seemed that Robert, the Chancellor, had arrived with three clerks and four servants, and had immediately begun issuing instructions from his chamber. They must have everything ready for the Chancellor's first meal before he returned from saying Mass in the church by the well, and it all had to be exactly as he ordered.

"Not even the King is so particular," the baker complained, setting food and drink hastily on a tray and spilling much of it.

There was no sign of the Chancellor, or anyone else, as she passed through the hall, but everywhere there were voices. Inside the chamber, Richard was propped up, reading the red book. Illesa closed the door behind her, feeling sad that the brief sanctuary they had found was already gone. Richard seemed to feel the same. Even when he took her hand, it was without a smile.

"Have you seen my uncle?"

"No, but he is already making his presence felt. The cook is working at twice his usual speed." She put some pottage on the end of the spoon and held it out to him.

"I'll feed myself. Help me to the chair." He put his arm on her shoulders and hopped across the room.

The sound in the hall was suddenly much louder. Chairs scraped on the floor and she could hear the familiar cadence of a prayer. Richard looked towards the door.

"That's him. He will eat before coming to see me. Bring over that little table and the tray. He will want an account of the accident. Have you heard anything of the Prince? Is he any better?"

Illesa shook her head.

"Uncle Robert won't be pleased. This was his idea, originally," Richard muttered, his mouth quite full of bread. "He explained to the Queen how the play of King Arthur's court could impress the foreign knights and cement the loyalty of the earls." Richard looked up at her. "It would be better if you did not tell him how you have come to be involved."

Illesa's stomach jumped. If the Chancellor had been at Acton, he would have heard about the girl they were seeking. All the events of the past month could gather themselves now and leap upon her, like a cat on a mouse. She ate a piece of meat and sipped her ale. Her fingernails were ragged and her clothing was stained and frayed. She looked like a poor villein. Perhaps if she kept out of the way, the Chancellor would not notice her at all.

"When he has finished his meal, I will go. I need to visit the church."

Richard looked up suddenly.

"You are not changing your mind?"

"No, but I must go. I need to pray." It was partly true. She must be prepared to face Kit, and to do penance for the sin that would come from loving Richard. But without the book, prayer was a dance without music. The words left her mouth but dropped to the earth like stones.

Illesa waited with Richard in awkward silence, listening to the constant murmur of indistinct words evenly spoken, without emotion. Finally someone intoned a grace.

She crossed the room and opened the door cautiously, shutting it behind her. Groups of well-dressed men talked by the table as the servants cleared away the remains of a large meal. The

Chancellor was in plain robes, not those he would use as a Bishop. She did not allow her eye to linger on him, but slipped along the wall towards the front door and walked purposefully outside.

Glancing all around, she began down the track to the spring. She had no good reason to feel nervous. Sir L'Estrange had not been in the group of men at the table. He had probably been given a task that sent him elsewhere. And in any event, with the Bishop Chancellor in charge, lawless behaviour was unlikely.

Illesa forced herself to wash and to drink, but the worry did not lessen. She knelt and stared unhappily into the stone-lined well. It would not work. Already greater concerns had overtaken their happiness. She was not Laudine, the Lady of the Well, and she could not pretend to belong to that world. Richard's ardour would die. His uncle would certainly not approve. It would be better to hide, or return somehow to the place she knew. She could take Tom's horse back. He might even marry her. He seemed like a good man.

She shivered and backed away from the water. There was something moving in it. A shape curved under the ripples of the inflow, dark and long, like a snake. She leant forward, watching it. The form rose to the surface, its wide mouth open, its skin catching the light, as if it were bronze or some newly forged hybrid of flesh and water. Then the eel curled away into the dark.

No, it would be no better. She was neither one thing nor the other any more, neither croft nor court. Like the eel, she was moving between two elements. Whatever she did now would be a betrayal to someone. But she would not betray the man who had shown her love, and who made all others seem as insubstantial as smoke or dust.

Her mouth was too dry for prayer. Only her fingers moved over her skirt as if across the words of the book, and her heart beat the time, mis-er-i-cord-i-a, have mercy on me, all the way back to the manor.

The hall was empty. Illesa listened for a moment at the chamber door, but heard no voices. She pulled the latch and the door opened swiftly, as if taken by a strong gust. Inside stood the Chancellor, his hand on the other side of the latch, a look of mild surprise on his face to find her tripping on the threshold.

"Ah, it is you," he said jovially, taking a step back to allow her in. "I was hoping to speak with you. I have been hearing of your skill." He held out his ring of office, a large, deep blue sapphire set in gold, for her to kiss and waved her towards the chair by the window.

"Richard was not certain when you would return." The Chancellor adjusted his robe across his broad chest and sat down adroitly on the carved chair opposite her, smiling. "I am afraid I have tired him, he needs to rest, but otherwise seems remarkably well." Robert Burnel's brown eyes looked at her candidly. "He gives you much praise."

Illesa glanced at Richard on the bed. His eye was closed. Perhaps he really was asleep.

The Bishop's face had taken on a new expression, an intense watching gaze that did not leave her face. His mouth opened slightly, and shut. Then blinking, he fingered his ring of office, turning it round and round.

"I owe you a debt," he said slowly, "for by all accounts you have preserved the life of my nephew."

She cleared her throat.

"You do me great honour, my lord. It is God who has provided the medicine and the spirit to heal him."

"Indeed, the Lord is merciful," he nodded, his eyes fixed on her. "Where do you come from, girl, that you have such skill."

Illesa looked over at Richard, but his closed eye told her nothing.

"I was taught by my mother. She was a midwife, before she went to the Lord," Illesa evaded.

The Bishop glanced at the bed.

"Let us leave the invalid to his rest. I will see you in my chamber where we can speak freely without disturbing him."

He got up and walked to the door ahead of her. One of the clerks was waiting outside.

"Lord Chancellor," he began.

"Later, if you please, Reginald. I am not at liberty yet." He swept past him and up the stairs, as quickly as a younger, lighter man. In his chamber were two further men, busy at parchment in the light from the window.

"Adam and John, finish your work in the hall if you please." He ignored their enquiring looks, helping them to gather their parchment, ink and quills. "You may return when you are sent for." And he shut the door on them.

He drew a stool up to the table, pointed her to it, and sat in the chair just vacated by the younger clerk.

"Let me give you a cup." He examined the cup on the table, seemed to find it acceptable, poured ale into it from a large jug, and pushed it towards her.

"Thank you, my lord," she whispered.

"Now I wish to know a bit about you, my girl," he said. "There is no reason to be frightened. Richard was as jumpy as a young foal about you, so I understand what his feelings are." The Chancellor leant back in his chair, fingering his ring as before, and then looked up at Illesa. "Where are you from?"

"Holdgate, my lord."

"Your parents?"

"A smith and a midwife, both dead."

"Did they always live in Holdgate, under the Templars?"

"No, my lord. For a time they lived in Acton, and served Lady Rose and her family. That was many years ago. My brother knew Sir Richard, and that is how I came to be part of the play for the King."

"Your brother is - ?"

"Christopher Arrowsmith."

The Chancellor folded his hands.

"Yes, I recall now. He helped Richard in Wales, is that right?"

"Yes, my lord."

"Where were you born and christened?"

"At Acton, my lord."

"How old are you?"

"I will be eighteen in a month."

He leant forward, his hands on the table.

"And what is your name?"

"Illesa."

"Yes," he said quietly. "It is." He said nothing more for a moment, looking at her, elbows on the table, his clasped hands resting on his lips. She could not bear it.

"My lord, I know there is a summons for me, but Sir Richard will tell you that I was innocent of the theft, by God's blood, I swear to you."

The Bishop looked bemused.

"What are you talking about? A summons? What for? Oh dear, please do not start that. Here take a sip." He pushed the cup towards her. "It is good ale, from the abbey."

Illesa wiped her eyes and brought the cup to her lips. The Bishop was smiling at her as if she were a little girl who had fallen over and scraped her knee.

"My dear girl, I know nothing of a summons. Tell me what the problem is."

She was surprised at how easy it was to talk to him. He listened with his head inclined, or nodded and only occasionally interrupted with a question.

"So I asked Sir Richard to take me with him, as I would have been put in gaol if the bailiff or constable had found me. He made me part of the play for the Round Table, and has treated me kindly. I am glad to have been able to help him in return," she finished.

The Bishop's expression was hard to read. He placed his hands flat on the table and stared at them for some time.

"You have been through many trials, Illesa. Have you kept your faith in God who preserves your life?"

"Sir, I am trying. It has been hard without the book. Although I know it isn't mine, it was always my habit to pray with it to Saint Margaret."

"Your mother taught you the letters?"

"Yes, she said I should learn, and that I should always keep it safe and hidden, to receive the Saint's blessing."

"She did well," he said, his face averted. "Did she ever tell you where the book came from?"

"No," Illesa hesitated. "Not directly."

"What did she say about it?"

Disgrace was already flushing her cheeks.

"She said it was from my father's family. Not her husband."

The Bishop's head was nodding slightly, all joviality gone.

"And you have felt shame for her, all these years."

"She was a good woman, my lord," Illesa said through fresh tears.

"I know she was, Illesa." He leant forward and took her hand. "You should not be ashamed of her. She did what she was told to do."

Illesa looked up at him and had to glance away at the sympathy in his face.

"You are very kind, my lord. I know it is a strange tale."

"Stranger even than you think. I met you and your mother, a month or so after your birth." The Bishop looked out of the window. "You were a heavy, well-fed baby, not like the tall, thin lady you have become." He smiled a little. "I even held you for a moment." He turned back to her, and Illesa clutched her hands together in her lap.

"You think it odd, no doubt. Why would I, the clerk to the Prince, be holding a baby? Do you know?" His look was almost embarrassed.

Illesa let out her breath. She shook her head, although she knew what he would say, as each piece of the past lined up in her mind, joining together to form the impossible fact.

"Your mother was as beautiful as you are, but she died in childbirth. Guiliane, full of joy." He shook his head. "I never thought that she would suffer. She seemed the essence of life itself." He turned his hands palm up on the table. "And of course your sinful father is myself."

Silence filled the space between them, as heavy and still as a millpond.

"Ursula passed you off as her own child for several reasons, some sinful, for which she did penance. She was grieving for a baby she had just lost and perhaps wasn't quite in her right mind. When she confessed to me, I told her to keep you. You were well and cared for, and of course, it was not advisable for a clerk in holy orders to be known to have a child." The Lord Chancellor, who was her father, paused. "It was a sin I was not able to acknowledge to the world. But now that I am in this position, I do not need to be so cautious. So you see, if you should be ashamed of anyone, it is your father, the Bishop."

He smiled broadly.

"Confession is a marvellous sacrament. But I see you are shocked. It will take some time to understand it all. Ursula did well with you, and you have shown yourself to be as brave and beautiful as any lady." He patted the table where he hoped her hand would be. "It will all be different now. I can help you as I have helped my other children. I will be able to match you comfortably, and give you a good living. What is it? You want to say something?"

"You have other children?" Illesa asked, in a voice not her own.

"Yes, my dear. I am weak in this way. It is a failing that the King accepts in his mercy, and that I will one day have to account for to the Great King of Heaven." He held up the fingers of his right hand. "I have four others, all well cared for. William, John, and two girls. Their mother stays in London now. She has no desire to visit Acton and receive a lashing from the tongue of the Anchoress." He smiled wryly. "She leaves that pleasure to me."

The Bishop pushed himself back from the table and put his hands on his knees.

"So, you should have some time to think, and then we may discuss this further. I will be at your disposal once I have seen to the business of the day and attended the Prince." He stood up and took her hand again, pulling her gently to the door.

"I knew as soon as I looked into your face, although it is eighteen years since I saw Guiliane, and I had no portrait. As soon as I saw you, there she was again, as bright as a gillyflower, but obviously in need of new petals," he said, indicating her frayed clothes. "I will attend to that very soon." He gave her a gentle push out of the door. "And please tell the clerks that they may return to the chamber." He made the sign of the cross in front of her and shut the door.

Chapter XVII
The 3rd day of August, 1284
Neigull

A storm had blown in during the night and Illesa's first impression of the day was rain lashing at the window. She turned over on her pallet and shut her eyes. A new Illesa had experienced the events of yesterday. She wanted to be the old Illesa, an ignorant child, without family. But free. Free to choose.

And free from the terrible anger that felt like a fever. She had barely kept it in check while listening to the Chancellor speaking so glibly about the reasons, the unfortunate circumstances, and the ways he was going to make everything well. Her next meeting with him had been after his dinner, and he was even more jovial than before. He had apparently instructed Ursula to teach Illesa to read the book. He seemed quite proud of this idea of his, as if he had himself taught her all aspects of natural philosophy. God had brought Illesa to him, he claimed, and now he had a chance to make things right. His plans for this were unformed, as yet.

To add to her bad temper, Sir L'Estrange had been at supper with the Chancellor, having returned from a provisioning mission to Caernarfon for the Prince. A spacious wagon newly equipped with the most comfortable furnishings, and with six of the best carthorses, was waiting in the barn. The Prince would be leaving this day. Perhaps going all the way to Windsor, where he would be housed comfortably during his convalescence. No other nearer place would be suitable, said the Chancellor. A period of time in Caernarfon was likely to make him worse, in its current state of disarray.

Sir L'Estrange seemed rather taken aback by the presence of such an important person. He glanced at Illesa from time to time, no doubt trying to understand why the Chancellor was keeping her near to him and smiling at her so warmly. The knight spent a great deal of his conversation trying to present a convincing case to the Chancellor for the extension of the terms of a significant debt.

And Richard himself had taken the news in a way she had not expected. He had listened to her angry account during his lunch, had stopped eating as she explained about the meeting between Ursula and Robert, his pale face sombre.

"God's wounds. That is my uncle. I suppose we should have guessed," he said in a tone of resignation.

"How could we have guessed? He made sure that no one would know!"

"Perhaps he should have kept it to himself."

"You mean never tell me?"

"No." He put his hand out at her furious tone. "That would not be right either."

"Well, he is perfectly happy now. He thinks he can make everything right by giving me a husband and a living. He has no idea what it did to our family. It broke Mother and Father apart and took Kit away from me. It made my mother live in fear for years." Angry tears were running down her cheeks again. "He cannot make that right. They are dead."

Richard turned his knife over in his hand.

"There is little that Bishop Robert the Chancellor of England cannot do if he puts his mind to it. I would not be surprised if he has your Ursula beatified."

"Don't make light of it!" she shouted.

"Very well. I am only warning you. Resisting my uncle is not easy, especially when he wishes to help. He will bring every power and resource at his disposal to bear."

After that he listened to her complaints for a few more moments and then said he wished to go to bed. She had fumed even more at that, as she needed someone to listen, to help her make sense of how she felt. He did not kiss her, only took her hand as she made him ready, silently stroking the line of her thumb with his finger.

After her dinner with her new father, she had lain awake most of the night in a state of rage.

Illesa turned to the bed. Richard had changed position. He was awake, but choosing to be silent. She could understand his silence and his worries, now that her mind was not so clouded with fury.

She got up and knelt by the bed.

"Sir Richard."

His eye opened, but he didn't smile.

"Yes, Lady Burnel?" He pushed himself up a little on the cushion.

"I do not want to marry."

"Don't you? I thought that was your dearest wish."

"No." She ran her finger down the scar from his eye to his lip. "How can I stop your uncle from marrying me off to some stranger?"

"I do not know. The nunnery is the only alternative I think."

She laid her head on his chest.

"I don't think that life would suit me."

"Really? I thought you might find it quite satisfactory." His hand stroked the short hairs at the nape of her neck.

"No. I am not of sufficient faith," she murmured.

"I think escape is the only option then," he said. "You need to ride as fast as you can to the end of the world."

"If I do that, how will I look after you?" she whispered.

"I would need to come with you, except I cannot."

She listened to the beating of his heart, loud and regular. He would live; he was strong enough.

"I have an idea, but it is sinful," she whispered.

"That is not possible. Not from your fair mind."

"I will sin and you must too," she said, looking up at his face framed by its messy halo of hair.

"Tell me, my little devil," he said softly.

It did not take long. The Bishop called her before the hour of sext. He had already been busy requisitioning her garments, as well as celebrating Mass and ensuring the good ordering of the Prince's arrangements. This time he greeted her at the door of his chamber with an embrace before holding out his ring for her kiss.

"Come and sit down, my girl. Soon your new clothes will be ready, and then we can begin to get you settled. Now I want to hear about Holdgate, as I understand it is a Baron's seat and likely to sell. You say that your home there has been taken? I should be able to rectify that quite quickly. The Templars and I have had many business dealings in the past. What is the land like? Quite fertile with woodland too, you said?"

"Yes, my lord. It is good land."

"Excellent. I will go there and visit it soon, perhaps next month, and the arrangements for purchase will not take long."

"Do you mean to buy the manor, my lord?"

"Yes, I think that would be best. If you are fond of the place?" He looked at her, his face suddenly full of doubt.

"Yes, my lord. It is the only home I remember."

"Excellent, well even when you are married elsewhere, this will ensure you always have a place you feel comfortable. I have always valued being able to return to the family seat. It is a comfort when life in the town becomes a burden." He began writing on the parchment roll in front of him, the quill scratching loudly in the quiet room.

"My lord," Illesa began, and licked her dry lips.

"Yes, my dear, just a moment. I am making a note to the clerks of what to write to the Templars. Then we will discuss the other matters."

"I must tell you something, Father," she said deliberately. She looked at him steadily as he put down the pen.

He smiled, hiding his annoyance quite well.

"Yes, what is worrying you?"

"I cannot marry."

"What?" he pushed himself away from the table, almost as though he were angry. "What do you mean?"

Illesa put her hand on her belly.

"I have not yet told Sir Richard."

The Bishop swallowed. His cheeks reddened. He put his hands on the table and rose to his feet.

"What is this? You are with child?"

"Yes, Father. It is early, but I know the signs very well."

The chair fell over as the Bishop strode to the window, and he did not right it.

"You were quick about it," he said, his voice tight and high. "You can't have known him long. Didn't your mother warn you of the dangers of being un-chaperoned with a man?"

Illesa did not reply. She folded her hands over her stomach. The Bishop looked out of the window. His hands clutched the edge of his cape.

"I wish to stay to look after Sir Richard, Father, for as long as he requires my care."

"Do you? And Richard is glad of it, I'm sure. Until he is well again and can range far and wide."

She kept her eyes lowered.

"I thank you for all your kindness, Father. I wish I had met you earlier in my life. Perhaps things would not have happened this way."

He looked at her, and then had to look down.

"Well, we are all in the hands of God. We cannot know his plan."

He returned to the table and poured himself wine from a flagon. The cup clattered on the wooden board when he finished.

"You are related you know," he said, waving his finger at her. "Not closely. Your union would not be forbidden, but even so, it is not advisable."

She nodded and kept her head bowed.

"We did not know it at the time, my lord. No one else needs to know that I am your daughter, now. The shame of it will not reach you."

He looked suddenly old and burdened.

"You should not have given in to him. Men will come up with all sorts of flattery when they are in the grip of lust. Surely you have heard the Priest explain."

Illesa raised her eyebrows.

"Of course you have," he muttered.

"Will you say a Mass for Ursula and Hugh, Father? They suffered much in life. I do not wish them to suffer in death."

His face worked silently for a moment, then he seized a roll of parchment.

"I will make a note to include it in the chantry of the Chapel Royal every year."

"I give you thanks." She curtsied, and waited.

"You may go," he said abruptly.

Illesa went to the door and, as she turned to shut it, saw her father at the table, staring at the wall.

She swept into Richard's chamber without knocking. Richard was in his chair by the window. As he turned to her, he looked almost guilty. A man stood in front of him. They had just stopped talking as she came in. It was the workman she had last seen on the platform, recruiting Kit.

"Sir," she began.

"Illesa, sit down," he ordered. "David, tell this lady what you have just told me, but spare the detail."

"Yes, sir," the man said, unhappily. "The man we took from here, the smith, he has died."

Richard reached out and took her hand, squeezing it tightly.

"What?" she choked.

"Here, drink," Richard said, thrusting his cup at her.

She pushed it away. The man was looking at his thick, sand-covered boots.

"He was hit on the head and drowned in the sea," he concluded.

"Are you sure it was Kit?" Illesa appealed to Richard.

"It seems so. He was the tallest recruit, and hard to mistake. Although, apparently he called himself by another name," Richard said quietly.

"What name?"

Richard turned to the workman.

"Ah, he called hisself John. I came here to see if anyone knew him, if his family was hereabouts. We had to bury him on the island. The King paid for the candles," he said, sounding awed.

The sun was too bright. It shone on the man's freckled, weathered face. He looked real, but this was surely some sort of waking nightmare.

"He is buried already?" Illesa asked.

The man called David nodded.

"Buried yesterday, he was." He scratched under his cap. "We would have kept him on; he was a good worker."

"You say he was hit on the head?" said Richard.

"Yes, sir, he must have been."

"He didn't fall into the sea, drunk?"

Illesa gave a bark of laughter and covered her mouth. David looked at her uncomfortably.

"Couldn't have, sir. We were only given the weakest of ale. It was a fast every day we were there. The monks are very strict about it. John, or Christopher you say, went out to relieve hisself the night before last and never came back. We found his body next morning, caught by the rocks. It took four of us to drag him up, sir."

Richard cut him off.

"You have all the men you took with you still on the boat?"

"All the ones that came from here. Told them to stay by the shore, as we are to go to Criccieth now. But there were many others that came from Nefyn. They are going straight to Caernarfon, sir, on the King's orders."

"Has anyone been accused?"

"No, no one saw anything. Couldn't think why it would happen. Everyone liked him."

Richard glanced at Illesa. She held her hands over her mouth as the sobs began.

"Have you any soldiers or guards?"

"No, sir."

"Right, David, go out into the hall and find a servant to run a message for me."

The man returned with one of the kitchen boys.

"Boy, go to the guard by the stair and tell him I have urgent need of four armed guards to bring a company of men from the beach. David, wait outside for them to gather and then lead them to the boat. All your men are to come to the hall without delay."

"Yes, sir," David said, unhappily. His journey to Criccieth would not happen this day. He shut the door behind him.

"Now, Illesa, you must gather yourself. You need to see these men and tell me if any of them worked for the Forester. I think that is the only likely explanation. The Lord Forester would not suffer the humiliation he received without some form of revenge."

She hugged her shoulders tightly trying to control her shuddering breath. It was not possible, after everything, all their trials, that Kit should just be dead, his body buried on an island she could never visit.

"You think he sent someone all this way?"

"I don't know," Richard sighed. "But I would not be surprised if the Forester left one of his men at Rushbury and instructed him to kill Kit as soon as he had a chance. Little did he know he would have to travel so far."

"I don't believe it."

"Nor do I," said Richard quietly. "But we will try to get to the truth of it."

By the time the men had walked from the beach, Illesa had stopped crying, drunk a cup of spiced wine and was sitting by the window. The light outside hung golden in the air, reflecting on motes of smoke and sea mist. She could not see the holy well or the chapel. It was as if they were on an island themselves, surrounded by a misty sea in which they would drown and disappear.

She felt the catch of breath that would bring more tears if she did not control it. No more thoughts of the island, or Kit buried there alone. A guard led one of the men in and blocked the door behind him. He was a short wiry man, belted for work, his cap stained with seawater; no one Illesa recognised. She shook her head and the man was led out. The next two had unfamiliar faces, creased with sun and wind.

The fourth man who came in had a thatch of black hair, broad strong shoulders and a flattened face. He looked frightened. The man who had been at the hanging. She knew him now.

Eadwick, who had been in the Long Forest with Jarryd and had lost his hired mount. He stood in front of her, squeezing his cap in his fist, his eyes darting around the room. Eadwick was too simple to have come on his own. Short Jarryd would be somewhere, hiding. He must have kept out of Kit's sight on the road. Jarryd would have told Eadwick to volunteer for the same job as Kit, sending him to the island. Where had Eadwick found the courage to strike Kit? He must have been threatened to the point of terror.

Illesa immediately felt sick.

If she accused him, he would hang, like the others, while it was the Forester who coerced and threatened. It was the Forester who should go to hell.

"Illesa," Richard jogged her shoulder, "Illesa, do you know this man?"

"No," she whispered. "I do not know him."

The rest of the men came and went, and Illesa shook her head at them all, and left the room without a word. She went outside with nothing. The sea rolled in the distance, vast and pitiless. Her legs moved. She was alone behind the last outbuilding of the manor, staring at the shifting waves. Voices came to disturb her. She moved away.

Illesa found herself at the door of the old, squat church. It was dark and empty inside, and she knelt down on the rushes. It was so, yet it could not be so, just as he was, and was not her brother. Dead in the sea. If he was unconscious when he drowned, he'd had no chance to ask for mercy. When was the last time he had confessed or even been to Mass? What would happen to his un-shriven soul? Prayers came at last, a torrent of words flying into the dim air. When they stopped, she rose from her aching knees and left the church.

The sun was setting, and a robin was singing in a clump of elder. If Kit had been walking next to her, he would have copied its tune perfectly. But he would never again whistle to tempt a bird from a briar. Her big, capable, infuriating brother was gone.

It was as if they all, mother, father and brother, had embarked on that boat, and sailed off to the island, leaving her to this strange new family that she did not understand, peopled with bastards just like her; half-brothers, half-sisters, and a father for whom she felt nothing. Far from the Lady of the Well, she was now a strange mixed creature: child-woman, common-noble, virgin-mother. Her choice might be wrong, but there was no one left to her in this world but Richard. All the others she loved had gone.

By the time she returned to the manor, it was almost dark. In the hall only one boy was still clearing the tables, flicking a cloth over the polished wood as he went. There was a guard, standing by the open back door, leaning heavily on his pike. The Prince must have gone. Her father, the Chancellor, was perhaps at prayer or doing business. She was glad not to have to face him now.

The door to Richard's chamber opened soundlessly, and she slipped in. At least here they had kept the fire stoked, and the remains of a meal showed he had not been neglected in her absence. The boy who had watched him that first day was sitting, hunched by the fire. Richard lay motionless, his arm outstretched and white as bone.

She ran to the bed and lifted Richard's hand. It was warm, and the blood was still flowing in his veins. His eye opened.

"You look like death," he said and reached to touch her face. "I thought you had run away."

She turned to see the boy, standing, holding out a cup, ready to help. Illesa took it from him.

"You may go. Thank you," she said, her voice unsteady. She lit a lamp as he left. She wanted to see Richard's colour, his wound. Make sure he really was well.

"Come here," Richard called. "You have been gone all afternoon. Whatever you are doing, it can wait."

"I am just making you something."

"You and your blessed physic. I am fine, I tell you."

"Well, you sound like your old self." Her voice was still cracked.

He was quiet, for a moment.

"You knew that man, Illesa."

"What man?" she asked. She did not look up from stirring the infusion over the coals.

"The simpleton, black hair. It was obvious you knew him. Why wouldn't you say?"

"Where is he now?" Illesa whispered.

"I let them all go. There was no reason to keep them and they would have eaten up all the stores."

She came to the bed with the steaming wine, sat down next to Richard and put the cup on the table.

"He wasn't one of the Forester's men. I saw him when we were running to the church for sanctuary. The Forester took his mount, and wouldn't give it back until he brought Kit in. He was terrified." She stared at the dirty lines creasing her palms. "Why should he die? It is the Forester who ought to hang for all the sins he commits every day."

Richard took her hand.

"You will have to leave the Forester to God's justice, Illesa. There is no court on this earth that will convict him."

She let out an angry breath.

"I know that." The tears dripped into her lap.

"But my uncle has reminded me of something that you may not know about."

"What?" Illesa said, her voice more angry than she intended. She squeezed his hand in apology.

"Because of the very holiness of the ground on Bardsey Island, so full of the bodies of the saints, it is known that no one who dies there goes to hell or purgatory, but straight to the presence of the Lord in heaven. So you see," Richard continued gently, "Kit has escaped again. Even the judgment of God."

"Is this the truth?"

"You have it from the lips of a Bishop."

Illesa covered her eyes with her hands.

"But I can never go there, never see the place where he is buried."

"You would not want him moved, Illesa? He is in the most holy ground. Only in Rome or Jerusalem would he be better housed in his six feet of earth."

He did not belong in the ground, but striding over it, whistling, swinging his pack of tools.

"Illesa." Richard was reaching for her hand again. "You have not changed your mind?"

She turned to him and shook her head. It was too hard to speak.

"I will have to do penance for corrupting your good nature," he murmured, stroking the area of soft skin in the middle of her palm.

The silence was warm with the sound of the logs hissing and cracking. Illesa sniffed and felt the wave of grief begin to subside.

"My uncle has talked to me about what you told him," Richard said, after a while. "He had some very harsh words to say about my lack of temperance and self-control. He berated me at length for my loose living. Gave me examples from his own life of the price of such indulgence. However, he has decided that he will not give up on you. As I said, once he has decided something, he will bring all his force to bear."

"I will not go to a stranger," Illesa began, "I don't care what he wants."

"Gentle falcon, don't bate so," he squeezed her hand in his warm fingers. "Listen. My uncle knows that many grasping families will line up to betroth their maids to me when they believe I will not live long, in order to inherit Burnel lands and take his estates. But he also wants me to have an heir and for the family name to continue, so he insists, with all his authority, that I marry you as soon as I am well enough to stand in church."

Richard's expression was amused.

"You are making sport of me," she said.

"I am not indeed. He fears that I would desert you, if we were not bound by marriage. His opinion of my loyalty is almost as damning as yours." He smiled broadly, but she could not return it.

"I think the thought of you being abandoned again was agony for him," Richard concluded softly.

Illesa kept her face turned to the fire.

"Where is he going? They are packing all his things into a wagon."

"He rides to Portmadog in the morning to meet the King and Queen and report on the state of the Prince."

Illesa swallowed, her throat dry.

"So, is this what you wish, Sir Richard," she whispered, "or will you do what your rich uncle says, because to refuse would mean the loss of his favour?"

He looked at her calmly, and brought her curled fingers to his lips.

"You are a strange one," he said. "You are like a falcon chick taken too late from the nest, unwilling to trust the one who would care for you. When else in my life have my duty and my pleasure been so well mixed?"

Chapter XVIII
December   AD 558
Fortress of Meirchion

The dogs were barking and squealing with excitement. Someone was at the gate. A low, cloudy half-moon gave little light. Manon turned over in bed and looked at her sleeping baby. She would not hope. There had been no message of victory, no message of death. It would drag on and on. They would continue their fighting until no drop of blood remained unshed that could enrich some future farmer's soil.

She could not rest. She lay each night on the yellow ox hide, listening to the soft noises of her children sleeping, but it did no good. Sleep ran from her. The curse on Owain would never let him return. It ensured her own misery.

The childbirth had been nothing but pain and blood. She had burned with fever a few days later, and a wet nurse had kept Gwenwyn alive. Manon had felt nothing. When she came back from the place of dreams, her daughter was a stranger. There was no warmth in the world, no meaning in the sky. All love was gone.

Gradually some light had come back. She had enough strength to go to the spring now. But still sleep did not come. It flew away whenever she shut her eyes, making them heavy when she was awake, and dry and sore at night. Something had gone wrong when she wrote the curse, or when she gave it to the goddess in the spring. It had rebounded on her.

That would explain why she felt so cold and shrivelled inside. Her visions from the goddess were longer and darker. Sometimes she fell to the floor, sometimes her mouth filled with blood and her tongue was swollen. It happened when she was in bed with Gwenwyn, and it was only Eluned who pulled her off and stopped her from smothering the baby in the frenzy.

For months she had not held her son, nor kissed her daughter. She feared touching any of her children in case the curse spread to them. They had stopped coming to her now. They sat on Eluned's lap instead and nuzzled her, their fingers interlaced around *her* neck.

Two days ago, Eluned had told Manon of a man called Beuno, who lived nearby in a small cell in the clan land of Urien. Two other men had gone to join him, and they lived as Christians. They prayed in their small stone enclosure, and worshipped the god who had died.

The man could stay in his hermit's enclosure, Manon had told her. She had no need of the council of Christians.

Eluned nodded.

"They say that he has the power of healing."

"Fools will believe what they like."

"If he does not show you due respect, then send him away."

"Why should I see him in the first place?"

"He has been in the north and has seen the fighting. Urien's men say he has seen Owain."

Manon held Eluned's blank gaze for a long moment.

"Very well, bring him to me."

He had come that day, a tall man, not much older than herself. He walked steadily towards her, and she was rather surprised when he suddenly stopped short, bowed and straightened, with his palms slightly raised in a gesture of prayer. His eyes were dark and heavy lidded.

"You are welcome here, Beuno, after your journey from the north," she had said. She had been suddenly full of hope that he would bring news and break her despair.

Then he began to speak.

What he believed was certainly a delusion. The gods would not do her will without sacrifice, without ceremony. What kind of god would answer prayers and requests without payment of some kind?

"The Lord Jesus is the saviour and the sacrifice," Beuno had claimed.

What madness was that? The gods needed food. The earth, the sea, the sky, all were bidden by them and as with any patron, master, father or mother, for their protection and service, offerings and service must be given in return.

"But there is one Father," Beuno had said, "and he only wants your faith, not your blood."

He had come close to her, spoken softly.

"I know your story. You are strong, but your goddess is not as strong as you. Curses cannot bring justice. They will destroy you. If you follow the Christ, then the curse will be broken."

Manon had sent him from the room without a word, and then she had shouted at Eluned. Had she said anything to this fool? Eluned denied it.

Afterward Manon was angry with herself. She had not questioned Beuno about Owain and the north. Now she would have to invite him back to find out what he knew, even if it meant listening again to his lies, his happy lunacy. A god so weak he could be killed by men. What help would that be to anyone?

Manon curled herself around her baby, not touching her little head or her open lips. She was a pretty baby. Already her golden hair curled at her neck. She did not often cry, but neither did she smile. Another condemned to sadness and emptiness.

The dogs were still barking, and now there were voices. She should get up, but it was so cold, and even as she was listening to the noise, sleep was shutting her eyes and lying heavy on her limbs.

Someone was coming in. Manon lifted her head. It must be one of her women, but the tread was too heavy.

"Who is it?"

She swung her feet out of bed. The figure was just coming through the hanging, a waft of smoke drifted around his form. He came forward and she threw up her arms to repel the intruder, her mouth forming a curse.

"Manon," said Owain, holding her raised arm. His face was hardly visible. "It is me, Manon."

Her breath juddered.

"What has happened to you?"

A scar stood out on his cheek, pulling his mouth askew. His voice was strange and he moved differently, as if there was a stone lodged in his shoe.

"What did they do to you?"

"Not as much as I did to them." He sat next to her on the bed, bringing her hands down from his cut face to her lap.

"They told me the baby is a girl," he said in his new slurred voice.

She felt the tears dropping into her lap.

"Gwenwyn," she said. "She is asleep." Manon turned to look at the baby, as if seeing her for the first time.

"I could not come to you before. Forgive me," he said, touching the curl of hair by his daughter's cheek. "Has she been well?"

"The babe is well," she said, her hand returning to his face. "You are here. Why didn't you send word you were coming?"

"I did not think you would see me."

"I should not have," she said.

"A week after the time I should have returned to you, they cut me here," he said, touching the scar on his face. "And when I fell to the ground, they stabbed my leg."

He stretched out his right foot, but it would not straighten.

"I could not come back until my legs were able to bear my weight."

Owain took her hand.

"It happened as you said. Your power is strong," he whispered.

"I do not want it. I renounce it," she said. "What has happened to your lips?"

She touched them with the tip of her finger.

"They have not kissed you for over a year and are withering. By God, I have missed you."

Chapter XIX
The 18th day of August, 1285
Acton Burnel Manor

Illesa opened the door slowly, expecting swirls of dust, but the room had been cleaned, and the furniture gleamed in the light from the glazed window, softened by the red hangings on the bed and the tapestry on the wall. The scene was unfamiliar. A woman stood by a pool of water, naked but for her golden, flowing hair. A man crouched behind a tree nearby, watching, fully clothed. She had not noticed it when she came here last, over a year before.

Cecily was waiting for her below, probably chatting to the cooks. She had a good understanding of birth and herbs, and she wasn't afraid to learn. Thank the Lord they had found her before Richard was called away to London.

Now that Illesa stood in the chamber, she wished she had brought the maid up with her, with her easy laugh and matter-of-fact ways. The un-made bed looked barren and spectral, and everything was so still.

Illesa shook her head. It was the year's mind of the death of Prince Alphonso in the church this morning that had upset her thoughts. The prayers for the Prince had made her cry. There had been so much goodness and honour in him, and yet he had died. What could any of them hope, if even a boy so treasured could be taken by a pointless accident?

And whenever she thought of that time, Kit came before her eyes.

The key was hidden in the same place on the prie-dieu. She slid her hand down the wood and twisted it off the nail where it hung, thinking of Richard's hand doing the same a year before. Then he had been filled with fury, and she with fear. Running, fleeing, always at a gallop. Now it was an effort just to walk, she was carrying the baby so low.

She was late coming for the book, should not really be away from home. Many times she had thought about it, but for some reason had put off the journey. But this room and the book had not been responsible for her mother's death. Those were just silly superstitions.

Illesa went to the cabinet, pushed the key in the lock and turned it. The book of the Saint was just where Richard had left it. The feel of its pale leather binding sent a jolt of recognition through her. She gathered it in her hands and held it to her breasts. But she would not open it here. She would take it to a new place, where she was happy; the room at Langley where they had made this baby. She would open it there and read it, and then the fear would go. Illesa moved to close the cabinet, when her eye caught another familiar binding, red tipped with gold. The story of the Lady of the Well.

It would give her something to do while she waited. Perhaps she could even recite it to Richard when he got back, if she put effort into learning to read the French words. The memories would please him: Gaspar in his dress, smiling wickedly, Balthazar, the man-bear, holding off the amorous knights and she, fumbling with her headdress, struggling with the horse and falcon.

The point in time when everything had changed, fallen apart and come together in new hybrid forms of angels and monsters, happiness and disaster.

Illesa picked up the red book, shut the painted cabinet door and turned the key. The two books lay on top of each other in her hand, one the colour of milk, the other of blood. Then she looked around the room and whispered the prayers that were ready on her tongue.

She prayed for the souls of her mothers.

She prayed it would be different for her.

Notes

Robert Burnel (died 1292), Chancellor and Bishop of Bath and Wells, along with Richard, who was the son of his cousin, are real historical characters in this narrative. Little information survives about Richard, who was a beneficiary of Burnel's largesse. He is recorded as being born around 1230, crossing the sea with Edward I in 1297 and dying in 1313. I have taken some liberties with his biographical facts, and created a son called Richard who was born in 1260. Due to the historical Richard's unusually long life, it is possible that a son, who was named Richard as well, was simply not recorded.

In his youth, Robert Burnel appears to have been close to Thomas Corbet, the overlord of the Burnel estate, as they both got into trouble for stealing a deer from the King's forest in 1258. Robert Burnel amassed a huge personal fortune and many estates during his career in the service of the King. He was known to keep a mistress (at least one was known as Julianne) and to have several illegitimate children who he married off to minor members of the aristocracy and judiciary. It was this stain on his character that prevented him from becoming Archbishop of Canterbury, despite being put forward for the job twice by Edward I. Robert Burnel was also known to hold the place of his birth in great affection and to have spent much time there. He was allowed to take oaks from the King's own forest in 1284 to build his fortified house. He bought the baron's seat of Holdgate in 1284.

It is not known whether Acton Burnell Church had an anchorhold or not. The small window in the chancel could be a leper's squint. Thomas, the Parson of Acton Burnell, died between 1286 and 1288, killed in a fight with a chaplain called William Petyt.

Heart burials (and the burial of other organs separate from the body) were relatively common in Medieval times among the nobility. A person may die and be buried far from home, for example on crusade in the Holy Land, but their heart could be preserved and returned to their home or place of birth.

Sir Perkyn is based on the legend of Ippikin, a medieval bandit living on Wenlock Edge.

Wenlock Prior, John de Tycford, moved to Bermondsey Abbey in 1284, having sold, in advance, all the wool crops for the next seven years. He took the money with him.

Saint Margaret (known as Marina in the Eastern church) was one of the most popular saints in Medieval England, mainly due to her role as patron saint of childbirth. The legend of her life was already deemed to be apocryphal by the late 5th century. Despite this, she became famous in the time of the Crusades and her story was included in *The Golden Legend* by Voragine. Many manuscripts were produced telling the story of her martyrdom (Passion) and her promises to those who prayed to her, one of which was that those who read her Passion and their babies would be protected during childbirth.

Margaret was said to be the daughter of a pagan priest in Antioch during the reign of Emperor Diocletian, and to have been converted to Christianity by her nursemaid. Her feast was celebrated on the 20th July in the West. Her cult was suppressed by the Holy See in 1969.

The story of Moses holding his hands in the air to ensure the victory of the Israelites is told in Exodus 17: 10-13.

The two stories that inform Part Two are 'The Knight with the Lion' from Chrétien de Troyes' *Arthurian Romances*, and 'The Lady of the Well', from *The Mabinogion*. Both of these stories follow the adventures of Yvain/Owain, as he learns lessons in honour and love. Owain was a real historical person, son of Urien of Rheged, and far from the chivalrous character we meet in the romances. His extended family had territory in North Wales and along the Border region of Scotland/England.

In the sixth century, Christianity was only beginning to take hold in the Celtic regions. After the departure of the Romans from Britain, most of the population had returned to their Celtic pagan practices, which often centred on sacred springs and holy wells.

The Monastic Chronicles report that during the Round Table Tournament that Edward I personally organised at Nefyn in July 1284, a dance floor collapsed, killing and maiming many of the nobles who had come to the Tournament from all over Europe. Approximately two weeks later, the heir to the throne, Prince Alphonso, died at Windsor. He was said to accompany his Royal parents to most important ceremonial occasions, and so I have postulated a link between these two events. Alphonso was buried at Blackfriars in London and when his mother, Eleanor of Castile, eventually died, her heart was buried with him in that Abbey.

The King and Queen, along with their many courtiers, did visit Bardsey Island after the Round Table Tournament. During their stay there, a tent man called John died. The King met the cost of the candles at his funeral.

Text References

* These passages come from the *Passio of St Margaret*, BL MS
Egerton 877, held in the British Library and translated into English
by Professor John Lowden, Courtauld Institute of Art, who has
generously allowed its publication here.
https://www.bl.uk/catalogues/illuminatedmanuscripts/TourKnow
nB.asp

Texts taken from *Selections from the 'Carmina Burana'* translated by
David Parlett (Penguin, 1986)
Reproduced by kind permission of the translator
1. from CB1 – 'Bribery and Corruption'
2. from CB196 – 'In the Tavern'

3. 'Le Chevalier au Lion (Yvain)', by Chrétien de Troyes, lines
2549-2557
4. This translation appears on page 327 in 'The Knight with the
Lion' in *Arthurian Romances*, Chrétien de Troyes, William W. Kibler
trans., 1991, Penguin Classics
Reproduced by kind permission of the translator

Glossary

alb – the white, usually floor length, robe worn by all clergy

alms - charity for the poor

ampulla – a small container for holding holy water or oil, sold as souvenirs to pilgrims

anchoress – a recluse often enclosed in a small cell adjoining a church

aspergillum – an implement for sprinkling holy water

bailey – the courtyard within the walls of a castle

bailiff – a justice officer under the sheriff who would collect rents

boon work – extra work done for the lord of the manor at harvest and haymaking

braies/breeches – undergarments for legs and loins worn by men and women

burgage plot – land in a town or city held in tenure of a lord for service or rent.

buskins – high leather boots

cadge – a wooden frame used as a portable perch for hunting falcons and hawks

chantry – a chapel or altar endowed for the saying of prayers and singing of masses for its founder

chausses – close fitting coverings for legs and feet

coney - rabbit

cope – a long coat or cape/special garment of a monk

cotter – farmer of small plot of land owned by a lord

court tour – justices sent from the royal court on tour around the kingdom to administer justice on large matters

cowl –hood of the garment worn by monks

crenellate – to provide embattlements or fortifications to a building

demesne – manorial land retained for the private use of a feudal lord

ewer – a jug, usually of metal

falchion – a curved broad sword

gambeson –tunic of heavy cloth or hardened leather worn as protection

groat – coin first issued by Edward I in 1279 worth 4d

hastiludes – jousting in a tournament

hose – tight fitting leg covering mainly worn by men

hue and cry – the cry to chase a criminal and the chase itself

jerkin – over jacket

jesses – straps attached to a hawk's legs

kirtle – a woman's loose gown

lych gate – the gate into the precincts of a church yard

Manon – Welsh name meaning 'Queen'

manorial court – each manor held its own court approximately every 3 weeks, which was mainly for petty offences

maslin – bread made from mix of rye and wheat

mêlée – mock battle between sides of armed horsemen

mews – a cage or building used for keeping hunting birds

mummer – actor of short entertainments, often masked

palfrey – a small horse, often used by women

peregrinus – (Lat.) a pilgrim or sometimes a crusader

peristyle – courtyard inside a roman villa

pie powder – from 'pieds poudrés' – French for 'dusty feet'. A court specifically for administering justice at fairs where there were many itinerant people

piscina – niche containing a stone bowl or drain which is usually built on the wall of a chancel for washing hands and sacred vessels

pottage – stew usually of vegetables

poultice - a soft, moist mass of cloth, bread, meal, herbs, etc., applied hot as a medicament to the body

prie-dieu – literally 'pray god', a stand for a book which has a ledge for kneeling for private devotions

privy – lavatory/toilet

scullion – lowliest domestic servant

shift - a body garment or shirt of a washable material such as linen, cotton etc.

shrive/shriven – to forgive/ be forgiven

simples – herbal remedies

solar – a private chamber, often an upper room designed to catch the sun

squint – an opening in a church wall to allow sight of the Host during the Mass

squire – a young man, usually noble, who is training for knighthood

surcoat – outer coat of rich material

tithing – ten householders, a division of a hundred which formed local government

toft – site of a homestead and its various outbuildings

tourney – shortened form of 'tournament'

villein – peasant occupying land subject to a lord. They were tied to the land.

wimple – headdress worn by women from the 12th – 14th century

Acknowledgements

My thanks go to:

Ann Mason, who shared her editing skills so generously, and whose interest and support have kept me going for all these years.

James Wade http://jameswade.webs.com for the beautiful and detailed maps - and his great patience.

Mike Ashton of MA Creative, for the cover design and skilful formatting.

Christine Evans, who openheartedly provided important information about Lleyn and Bardsey Island.

The Shrewsbury Library and the Shropshire Archives, important repositories of information and peace.

Writing West Midlands and my colleagues on the Room 204 Writers Development Programme, for all their support and advice.

Anna Dreda and Manda Scott, for their encouragement.

All those friends and readers who cheered me on with their enjoyment of the story, especially: Karen, Lou, David, Heather, Liz, Ted, Catherine, Camilla, Lisa, Hal, Katriona, Cath, Sarah, Kate, Jancis and Alison.

My three children whose daily presence blesses and inspires me.
My mother, for her powerful and constant love.
My mother-in-law, for her acceptance and enthusiasm.
My sister, for sharing the remembrance of things past.
My father, for his provision of humour and research materials when they were needed most.

And finally - Michael, whose support for this absorbing and time-consuming project has never wavered.
I thank you with all my heart.

Selected Resources

Printed:
Celtic Goddesses, Miranda Green, 1995, British Museum Press
Medieval Women, Henrietta Leyser, 1995, Phoenix
Eleanor of Castile, John Carmi Parsons, 1995, St Martin's Press
Women Defamed and Women Defended, Alcuin Blamires ed., 1992, Clarendon Press
Silence, Sarah Roche-Mahdi trans., 1992, Michigan State University Press
Medieval English Verse, Brian Stone ed., 1964, Penguin Books
Medieval Comic Tales, Derek Brewer ed., 1996, DS Brewer
Medieval Ghost Stories, Andrew Joynes, 2001, The Boydell Press
The Time Traveller's Guide to Medieval England, Ian Mortimer, 2009, Vintage
Life in a Medieval Village, Frances and Joseph Gies, 1990, Harper Perennial
The Tournament in England: 1100 – 1400, Juliet Barker, 1986, The Boydell Press
The Book of Beasts, TH White ed., 1954, Jonathan Cape
The Monks on Ynys Enlli: Part One c.500 A.D to 1252 A.D.; Mary Chitty 1992
The Monks on Ynys Enlli: Part Two 1252 A.D. to 1537 A.D.; Mary Chitty 2000
The Thirteenth Century, Sir Maurice Powicke, 1962, Oxford University Press
Arthurian Romances, Chrétien de Troyes, William W. Kibler trans., 1991, Penguin Classics
The Mabinogion, Sioned Davies trans., 2007, Oxford University Press
Selections from the 'Carmina Burana', David Parlett trans., 1986, Penguin Books
Edward I, Michael Prestwich, 1988, Methuen
Birds in Medieval Manuscripts, Brunsdon Yapp, 1981, The British Library
Images in the Margins, Margot McIlwain Nishimura, 2009, The J.Paul Getty Museum and The British Library
Pilgrimage in Medieval England, Diana Webb, 2000, Hambledon and London
The Welsh Wars of Edward I, JE Morris, 1901, Alden Press
Castle Diary, Richard Platt/Chris Riddell, 1999, Walker Books

A History of Much Wenlock, Vivien Bellamy, 2001, Shropshire Books
The Political Career and Personal Life of Robert Burnell, Chancellor of Edward I, Richard Huscroft, 2000, Submitted thesis for Degree of Doctor of Philosophy at Kings College, University of London

Websites:

https://www.bl.uk/catalogues/illuminatedmanuscripts/TourKnownB.asp
http://www.victoriacountyhistory.ac.uk/counties
https://www.bl.uk/manuscripts/
http://www.gallowglass.org/jadwiga/herbs/herbhandout.htm
https://en.wikipedia.org/wiki/Trotula
http://www.earlyenglishlaws.ac.uk
https://en.wikipedia.org/wiki/Court_of_Piepowders
http://www.english-heritage.org.uk/visit/places/#?place=Stokesay%20Castle&page=1
http://www.sacred-texts.com/neu/eng/vm/vmeng.htm

38212807R00236

Printed in Great Britain
by Amazon